Eddie's Penguin

Alan Grainger

Eddie's Penguin 2015 Edition

Also by Alan Grainger

The Tree That Walked
The Klondike Chest
The Rumstick Book
It's Only Me
The Learning Curves
Father Unknown
The Legacy
Blood On The Stones
Deadly Darjeeling
Deep & Crisp & Even

ISBN 978-1467945608

Que messieurs les assassins commencent!
(Let our respected friends the murderers begin)

.

Dedicated
to
Lorenzo Tonti
and
The Pardurmon Society

The first for inspiration,
the second for more inspiration

The Searchers

*

Sophie
Eddie

****

**The Members of the L.M.S. Club with their nicknames,
their children, and where they live.**

*

Jonathan Melchitt (Ghandi),
Mungo, Boris and Dudley,
Horsham, Sussex.

*

George McPhee (Jock),
Sandy, Eva,
Lewes, Sussex.

*

Rory Brett (Ginger),
Angus, Rex,
Beaconsfield, Buckinghamshire.

*

Henry Byrd (Dicky),
Eddie, Sophie,
Islington, London

*

Roland La Tour (Frog),
Angela,
Islington, London.

****

**The Detectives
New Scotland Yard**
Commander Bill Simpson

Sussex CID
D.C.I. 'Foxy' Reynard
D.S. Lucy Groves
D.C.'Next' Best

North Yorkshire CID
D. I. 'Tank' Sherman
D.S. Malcolm Bellamy

Buckinghamshire CID
D. I. Greg Lightfoot

Alan Grainger

8, Belvedere Crescent, Islington, London N1 1QBWednesday 8th March 2006. 4.00 p.m.

S ophie wondered if she had the courage to go through with it. It had been fine back home in Trinidad when she'd made up her mind to tackle him but, standing here on his own doorstep, she wasn't quite so sure. Had she the stomach to face him, to tell him she was his child, the daughter whose existence he'd purposely wiped from his memory. It was why she'd come though: to track him down and confront him, so she'd have to stick it out and do what she'd always intended … find a way to make him pay for ruining her mother's life, and her own.

The street was quiet. It was a murky day, and late in the afternoon. There was little in sight in either direction other than a few parked cars, a taxi driver picking up his fare, a short round woman waddling along with a load of shopping, and two giggling schoolgirls bending under the weight of their heavily laden satchels. With the daylight beginning to fade the street lights had come on, already they were casting a yellow glow on the stone flags in front of the houses of Belvedere Crescent and illuminating the trees of Belvedere Gardens opposite.

As she stood on the top of the chequerboard tiled step of her father's house, with her reflection caught in the painted surface of his shiny front door, she caught a drift of the tantalising odours emanating from a nearby cluster of French bread shops, ethnic restaurants, and continental delicatessens. Islington, with a renewed air of sophistication, was once again becoming a Mecca for winners. If her father lived here he was doing all right.

Number Eight was obviously different to the others

though, having remained a single residence from the day it was built. Well cared for, it had survived in one piece through times when all around were being divided up. The front door was panelled and painted black, and it had Virginia creeper trailing across it from above the pediment. In its centre was a door knocker in the shape of a lion's head. She raised the heavy ring in the effigy's mouth and let it fall on the stud. From the resulting hollow echo which followed she sensed the house was unoccupied but couldn't make up her mind whether she was relieved or disappointed. She tried again, no answer. As she lifted the knocker for a third attempt her attention was unexpectedly caught by a female voice coming up from behind her.

The woman with the shopping, who she'd spotted only a minute or two earlier, was standing on the bottom step.

'There's nobody in dear, 'e's gorn away.' the woman said, putting down her heavy shopping bags. 'Lookin' fer Mr Byrd?'

'Yes … Mr Henry Byrd, he's not about?'

'No, 'e's in Mexico … paintin'. Won't be back fer free or four mumfs. Can I do anyfin'? I look after 'is 'ouse when 'e's away. Jer want somefin?'

'I … 'er … well I just hoped to meet him really, to pass on a message from someone in Trinidad.'

'Oh, Trinidad? Right. Yers, 'e's been there.' the woman said, noting Sophie's sleek brown skin. 'Tha' where y'from then - Trinidad?'

'Yes, I only got here two days ago.'

'Trinidad … I see … yers.' The woman, paused, nodding her head as though she was having difficulty in taking it all in. 'Right … well, y'must be cold, standing out 'ere on the step. If yer'll let me pass I'll open up and yer can come in fera bit if y'like. I'll find some paper so's y'can write 'im a note. Orlright?'

'Thank you, yes … good idea, because I'll more than likely be at home by the time he gets back.'

'In Trinidad?

'Yes, I'll be there in two weeks' time.'

By then the door was open and the woman went ahead to put on the light before coming back for her shopping.

'Here … let me help.' said Sophie, picking up three or four of the polythene supermarket bags.

'Oh fanks.' the woman replied. 'By the way, I'm Mrs Flower

... Ada Flower ... 'e calls me Mrs 'F'. Y'can do the same if yer like.'

'Oh ... right, OK. I'm Sophie Sweetman.'

'Lovely name.'

'Oh ... huh ... I don't feel so lovely with all these goose pimples!'

'No, 'course yer don't. Come on then, dahn the kitchen while I put the kettle on. Yer'll 'ave a cuppa tea won'tcha ... while yer writin' the message like? I s'pose you met 'im when 'e was in Trindad lars year?'

'I didn't as a matter of fact, Mrs Flower ...'

'Mrs 'F' 'll do.'

'All right, Mrs 'F', and ...'er ... no I've never actually met him ... it's just ... well, I know people who know him, if you understand what I mean?'

'Pity 'e's not 'ere, 'e'll be sorry 'e's misstcher.'

'Will he ... I wonder?' said Sophie, shaking her head as she put the bags down.

'Course 'e will, 'e likes young women,' chortled Mrs Flower, 'even if 'e is gettin' on a bi'!'

Sophie's eyebrows shot up. 'Oh really.' she answered, pinching her lower lip between her finger and her thumb. 'And what about Mrs Byrd, I suppose she's with him?'

'There ain't no Mrs Byrd dear. Never 'as been, not ter my knowledge, didntcher know?'

'No ... but I'm not surprised.'

'Go on, why?'

'No reason, it's just my friend said to keep my distance, 'Drop in, leave the message, and go.' She was joking I expect.'

'Hmm ... was she? I'm not so sure.' said Mrs 'F' to herself, as a look of puzzlement began to cross her face. 'Any road up ... as far as I know ... there's never been no Mrs Byrd, 'e's far too cute fer tha'! 'Ere, wha' am I saying? I 'ardly know yer. Anyway the tea's almos' ready, let's take it frough and, while we drink it, y'can write the note... righ'? Bi' o' cake?'

'No the tea will be fine, thank you Mrs 'F'; I'm trying not to eat too many sweet things.' Sophie said, taking the tray Mrs Flower had loaded, and following her back through the hall into the sitting room.

'You take tha' one over there.' said Mrs 'F', pointing to an arm chair beside the marble fireplace, 'and I'll pull over a table so y'can pu' the tea fings on i'.'

While Mrs 'F' was pouring, Sophie took the opportunity to look round ... everywhere, as far as she could see, bore signs of his wealth, and it sickened her. This was worlds away from the little wooden worker's cottage on South Bay Sugar Estate in which she'd been raised, and more than enough to make her writhe in anger. The room they were in, the drawing room, was in the front of the house, it was square shaped, with folding doors leading into a second, smaller, living room, overlooking the back garden. Both were painted in a rich plum colour which set off the elegant furnishings and the glittering array of polished silver photograph frames crowding the mantelpiece. The walls carried only a few framed pencil sketches but, over the fireplace, there was a large oil painting dominating the room. It was the picture of a reclining female nude, a fantastically good looking black woman, thirty-ish with glistening skin, lying on a divan, and displaying enough of a knowing smile to dare any observer to guess what might have just taken place.

Mrs 'F' saw Sophie's attention had been drawn to the voluptuous image. 'Bit 'iffy' dontcher fink luv? Done it 'is self y'know. Y'can see 'is name in the corner, near where 'er clothes is chucked on the floor. Makes yer wonder don't it ... if yer know wha' I mean?'

'Oh yes Mrs 'F', I know exactly what you mean.' said Sophie, staring in horror at the erotic portrait *of her mother!*

'She looks a bit like you.' said Mrs Flower, as a beam of enlightenment crossed her face. 'Yers ... she really do.'

'Like me?' said Sophie 'I don't think so, I'm just an ordinary girl, she looks as though she'd a model ... did you find any writing paper?'

'I'll look now,' said Mrs Flower, crossing to the bureau and starting to rummage in it. 'Sorry, luv ... there ain't nuffin' 'ere ... I 'ave a pad in the kitchen, I'll go an' geddit.'

As soon as she'd left the room, Sophie went over to the mantelpiece and picked up a framed photograph she'd spotted a moment earlier. It was one of five young men standing outside a terraced house, and looked identical to one she had in her hand bag.

For no reason she was ever subsequently able to fathom, she unclipped the back of the frame and took the photo out. It seemed to be the same as her own, the one her mother had given her, the only picture of her father she'd ever seen. But when she turned it over, she found a there was an important difference; they'd all signed this one with their nicknames.

She listened for moment, checking for the sound of Mrs Flower returning from the kitchen with the writing pad. When she heard nothing, she took the print from her hand bag and put it in the frame which she then replaced it on the mantelpiece.

The signed one, the one she'd taken out of the frame, she slipped into her handbag just before Mrs 'F' reappeared.

'Sorry I took so long, will these do?' Mrs 'F' asked.

'Perfect.' answered Sophie, taking the pad Mrs 'F' gave her, and scribbling a few words on the top sheet, before tearing it off and putting it in the envelope she'd also provided. 'I'd better be going,' said Sophie, 'I've a friend picking me up at half past five from a B&B I'm staying in, in Clapham.'

'Yer've 'ardly touched yer tea?' Mrs 'F' said, as she topped up her own. 'I'll put some 'ot in, if yer like.'

'Thanks but 'No', I must be on my way … you won't forget to give Mr Byrd the letter, will you?'

'Trust me.' Mrs 'F' replied, sniffing noisily, and beaming a toothy smile before getting up and conducting the young visitor out into the early evening mist.

Back in her B&B an hour later, Sophie was finally recovering from the tension of her visit to Belvedere Terrace. Ever since she'd returned, she'd been studying the faces of the men in the photograph and trying to remember their names … new and positive clues to her father's background. It may not have amounted to much but it was enough to drain away the guilt she'd been feeling since she swapped the photos. With such a lucky start to her search she might have a better chance of finding out more about him prior to meeting him.

She lay on the bed and tilted the photograph towards the window to see their faces better. The look of arrogance on her father's sickened her, and she couldn't help wondering how she'd react when she finally confronted him face to face. If she'd seen herself in the mirror she'd have known, her teeth were clenched and she was beating her thigh with her fist.

A few minutes later, with her anger subsiding, she put down the photo, lay back, closed her eyes, and began to go over the chain of events which had brought to London, and her father's door …

Her father's father, her paternal grandfather, Gerald Byrd, had been well off and, when he and his wife, Mona, were killed in the London Blitz their estate went into trust for their only child, Henry, who was subsequently raised by Mona's unmarried sister, Imelda, in their home at Belvedere Crescent.

Henry had been a wild boy from the start, and all but beyond the control of his despairing aunt by the time he was sixteen. When he was twenty and having, by then, come into ownership of both the trust and the house, he'd abandoned his doting aunt and his studies, and set off on a life of nomadic profligacy. He professed to be a painter ... and was one, but only in an uninspiring and amateurish sort of way because of his inferior draughtsmanship. Now and again he'd get lucky and, on those occasions, much to his own surprise, as much as anyone else's, he was liable to produce quite a good painting ... the portrait of Sophie's mother being an example.

That his work was generally mediocre never troubled him, for his real and consuming interest wasn't painting at all but the passionate pursuit of young women. When he arrived, uninvited, in Trinidad, to stay with his mother's other sister, Kitty, wife of Harold Sweetman, a local sugar planter, he was immediately on the lookout for what he called 'a bit of fluff' and, in next to no time, he had Harold's illegitimate, but acknowledged, daughter, Gentle, an attractive young half breed West Indian girl, in his sights.

Nine months later, and while Gentle was giving birth to his child, Sophie, Henry was thousands of miles away in pursuit of his next quarry. Gentle and Sophie never saw him again, having successfully dodged his responsibilities in Trinidad, he was up to his tricks again, in Brazil.

As far as Sophie knew, he never attempted to make any further contact with her mother, and he certainly never showed the slightest interest in her. From his standpoint, she might never have been born. Her burning anger at this brutish behaviour had come to a head at the time of her mother's death, a few months earlier and, funded by her own savings and the few dollars her mother had left her, it became the driving force behind her mission of retribution.

In view of what Mrs Flower had told her about him being in Mexico, it was beginning to look as if their paths wouldn't cross yet. Still, there were ten more days before she'd be heading home, and she resolved to get the best out of them by talking to anyone she could find who'd ever known him.

She picked up the photograph again, hoping for inspiration. It was old and badly discoloured, but even so, when she examined it closely, she could see it had been taken outside a terrace house not dissimilar to the one she was staying in Clapham. There were hundreds of similar ones all over South London.

From the young men's facial appearance, and from their clothes, she gauged it to have been taken in the nineteen fifties. It might possibly have been when he'd abandoned college to go on his rampage around the world. With a bottle in one hand and a glass in the other, it could even have been the actual the day of his departure. She turned to the signatures on the back and, by flipping backwards and forwards to check her memory she soon knew she'd every name and face fixed firmly in her mind. On the extreme left of the picture was 'Ghandi', a tall, thin, prematurely bald young man, with rimless glasses. He was wearing a short sleeved white shirt over white trousers, as was the other tall but sturdier man at the other end of the group, a man with the look of a sportsman, who'd signed himself 'Ginger'. Both had on white pullovers with stripes around the neck line and waist, and looked as though they'd just come in from playing cricket.

Between 'Ghandi' and her father was 'Jock', the shortest man in the picture, and the plumpest. He looked like a man who'd shun anything remotely physical and had a foolish inebriated grin on his face. Like Henry, he had a bottle of champagne in one hand and a half full glass in the other. In the middle of the group stood her father, he'd signed himself 'Dicky'. A nickname she knew was often given to anyone called Bird or Byrd.

Between him and 'Ginger' was 'Frog', another low sized man who, like Jock, favoured corduroy trousers and a polo-necked jumper. He had long, windblown, blonde hair, half covering a heavily bearded face, and was wearing open toed sandals. Above the names, someone had printed:

The LMS Club.

So there they were, her father and his four best friends - Ghandi, Jock, Frog and Ginger. If she wanted to know more about him, all she had to do ask them.

4, Balaclava Street, London SW11 1JX
Thursday 9th March 2006. 9.30 a.m.

Ask them ... yes. But, to do so, she'd have to find them first and how would she set about doing that? She had little to go on beyond the photo, the tips she'd got from her eighty year old grandfather, Harold, and a few snippets of information she'd gathered from her mother, who'd only known her father long enough to discover the way to his bed.

Breakfast in the B&B the next morning was over long before she got up. She was still trying to come to grips with the disappointment of the previous day's anti-climax and had spent a restless night grappling with the memory of the wretched painting of her mother, only getting to sleep well into the small hours.

The shower was powerful as Mrs Perkins had said it would be, and she stood with her face in her hands, the refreshing jets of hot water cascading over her as she thought about her father. His father, her paternal grandfather, had suggested she initiate the search at Eight, Belvedere Crescent, his late wife's childhood home, the house where her unmarried older sister, Imelda, had brought Henry up. But he had no idea whether Henry was still living there. Indeed, he had no idea where he was at all; it had just been a suggestion to give Sophie a starting point.

If the surprise she got when the first person to whom she'd spoken knew her father hadn't stunned her so much, and the excitement of getting into his house and sitting in his chair had been less numbing, she might have reacted with less obvious shock to the portrait of her mother over the mantelpiece.

Seeing her mother lying there, unclothed, and draped across the couch with that awful smirk of satisfaction on her face, made her feel sick. Not surprising ... what child would not be upset when confronted by the public exposure of its mother's unlikely behaviour? It was why Sophie had shot off so hurriedly, a decision she'd begun to regret as soon as she was through the door … she should have stayed longer and ask more of Mrs 'F', and she knew it.

She got out of the shower, a white towel turbaned round her wet hair and sat in her bathrobe on the end of the bed, looking at herself in the wardrobe mirror and thinking again of the events of the previous day. After a few minutes she unwound the turban and rubbed her hair until it was nearly dry then, shaking it loose, stood up and went over to the window.

Outside a watery sun was breaking through the clouds, giving a shine to the ivy leaves shrouding the window frame and creating a reflected image of the room in the window glass. Right in the middle of the picture she could see the end of the bed. Beside it was an untidy scattering of her clothes. The whole scene brought the disgusting painting of her mother straight back to her mind.

She walked over and piled the pillows in the middle of the bed, dropped her robe to the floor, and flopped back naked in an unconscious re-creation of her mother's erotic pose. She couldn't have said what prompted her to do it, or why she capped it all by putting on the same look of lust which had been on her mother's face, but the likeness was amazing. From the fall of her breasts, the length of her legs, the rich hazelnut colour of their skin and, above all, the disgusting leer on her face, she was so like her mother it was frightening.

She sat for a while examining her image in the mirror, noting two of the characteristics which marked her ancestry - a straight Anglo Saxon nose and full Afro Caribbean lips, her lineage was defined in her face.

The lascivious smile she'd put on had gone by then, her self-torturing over. She sat up staring into the distance, subconsciously smoothing the skin of the flat of her stomach and running her hands repeatedly up and down her thighs. And then she drew a deep breath and lay back to stare at the ceiling. As she began to drift back to thoughts of her mother once more, the tranquillity was unexpectedly shattered by a loud knock. 'Yes.' she said, snatching up the bathrobe and pulling it on again. It was Mrs Perkins, the landlady. 'You alright dear? When you didn't come down for breakfast I got a bit worried.'

'I'm fine thank you Mrs Perkins, just tired. I think it's the jet lag catching me up.'

'Yes, it probably is. If you're alright then I'll leave you. It was just ... well ... I got a bit concerned y'know, when I didn't see you downstairs.'

'It's kind of you to think of me Mrs Perkins but I'm OK. I'm just getting dressed at the moment, and I'll soon be going out for the day. I'll give you a shout when I leave.'

'Oh ... right ... have a nice day then.'

Half an hour later, she was in the café adjacent to the delicatessen from which she'd bought the previous evening's snack. She'd a large cappuccino before her, a pain-au-chocolat in her fingers, and she was staring at the slow moving traffic. Not that she was conscious of either the people or the vehicles, she was thinking of her next move. There really was nothing for it; she'd have to go back to Belvedere Crescent for another session ... the photograph, the house, and Mrs 'F', were still the best leads she had.

She took a bite from the flaky pastry, gave slight shudder at its staleness, and put it back down on her plate. Then, having drunk her coffee and paid her bill, she made her way to Clapham Common Underground Station.

Belvedere Crescent, Islington, London N1 1QB Thursday 9th March 2006. 11.15 a.m.

When Mrs Flower had seen Sophie go down the steps and set off in the direction of the tube station the previous evening, she thought she'd seen the last of her, so it was quite a surprise when she'd answered the door bell the next day to find the girl waiting there.

'Well, well, it's you again is it, luv? D'yer want somefin'? Yer'd better come in.'

'I did ... I forgot to ask you several things, and I only remembered them on the way to Clapham.'

'I see,' said Mrs Flower, leading her back into the sitting room. 'I can't give yer long; I've an appoin'ment at the 'airdresser's in 'arf an hour.'

'I promise not to be long, five minutes. Can you spare that?'

'Ten ... and notta second more. I'm not so quick as I used ter be. Wha' is i' yer wanna know, then?'

'It's difficult Mrs 'F', what I didn't tell you yesterday was ... I'm a columnist on the Trinidad Echo.'

Mrs Flower's eyes lit up. 'Oh a repor'er, I never met no one from no newspaper before.'

'I'm not a reporter, I'm a columnist. I write a piece every week on whatever I think might interest our readers.'

'Ooh.'

'And I'm getting something together about painters who've submitted work for inclusion in an exhibition which will tour the Caribbean later this summer; Henry Byrd is one of them. The finished works of most of the artists who have visited the islands to paint have never been seen in our part of the world. They're usually exhibited and sold in London or New York.'

'I see. And 'ow can I 'elp yer?'

'Well Mrs 'F', said Sophie, taking out a notebook and pencil, which she'd bought at the news agent's shop at Clapham Junction station expressly to give authenticity to her role and, flipping back the cover, asked, 'Can you tell me much about his childhood?'

'Mr Byrd's? Oh dear, no I carn, even though I've been workin' forrim fer fifteen years. Sorry.'

'What a shame, I was sure you'd know. Never mind ... what about women friends then ... you said he wasn't married?'

Mrs Flower shook her head. 'Carn 'elp yer there neiver ducks, and I'm not sure I should, even if I could.'

'Fair enough, does he have any close friends at all, or brothers or sisters?'

'Not tha' I know of ... 'e was an only child I believe. E's 'ad a few friends call 'ere from time to time but I don' know much abaht 'em, in fact I don' know nuffin' abaht 'em.'

'What about anyone in these photographs?' Sophie asked, reaching over to the mantelpiece and picking one up at random.

Mrs Flower took the picture and gave it a brief glance 'No. I don't know 'em.'

Sophie nodded and put it back before taking up the frame from the back into which she'd inserted her own photograph the day before. 'What about these men, who are they?'

'Notta clue, luv.'

Sophie pushed the picture towards Mrs Flower and asked again, 'Are you sure you don't know any of them?'

Mrs Flower squinted at the five men in the photograph. 'Lef' me glasses at 'ome this morning bu' no, I don' know none of 'em ... excep' ... perhaps this man 'ere.' she said pointing to the bearded face. 'E does look a bi' familiar now I come to fink of i', if it's who I fink i' is, 'e used to teach Ar' down at the Comprehensive. 'E taugh' my daugh'er. I'd ring her but she's on 'oliday until next week - in Greece.'

'Know his name?'

'Nah, I can't remember, i' would've been a long time ago, she's gettin' on fer firty. Now wai' a minute, I tell a lie, I do remember - a French name I fink. 'E's dead I believe - I fink 'e was knocked down by a bus.'

'No use my worrying about him then ... and you know

18

none of the others.'

She shook her head. 'Sorry I gotta go.'

'Don't apologise, you've helped me a lot.' said Sophie, getting up from the chair in which she'd been sitting, and picking up her coat to leave. 'Thanks again for your help. You'll remember to give Mr Byrd my note.'

'Y'never arst me abaht 'is son.' Mrs Flower answered, rising to go herself.

Sophie's thin black eyebrows shot up. 'He has a son?'

'Only seen 'im the once, but 'e's got one orlrigh'. They don't ge' on - 'im and his dad - don' ge' on a tall.'

'D'you know much about him?'

'No, nuffin' - I jus' remember 'e came 'ere one day an' five minutes later 'e was gorn. Mr Byrd slammed the door when 'e lef' - nearly took i' off of its 'inges. He was 'opping mad, tol' me never ter let the boy in if 'e came again. Said 'e was an imposta after 'is money. But I don' reckon 'e was no imposta. No, 'e was 'is son orlrigh', the likeness was amazin'. Come ter fink of it, 'e was the spittin' image of the young man in the middle of tha' pitcher on the mantelpiece, and 'e's Mr Byrd, isn' 'e? Look I gotta be going.'

'Mrs 'F' I could hug you. You've given me two people to follow up - his son and this French art teacher, provided he isn't dead. I only need one anyway. Sorry I've delayed you so much.'

'Well I'm glad yer pleased. Send me a copy of yer newspaper article when it comes out will yer? Look, ducks, I've gotta rush or I'll lose the appoin'men'.'

'Don't' worry Mrs 'F' I'll walk down the road with you.' said Sophie, her face wrinkling into a slightly disbelieving expression as she considered the fact she had a brother, albeit a half one.

They walked down to the junction where Mrs Flower turned off for the hairdresser's. Sophie went in the opposite direction to see what she could discover at St Simon's, the local Comprehensive School, on Liverpool Road.

Miss Tempest, the school secretary, was very helpful. She recognised the man in the photograph straight away. 'That's Mr La Tour, he used to teach Art, but he's not with us any longer.' she said, tapping her forefinger on the picture of the bearded man between 'Dicky' and 'Ginger' and, going over to her computer, scrolled back through the records until she found the address at which he'd been living when he'd been teaching there.

'Lucky your data goes so far back.' Sophie observed.

Miss Tempest shook her head. 'I've got everything from the day I started, nearly twenty years ago.'

'And do you know Mr La Tour well?'

'Did - he's dead, killed in a road accident years ago, leaving his wife to bring up their daughter. It's a bit unkind I dare says, but the smell of whisky's what I always associate with that man.' She paused for a moment, thinking, and then went on to recall in some detail what had happened on the day he'd been knocked down and killed. Apparently he'd been in a rush to get home and had stepped out into the road to get past a group of dawdling school children. He didn't seem to have seen the bus at all, and the unfortunate driver had no time to apply his brakes fully.

'It wasn't anyone's fault other than Mr La Tour's,' she said, 'and the rumours of alcohol were quashed for the sake of his wife.'

His old address, which Miss Tempest gave her, was nearby in Primrose Mansions. It turned out to be in an ugly and badly run down early fifties block of flats. The whole surrounding area couldn't have been more different to the nearby leafy elegance of Belvedere Crescent. In comparison to it, the Primrose Mansions flats gave the distinct impression of being totally unloved. She went up in a graffiti decorated lift, walked along the landing until she reached number Thirty Four, and knocked. A young woman in her late twenties with a baby in her arms and a toddler clutching at her skirts with one hand as he sucked the thumb of the other opened the door, permitting the steamy smell of clothes being washed to gust out from behind her.

'Yeah?'

'I'm trying to contact anyone who can tell me where I can find the family of a Mr Roland La Tour who, I understand, used to live here.' said Sophie.

'Why's tha' then?' asked the woman, glancing down and removing boy's thumb from his mouth. 'Who wants ter know?'

'My name's Sophie Sweetman, I'm from Trinidad, and I'm over here trying to trace my father and his family. Mr La Tour was one of his friends when they were at college.'

'I never 'eard of no Sweetman, so I carn 'elp yer.'

'Are you a relative of Mr La Tour's?'

'Wha' is it ter you?' The woman reached for the edge of the

door and started to retreat inside.

Sophie held out an open hand, begging an answer, 'It's important to me because my father abandoned my mother before I was born. I want to know all about him and find out why he did so.'

'Right ... right.' said the woman, opening the door slightly wider again, and dropping her free hand to her son's head to ruffle his hair. 'Bit of a one, yor dad, was 'e? Knock you and yer mum abaht a bit?'

Sophie smiled. 'Walked out the minute she told him she was expecting me, and shot off to Brazil the next day. Mum never saw him again. Can I come in for a moment, it's hard talking out here?'

As if to confirm the point, the door of the adjacent flat opened and the neighbour stuck her head round it giving Sophie a black look and asking the woman with the baby if she was 'orlright.'

'Yeah, I'm OK, Lil.' the woman answered, and turning back to Sophie said, 'Yer'd betta come in then.'

As they walked down the hallway into the kitchen at the back of the flat the young woman introduced herself. 'I'm Roly's daugh'er ... Angela - 'Angie' if yer like, Angie La Tour.'

The kitchen was tiny, with condensation streaming down the window panes. Below it the draining board and sink were piled high with used mugs, plates, saucepans ... and baby's bottles. Underneath them the washing machine stood open, with damp clothes tumbling from it. The place was a mess, so was the huge unshaven man, sitting in his vest and boxer shorts at a small table attached to the wall eating a plate of sausages and chips. He was wearing a black baseball cap with a Nike sign on it and hardly looked up as they entered, just concentrated on his reading and his food, a large proportion of which was poised in front of his face speared on his fork.

'Tha's Wayne,' said Angie, waving her hand in the man's general direction.

He totally ignored them as he chomped, open mouthed, and continued to read the racing page of what looked like the Daily Mirror, propped up against a topless bottle of Heinz Tomato Ketchup with dried out dribbles running down its neck.

'Hello.' said Sophie, smiling, and trying not to stare at the repulsive sight.

"Ere grab hold of Lance will yer?' said Angie, holding out the baby. 'I'll shove this stuff in the dryer and we'll go inside.'

As she transferred the washing to the dryer, and the baby to Sophie, she continued to ask questions. 'So why did yer want ter speak ter my dad then? Didn' yer know 'e was dead?'

'I wasn't sure.' said Sophie, handing the stinking child back to its mother when they entered the living room, and making for the only chair not covered with clothes. The little thumb sucking boy, who'd followed them in, climbed straight up onto her lap.

'Yew orlright alrigh' there wiv Garf? I'll send 'im in ter Wayne if 'e's a nuisance. ... Yeah, my Dad, died a long time ago, 'e was knocked dahn by a bus.'

'Really, that's awful. How old were you then?'

'Firteen. 'Ere, wha's this all abaht?'

'Me. It's all about me really. I told you; I want to ask my father why he ran off.'

'So wha's tha' got ter do wiv *my* dad?'

Sophie took a big breath and told Angie the whole story, ending by explaining the connection she'd made after seeing the photograph with the names on it.

'Le's get this straigh' then,' said Angie, 'yer want ter track 'em all dahn and find out what sor' of a geezer your dad was before yer tackle 'im.'

'Right.'

'And 'is name's 'enry Byrd right? And 'e was a mate of my dad years ago when they was all schudents.'

'Correct.'

' 'E's a miserable bastard.'

'Who is?'

'Your dad ... 'enry Byrd ... 'e's a bastard - a toffee nosed bastard. I know 'im, oh yes, I know 'im orlrigh', 'im and tha' big house 'e lives in. No time for me though, when I needed a bit of 'elp after my mum went an' died.'

'You've lost both your parents?'

'Alcos both of 'em, 'e fell under the bus when 'e was out of his mind with the drink. And she ... well poor cow ... she drank 'erself ter deaf. It was around then when I went rahnd ter ask your old man fer a bob or two. I'd been 'in care' fer a while and I 'ated i'. When I was fifteen I tried ter run away. Bastard wooden 'elp me though, your dad.'

'How did you work out the connection between them?'

'Easy ... same as you, we 'ad a photo, wiv all their names

on, on our kitchen dresser when I was a kid. I've still gorrit' ... over there be'ind Wayne's birfday cards on the top of the 'tele'.'

Sophie looked across and sure enough there it was, in a wooden frame instead of a silver one, but otherwise identical. 'And did they all sign yours?'

'Yeah ... jus' wiv their nicknames though ... but I know who they all are, 'cos my dad once tol' me. Tracked 'em dahn I did, same time I tracked dahn your dad. None of 'em gave me a tosser.'

'You found and spoke to them all?' Sophie couldn't believe what she was hearing. Here was a chance to jump forward a good few places.

'Every one of 'em except 'Ginger' 'e' was in 'orspital wiv a bad back and I never go' in ter see 'im.' said Angie, looking thoughtfully at the photograph in her hand, playing out in her mind the memory of the chilly and disinterested reception she'd got from those of the group she *had* met.

'Go on.' encouraged Sophie, 'tell me more.'

Angie took a big breath and sniffed again. 'They was all toffs yer see ... and my dad weren't. 'Ow he got mixed up wiv 'em in the firs' place I could never figure out ... Anyway they was pretty close at one time and they 'ad this drinking club ... says it on the back of the photograph ... 'The LMS Club'. Load of stupid rubbish. But they fough' it was great. I reckon i' must 'ave been the drink wha' brough' 'em together because tha's the only fing I can see they 'ad in common.'

'My father isn't an alcoholic I don't think.'

'Nor more was mine when the pho'o was taken, 'e just kep' getting worse, Mum tol' me. Ruined 'is life.'

'I'm sure it did.'

'Nah, tha's not what I mean'. Wha' I mean' was tha' i' ruined 'is life as a sculptor because 'is 'and shook so bad 'e couldn' 'old a chisel.'

'I'm surprised he managed to get a job as a teacher. How did he pass his exams?'

'Well 'e weren' a real teacher, par' time only. 'E'd been tryin' ter get on the wagon fer two years, an' 'e was beginnin' ter line up a few bits o' stone, when 'e went an' fell.'

'In front of a bus ... yes I know.'

'No before tha'. 'E fell from off of 'is pedestal. Got totally 'Brahms and Liszt' one nigh' and never really got off the drink again, or even tried, until the day 'e died.'

'That's a dreadful …' Sophie was about to say, when Wayne burst into the room.

'Goin' dahn the Nag's.' he grunted, and disappeared again.

'The Nag's 'ead … it's our local.' Angie said by way of explanation. ' 'E spends most of his time dahn there.'

'You do have problems don't you?' said Sophie, as she tried to ease her arm free of Garth, who'd worked his way into a comfortable position nestled into her bosom, and was quietly snoring. 'D'you have any brothers or sisters?'

'I gotta narf bruvver - Eddie.' replied Angie, scratching the top of her head.' And d'yer know wha'? I was jus' finkin' … 'e must be yourn as well.'

Sophie's eyebrows shot up 'Mine? … How?'

Angie started to giggle and began slapping her knees as she rocked in the chair at the news she was about to deliver. 'Shaken yer 'aven't I? You didn' know abaht Eddie didja?'

'No, not specifically. I knew I had a brother, Mrs Flower told me yesterday when I called round to the house. She didn't tell me his name though. So, if my father is Eddie's father as well … who's his mother?'

'Tha's it, innit? … 'Is muvver was my Mum.'

'Your Mum was his mother? … Oh, now I see it, after your father's death, his wife …'

'Yeah, yeah, a year or two after *my* Dad died, Mum got tergether wiv *your* Dad. Next minute Eddie was on the way!'

'They never married - your mother and my father?'

'Married? Yor Dad and my Mum? Nah, you must be jokin', 'e shot orf.'

'What do you mean?' asked Sophie, still struggling with Angie's impossible Cockney accent.

'Deser'ed my mum like 'e deser'ed yourn, 'e did.'

'As soon as she got pregnant?'

'Yeah … I tol' yer 'e was a bastard.'

Sophie nodded slowly; absentmindedly stroking Garth's hair as she tried to digest the information she'd been given. Based on what Angie said, it seemed likely her father had gone to Trinidad immediately he'd got wind of Angie's mother's pregnancy. It also appeared to her that she and Angie must somehow be related, and she wondered if Angie had come to the same conclusion. 'What d'you think it makes us?'

Angie obviously had thought about it and started chuckling. 'Notta clue darlin' ... I ain' gotta flippin' clue. 'Ere, are yew orlright wiv 'im?'

'Garth? Yes he's fine. I was just wondering though, does Mrs Flower know about you, as well as Eddie?'

'Old Fanny Flower?'

'His house keeper.'

' 'Ousekeeper! Fanny Flower! ... Don't make me larf, she lives one floor dahn from me. 'She's a cleaner, tha's all - buckets and mops - 'ands and knees ... 'ouse keeper, my arse! So wha' did she tell yer abaht Eddie?'

'Nothing really, it was just as I was leaving. Not his name anyway ... she told me he crashed into her one day just as she was coming out of the front door.'

'And wound up 'ere ten minutes la'er like you did. Must be somefin' abah' this place.'

'You in touch with him at all?'

'Eddie? 'Course I am, 'e's my bruvver.'

'It'll take a bit of time to get my head round all this Angie. Do we have any other half brothers and sisters tucked away anywhere?'

Angie grinned. 'Not tha' I know of.'

'And you and Eddie were brought up together.'

'We was no'.' she said indignantly, 'We was taken from Mum and Dad because of the drink, and pu' inter care.'

'From which you both ran away, right?'

'Wrong; I did. I run away a good few times - but Eddie didn' - 'e was too young. 'E got adopted eventually ... by the couple wha' foster dim. 'E was lucky.'

'And do you see much of him?'

'Oh yeah, Eddie offen comes up fer the weekend. 'im and Wayne ge's on like an 'ouse on fire ... West 'Am.'

'West what?'

' 'Am ... oh orlright ... Ham, West Ham' she said, carefully pronouncing the 'H', 'itza foo'ball club. They're suppor'ers ... foller them all over the place.'

'And where does Eddie live, I'd like to try to meet him before I go back to Trinidad.'

'Portsmuff, tha's wher 'e lives. I'll give yer 'is address if yer like. But 'e's easy ter find, 'e works in the gardens dahn the sea fron'. The Esplanade Gardens. There's a boa'ing pool there and flower beds and tha'.'

'So he's a gardener.'

'Charge 'and ... Knows 'is stuff .... Gotta job wiv the local council when 'e left school. Took to i' like a duck ter wa'er.'

'A happy ending then.'

'Yer jokin' ... look at me. I'm a mess and I'm only twenny nine, and there's tha' lot Dad used ter knock around with wiv, got money ter burn because of 'im ... an' they wouldn't give us a brass farvin' when we needed it.'

'Why do you say 'because of him', Angie?'

'Because they bought 'is work from 'im when 'e was skint, didn' they - and then made forchune out of it. Gave 'im buttons, and made fahsands when they sold it - miserable sods.'

'Really, I don't understand.'

'Ah, well, tha's another story. Dad's stuff went and got popular yer see - only a year or two before 'e died - when 'e was on the drink. All 'is sculptures sho' up in value and those bastards 'ad most of 'em ... made a flamin' stack o'money they did. My dad didn't 'ave nuffin' lef' ter sell, didn't even 'ave the price of a pin' when 'e died. 'Ere, I've got ter ge' on wiv the tea for these two, and when I've gottem fed I gotta leave them wiv 'er next door so's I can ge' ter work.'

'Oh, I'd better go then. What do you do?'

'I'm on 'the cash', six ter ten every nigh', dahn the Spar supermarket on the corner.'

'Tough life.'

'Tell me abah tit!'

Sophie slid out of the chair without disturbing Garth, who'd gone to sleep again, 'I think I'll go down to Portsmouth try to find Eddie tomorrow.' she said, 'I can get there and back from London in a day can't I?

'O'course you can, I tol' yer, 'e often comes up fer a match of a Sa'urday. Don't ferge' - The Esplanade Gardens - and 'is name's Eddie Parsons since 'e got 'imself adopted but remember, 'e ge's touchy if anyone mentions anyfin' abaht my mum and your old man, and tha' stuck up LMS lot.'

'I can't say I'm surprised.' Sophie replied.

The Esplanade Gardens, Portsmouth, Hampshire.
Friday 10th March, 2006. 11.30 a.m.

Sophie got off the bus and crossed to the other side. In front of her the public recreation area took up the whole space between the road and the promenade, beyond which white topped waves could be seen rolling down the Solent and out into The English Channel.

Across to the south west a couple of miles away, and almost invisible in the hazy blue-grey light, she could see the low profile of the Isle of White. While up to the right and in a north westerly direction, was the long stretch of Southampton Water, gateway to the oceans of the world for ships sailing out of the famous port, home to Britain's passenger fleet.

Nearer at hand she spotted the dull grey painted super structure of warships either anchored or berthed in the nearby harbour of Portsmouth, or 'Portsmuff', as Angie pronounced it, a place known to the men of the Royal Navy as 'Pompey'.

As if to underline the importance of Sophie's visit one of the greatest ocean liners of all time, the Queen Elizabeth II, more popularly called the 'QE2', was emerging from the sea mist and moving majestically towards her moorings at the end of another transatlantic crossing. Sophie shook her head in near disbelief at the ship's towering height.

On the other side of the railings, separating the park from the road, a dozen rowing boats tied to iron rings on the boating lake's wooden quay, waited for the summer and the hordes of children who would splash about in them as soon as the weather warmed up. An elderly man and a small boy were watching the child's yacht racing across the water, its sails skimming tiny wavelets whipped up by the breeze. Sophie watched too, not for the progress of the child's boat, but for a sight of anyone working in one of the flower beds beyond the lake, for this was where Angie had said Eddie Parsons might be found.

There *was* a man there. He'd been digging between the shrubs in an ornamental display of miniature evergreens and was busy scraping clay from the tines of his fork with a twig when she spotted him. As she peered across he looked up, somehow sensing he was being observed. She knew it was Eddie straight off. She'd never seen a picture of him or thought of asking Angie what he looked like, but she knew him immediately, and set off towards the gate into the park. He watched her for a while then, stabbing his fork into the ground, walked to meet her.

As she approached he began to smile and nod slowly. 'It's Sophie isn't it?' he asked, as they drew closer.

She bit her lip, to cover her nervousness, and nodded back. 'How did you know?'

'Angie.' he answered, stopping a few feet short of her, and making no move to reach out. 'She rang me last night. I've been expecting you since mid-morning.'

'I'm glad you got some warning.' Sophie replied, awkwardly, wondering at the same time if she should offer her hand then, thinking better of it, asked, 'Any chance we could get a half hour to talk before I go back up to London.'

Eddie burst out laughing. 'Half an hour to talk to a sister who didn't exist yesterday, 'course I can. Look I'm nearly finished the job I'm doing here, and I usually knock off early on a Friday. If I work through my lunch break I reckon I can finish at about half two. I'd stop now but I'm in charge of the lads on this stretch. If I slope off they'll all be doing it.'

Sophie was impressed. 'OK. That's fine. Where shall we meet?'

'Can you see the café over there?' said Eddie, gripping her elbow lightly with one hand and pointing with the other.

'The Rainbow Room?'

'Yeah … I'll be there at two thirty. How's that?'

'OK. At half past two.' she replied, as he walked back to the flower bed, pulled up his fork, and moved on to where Sophie could see the backs of two other green overalled men kneeling between the plants.

Eddie had been a surprise. After Angie, she'd been

expecting to have to decipher *his* cockney accent and idiom; but he was quite different, lucid and easy to understand. He had a London accent, but not one as puzzling as Angie's: no weird expressions, and not so short of tees and aitches she couldn't comprehend him. Why was there such a big difference between them?

She strolled down the seafront path for the best part of two miles before turning back to the pavement of the Esplanade and heading for the café.

The sun, which had appeared briefly, had been gobbled up by the clouds by then, and it was very cold - not much like a winter in Trinidad. Tugging her white woolly hat down to cover her ears and pulling some gloves from her pocket, she snuggled into the pale blue Puffa jacket she'd bought in Gatwick Airport and strode out for the café, counting off the steps as she went. When she got to the door she shoved it open and walked to the back of the room, where she slid onto a bench seat as far as she could get from chilly winds outside. Barely had she settled when Eddie came in.

He was extremely smart, his rubber boots exchanged for highly polished black brogues, and his overalls replaced by a leather jacket worn over a pale grey polo necked jumper and similarly coloured trousers. The baseball cap had gone too, and his brown curly hair wet from a recently taken shower was shining under the neon strip lights as he slid along the bench opposite to her. He was an impressive looking young man, and he looked to be anything but a corporation gardener.

Sophie nodded and inclined her head in approval. 'You're quite a surprise. Nothing like I expected from what Angie told me.'

'Well, Angie's lost it. Stuck with that lump of lard she's tied herself to it's no surprise is it?'

'I thought he was your friend.'

'Wayne Tyler! No way. He's a lazy slob. I just used to go up to stay with her in the football season so I could watch West Ham on a Saturday with a couple of mates I've known since school.'

'She told me you and Wayne went together.'

'Yeah, he used to come with us sometimes if we couldn't lose him, bloody limpet. I used to try to freeze him out but the guy's too thick to notice and, as the last thing I wanted was have Angie on my back, I usually let him tag along with us. Angie never ceases trying to shove us together. I stopped going in the end, I haven't been for ages. How is she?'

'She's alright I suppose, but from what I saw Wayne's not much help to her.'

'He's useless, but she doesn't see it. She's always on at me to get together with him and sort out that 'LMS' lot, she's really got it in for them. It's amazing, she blames them for *all* her troubles, and she expects me and Wayne to give 'em a good smacking.'

'A good smacking?'

'Ah, it's an expression - means give them a good hiding, you know, teach 'em a lesson.'

'And you don't want to do it.'

'Why should I? I've no problem with them.'

'No bitterness?'

'Against them as a whole? No. My problem's just to do with one of them - the bastard who ditched my mum.'

'And mine!'

'Yes, sorry, and yours … tell me about it! In fact, what about joining forces to take him down a peg?'

'It's a tempting idea Eddie, but we hardly know each other do we? We need to talk a lot more before we go down that road. So come on, tell me your side of the story and I'll tell you mine.'

'Get straight to the point you mean?'

'It's why I'm here.'

'OK. Let's have something to eat and then we can talk for as long as you like.'

'Or until the last train leaves for London.'

'Fair enough.'

Three hours, a couple of plates of beans on toast and several pots of tea later, she had his story. It was much as Angie had already told her, he'd come into the world as the result of a one night stand between Henry Byrd and Angie's mother, Mary La Tour, the widow of Henry's late friend, Roly, who'd been killed by the bus. When Mary told him she was pregnant a few weeks later, he couldn't escape quickly enough. He gave her a handful of cash and vanished, leaving her to cope with raising two children, Angie and Eddie. It was a familiar story! Even when he returned to London a year or so afterwards, he never made any attempt to re-establish contact and she resorted to alcohol for comfort, as had poor Roly before her. Not surprisingly the home fell apart and the children were taken into care.

By the time Eddie had finished his life's story he was as grey as the clouds outside and was staring glumly down at his white knuckled hands gripping the edge of the table. Sophie couldn't resist stretching across the table to lay hers on them, causing him to look up. The baleful expression on his face had aged him; he seemed ten years older than he had when he'd joined her an hour earlier. Then, quite suddenly, he smiled.

'Your turn,' he said, 'come on, tell me your story.'

'Let's have a rest from stories for a bit Eddie, I'm finding all this rather difficult.'

He nodded. 'When're you going back to Trinidad?'

'Middle of next week.'

'You can stay with me if you like, after all you are my sister, I've got a little flat. There's a spare bed if you want it.'

She shook her head. 'I'd love to, I really would, but I'm going to spend a bit of time trying to find some of those friends of his in this LMS Club thing. Get to know more about him, I need to know exactly what sort of man he is before I tackle him.'

'Tackle him or throttle him? I'll bet you'll discover he's always been a bastard.'

'Maybe I will, but I still want to talk to any of them I can find. Do you know who they are?'

'Yes, Angie winkled 'em all out.'

'And have you met any of them?'

'Not me, but she has. I'll give you the list she wrote for me, if you want. We'll have to go back to my place to get it. It's just round the corner from here - five minutes.'

On the way there Sophie worked out why Eddie and Angie were so different. He seemed to have recognised how their childhood attitudes hadn't got them anywhere, and had resolved to pull himself out of the mess he'd been making of his life. Separated from Angie after he'd refused to run away with her for the fourth time, he'd already unknowingly made the most significant decision of his life and, within a few months, under the supportive influence of his new foster parents, George and Sylvia Parsons, he'd begun to prosper. When they saw the change in him they went the extra step and adopted him.

He'd attended school regularly and his teachers had quickly recognised untapped ability. After that there was no stopping him.

When he left school he secured a job as trainee in the Parks Department of Wandsworth Borough Council in what amounted to an apprenticeship, and backed it up with night classes, at Kew Polytechnic to study for a diploma in Public Gardens Management. Once he'd finished his training and received his certificate he was ready for promotion. The opportunity came when he was engaged by Portsmouth City Council as charge hand responsible for all The Esplanade sea front gardens - he was on his way. Before he was finished, he hoped, he'd be a Parks Superintendent with a nice little house to go with the job.

Angie, it seemed, had gone the other way and wound up with the same drink problem which, one way or another, had been the undoing of her parents.

Uncontrollable at school, uncontrollable in the foster home where she'd wound up after absconding so frequently from others, she'd quickly slipped down to the lowest level of human behaviour with a chip on her shoulder which would have crippled an ox. Oddly enough, Wayne Tyler had been her saviour.

Wayne, who nobody else could stick, had been an abandoned child himself but somehow he managed to retain a little bit of self-respect and had taken Angie under his wing when he'd found her sleeping under a railway arch.

Between them they'd dragged themselves from the bottom of the pile and when the first child arrived they'd continued to slowly lever themselves up.

Currently, after years 'in the gutter', they'd achieved a level of self-respectability and family responsibility they would have scorned when they first met. Both twenty nine years old, and with a second child to help concentrate their minds, they'd probably got as far as they ever would, but it was still a lot farther than they'd have dared to dream of five years earlier. All that was left of Angie's old attitude was the burning anger at what she perceived to be the injustices perpetrated on her father, and hence on her mother and herself, by what she called 'those miserable lousers in The LMS Club'. She was as determined to get her pound of flesh out of them.

By the time they got to the flat Sophie had a good idea of what made the English side of her extended family tick, and she could see she'd be better distancing herself as soon a she could from Angie, while giving Eddie time to expand his thoughts on taking their father down 'a peg or two'. Only then, could she decide whether or not to join forces with him.

'What time's your train?' he asked, putting his key in the front door Yale lock.

'I'd like to be on my way at eight if possible. There are quite a few going through Clapham Junction which depart around then.'

Eddie shoved the door open and stood back to let her pass. 'Go right through. I'll put the kettle on. We needn't leave here until seven thirty ... that'll give us plenty of time. Come on now it's your turn, you've not said much yet.'

'OK, but no more tea for me. I wouldn't normally drink what I've drunk today in a year. Have you coffee?'

'Not your sort of coffee, just the granule stuff.'

'It'll do. So what do you want to know about me then - there's not much to tell. I had a happy childhood thanks to my Trinidadian grandmother and my English grandfather, who between them saw my mother through her most difficult days. We lived on my grandfather's sugar plantation in our own 'chattel', which is what a cottage is called in Trinidad, and everyone worked on the estate in some capacity or other. I wanted for nothing, except for a father, and it was only when I grew up I began to get curious about him.'

'And you woke up to life!'

'I suppose so. But, as the facts were trickled out to me, I began to get more and more angry, and when my mother died I resolved to come over here to find him. What I'll say to him, I don't know, except he'll be sorry he ever went to Trinidad.'

'So you are like Angie and me after all - you need your pound of flesh as much as we do.'

'A pound of his flesh. I'm not bothered about the others in his silly club except to get information out of them.'

'And you'll come back when you've worked out a plan will you? That'll cost you - what do you do?'

'Well, I told his housekeeper I was reporter for the Trinidad Echo ... but I'm not ... I'm an Air Stewardess with Continental Airlines. I've been on the Chicago run for the last two years but I'm trying to get into BA on their London route.'

'Which'll get you to London from time to time?

'Yes it will. I'll have to move to Tobago if it comes off, but I won't mind, Tobago's a lovely place and I'll be able to get over to Trinidad on a staff discounted flight easily enough when I need to.'

she said, glancing at her watch, 'I reckon by late summer I'll be here twice a month. But right now I've got to go; have you the list?'

He went over to the side board, took out a piece of paper torn out of a school exercise book and gave it to her. 'I hope you can understand Angie's notes. Give me a call before you go back home and tell me what you've made of it.'

She took the sheet of paper over to the standard lamp and read through the entries someone had typed on it.

The LMS Club Members
(nicknames, names and addresses)

(Ghandi) - Jonathan Melchitt, 'St Anne's House, Horsham Common, Sussex - Publisher

(Jock) - George Mc Fee, 'The Malthouse', Point Hill, Lewes, Sussex - Stockbroker

(Ginger) - Rory Brett, The Mede Manor Hotel, Beaconsfield, Buckinghamshire - Hotelier

(Dicky) - Henry Byrd, Eight Belvedere Crescent, Islington, London, N1 1QB - Artist

(Frog) - Roland Latour - 34, Primrose Mansions, Islington, London, NI 7AS - Sculptor (died 1989)

'So that's them is it? The LMS Club - they sound like a weird bunch don't they?' she said, looking at her watch again and zipping up the Puffa jacket. 'Look Eddie, I've got to go, I'll ring you after I've tracked them down and made up my mind. You never know, we might join forces after all.'

Five minutes later she'd gone, leaving Eddie to wonder what had hit him.

The Odeon Cinema
Leicester Square London WC2H 7JY
Sunday 16th July 2006. 7.20 p.m.

The crowd was immense; the manager reckoned they hadn't had one like it since the previous 'Harry Potter'. 'Premières', he hated them all; thousands of screaming fans fighting for a place at the front to watch the arrival of dozens of 'prominent' guests, of whom no one had ever heard … and all expecting to be fawned on. The press; nothing but a load of anorak clad hooligans.

Worst of all of them were the stars - petulant, self-opinionated, bad mannered egocentrics, so full of their own importance they usually wound up tripping over it … yobs the lot of them, he reckoned. He couldn't wait for Monday morning to see the City of Westminster road sweepers move in to brush away the mess they left behind.

'Boss's looking a bit grumpy tonight ain't 'e Fred?' said the chief projectionist to his assistant.

'We'll steer clear of 'im then; go down the canteen and 'ave a cuppa. There'll not be much 'appening 'ere for another hour.'

'Double checked our stuff?'

'Treble checked it.'

'Right … canteen then.'

An hour later and, just as Fred had predicted, things started to happen.

Two hours later again, matters were peaking outside for the minor celebrities were all 'in' and only the really big names - the actors who starred in the film - had yet to come. They arrived late, in a cavalcade of cars which had picked up them and their 'hanger's on' at The Dorchester Hotel, where they'd been taking on a few nerve calming drinks.

As the cars drew up the crowd, mostly of placard or autograph book carrying young girls, bounced up and down in a frenzy of waving arms and chanting voices.

Lining the route in front of the fans were the security guards; big shaven headed men with no necks, whose huge muscles were straining to burst the seams of their improbable black bow-tied evening attire.

Here and there, between the security cordon and the rope to restrain the fans, press men, cameras at the ready, jostled for position. When the leading car stopped and the door opened the crowd roared in anticipation of a close up of the occupants. It died to a moan though, when they didn't recognise either of the people who alighted. As the minutes ticked by, and more cars drew up to discharge their passengers, the crowd's excitement began to rise again. Finally the car they were all waiting for drew up and the fans went mad, yelling for their hero ... 'Rex' ... 'Rex' ... 'Rex'.

This extravaganza was part of the publicity for Rex Brett's second film - 'My Love, My Love' for which the pundits were forecasting massive world-wide acclaim. His first - 'The Lonely Garden' - had already brought him into the public arena, this epic could rocket him to international stardom.

As he stepped from the car the screaming rose even higher. He pretended not to notice, tried to appear aloof ... but the glint in his eye gave him away ... he was thrilled to bits.

A beautiful young woman, half his age, emerged from the limousine next and took his arm as they slowly walked through the throng. Just before they got to the step leading to the theatre's foyer he half turned, presenting the profile which featured on every hoarding in London, and the crowd went wild. Then, as he was about to mount the step, a reporter pushed through the security guards and leapt to his side.

'Who's the new girlfriend Rex ... where's Eva?'

A thunderous look replaced the fixed smile on the actor's face and he drew back his fist and threw a straight left at the press man, dropping him to the ground with blood trickling from his flattened nose. The press corps, to a man, shoved forward. The crowd surged after them. The screaming rose to a crescendo and the whole colourful pageant descended into chaos.

The dawn sunlight was shafting through a gap in the

bedroom curtains by the time the cinema manager eventually got back to his suburban home in New Malden. As he slid into bed, alongside his wife, she half turned. 'Go alright, did it?'

'Alright?' he exclaimed, in a loud whisper. 'Only the best bloody première we ever had. Rex Brett floored a guy from the Daily Mirror and started a riot which spread all over Leicester Square. Can't wait to see what the papers make of it.'

The Mede Manor Hotel
Beaconsfield, Bucks.
Monday July 17th August 2006. 9.45 a.m.

Bloody Rex! He's in the news again.' said Angus Brett, Rex's older brother, putting down the newspaper he was reading and drinking the last of his coffee.

Around him was the debris of his breakfast. Opposite to him was his yawning wife, still in a dressing gown and blinking in the smoke which was drifting up from a cigarette held between her nicotine stained fingers. Not a pleasant sight at that time in the morning. Not an unusual one either after the hard night's drinking which went on behind the bar as they'd waited for a clientele who no longer appeared and thought of the halcyon days when the place had throbbed. But those days were gone, and they had no-one to blame but themselves.

All the warning signs had been there from the day they'd taken over yet, when they'd unravelled the figures and found the cupboard bare, they, like Angus and Rex's popular father, 'Ginger', had looked the other way.

The cash had been flowing in the wrong direction for years under Ginger's captaincy and all he'd done was cast his hard won profits into the torrent in the hope they'd stem it, a singular act of irresponsibility which would have had his own father turn in his grave. Reserves carefully garnered in the past to fund development, had been plundered by him to support current expenditure which was out of control. And then, after his father's death, and Angus and Betty had taken over, they'd done no different. They'd carried on, blindly squandering money oblivious to the threat of rising new challenges - only to find themselves on the wrong foot when one appeared - a new motorway.

By the time they woke up to the fact it was almost too late.

They'd done nothing to defend their position when the new road was first mooted, and nothing again when the bulldozers started shoving the landscape around. They'd only actually come to life when their competitors changed their style of operation to suit the new circumstances and vacuumed up all the remaining business in the town. By then Angus and Betty were facing disaster - and blaming each other for it.

None of this would have happened at all if, despite the financial weaknesses they'd inherited, he and Betty had faced up to the problems and used their heads.

They had all the necessary expertise and experience to weather the storm, Angus had trained in Hotel management, held a degree in the subject from London University as had his father 'Ginger', and he'd worked for two years in a major hotel chain in France. Betty had been a Pru Leith student around the same time and followed it with a stint in the kitchens of La Bonne Bouche in Chelsea. When they took over the hotel, not long after their marriage, it was still a business they could have rescued. With her culinary excellence and his effusive and quietly efficient manner, customers would have come in droves to hold their weddings, birthday celebrations, re-unions and anniversaries.

They should have captured a large share of everything which was going in Beaconsfield and, if they'd done so and hung onto the remaining profitable elements of the business left by Angus's grandfather, a good bar trade and an average of seventy per cent occupancy of their ten bedrooms, they'd have had a thriving business. But they didn't utilise their attributes. Instead they stood back from a 'hands on approach' which would have worked, emigrated to the customer's side of the bar, engaged others to do the work they should have been doing themselves, and wound up managing their own downfall.

The crunch was coming though; with a few more months like the last six they'd be finished. Something had to be done. Rescue money had to be found.

The biggest shock had been when the bank refused to sanction an increase in their overdraft or give them an additional fixed term loan. Strangled by lack of cash they were heading for disaster at a rate of knots.

Not that a casual caller would have noticed it for on the surface everything was fine and the cheerful ebullience of the landlord, back behind the bar by then, would have soon dispelled doubts about financial viability. Anyone hoping for a meal such as had been available in the past might have been more suspicious though, for in the food department the decline in their fortunes was more obvious. Betty had abdicated her responsibilities there to such a degree the best on offer was selection of factory made meals taken from the freezer, heated up in a microwave, and served in the bar.

The question was, could they find a way of staving off what now seemed inevitable?

'Are you going to sit there all day?' Angus asked, rising from the table. 'I'm going to try the bank again.' He walked over and stood facing her across the table. 'Come on, pull yourself together for God's sake Betty, do something to help me for a change.'

But she ignored him and, shrugging her shoulders, drew in another lungful of smoke, before dissolving into a fit of coughing. Angus glowered at her and stamped out to his car.

The bank manager wouldn't budge. He repeated his previous thoughts and outlined the bank's non-negotiable position, there'd be no money advanced until Angus put more capital into the business himself. If *he* did so, then *the bank* would consider matching it pound for pound with a loan of up to fifty thousand. It was the best that could be done.

Sitting in the car, parked in a lay-by half way home, Angus briefly thought of trying to find a completely different source of funds, but as quickly dismissed it as a pointless idea, reasoning that if his own bank manager wouldn't play, no other financial institution would be likely to do so either. He had to get fifty grand from somewhere though, and then hope the bank would double it.

But from where else might the money come?

Rex, his young 'film star' brother, had plenty; but would he part with any of it? Not likely, not to him anyway, there was a better chance of getting it from the bank!

A few years earlier when he'd got the hotel after their father's death, Rex had been left a large block of shares ... they'd almost immediately lost their value and Rex had never got over it. How could Angus now admit that, because of his own poor stewardship, the hotel was all but finished too? No, he'd just have to get the cash from somewhere else. He slumped down in his seat and closed his eyes. How had it all gone wrong? He should have done something about the poor state of the company the day he'd taken it over but he hadn't, he'd looked the other way. And when the motorway was being talked about he'd done nothing about that either.

Even as recently as four years before, the business had been profitable - just, but when the Motor Inn opened up it had creamed off all the passing business and sealed their fate. At the same time The Jolly Farmer and The Roebuck, two local pubs, raised the level of their catering from Pub Grub to Haute Cuisine and robbed him of all his Function and Sunday Lunch trade. Maybe their competitive success would turn out to be transitory but he couldn't afford to wait to see if it was. He was in 'last resort' territory, every possible source of cash had to be identified and considered.

For the previous nine years he'd been a member of the Small Hotels Association, and always considered its annual conference in Harrogate to be more of a social event than anything else. When The Mede Manor Hotel had the outward appearance of success, he'd believed it himself; never feeling the need of advice or assistance from others. This year the situation was different. Might the conference provide a route to his salvation? Was it possible he'd be able to tempt a competitor into buying him out? There'd surely be plenty of opportunities while he was there.

The more he thought about it the more attractive the proposition became. Absentmindedly he keyboarded his fingers on the steering wheel and started humming then, leaning forward he turned the ignition on, slipped the car into first gear, and edged out into the traffic.

A few minutes later the sight of a boy on the kerb wearing cricket whites and about to step onto a pedestrian crossing, brought him to a halt. As he watched the tall gangling youth amble across in front of his car swinging a bat, he was reminded of a photograph he'd known since childhood. In it, his father, dressed for cricket, was standing at one end of a group of college friends. They were in a celebratory mood and had signed the back using their nicknames - his father's was 'Ginger'. What would *he* have done if *he'd* had to raise fifty thousand pounds? How would *he* have gone about it?

The car behind him beeped its horn and jerked him back into reality. He looked to see where the boy had gone, but he'd disappeared. The memory of his father and his tipsy college pals hadn't though, nor had the yarn his father had spun about them. As he drove home the words came back; he hadn't thought about them for a long time.

'You need to be last to win this one.' his father had said, tears of laughter trickling down his cheeks. Then, looking from side to side as though he was making certain they weren't overheard, said, 'You'll find it all in an envelope, locked in the deed box in my office after I'm gone. It might be worth a few quid by then.'

What could he have meant? Did he mean anything? Had he just been concocting a bit of mystery to amuse a bored kid demanding to be entertained? No point in reading too much into what was probably no more than a children's story, that'd really be clutching at straws. He'd need more than a fairy tale to get him out of trouble this time.

All the same …

Later that night, once Betty was on her way to bed with her customary triple vodka nightcap, he shut himself in the office and took out the deed box from the lower shelf of one of the cabinets. He knew it contained a lot of family stuff, birth, death and marriage certificates, together with wills and other legal papers relating to the past. Right on the bottom, were his grandfather's First World War medals, including an M.C. awarded to him for 'exemplary gallantry' on the North West Frontier. Once worn with pride, they'd been condemned to languish in a cardboard box. He picked out the tarnished silver cross with its purple and white banded ribbon, straightway recalling all the stirring tales of the Khyber Pass his grandfather had told him.

And then he remembered the purpose of his hunt, and began to forage through the papers in the hope of finding some confirmation of what his father had told him … maybe even the envelope he'd mentioned.

The Promenade, Brighton, Sussex.
Monday 31st July 2006. 11a.m.

Eva McPhee, 39, sat hunched in the corner of a wrought iron seat looking at the waves pounding the stony beach in front of her, and she was quietly sobbing. It was four o'clock in the afternoon and she'd had yet another rotten day. In fact they'd all been pretty awful since Rex had walked out. When he'd gone, her luck had gone with him. Over the previous few days it had finally begun to sink in; the hope he'd somehow miraculously re-appear and take her in his arms again, replaced by a twenty two carat certainty he wouldn't, and without him she was lost - a stray animal waiting to be put down.

They'd been together for nearly twenty years - since the day they'd both started at RADA, The Royal Academy of Dramatic Art, nursery for stage stars of the future. He'd been the most promising student in their year; she'd been the best looking young woman. Two people who stood out in an establishment brimming with talented actors and good looking girls. It was almost inevitable they would get together. And now he'd gone off with a girl exactly half her age. The louse.

A God given talent to act convincingly, an ability to change character by simply altering his expression, coupled with the ease with which he could pick up an accent, ensured he was always in demand. Not so her. 'Competent' was nearer the mark in her case. And when her looks faded, her competence did the same. It was a month since he'd gone and the harsh realities were setting in.

At the audition, not two hours before she'd tearfully made her way to the seat on the seafront, she'd heard the damming words again - 'I'll let you know'. It was the third time she'd been demolished so cruelly. Up until then it had never occurred to her any success she'd enjoyed had been solely because Rex had engineered it, never seen that for years she'd been little more than a passenger on the roller coaster ride marking his success. Casting directors wanting him had had to take her or the deal was off. Every part she'd ever played since coming out of RADA had been obtained by his blackmailing someone to get her 'in'. Now he'd gone she was beginning to realise that, without the pressure he'd applied, her chances of employment in the theatre world were fast disappearing

The director's concluding remark following her audition, had brought it home - 'I'll let you know' - she knew what he meant. This latest rejection was simply a reflection of what had happened elsewhere in her life; she was too old for the part, and she was too old for Rex. The casting director at Brighton's Theatre Royal and Rex both seemed to need twenty year old ingénues. And at thirty nine there wasn't much she could do about that.

A small child came and sat beside her, the huge pink and white ice cream in her fist, dribbling, in a sticky trail, down her wrist. D'you want some?' she said, stretching out her arm in Eva's direction.

Eva smiled and shook her head. 'No thank you.'

'You've been crying, your eyes are all red.'

The child's directness made Eva laugh. 'Yes I was a bit. But I'm alright now, thank you.'

But was she all right? No she wasn't, she was far from all right; her life was disintegrating.

The child slid from the seat and ran off to join a young woman pushing a pram, and Eva turned back to stare at the sea.

Over nineteen years together and dumped for a twenty year old. The miserable bastard! She spat out the words as she stamped her feet in mixture of anger and despair.

They'd first met in the Marlborough Arms, a pub near RADA frequented by students of the college. A big noisy crowd of them had gone there at the end of their first day's tuition, a happy bunch of overgrown kids, full of hope they'd soon be up to their necks in glamour, excitement, and fame.

She was with another girl who she'd just met for the first time that day, having first noticed Rex when the class was assembling. All throughout the introductory talk she'd been surreptitiously watching him, but when the class broke up she lost sight of him in the crowd as it left the room. Twenty minutes later she spotted him again, down at the pub. He was leaning with his back against the bar surveying the room, a glass of champagne in his hand. She'd never in her life seen anyone who looked so breathtakingly sophisticated.

The relationship which had started on that first day at RADA had never faltered until recently when she'd sensed something was troubling him. What it was - she soon found out - he'd fallen for a young woman in the film he was making, someone who could have been cast from a mould labelled 'Eva McPhee at Twenty', someone so strikingly like she used to be, it made her toes curl up. She should have guessed what would happen next but she didn't and, three weeks later, when she returned from a visit to her father in The Cottage Hospital in Rottingdean where he was recovering from a stroke, she found Rex packing. Half an hour later he'd gone, leaving her distraught and confused.

Where he was at present she didn't know, and her pride wouldn't let her try to find out. Her friends, bar one; her next door neighbour, a widow in her sixties, who'd been deserted herself some years earlier, shied away from her, unable think of how to respond to her sorry situation, unwilling to take sides. Whatever pity they might have had for her they daren't risk falling out with Rex. Any sort of friendship with him had real cachet and the potential of being invited to share in his success.

A sea breeze un-noticed previously was building up and already tearing the tops off the waves. Eva drew her coat around her, got up from the seat, and walked to the railway station. It was a good opportunity to visit her father, back home again in Lewes by then and recovering quickly from his illness. Sooner or later she'd have to tell him what had happened between Rex and herself, maybe she'd stay the night and just 'hope to God' her brother Sandy wouldn't turn up and say 'I told you so'.

And then, as luck would have it, walking into Brighton station, she came face to face with a poster advertising Rex's latest film, the one she'd thought she'd be in with him, and it brought her straight to tears.

'My Love, My Love'

starring

Rex Brett

She stamped her foot in fury and frustration. Half hidden behind the film's title he seemed to be sneering at her, the full treatment, his famous 'supercilious look' focussing directly on her.

She knew there and then she truly hated him, hated him so much she could kill him.

Room 322, The Grand Hotel
Harrogate, Yorks.
Monday 31st July 2006. 4.00 p.m.

Angus Brett unpacked his bags and sent for a plate of sandwiches and a pot of coffee. There was a long night and a long day before him if he was to manage to get back in time for the first session of the conference on Wednesday. Hopefully there'd be a few opportunities between then, and when it wound up, for him to filter out the news that he was putting his hotel on the market. In the meantime he'd need to make the best use he could of the coming forty two hours, to settle the details of the fall back plan he'd devised after studying the interesting contents of the envelope he'd eventually found amongst his father's papers a couple of weeks earlier.

Before finalising his plan though, he needed to make a round trip to the island of Skye, one which might take him most of the coming night and the next day. On the way back he hoped to have enough time to divert to Richmond, also in Yorkshire and only twenty miles from Harrogate, where he needed to assess the rest of his prospects.

If everything went according to schedule he'd be back in time to for the first session of the conference without anyone realising he'd left the hotel at all. It wouldn't be easy but the stakes were high. He had to make the attempt.

He was in the lift at three pm, and going down.

Dressed in a navy blue track suit, he carried a grip in which were: a flask of tea, a pack of sandwiches, a bottle of water and a couple of apples. Before he left his room he hung a 'Do Not Disturb' sign on the door and pushed a note under the chairman's, pleading a 'stomach upset' as his excuse for having to miss the next day's opening cocktail party.

The main reception area was crowded: business men, leaving after a retirement lunch were trying to push their way through a group of animated Japanese Agatha Christie fans, as they waited for their rooms to be made available. The hall porter, heavily laden with suitcases, was helping an elderly couple to board a taxi. Nobody saw Angus leave.

He had the route planned: up to Scotch Corner on the A1, across the Pennines on the A66, and then up to Scotland via the M6. After Glasgow it'd be the A74(M) and then, sticking to the main roads in the interest of speed, the A82 to Invergarry, just short of Lough Ness. Finally, it was just the home run to The Isle of Skye on the A87. The weather was fine and the traffic surprising light, other than in the environs of Glasgow, which were busy even at eight fifteen in the evening.

By eleven he could see the lights of Portree in the distance. Nearly there. The moon was rising in a cloudless sky as he drove through the town it lit up the landscape like a stage set. He glanced at his watch. Perfect. He hadn't stopped apart from a short break outside Glasgow. His joints were stiff, but though he felt completely exhausted he daren't let up while there was good light for him to check the terrain and timing.

On the other side of the town he came upon a man walking unsteadily along the road. He stopped and asked him the way, immediately wishing he hadn't for, as well as having to recoil from the man's whisky laden breath he could hardly understand what he said. Finally, with much gesticulating, the man did manage to convey the directions, and he was soon parked outside The Glencarraigmor Country House Hotel.

It looked bleak and unwelcoming; perhaps that was why the Small Hotels Association often used it. Singularly remote, it was the perfect place for them to decide, the following September, on the secret pay strategy of the association's Labour Relations Committee, of which he was a member. All he had to do on the present visit was scout around until he found a suitable location to stage the 'accident' which was to be his alibi. By two a.m. he was through. The notebook he'd brought, in which his movements were outlined, had only to be fleshed out with the final details of what he'd seen and measured 'in situ'. It would work alright … it had to.

He poured the last of the coffee into the plastic top of the flask and sipped it as he sifted through the pencil jottings, amending them where necessary. Then, forcing himself to relax despite the turmoil in his head, he let back the seat, pulled a rug over himself and, hoping to get some sleep, closed his eyes. He did drop off, but not for long and, far too soon it seemed, he was rubbing his arms and struggling to get fully awake. He looked at his watch; two hours was all he'd had.

A quick walk down the road, a sluicing in the cold water of a burn running alongside it, and he was ready for the return journey.

By eleven o'clock in the morning, having taken only a brief stop for coffee and a crispy bacon sandwich, he was back in Yorkshire again and crossing the Pennines.

Light traffic, other than in Glasgow, had ensured he was well inside his planned timings and he risked taking another two hour nap in the car park of a roadside restaurant.

Before one pm he was pulling into the yard, behind The Queen of Scotland Hotel in Richmond, and tugging his notebook from his pocket. This bit was going to be trickier. He locked the car and walked through an alley into the square. Opposite was the police station. He crossed over and went in. The desk sergeant greeted him with a quick lift of his chin. 'Can I help you?'

'It might be nothing,' Angus said, 'but as I came into the town I saw what I think might have been a car theft.'

'Whereabouts, Sir?'

'Ah, that's it; I don't really know the area very well, but I've just come from Scotch Corner.'

'Ah, right … and what did you see?'

'It was odd, there were two men with black balaclavas covering their faces, one of them smashed the car's window and then they both jumped in and shot off like lightning in the direction of the A1 motorway.'

'I'll try to get a squad car after them' the sergeant said, picking up a 'phone. 'Did you spot the make?'

'Mercedes. A new one. Black. Highly polished.'

'I don't suppose you got the number?'

'Sorry. Anyway, by the time I realised what was going on I

was past them. The last thing I saw, in my rear mirror, they were racing off in the other direction.'

'Hmm ... yes ... we've had quite a few car thefts recently; it'll be the same lot I expect. If you don't mind I'll get CID to talk to you. Hang on, here's the very man, Sergeant Bellamy.'

The sergeant and Angus were soon deep in conversation and, by the time he left the station, he'd drunk the best part of a pint of tea as well as the receiving personal thanks of the station's commander, Chief Superintendent Dudley Melchitt, into whom they'd bumped, as they walked along the corridor. He could hardly believe his luck, he'd extracted everything he needed to know about Richmond CID, and then met the very man he'd come to research! All he'd given in return, and under an invented name at that, was some fictitious information about a phoney car theft.

On leaving the police station, he stopped at a pharmacy to purchase a disposable camera after which, in an adjacent café, he sat drinking coffee and planning the last leg of his marathon journey.

Half an hour later he was on the ancient stone bridge and looking down on the surging waters of the River Swale. The sun had slipped behind the trees but it was still light enough to take a few shots of the scene to study later.

Then, just as he was about to leave, he spotted a man swathed in fishing gear and with a rod in hand, making his way along the bank below him. It was the senior police officer he'd met not much more than an hour earlier, Chief Superintendent Melchitt.

James McPhee and Son,
Stockbrokers,
3, Lombard Street, London EC3V 9AA
Tuesday 1st August 2006. 8.00 p.m.

S andy McPhee, the telephone to his ear, rocked back in his big leather chair, raised his feet onto the desk top and tried not to laugh. 'Maybe she'll get some sense now.' he said, as his father relayed the news of his sister's break up with Rex Brett. He'd been on the point of leaving for home when the call came through. Everyone else had gone and he'd been on his own for the previous two hours in the small top floor suite of offices he leased from Banco Real d'Espana which occupied the rest of the building. He'd had another worrying day; before long he have to face up to some crunching decisions which might mark the end of McPhee's, the business founded by his grandfather James, continued by his father George (known to all as 'Jock'), and now by him. It had never been a company to make much profit, but nor had it ever experienced the losses which, sooner or later, come the way of all gamblers, including professional ones like stockbrokers and insurers. His grandfather's strict Presbyterian upbringing had seen to that, by ensuring 'Prudence' had been the company's watchword.

Curiously, old James McPhee's cautionary approach had only come about after he'd taken a massive gamble by starting the company during the Wall Street Crash. At the time, he'd been a junior partner in another long established company of stockbrokers and, having identified some tempting prospects amongst companies whose asset value had been decimated, he dived in while his colleagues were still down behind the parapets hoping for the best. As they preached caution he sensed opportunity and, though his daring would later turn to the other extreme, he took a chance, went out on his own, and plunged into the developing bear market.

Not waiting for the market to bottom out, he picked up quality stocks with sound fundamentals at bargain prices, investments which were to become the foundation for a business which, amusingly, would later enjoy a reputation for taking no risks.

Following his successful early years he bought an old malt house in Sussex which he converted into a fine residence. Here, he and his wife raised their sole child, George. Twenty years later, on the deaths of his parents, George, who by then had become known as 'Jock', and his young wife took The Malthouse over and there raised their children, Alexander (Sandy to his friends) and Eva.

Married at twenty two, divorced at thirty, and now forty six, Sandy mostly lived midweek in a flat in Earl's Court, but he spent every weekend at The Malt House, with his widowed father, Jock, from where he trotted down to Brighton to drink at the golf or sailing club if he wasn't propping up the bar down the road at The Coachman's Inn. His comfortable style of living was likely to be disrupted though for he'd abandoned the strict rules his grandfather had laid down regarding the investments to be recommended to clients who managed their own portfolios, or included in those of which they were the discretionary managers.

In nine weeks' time the half yearly performance reports were due to be published and he already knew what shocking reading they would make. Just over two months then, before the knuckles of dozens of the company's most loyal and soon to be most wrathful clients, or their legal representatives, would not only be looking for his blood but banging on his door to signal the demise of James McPhee, Stockbrokers, and more than likely trigger another stroke for his father, Jock. He'd spent many hours over the previous weeks sitting like this, behind his father's desk, worrying about such an eventuality, racking his brains, hoping to dream of a way out. Every evening he'd be there, long after everyone else had gone, trying to assemble re-assuring words to say to the staff the next day, words he hoped would drive from their minds any thought of telephoning 'the boss', recuperating at home from his stroke, to tell him what was going on.

Every morning the waste paper basket would be full of torn up plots and plans, all with fatal weaknesses. For hours, sometimes until near midnight, when all the lights in the surrounding offices had been extinguished, he'd still be there listening to the muted sound of the last of the homeward bound traffic and praying for an inspiration. But none had come.

Not until this evening that is, for only an hour before his father had 'phoned to tell him about his sister Eva's problems with Rex, he'd stumbled across something which might just get him out of trouble. He'd been idly sliding one of the top drawers of his father's desk in and out when he briefly saw something which looked vaguely familiar - a photograph. He hadn't seen it for years, not since he'd been a child sitting at the same desk one Saturday morning with a colouring book and crayons while his father caught up with all the correspondence which had accumulated while they'd been on holiday. The photo was faded and yellowing, but he'd remembered it well and what his father had told him about it.

They were all student pals it seemed, including the tall man in whites at the end, the man his father had called 'Ginger', the man he now knew to be Rex Brett's late father. He didn't know the others. When he'd turned the print over he saw the inscription and nickname signatures, remembered them from the last time he'd handled the photograph nearly forty years before. And then, as he'd gone to put it back to where he'd found it, he'd spotted the envelope. 'The LMS Club' was written on the outside, in his father's handwriting. He'd turner it over but it was sealed and, stifling his curiosity, he'd put it back.

That had been an hour earlier, and since then he'd returned to thoughts of how to recover some of the company's losses without winding up worse off, but it was getting late, and he was still no nearer a solution to his problems. He glanced at his watch; time to go. As he yawned, the image of the sealed envelope flashed through his mind again. He opened the drawer and took it out.

His father had signed it Jock McPhee on the back. Across the seal was written: Not to be opened in my lifetime

Trying to partially collapse the envelope in order to see through the gap under the glued flap didn't help him discover much about what was inside. The only thing visible was what looked like another envelope. His chin was itching and he rubbed it thoughtfully. Then, rocking back the chair, he rose and went over to the Cona Coffee percolator his secretary ensured was always charged. One glass jug stood on the warming plate half full of coffee. Nestled into the heating mantle alongside it was the other, it was half full of water. He flipped the switch, went back to his desk, picked up the envelope, and sat waiting for the steam to arrive.

83 Hope Street, Tarapuna, Trinidad, Saturday 12th August 2006 1.15 p.m.

Sophie didn't often get Saturday off, and when she did she usually went to the beach after she'd done her shopping. When her mother had been alive she'd regularly gone over to South Bay to see her but she hadn't really enjoyed the visits at the end, and invariably returned to Tarapuna in a sorry state of mind.

Surrounded by hundreds of acres of swaying sugar cane in her childhood, their picturesque little cottage had, in recent times, become hemmed in by warehouses and pig farms, and she hated it.

This Saturday it would be different though for, with her switch to British Airways imminent, and her associated move to Tobago only round the corner, she'd decided to make a start on packing up her stuff.

It was a hot sticky afternoon and she went out into the tiny garden behind the little rented house near Piarco Airport into which she'd moved when she'd started flying. It had been difficult leaving her childhood behind her on the South Bay Sugar Estate, but with all the changes since Europe switched from sugar cane to sugar beet, she was a glad she'd done so. Dragging a white plastic lounger into the shade of the mango tree she returned to the kitchen and collected the dish of fresh pineapple she'd prepared for her lunch.

On her way back out she picked up a folder containing two things she'd brought back from England - a map and the list she'd got from Eddie.

Overhead a plane climbed up noisily from behind the coconut palms and swung northwards. She knew its livery; Caribbean Airways. Without thinking she glanced at her watch, it had to be flight BW 302 to Barbados, the connector for BA 657 to Heathrow, the very thought of which brought to mind how soon she'd be off herself; to her new job, her new home, and her next visit to London. Three more weeks and she might see her name on the duty roster for Gatwick, four maybe, before she'd be back on the hunt for her father's friends. She leaned back on the cushions, popped some pineapple into her mouth, and reached for the folder.

A glance at the road map she'd picked up in London had tested her limited knowledge of English geography earlier. Even so, she'd been able to roughly place all the addresses Eddie had given her. None was more than an hour from Gatwick; two were within a few miles of each other. She put down the map and pulled out Angie's neatly printed second list, turning immediately to the notes on the back which she'd spotted the day before. On it were the names, nicknames and approximate locations of her father's friends, followed by the names of their children.

She'd pencilled '*and Sophie!*' next to that of Eddie, for Angie wouldn't have known of her existence when the list was made. Surely she now had enough to accomplish her mission.

The L.M.S. Club

Names, Locations, Nicknames and Children.

Jonathan Melchitt (Ghandi) - Horsham, Sussex.
Mungo, Boris, Dudley.

George McPhee (Jock) - Lewes, Sussex.
Sandy, Eva

Rory Brett (Ginger) - Beaconsfield, Buckinghamshire.
Angus, Rex.

Henry Byrd (Dicky) - Islington, London
Eddie *(and Sophie!)*

Roland La Tour (Frog) - Islington, London
Angela.

As she studied the names she couldn't help but wonder what reaction she'd get when she turned up un-announced on their doorstep and said who she was.

Glencarraigmor Country House Hotel, Isle of Skye, Scotland. Monday 4th September 2006. 10.15 a.m.

Angus had arrived at the hotel at around ten, having flown to Inverness the previous evening. He'd hired a car at the airport and driven down along the full length of Lough Ness to Fort Augustus where he'd spent the night in a B&B before completing the journey. The route had been chosen to gain over a day for himself before having to join the rest of the Small Hotels Association's Remuneration Committee at the meeting called to prepare the Association's position in advance of negotiations with the trade unions in London at the end of the month.

Other sub-committees were also assembling in the hotel in line with the Association's custom of holding its business meetings in member's premises, all over Britain.

This year it was the turn of the Glencarraigmor, up on Skye; next year it would be the Lord Nelson, down at Cowes.

Angus had told his wife the previous afternoon, as she coughed her way through a mug of tea secretly laced with Vodka, he was going to Scotland early because he needed some time on his own to think out all the implications of pay increases for future of their own business. But that wasn't his real intention at all, it had been to create enough time to drive the 360 odd miles from Skye to Richmond in Yorkshire, kill a man, drive back again in time to attend a meeting, and get away with it.

Many times, since discovering the envelope in his father's deed box he'd thought back to the conversation they'd had all those years before. He'd been six years old at the time, 'So,' his father had said, throwing an arm round his shoulder. 'all you have to do, Angus my boy, is make damned sure you're last, because it's a funny old competition this one, and the last man'll win it.' His father's words had puzzled him for a long time afterwards but, gradually, as he grew up, he'd forgotten them. And then, recently, when the youth in the cricketing whites carrying his bat had strolled across the road in front of his car, they'd all come back.

Well he wasn't puzzled now, not since he'd opened the envelope and done a bit of research. Oh yes, he knew how he could make sure he'd be last and, in doing so, eradicate all his problems. He hadn't told Betty what he'd found out, and he'd had to struggle long and hard with his conscience before deciding to do anything at all. It was the letter from his accountant, pointing out how close he was to insolvency, which tipped the balance. He had to get his hands on some serious money, and quick … if that meant removing anyone who stood in the way, he'd remove them.

He'd set out his priorities, done the necessary research, made several scouting trips, identified his initial objectives and made Phase One of his plan. Everything was based on the facts he'd gained from the hurried overnight visit to Skye and back from Harrogate via Richmond a month or two earlier, and appeared to have come together rather well. In twenty four hours the first of his unsuspecting rivals would be out of the picture and, with a bit of luck, he'd be in the clear.

He looked at his watch … ten thirty … time to be going. He handed his key to the receptionist and told her he was going to take a scenic drive up the coast. 'I won't be back for lunch and probably not for dinner.' he said.

'Ah, well then,' she replied. 'You'd better take a front door key … just in case … because we have no night porter.'

Angus smiled his thanks and took the Yale key she handed him. 'Good idea,' he said, 'I might need it.'

By lunchtime he was well on his way to Glasgow and making good time. If all went well he'd be in Richmond by late afternoon - perfect to be in position, on the river, by six pm.

Aysgarth Falls, River Ure, North Yorkshire.
Monday 4th September 2006. 6.15 p.m.

Tony Bloxham, head chef at The Royal Hotel in Richmond, was on his way back home. He'd taken enough shots to give him ample choice when he came to select the three best to submit for the end of season Photographic Festival and Exhibition in Richmond Town Hall which was due to start on the second of October next.

He'd spent most of the afternoon at the falls - a favourite spot for him - though on Mondays, his day off, he might be found anywhere on the River Ure or the River Swale, facing the challenge of photographing moving water. The results he got won him many prizes but, so high was his standard, he was seldom satisfied. He must have taken a hundred images during the afternoon and, though any one of them was worth one of the 'Highly Commended' certificates, he wasn't sure whether he'd got one good enough to give him a chance of winning the highest accolade of all - 'Photographer Of The Year.'

As he neared Richmond, and was thinking of a pint more than a picture, he came to a lay-by near the stone bridge over the river just short of the town. The light was perfect, giving a golden glow to the leaves of the early turning Beech trees as they cast shadows on the stone parapets. He glanced in the mirror. There was no one behind. He stopped, got out, and went over to the wall to look down on the water leaping and surging through the rocks below him. Here surely was as good a chance as he'd ever get to capture a winning picture.

By the time he'd got his gear set up, and the camera ready to start shooting, he knew he only had minutes before the shadows would lengthen and cast darkness on the shimmering water. In consequence, he hardly noticed that since he'd first glanced down on the scene a fisherman had appeared and was, by then, standing in the shallows, very still, rod raised to cast, and studying the dark pool immediately below where Tony had positioned himself ready to shoot what he sensed would be the best picture of the day.

As he released the shutter - a fast moving cloud killed the light. He took a couple more as back up, wondering if he'd left it too late, for there was no way of telling until he had a print in his hand. Time to go. He picked up his stuff and began putting it back in the car, not noticing the fisherman had disappeared. Even if he had, he'd have assumed the man had just moved somewhere nearby downstream and was out of sight on the other side of one of the bridge's buttresses. In truth he never gave him a thought.

Fifteen minutes later, as he was pulling away from where he'd been parked, a man scrambled over the parapet, ran across the bridge, and almost collided with the left wing of his car. He stamped on the brakes, brought the car to a halt, and jumped out to remonstrate. But the running man was fifty yards away by then, and getting close to a stationary silver coloured vehicle facing in the opposite direction.

What the hell's going on? Tony wondered, shrugging his shoulders philosophically and climbing back into his old Riley Elf and starting the engine. As he drove off he glanced in the mirror; the silver car had gone.

'That's funny' he thought, 'I wonder what his rush was.'

Best-in-the-North Transport Café, Leeming. Yorkshire Monday 4th September. 7.12 p.m.

Sandy McFee sat, elbows on the table, a mug of tea between his hands, and shaking like a leaf as he went over the afternoon's events in his mind. All around was the football chatter of men at ease and taking their break. He was taking a break himself, but he wasn't at ease - far from it.

'Who'd have believed it?' he thought, 'I'm not ten minutes in the town at the start of my first recce, and who comes round the corner and nearly knocks me for six but bloody Angus Brett! Lucky his head was well down and he was in a hell of a hurry himself or he'd have spotted me. Not that he knows me really, except as Eva's brother, but if he'd seen me, what could I have said ... 'I was spying on the local Police Superintendent?' Christ, I think not. Just as well I followed him though. Just as well I managed to keep up with him without being seen. Just as well I saw what he was up to. If anyone had told me I'd bump into a guy who was about to do the exact same thing I was planning to do I'd have said they were nuts. My God, I was blessed when I took a short cut and got ahead of him. And blessed again when I scrambled in behind the bushes, seconds before he appeared. It all happened so quickly after that, just as he walloped Melchitt, who was exactly where I guessed he'd be, the flaming camera up on the road flashed and put the heart across me, I can't imagine what it did to Angus Brett, he was off like a startled rabbit ... leaving me stuck behind the bushes, wobbling like a jelly.

Amazing. He never even looked to see what damage he'd done, I had to. Just as well I did too - bloody Melchitt was still alive. And then to nearly run into the damned car, well...

Christ what a day. I'll just sink this tea and then Richmond won't see me for dust.'

Market Place, Richmond, Yorks.
Tuesday 5th September 9.30 a.m.

As soon as the last breakfast had been served Tony Bloxham slipped out of his chef's garb, pulled on his jacket, walked quickly out of the back door of the Royal Hotel and across the road to the camera shop in Finkle Street. It was owned by Barry James, Vice Chairman of the Photographic Society, Tony's principal rival in black and white imagery.

Pulling the cassettes from his pocket and placing them on the counter he didn't mince words in addressing the man who picked them up, 'Muck any of them up, Barry, and I'll have your guts for garters.'

'I see; good are they?' Barry jested, as he winked at a second customer farther along the counter, a youngster who by his grin had obviously heard Tony's comment. 'I'd better take care then. They might be your ticket to fame.'

Tony couldn't keep a straight face, 'They'll be good enough to see your efforts off, mate … but fame … I hardly think so.'

'What are they of this time?'

'Oh, my usual stuff, water and trees.'

'You should try something a bit more exciting, Tony. Get your trees and your water shots in, but as a background only - add something else to give your pictures more purpose - put in something to suggest a story which is about to unfurl, tease the viewer, leave clues rather than show something specific.'

'Make 'em like yours in other words!'

'Sure … more like mine … but better!'

'Nah, I don't think so Barry. They wouldn't be me … I'm a water and trees man - always have been, always will be.'

Swaledale, North Yorkshire.
Tuesday 5th September 2006. 5.00 p.m.

The sun glistened on the wet golden leaves of the trees lining the river bank as the breeze rustling through them blew away the autumn shower. Overhead the sky, cloudless and blue, would make anyone wonder from where the rain had come. All around midges darted about trying to avoid wisps of steam rising as the dampness evaporated from granite boulders standing in or beside the peat stained water.

Face down, and caught in a cleft between two big rocks, was the body of a man. From upstream of him, the built up water spilled across his back in a smooth flowing waterfall. A few feet away, his rod lay in the river but his rain hat, covered with dozens of flies he'd tied himself, having floated away, had been caught by a swirl of current and beached itself on a nearby patch of gravel.

Two young boys, brothers, Billy and Brian Dugdale, their eyes staring fixedly into the water, had walked right past the hat as they'd made their way tentatively upstream between the boulders, fishing nets in one hand, jam jars swinging on loops of twine in the other. A stickleback in one of the jars, with no other option but to swim around in circles, looked down forlornly at the water racing beneath it.

Billy was just about to stand on the man's body when he realised the smooth little waterfall in front of him was different to the others he'd been wading through all morning. His shriek, and that of Brian when he saw what Billy had nearly trodden on, attracted the attention of their parents Johnny and Beryl, sitting at a picnic table on the other side of the arched bridge bearing the B 6270 to Upper Swaledale.

Their prompt response had police and ambulance service quickly on the scene.

Arriving in the first wave was Detective Inspector Ronnie Sherman, known behind his back as 'Tank', partially because of the name association, and partially because of his bulk. He was soon slithering down the bank on the seat of his trousers to join the group of people clustered round the waterlogged corpse. Behind him Detective Sergeant Malcolm Bellamy stumbled through the rocks too, as he chatted to the police surgeon.

By then, Johnny and Beryl were perched on a flat rock waiting to be interviewed. But the boys, restless and wriggling impatiently, whispered and nudged each other as they tried to work out who was who. They soon found out.

'Bloody hell!' exclaimed D.I. Sherman, stepping back in shock when he saw the face of the deceased, 'look who it is 'Malc', it's the Super.'

Hearing his outburst, Sergeant Bellamy leapt forward to see what had prompted the D.I.'s remark. When he did, he was so shocked, he puked.

One of the ambulance men, having grasped the dead man's hand, was trying to free him from the grip of the rocks but he was wedged too firmly for the ambulance man shift on his own. A colleague stepped forward to help but the inspector shoved him to aside, 'Here, let me.' he said and, wading out, took a hold of one his late Superintendent's feet. Bellamy shook himself back to reality, leapt to Sherman's side, and grabbed the other leg. Between them they managed to get all that was left of Chief Superintendent Dudley Melchitt over to the bank where they lowered him gently down on the trampled grass.

'Stone me.' muttered D.I. Sherman, letting go the foot he'd been holding, and shaking his head in disbelief. 'Whoda believed it?'

'Who indeed?' said Bellamy.

Melchitt House, Golden Square, London W1F 9JB
Wednesday 6th September 2006. 3.00 p.m.

Mungo Melchitt twisted his fingers through the last few remaining strands of hair on his sunburned scalp. At forty seven he looked little different in appearance to the way he'd looked eight years earlier when he'd taken over the running of the family business from his dementia stricken father Jonathan (Ghandi to his contemporaries), and with it the responsibility of ensuring the dividend income which sustained the family comprising his father, himself, and three maiden aunts, as well as bolstering the sporadic earnings of his two profligate cousins, who, as he put it, 'never did 'a tap' of honest work.'

He sat at one end of the boardroom table.

His principal supporters, Aunt Violet, Aunt Rose and Aunt Daisy grouped themselves at the other end. On his left was the company's long serving secretary - Miss Eunice Pink. On his right, Mr Swayhurst, the auditor. Halfway down the table, and opposite to each other, were his cousins, Julian and Jarrold, twin sons of his father's late brother - Jackman Melchitt.

The AGM of Melchitt House Publishing was nearly over. The accounts had been passed, the auditors re-appointed. Only the level of dividend had to be agreed. Tension had been rising since the meeting began, for the previous year's accounts, received in advance of the meeting, told the sorry story of a disappointing period, and signalled a reduced dividend as well as the need for an urgent change of direction.

Though Melchitt's was a family business, it had to be said it was not a happy one. Jealousies had soured relationships for years compounded by the fact that, of the founder's five children, only Jonathan worked in it.

Jackman, a man with the reputation of being a playboy, and wrongly believing he'd always wind up playing second fiddle to his older brother Jonathan, had refused to take a position in the company when he came out of the army. Instead he'd set himself up in the risky business of dealing in vintage motor cars from a lock up garage in Crawley where he traded as 'Melchitt Classic Cars'. He'd always struggled to make anything of the business and was permanently jealous of Jonathan's success in the family firm.

Oscar Melchitt, who'd started the publishing company, hadn't live long enough to see the rancour developing between his sons, while his daughters, Violet, Rose, and Daisy, had wisely kept well clear of trouble by staying at home to look after him.

After Oscar died, his shares had been divided equally between his five children. Unfortunately this only further exacerbated the problems. Violet, Rose and Daisy supported their brother Jonathan by giving him their proxies to add to his twenty per cent, which meant he had overwhelming control and made it easy for him to frustrate his brother Jackman's wish to sell the business and use his share of the proceeds to develop Melchitt Classic Cars.

Jonathan had three sons: Mungo, Boris and Dudley. Jackman had two: Julian and Jarrold.

In due course Mungo joined his father, Jonathan, in Melchitt's, quickly rising to be his deputy. Boris went 'walk about' in the far corners of the world and wound up living the life of a recluse on an old World War II motor torpedo boat moored in a slow moving backwater creek near Rottingdean, while Dudley joined the Police Force.

Both Jackman's boys teamed up with their father in Melchitt's Classic Cars and with their opinions well coloured by his attitude, and further compounded by their combined inability to make any sort of a living from the clapped out old bangers they actually traded in, they invariably looked at their successful cousin Mungo with ill-disguised envy.

When Jackman died, Julian and Jarrold each inherited half of his shares in Melchitt House Publishing, and immediately set about a campaign of sniping at their Uncle Jonathan whenever they got the chance. This only served to antagonise their great aunts: Violet, Rose, and Daisy, who backed Jonathan even more resolutely.

Then, when Jonathan's health deteriorated with the onset of dementia, Mungo took over his executive function. He still didn't own any shares though, nor would he as long as Jonathan was alive, an awkward situation, for Julian and Jarrold each owned ten per cent, being of half their late father's shareholding. Open war within the family broke out.

The atmosphere on the day of the AGM had been tense from the start, only frosty nods being exchanged as the shareholders assembled. When the meeting got under way, Julian and Jarrold lost no time in making a point of questioning everything Mungo said, interrupting him whenever they got a chance, challenging him over every line in the Profit and Loss Account and generally irritating him as much as they could in their attempt to disrupt the proceedings.

Mungo's patience was stretched to the limit by the time they got to the crunch issue of dividend. Standing up, he slowly looked around at each of them before expounding his views on what he believed to be the most appropriate course for future development.

'So,' he said, 'As you have seen from the accounts, and as you have heard from me in the report attached to them, we need to treat this coming year as a year of retrenchment - a year in which we put behind us the unfortunate failure of two major book launches and seek new writers capable of restoring our profitability. We might also add an additional genre to our list - Crime. To achieve this I have set in motion negotiations to attract a very senior and extremely successful editor of crime fiction currently under contract to a rival house. He has told me he may be able to bring some of 'his' authors with him. In order to secure this man I will need to provide a handsome incentive needless to say and, rather than enter into additional borrowings, I suggest we use what we might have paid ourselves in dividends to underwrite the cost of his recruitment.'

At this both Julian and Jarrold banged their fists on the table. 'You have to pay a dividend Mungo. Dammit, we have already pledged the equivalent of what we got last year for a project we're working on to export Bentleys to Saudi.'

'Whatever you do in Saudi Arabia has got nothing to do with this company.' said Mungo, impatiently. 'What you do with your money isn't of any concern to the rest of us. You're always getting involved in crack pot schemes, just as your father did - why don't you think before you throw away what I've earned for you here. You carp and carp, you contribute nothing, and you make a great song and dance every time you disagree with what the rest of us want to do. I'm running this company and I've made a lot of money for you in the past with little support from you. If you don't like what I'm doing - gather enough votes to replace me. But you won't be able to, so buckle down, for God's sake, and help us make a success of what we have here. It's a damned good business.'

Jarrold was on his feet by then, red in the face with rage. 'You don't mind about the rest of us you sanctimonious bugger. Look at the salary and bonuses you pay yourself with our money and you're not even a bloody shareholder. You're milking the company dry for your own good, and leaving damn all for the rest of us.'

Julian was nodding furiously in agreement, but Aunt Violet, had heard enough. 'Boys, boys, behave yourselves and mind your language. Mungo is right, we've had plenty of good years, and we'll have them again, but for this year we have to hold back and re-invest for the future.'

Aunt Rose and Aunt Daisy sat, button-lipped, but from the expression on their faces they obviously agreed.

'I'm putting it to the vote then,' said Mungo, 'it's the only way to settle the matter once and for all.'

At that precise moment there was a knock on the door and Miss Pink's assistant came into the room. 'Excuse me Mr Mungo …' she whispered, 'man on the telephone … says it's very important …'

'It's alright Miss Wallace,' Mungo said to her, 'I'll take it out there.'

During the few minutes he was absent not a word was said. The twins glared at the door through which Mungo had disappeared and hoped something would drop on him to prevent him coming back, the aunts stared at the table-top or each other, while Miss Pink and Mr Swayhurst just looked straight ahead. But all of this went from their minds when Mungo returned.

'It's Dudley.' he said. 'He's dead.'

The Memorial Hospital,
Isle of Skye, Scotland.
Thursday 7th September 2006. 6.00 p.m.

Nurse Niamh McNevitt appeared at the man's bedside as he lay silent and motionless gazing blankly out of the window and, reaching across him, took up his chart to fill in the details. Across the top it said,

Angus Brett …admitted 06.30 am 06/09/06. …. Dr Omundo

'Beautiful out there isn't it?' she whispered.

His expression never changed. She couldn't tell whether he'd heard or not. But he *could* see and he *could* hear and, as he unblinkingly watched it, the sun dropped below the horizon to leave only a rosy glow mirrored on the sea's dead flat surface.

She placed her hand lightly on the back of his bandaged wrist for a moment, sighed and shook her head. Then, reaching over to the flask of water on his bedside locker topped it up from the stainless steel ewer she'd just brought in with her; it took barely a spoonful.

'You've taken hardly any water again today Mr Brett, Nurse McEwen mustn't have tried hard enough. Come on now, you really must keep your liquids up.'

She raised his head from the pillow, put the drinker to his lips, and waited until she saw water dribbling from the side of his mouth. 'That's better,' she said. 'Keep trying, or we'll never have you right.'

She wiped his lips with a tissue, but she needn't have bothered for there was no response whatever from him. Then, putting the drinker back beside the flask, she shook the drip stand to release the bubbles in the tubes and checked the level in the bag of saline solution. All the time she was watching him, hoping to see some sign he was aware of her presence. When there was none, she shrugged her shoulders and pursed her lips, 'I don't know what we're going to do with you Mr Brett, I really don't. Everything's going well considering how long you were lying there before you were found. Your forearm isn't broken after all, the stitches will be out of the cuts on your hands and wrists in a week, and the bruises, well you could win prizes with them it's true, but they're doing fine as well. What I can't work out is what's going on in that head of yours. You've been here nearly two days and not a muscle have you moved. If there's no improvement by tomorrow Doctor's going to send you to Edinburgh.'

She bent to smooth the bedclothes where she'd leaned on them and then, swivelling round on her heel, click clacked out of his room, down the corridor, and back to the nurse's station.

As the noise of her footsteps faded away Angus let loose the breath he'd been holding and smiled. He was stiff all over and the back of his hands hurt like hell, but apart from that he was well on the mend. 'So far so good,' he thought, 'it's working out just as I planned; maybe I can risk starting to come round.

North Yorks Infirmary, Richmond, Yorkshire. Thursday 8th September 2006. 3.00 p.m.

Detective Inspector Sherman stood on one side of Mungo and Boris Melchitt, Detective Sergeant Bellamy stood on the other. It was their responsibility to establish all the circumstances surrounding the death of the man lying in front of them, their former boss, Chief Superintendent Dudley Mclchitt, the first suspicious death they'd been involved in for nearly two years.

Mungo had come up by car with Boris, who'd arrived in the office unexpectedly the day after the AGM. Now, with their brother's body before them on a mortuary trolley and covered with a sheet, an air of bewildering unreality had begun to prevail. That it was Dudley was beyond doubt, but with the wax like transparency of his skin, and the lack of expression on his face, this person didn't seem much like the Dudley they knew. Always the practical joker, the giggler, the leg-puller, the Dudley they remembered bore little resemblance to the dead man at whom they were looking.

Mungo turned to Boris, staring glassy eyed at the corpse, and tapped his arm.

Boris shook himself and smiled and Sherman, who'd watched both brothers' reaction as the sheet was pulled back, gave each of them an enquiring look.

Mungo nodded; it was Dudley.

No further words were said after that until they were back in Sherman's office when the inspector, flipping back the top page of pad of lined paper, asked if they'd mind if he took a few notes. 'There's a thing or two I need to know.'

'Ask whatever you want Inspector. We're here to help and

to arrange for Dudley to be brought back home for burial in the family plot.' replied Mungo. 'And we have some questions of our own we'd like to ask you.'

'Right,' the inspector answered, slightly taken aback at the prospect of being cross examined. 'You realise, of course, we have yet to positively establish the cause of your brother's tragic death?'

'The cause of his death? But it was drowning surely.'

'No, not surely I'm afraid. There are strong indications he might have suffered a considerable blow to his head before he died.'

'Before he died?' echoed Boris, doubt creeping into the expression on his face. 'Before he died?'

'Yes, though I'll need a clearer picture to emerge before I finally make up my mind. Hopefully the post mortem will deliver one which provides us with more to go on.'

Mungo leaned forward, his folded arms on the table. 'You've shocked us Inspector. D'you think he was assaulted then? Is that what you're saying?'

'We don't know what happened yet, but at the moment we have to consider it's a possibility.'

Boris leaned forward as well. 'Meaning?'

'This is difficult gentlemen. I'm not trying to be evasive, but clearly if there is a chance the Super was attacked it becomes a very different matter.'

'You can't mean someone killed him surely?' exclaimed Mungo, a look of horror on his face.

'It's as I said, Mr Melchitt, we don't have enough information to take a view at this stage. The post mortem is being done tomorrow and we'll be in a better position to see our way forward when we have the report.'

'So Dudley's remains will not be available to us.'

'Not yet, Sir, I'm afraid.'

Boris turned to Mungo. 'We should book in somewhere and be prepared to stay a couple of days.'

Sergeant Bellamy, who hadn't opened his mouth until then, suggested The Queen of Scotland Hotel. 'The Super used to stay there when he first joined us up here last year; y'know, before he found a place of his own.'

'And if the post mortem's tomorrow, how long will it be before we get an answer?' asked Boris.

'We should get it tomorrow as well, with a bit of luck,

maybe not the detailed written report, that usually takes another day. But hopefully we'll have enough information by lunchtime.'

In the end they stayed and, the following morning having spoken to a local undertaker, they went round to Dudley's house to assess what they'd need to do with his things. Enquiries they made by talking to the neighbours on either side of the house revealed nothing.

'Mr Melchitt kept himself to himself,' said Mrs Deakin, the elderly lady who lived on one side of him. 'Quiet as a mouse he was. Just his car coming in and out at all hours, otherwise we'd not have known he was there.'

Similar comments came from Mrs James on the other side. 'We hardly ever saw him other than when he was out cutting the lawn or the hedge. He seemed to like those jobs because the rest of the garden was looked after by a contractor.'

'So you really had no social contact at all?'

'None. If he'd had a wife at home all day,' the younger woman said, 'or a load of kids, it might have been different. But we were never in his house, and he was only in here the once, at Christmas, when he came round for a drink and gave my boys a box of sweets.'

Mungo nodded thoughtfully as he accepted the cup of tea the woman had made when they arrived. 'Poor old Dud,' he said, turning to Boris, who was stirring a third spoonful of sugar into his cup. 'He never got over losing Beatrice, did he? Blamed himself, and buried himself up here to try to forget.'

'Dudley's wife was killed in a hit and run accident a few years ago.' explained Boris to the neighbour, who clearly had no idea what Mungo had been talking about. 'They never caught the person who did it.'

'Couldn't prove it you mean. Dudley reckoned he knew who it was, but despite all the resources at his disposal he couldn't pin it on the man. And I agree, I've always thought it what was behind his shifting himself up here, a mixture of a sense of failure in not being able to point the blame positively, and the fear that one day he might be tempted to exact retribution himself.'

'What, Dud? ... Never, he'd too much self-control. But we shouldn't be talking like this.' Boris was shaking his head as he spoke. 'Not when we're only guessing.'

The younger woman, who'd been listening attentively, then asked if the Superintendent had ever had any children.

'No,' replied Mungo, 'None. He was always a loner, though not what you'd call lonely; just totally committed to his work. He put a few tough nuts away in his time.'

The woman went to top up their cups but they both refused and were soon driving back into Richmond where they had an appointment with the undertaker.

As they sat in the waiting room in the funeral parlour Boris ventured his opinion that they hadn't got much nearer finding out what had happened since they'd arrived the previous afternoon.

'And nor will we,' answered Mungo. 'until we have the post mortem report in our hands.

By 2 p.m. they were back at the reception desk at the police station asking for Detective Inspector Sherman.

Sergeant Bellamy came out to collect them, and conduct them to an interview room. On the way, he asked if they'd found anything unusual at the Super's house.

Mungo answered him. 'Not a thing. It was just like the house he had when he lived down South, more like a show house than a home. There wasn't a stick of furniture out of place and not a dish left on the draining board, only the minimum in the fridge, and everything in order. His late wife was the same - they both had a bee in their bonnets about tidiness.'

Bellamy smiled. 'He was the same here … drove us barmy!'

By then they were seated in the room they'd occupied the day before. Almost immediately the inspector burst in. 'I've got it.'

'The report?' Mungo asked, rising to meet him.

'The preliminary notes only; but enough to go on. They did the post mortem late last night. The one before it was completed quicker than they'd anticipated.'

'And?'

'And he was drowned.'

Boris joined them just inside the door. 'So we can rule out anything suspicious; it was an accident, pure and simple.'

'No, it's still not as clear as that I'm afraid. Sit down again and I'll tell you what they said to me.'

'Superintendent Melchitt definitely died of drowning, that much is certain.' the D.I. began, 'What is not so cut and dried though is 'why?' The pathologist was very interested in a large contusion on the side of his head, one we'd seen ourselves, and he reckons that though the blow didn't kill him, it would have been enough to render him unconscious. After being struck in such a way he could have fallen into the river and drowned; but there's something else as well - he had bruises all round his throat and neck. It looks as though he might have been held under. There's no proof of any of this, and maybe there never will be, but the sequence of events I've outlined is consistent with what we found. What we don't know, for sure, is how he got the blow on the side of his head ... or the bruises on his throat or neck.'

'The side of his head?'

'Yes, on the left hand side, just above his ear.'

'And you found him lying face down.'

'That's how he was when I arrived and I don't think he'd been moved. It was quite difficult to release him actually; he was jammed in between two boulders. This led us to believe he'd either fallen where he was found or he'd been swept there by the current.'

'You sure he didn't simply lose his footing and bang his head on a rock as he tumbled in? Boris and I drove out there last night and walked along the river bank. The bottom's very stony and it looked pretty unstable to us.'

'That wouldn't explain the bruises on his throat and neck. Other than for them your theory could be right, I know how slippery it can be. I fish the river myself. We all do.'

Boris sat upright in his chair immediately 'We? Who's we?'

'The Richmondshire Police Fly Fishing Club.' the inspector answered, defensively; bristling slightly at Boris's aggressive questioning. 'We have the use of the water from the farmer who owns the rights, have had for years. Sergeant Bellamy here's a member as well. We often go up there for a few hours for the evening rise. Super's been up there tons of times since he came here. Oh, he knew the water all right; you can take my word for it.'

'Ah, I see.' said Mungo, trying to lighten the tension Boris's remarks had set off. 'So the farmer lets you catch his fish and in return you catch his poachers. Is that it?'

A slight grin began to cross the D.I.'s face. 'Something like that, yes. But more to the point, we all know the river, and we all slip sometimes. But when we do we usually fall forwards.'

Boris was beginning to see what he was driving at. 'In other words Inspector, what you're saying is, he probably wouldn't have hit the side of his head if he'd fallen, he'd have hit the front of it.'

'Exactly.'

'What the D.I. is inferring is even more, Sir.' explained D.S. Bellamy. 'We know the river, as the D.I. said, and we've fished it dozens of times. The spot, around where he was found, is one of the best places because it's from there you can get at one of the most productive pools. He'd probably been standing round about where we found him, and he'd have been facing across the river, watching or casting into the pool on the other side, the one under the alders lining the bank.'

Mungo sat back, his arms folded across his chest. 'And someone came up from behind, stepped down from the bank, waded out, and hit him … surely he'd have heard whoever it was, wouldn't he?'

The inspector laughed. 'Mr Melchitt I assume you are not a fisherman. A man's in his own world out there if a fish is rising to his fly - he'd not notice a thing, believe me. And anyway, the water churning through the rocks would be making more than enough noise to cover the sound of anyone wading out behind out him. I was thinking about this as the sergeant spoke, and I don't reckon he'd have known a thing until he got that crack on his head and, by then, it'd have been too late.'

'And there're the bruises on his throat as well, don't forget them.' said Sgt Bellamy.

'Exactly, which just further compounds the mystery.' the inspector added, 'Anyway if nothing else turns up in the full report to change my mind I'll be recommending we investigate your brother's death as an unlawful killing - murder in other words.'

'And what does that mean?'

'To us it'll mean a long trawl back over what we know and what we can deduce. Then it'll be leg work, we'll need to search for forensic evidence, though I don't hold out much hope for finding any now. And then, of course, there's always the possibility of turning up a witness.'

'Someone who saw it happen?'

'Ah, I doubt we'll find anyone who actually saw the attack but there could be any number of people who saw something without realising its significance. And we're now faced with the question of 'motive' as well, and that'll mean digging into the Super's life, his family, his friends, his enemies and ...'

'Enemies? Never.' exclaimed Boris.

'All policemen have enemies of some sort, Mr Melchitt, we have to check every angle.'

As they'd got as far as they could and, as the Super's body wouldn't be released for several days, Mungo and Boris, decided go home. D. I. Sherman saw them out to their car himself. 'We'll be doing everything in our power to find out what happened to your brother, gentlemen, you can rely on it. I'll telephone you as soon as I have something new.'

Mungo shook his hand, thanked him and, with a long drawn out sigh, climbed into the car.

The Memorial Hospital,
Isle of Skye, Scotland.
Friday 10th September 2006. 10.00 a.m.

Dr Omundo dropped his head and looked over the top of his glasses at Angus, sitting on the edge of the bed, fully dressed and with his hands and head swathed in bandages.

'Hmm' he said, then grasping his chin and summoning up the gravest expression he could manage considering his youthful appearance, added, 'I can't stop you if you want to go Mr Brett, but I'd rather you had another day or two with us - just so I can be sure you are fully recovered. You took a severe knock you know, and I'd really like to be satisfied there won't be any repercussions. As it is, your progress has been remarkable considering the state you were when you were admitted.'

'I'll be fine doctor,' Angus replied, 'I know I will, I have no headache, no dizziness, nothing. But I do have a need to get home; my wife can only cope without me for a few days, certainly not for over a week.'

'She's not well?'

Angus shook his head, 'Never will be until she gives up smoking cigarettes and stops drinking.'

'Ah, I see, yes, she has a problem. Well it's up to you Mr Brett. You know what I think and I must tell you I'll be strongly emphasising my views in my report. Are you quite sure you won't stay until after the weekend?'

Angus thrust out his hand. 'I can't. I really have to go, but thank you so much for looking after me.'

Omundo grinned, 'I don't think you're ready to shake hands just yet Mr Brett. If anyone grips your hand in the next week or two I can assure you your eyes'll be watering!'

Angus nodded and turned to Nurse McNevitt, who'd just come in, 'My thanks to you Nurse … and to your colleagues.'

'You're a lucky man, Mr Brett.' she replied, handing him a plastic bag. 'Good job your friend from the hotel came round with a change of clothes; your old ones are in the bag but they're covered in blood and torn to shreds.'

'You're very kind. I'll probably ditch everything except for the shoes when I get home.' he said and, raising his hand in a half salute, swung round to hobble out to where Herbie Scott, another committee member, and proprietor of The Old Bell Hotel in Datchett, was waiting to collect him. Herbie was going to drive them back to Aberdeen in the car Angus had hired.

'Good meeting, Herbie? Angus asked, as they drove through the hospital gates. 'Sorry I missed it.'

'Waste of bloody time, hours of waffling and not a single decision taken. But what happened to you?'

Angus smiled. 'I don't know … it seems I fell.'

'Go on.'

'Well … I got up here a day early, I needed some time to think to be honest … I'm having a difficult time at home with Betty and I wanted to be on my own for a bit.'

'Ah, tough luck … so she's no better?'

'Worse; it's a bottle a day now. I'm at my wit's end, Herbie, I just don't know how to deal with the problem and I wanted to get away to work out our future.'

'Right … So how did you come to wind up wrapped round a rock; you were preoccupied, I suppose, and missed your footing; it's tricky enough up there.'

'I've no idea what happened, in fact I can't remember anything much. I drove up to the café intending to have a cup of tea before walking up to the headland to watch the sun set; I can remember that alright. I'd been driving around all day, you see, trying to clear my head, and I decided to finish up with an hour or two up there, it's a nice tranquil place with no distractions where I could work out where Betty and I are heading.'

'The tea rooms are closed, didn't you know?'

'No, but when I got there and saw everything locked up, I decided to go on up to the top anyway.'

'And was there nobody else about?'

'Not a soul …'

'And?'

'And nothing … I climbed up, had my time on my own as I'd planned, but on the way down I somehow slipped and tumbled down the slope out of control until I came up against one of those big rocks at the bottom. Can't remember any of it … not a thing.'

'And what time was all this?'

'Oh … around six, six thirty, I suppose.'

'And you lay there all night.'

'Must have, a young lad looking for some lost sheep found me early Tuesday morning. I was still unconscious.'

'And he sent for the ambulance?'

Angus laughed. 'He thought I was dead, I believe.'

'So what's the damage?'

'Cuts and bruises, lump on my head the size of a duck egg, and dented pride. I feel really stupid making such a spectacle of myself and causing a distraction for you guys, let alone frightening the wits out of Betty.'

'She knows?'

'Oh yes, the police went round. Sobered her up I can tell you, so maybe some good'll come out of it.'

'It's hard to believe you could have come through it all and recover so quickly.'

'I know, I can hardly credit it myself.'

'Bloody miracle I'd say.'

Angus nodded but he wasn't really listening; in his mind he was back at the riverside looking down at the body of Dudley Melchitt face down in the water, and trying to work out if someone hidden in the bushes had seen everything.

'You alright, Angus?'

'I'm fine Herbie, just tired, ignore me.'

'OK. Nod off if you want to old son, we've a long drive before we get to Aberdeen.'

'I will if you don't mind' he replied, lowering the back of his seat and closing his eyes. Soon he was drifting off into thoughts of what had happened over the previous few days, wondering why he hadn't waited to see if Melchitt was dead before taking off in a panic, worried there'd been someone in the bushes watching him. Gradually the noise of the engine and the movement of the car began to take over and, before ten minutes had elapsed, he was sound asleep.

The Camera Shop
Finkle Street, Richmond.
Tuesday 13th September 2006 9.45 a.m.

Barry James, a large magnifying glass held to his eye, was examining Tony's films. They'd all come out well. Amazing how black and white images brought the water to life when, on the face of it, the opposite would seem more likely. He had the proofs laid out on a bench and was checking them for flaws which might have crept in while they were being processed. With the two of them likely to be competing in the same category at the forthcoming exhibition he needed to ensure his work on his rival's photographs was faultless.

He'd developed dozens of Tony's negatives in the past, and most of them seem to have been taken around Aysgarth, for the waterfalls were in all of them in one way or another. Many were close-ups but he'd included some long distance shots too. In these, the darkness of the overhanging foliage and the deep tones of the smooth flowing water threw up the whiteness of the cascades in the most dramatic way. They were all excellent and Barry could see Tony wouldn't have a problem in finding three good enough for the competition.

The last four had not been taken at Aysgarth but near the bridge, over the River Swayle he'd have passed on his way home. They were all long distance shots and some showed a fly fisherman poised to cast. He picked one of them up.

'Hmm, this is more like' he muttered, 'he's asking a question here at last, getting the viewer to participate. If he really cottons on to the trick he'll soon be delivering stuff for me to worry about. Yes, there's no getting away from it, these last few are damned good ... too good for comfort.'

Outside Gatwick Airport, Sussex.
Monday 25th September 2006 8.00 a.m.

The flight had been full and Sophie and her colleagues in the cabin crew had been kept busy all night. As she emerged from the airport in the airline's minibus England immediately seemed to be more attractive than it had appeared when she'd arrived the first time in January. Then it had been all grey, this time it was bright and sunny. The Holiday Inn, her home for the two night stopover was quite close and before long she was in her room unpacking her bag. Once it was done, and as the rest of the flight staff were climbing into their beds, she slipped into the shower and let the jets of water flush the tiredness out of her.

By ten o'clock, and having eliminated all thoughts of 'Frog', who'd died, she was ready to start visiting her father's three remaining student days' cronies. She'd the best part of the day and the whole of the following one to do it, starting with George McPhee, or 'Jock'. With a bit of luck she hoped to find him at the address she had in her hand bag, the one she'd got from Eddie in March: The Malthouse, Point Hill, Lewes, Sussex.

The Budget car she'd booked was ready to for her to collect and by eleven o'clock she was driving down the A23 towards Brighton and the turn off for Lewes.

Thirty minutes later she passed a sign indicating she was within the town's boundary.

She stopped when she saw a man coming out of a gateway with a dog and asked him the way to Point Hill. His directions were clear and before long she was pulling up opposite a fine if somewhat unusual shaped house, standing well back from the road, behind a wide white painted gate bearing its name: The Malthouse.

Parked outside the front door was a hearse, and straight off she guessed her mission was going to be a short one.

An enquiry confirmed the disappointment when, having pulled in behind the funeral procession half an hour later, and followed it to All Hallows Church, she got an opportunity to glance at the mourner's attendance list in the church's porch waiting for everyone to sign.

At the top it said what she'd feared; the name of the deceased, it was George McPhee. Below the heading, half a dozen people had already signed in, but she recognised none of the names and assumed they were neighbours. There weren't many. Few people, it seemed, were going to miss Jock - maybe only his family - and that, as far as she could judge from the handful of people present, might consist of just one man and one woman. They were sitting in the front pew, stiff and unconnected, not looking like a husband and wife - more like a brother and sister. She glanced at the list Angie had made out; they had to be Sandy and Eva.

She left un-noticed before the service was over and returned to her car disappointed. She'd been building up to this confrontation for days and, now she'd arrived, she was too late. She drove back to Jock's house and sat waiting for the mourners to return. It was only when she got there she realised it might be hours before they'd be back, they could be burying him in All Hallow's churchyard or taking him to a family plot or crematorium miles away. She'd no option but to reassess her plans in light of the new situation and see if one of the other names on her list was near enough to try.

Somewhere between the house and the church, she recalled passing a pub called The Coachman's Inn, it would do. What she needed was coffee, strong black coffee, to fight her tiredness. The surge of adrenalin which had been fuelling her since she'd landed had started to drain away when she'd seen the hearse, and she was having a job keeping awake.

The Coachman's Inn was shut when she got there. A handwritten note stuck on the door said 'Open at Five'. Too tired to risk driving farther, she pulled over into the shade of an old oak tree at the back of the car park, locked the doors, let the seat back as far as it would go, and drifted off to sleep.

The sound of car doors slamming awakened her. A glance at her watch told her it was two thirty; she'd been dozing for nearly two hours. She ran her hands through her hair, repaired her makeup, and got out of the car. Half a dozen people were filing into the pub. Amongst them were the man and the woman she'd seen in the front pew. The burial, or cremation, was obviously over and they were preparing to send Jock off in style.

She waited until they'd all gone inside and then, after a decent interval, followed them in.

They were grouped at one end of the bar talking quietly to one another. Champagne was being poured. She made her way over to the other end of the counter and stood patiently waiting for the barman to notice her but, before he did, one of the funeral party spotted her. 'Young lady down there looking for a drink, Jackie.' he said to the barman, who came down and took her order for coffee.

'Take a seat Miss. We're not really open yet.' he said, 'I'll bring it over in a couple of minutes after I've served these people. It's a private party, one of our regulars has passed away ... they're his family and friends.'

She sat for a while watching and listening but it wasn't long before another wave of tiredness swept over her.

'You alright?' said the barman, putting down her coffee in front of her.

'Fine.' she replied, sitting up and trying to re-orientate herself. 'It's jet lag; I was flying all night.'

A man, one of the two chief mourners, who'd heard what she'd said, followed the barman over to her table and nodded his head understandingly. 'Come over and join us.'

She looked across at the rest of his party. They were standing in a semicircle at the bar, and talking much more loudly than they had been when they'd first arrived, their serious expressions and reverential tones, replaced by grins and giggles as the alcohol took effect.

'We've just buried my father and we're having a drink in his memory.' the man explained, holding out his hand towards her. 'Come on, I'll introduce you, we can't have you sitting over here entirely on your own. Dad wouldn't have wanted anyone left out.'

She hesitated. Should she say why she was in Point Hill, tell him she'd come specifically to see his father?

He smiled, 'They won't bite. They're just Dad's friends. I'm Sandy by the way and that's my sister Eva over there at the end on her own ... she's still a bit upset.'

Sophie nodded, and reluctantly followed him back to the assembled mourners; *they* didn't look upset, not with all the champagne flowing. Eva, meanwhile, seemed to be edging even farther along the bar in order to distance herself from the revelry.

A silence descended on the ring of mourners as soon as Sandy and Sophie joined them. 'Why on earth has he brought her, a complete stranger, to join us?' their expressions said, and it made her smile. When the introductions were complete they rudely turned their backs on her again and continued their previous conversations with each other.

Wishing she'd refused Sandy's invitation she slipped away from the crowd and went over to Eva who was sitting, head in hands, at the far end of the bar, looking morosely into the distance.

'Are you alright?' she asked.

'What do you think?' Eva replied.

'Well, obviously, it's tough losing your father but you're upset at all this going on as well aren't you?'

'It's Sandy ... they're all his pals. Most of them didn't even know Dad. It's disgusting.'

'Oh dear ... I know what you mean.'

'Do you. I wonder. Is your father alive?'

Sophie smiled, 'I think so.'

Eva dropped her hands to the counter and turned her head to look Sophie in the face. 'Funny answer.'

'I suppose it is but ... well ... I've never even seen my father. He'd flown before I was born.'

'Oh ... one of those was he?'

'I always believed so.'

'But now you don't?'

'It's what I'm trying to find out.'

Eve swung right round, her interest awakened by Sophie's remarks. 'Have a drink; it's all paid for ... you might as well.'

Sophie gave a little nod 'Why not? Yes, sure ... thanks.'

Eva tapped the bar and signalled for a glass of champagne to be brought over. When it came, it was accompanied by a plate of sandwiches.

'Oh good, food,' said Sophie, 'I haven't had anything since I got off the plane, I didn't realise how hungry I was.'

'Where have you come from?' Eva asked, perking up.

'Tobago.'

'Tobago? Nice. On holiday are you?'

'Not really, just two days stopover at the Holiday Inn at Gatwick before I go back. I work for B.A.'

'So how come you've wound up here? There are better places to visit than this.'

Sophie thought for a minute before answering. 'It may sound odd to you, especially in view of what's happened recently but, believe it or not, I actually came to Lewes to try to speak to your father.'

Eva's nudged her stool closer and raised her eyebrows. 'You're here to see Dad. Why?'

'To ask him about mine.'

'My father knew yours? Unlikely. I mean he was never in Tobago or anywhere else in that part of the world as far as I know.'

'They knew each other a long time ago, in their college days in London, I'm pretty sure of it.'

'Really?'

'Your dad was known as 'Jock' ... right?'

'Yes, but so are half the men in Scotland.'

'My father's called Henry Byrd, yours would have known him as 'Dicky'.'

'Oh ... well ... yes. Dad did know a man called Dicky Byrd, I remember the name. Hang on.'

She got off her stool and shouted across the room to her brother, 'Sandy come over here, you'll never guess who this is - she's Dicky Byrd's daughter.'

Sandy looked up as though he'd been shot ... and then he slowly blanched. 'Jesus,' he said to himself, 'Dicky had a child and nobody knew! What the hell's she doing here ... not ... not ... no she couldn't be.'

The Queen of Scotland Hotel
Market Place, Richmond, Yorks. Sunday 1st
October 2006. 12.30 p.m.

Barry raised his glass, 'Here's to you Tony, you're a worthy winner. I thought I had you this year with the black and white Friesians heifers I took in Leyburn cattle market, but your one with the fisherman in the act of casting was superb. I hope you'll remember it was me who gave you the tip which has lifted your work.'

Tony clinked his glass with Barry's and took a sip. 'Thanks. It was close mind you; I thought your cattle were terrific. But as to telling everyone about the tip you gave me, well I wish I could, but I'd be lying if I did.'

'Lying? What d'you mean lying. I remember distinctly giving you the advice on dozens of occasions, the last one being the day you brought them in. You told me you couldn't change your style, but you, you cunning blighter, you had me fooled completely; you'd already done it when you placed the fisherman in your shot. And look what bloody-well happened … you won. I gave you the tip and you won. You might at least acknowledge it.'

Tony shook his head. 'You misunderstand me Barry. I hardly noticed the man in the river. It was fluke. I didn't put him in on purpose. But you're right, his being there made all the difference.'

'A fluke you say… a fluke! Well I'm damned, beaten by a bloody fluke. And, to top it all, your picture will not only be the highlight of tomorrow's exhibition but I'll have to put a blown up version of it in …in *my* flamin' window!'

'Ah, come on Barry it's the custom and, what's more, it's usually one of yours.'

'It'll sicken me every time I look at it.'

'Bugger off.'

'I'm only joking. Let's have another and then I'm going back to enlarge the flaming' thing.'

The Camera Shop
Finkle Street, Richmond, Yorks,
Sunday 1st October 2006. 1.36 p.m.

Barry, who'd been bending over the photograph showing the fisherman on the darkroom table, suddenly straightened up. 'Good grief,' he mumbled, 'it's Dudley Melchitt. Why didn't I see it before? His arm's almost covering his face but I should have recognised him. I wonder when Tony took it, must have been only a few days before Dudley died; it might even have been on the very day. I'd better ring and check.'

Tony came straight round. 'I don't think I ever met Superintendent Melchitt, Barry, so I wouldn't have recognised him anyway. But all the films

I left in the day you were on at me about my changing my style had been taken the day before, which'd be the previous Monday, my day off.'

Barry looked at the calendar on the wall beside him. 'That's Monday the 4th of September - the day Dudley Melchitt died. Look, Tony, these pictures might be important, so we'd better get 'em round to the police to see in the morning. In the meantime let's have a look them again.' He went to the filing cabinet, pulled out an envelope and tipped out the contents. In a matter of seconds they'd picked out three photographs not entered in the competition.

In the first there was no sign of the fisherman at all. In the second he was there, but in the shallow water at the very edge of the river, his foot slightly raised as though he were about to take a step forward; and he was looking downstream, with only the back of his head showing. In the last photo he was leaning slightly backwards with his arm drawn back to make the cast. His face, no longer hidden in this picture, had on it a look of intense concentration. Barry saw immediately it was Dudley Melchitt.

Richmond Police Station.
Monday 2nd October 2006. 10.00 a.m.

Inspector Sherman, Sergeant Bellamy, Tony Bloxham and Barry James sat around a table, deep in conversation. Before them were Tony's photographs.

'It's the boss all right.' said the Sherman, 'Pity we didn't see these before - we'll need the negatives.'

'No problem they're in this folder.'

As the inspector took them he asked if the prints had been trimmed.

Barry nodded. 'Certainly they have, it's customary to slightly enlarge prints intended for exhibition and then crop them back to a standard size.'

'So the negatives might hold more of the original image than we see on these prints.'

'A little more, probably … I can't actually remember.'

'And you are sure, Mr Bloxham, you … Hey, wait a minute, haven't I seen you somewhere before?'

Tony laughed and nodded, he'd recognised Detective Inspector Sherman the moment he'd walked into his office. 'You might have done … through the hatch. 'Rare but not blue'. Am I right?'

'What?'

'Rare but not blue - your steak!'

It was the inspector's turn to laugh then. Barry James and Sergeant Bellamy looked at the two of them in total astonishment.

'Gotcha.' said Inspector Sherman, 'you're the chef in The Royal Hotel aren't you?'

'Guilty.' Tony replied.

'And you took all these did you?'

Barry answered. 'He took all these and many more on the same day Inspector. He was getting ready for the Photographic Exhibition over at the Town Hall which is opening later today. One of these photograph's already won first prize. I was about to blow it up for my shop window when I recognised Mr Melchitt in it.'

'You knew him?'

'Oh yes, I knew him alright, he was my next door neighbour.'

'Hang on.' said Bellamy, pulling out his notebook and flipping back through the pages. 'Here we are Sir, we interviewed a Mrs James and a Mrs ... 'er ... Deakin, after the Super's brothers had been talking to them.'

'So we did ... a couple of days after the incident, I remember.' said the inspector. 'And the Mrs James we spoke to is your wife, eh? Pity we didn't talk to you at the same time.'

'It wouldn't have made any difference if you had Inspector.' said Barry, 'At that stage Tony hadn't given me the negatives to develop.'

'Could you oblige us and make us a set of larger prints Mr James - untrimmed of course.'

'You'll have them immediately after lunch. I'll do them myself.'

'And talking about lunch.' Tony said, standing up, 'If you've finished with me I'd like to get on. I should be in my kitchen getting my vegetables ready.'

'I think you can both go, thanks for coming in with this information ... very helpful.'

When the inspector and the sergeant got back from their lunch in the canteen, the reprinted photos were on the inspector's desk. They each took one up.

'Nothing much here.' said Sherman.

Sergeant Bellamy looked up from the one he was examining and smiled. 'Yeah? Try this one then, you may find *it* interesting.'

Sherman took the photograph and, having barely glanced at it, whistled. 'There's someone on the edge ... Hang on ... it's someone walking along the bank! He was cut off from the other print we saw earlier. Recognise him?'

'I do not. Nor the other guy, but it's hard to say,'

'What other guy?' barked the inspector, snatching the print

back out of Sergeant Bellamy's hand.

'Here, tucked down behind the bushes, on the other side of the picture. This one's right on the other edge, I reckon he's watching the first guy.'

'Stone me, you're right Sergeant, there *is* somebody there. Hard to see whether it's a man or a woman though. Anyway whatever, or whoever, it is: man, woman, or child, we've got something to work on for a change. Let's see if our technical guys can do better than our friend Mr James, maybe they can sharpen it up enough for us to get them reproduced in a newspaper.'

'Will do, and I'm going back out to the river to take a look around the bushes where the third fella was. You never know.'

'Right, and I'll put pressure on the lab. We can compare notes later.'

The interval which had elapsed since the day of the murder had been long enough for evidence of the presence of anyone hiding in the bushes to have been obliterated or blown away, but Sergeant Bellamy did find one thing, a London Underground train ticket, an unlikely thing to come across on a riverbank in Yorkshire. He manoeuvred it into an envelope with a twig and put it in his pocket. Glancing back as he climbed the bank to the road, he couldn't help marvelling at the tranquillity all around. Who could have imagined a man had been done to death in such a lovely place?

As Inspector Sherman tidied his desk prior to going home, he'd a big smile on his face, it'd been a good day; the photographs had been enhanced and Sergeant Bellamy had brought in a valuable clue. For the first time in four weeks they had something to go on … not much but, with a bit of luck, enough to put him on the tracks of Dudley Melchitt's killer.

The Malthouse, Point Hill, Lewes, Sussex.
Wednesday 4th October 2006. 7.00 p.m.

S andy McPhee shut the door, walked back into the sitting room, and stood at the window watching his sister Eva's car until it disappeared down the drive out of sight.

It was a just over a week since the funeral and he was keen to get on with a final check before setting off on the next stage of his plan, but he'd been unable to do anything while she was still there. Now, with her chasing up a part in a Christmas Pantomime, he was at last on his own. Nevertheless he'd leave it for a few minutes before going over everything in the garage again; he didn't want to be caught should she come back unexpectedly to pick up something she'd forgotten.

The house was quiet and cold. He opened up the valve on a radiator, unused since the spring, and waited for the heat to come through. When a hopeful sounding gurgle announced the arrival of hot water from the boiler he gave a smile of satisfaction and went over to the drinks trolley where he poured a goodly measure of Laphroaig Malt Whisky into a brandy balloon. He liked it that way, liked the pungent fumes in his nose as he slowly sipped the smoky spirit from the Isle of Islay.

Sitting back in his chair he looked around, and he couldn't help but sigh; all this was in jeopardy. It had taken three generations to create it and now, if he didn't get out of the jam he was in, it would all be gone. In a few weeks' time he might have nothing left but a slow fading memory of the dark ochre walls, the antique mahogany and rosewood furniture, the soft leather seating, and, more than anything else, the pictures, black and gilt Hogarth framed ancient maps collected by his father, and bold contemporary water colours in highly ornate frames painted by his mother.

Here, in this splendid room, he was surrounded by the

evidence of a privileged upbringing, none of it more compelling than the sight of the two half-moon tables either side of the fireplace crammed with silver framed photographs.

Between the tables, in the hearth, a huge display of gold and red autumnal foliage collected and arranged by Eva brought a feminine touch which had not been seen in the house for a long time. His mother would regularly have done the same sort of thing had she been alive but, since her demise, he and his father had abandoned all such activities as being too troublesome.

Everything had been too much trouble when he thought about it and, being tied to the old man every evening after the nurse had gone had been worst of all. He wasn't cut out for it - baby-sitting - it deprived him of the chance to nip down to The Coachman's Inn occasionally, or to nip down to the golf or sailing club; they'd been out of the question for months. No, if he wasn't sitting in the office worrying himself sick over money, he'd been here in this very room looking at a dementia stricken old man who only opened his mouth to put food in. 'Not any more though.' he thought.

He took another swig and rolled the fiery liquid round in his mouth before swallowing it, savouring the peaty flavours as he thought about the imminent prospect of his world collapsing and the risky plan he'd been forced to adopt to ensure his survival. A hundred thousand pounds was all he needed to stave off trouble, short term, and ensure enough breathing space for him to work out a more permanent solution. That's what he'd have to get hold of - one way or another - a hundred thousand quid. There could be no turning back. He had no option but to continue with his plan and hope for the best. It would need to be meticulous though, and the execution of it immaculate, if he was to get away with it. Phase One had only been successful because he'd been lucky, Phase Two would have to be considerably better organised if he was to succeed with *it* as well.

He bit his lip and pondered on the near hopelessness of his situation as thoughts of what might happen in the future crowded in on him. Very soon, unless he acted, his financial manipulations would be exposed, for he'd started milking the client's cash deposits. Very soon some, if not all of those who'd handed their savings over to McPhee's for safe keeping, would discover what he'd been doing with their money.

He took another sip, put down his glass, and was shuddering when one of the silver framed photographs flashed in the sunlight. It was one which must have been taken on the same day as the one in the office - the picture of the LMS club. He went over and picked it up as he had done so many times over the previous couple of weeks.

What a lot, irresponsible and not bothered much about their studies, they'd have been more aware of the price of a horse at Ascot and the cost of a pint in the local, than they would have been of the name of the last Roman Emperor or the atomic weight of lead. The difference between him and them was they'd finally grown up, while he'd stayed a playboy.

A tired smile began to form, but he changed his mind before it developed into a laugh and leaned back, straight faced, arms folded across his chest, and closed his eyes.

'Where the hell is Eva?' he wondered, 'I'll give her ten more minutes. If she doesn't come back by then I'll get on with it. Yes ... the LMS Club. Great name, I remember the night the old man told me about it. It was in one of his few moments of lucidity just before he'd died. He didn't know I'd already opened the envelope. So what? The real question is how many others know - apart from Angus of course - he obviously does. For instance what about the girl who turned up at the funeral, Sophie Something - Dicky Byrd's daughter - I wonder if she knows? Is she onto the same thing?

It might all turn out to be a cat and mouse game of course, with everyone wondering if they're a cat or a mouse. Maybe we're all cats and all mice, that'd be a laugh! Maybe I ought to be locking myself in at night, watching my back, hoping I'm a cat and not a mouse! Ah well ... I might pop down to The Coachman's later ... when I've finished in the garage.'

He sat up, rubbed his hands together, and then rose, muttering, from his chair. 'I'll get on then, Eva won't be coming back now.'

Outside the double garage stood his silver Volvo, inside was his father's treasured old black Austin Princess, unused for decades and standing on flat tyres. It was covered in dust, as was the floor which had his footprints all over it. Beside the old car was a gleaming new crimson and cream Honda motor cycle. On top of the saddle were draped a set of almost new black leather overalls. He'd hired both from Rogers and Griffin Motor Cycle Hire Ltd., of

Redhill during the afternoon, having got off at Redhill station instead of continuing on to Lewes, from where he usually walked home. They wouldn't rent him a helmet, mysteriously saying it was for 'Health and Safety reasons'. In the end he'd bought one.

He'd been concerned as whether he'd be able to smuggle the bike and all the gear into the garage without Eva seeing him. However when he got home she wasn't there, so he simply drove straight in and locked the doors behind him, wondering if he shouldn't have done the same the previous time instead of using his own car.

Not that there was much point in worrying about that. He'd just have to hope he'd got away with it.

Richmond Police station.
Thursday 5th October 2006. 10.00 a.m.

The photos re-worked by the police laboratory had come back an hour earlier and D.I. Sherman, with Sgt. Bellamy, was at Sherman's desk studying them. 'Bugger all difference on this one, Malc, I still can't make the guy's face out.' said the inspector, putting down one of the prints.

'Pity, because I think we have something here, Guv.' replied Bellamy, handing him a different photograph.

Sherman took it and went to the window to get better light, immediately seeing that, as a result of the lab's enhancement, the man walking along the bank had become well enough defined to be recognised. The second man's face was still no clearer though, and mightn't even have been a face at all. 'This guy must have moved at the crucial moment.' said Sherman, stabbing his finger on the doubtful blur. 'But we've certainly got something to work on with the laddie walking along the bank. D'you know what, Malc … he looks familiar to me.'

'Aye, he does to me as well, but I can't think why.' Bellamy replied, 'I'm going to send copies to the papers and I've already asked the lab to circulate 'em round the county. If the lab can knock up extra posters I'll get 'em put up all round the town.'

'Good … and I want you to take this lot we have here round to the super's neighbours, not just the ones next door but the whole road, and the shops at the corner, and the nearest pub. See if any one recognises either of the faces.'

The Mede Manor Hotel
Beaconsfield, Bucks.
Thursday 5th October 12.15 p.m.

Y ou're back early.' Betty said, drawing on her forty third
cigarette of the day and sucking the smoke deep down into
her lungs before snorting it out like a horse on a frosty
morning. 'Did you get anywhere?

'How many of those things have you got through today?'
asked Angus, angrily ignoring her question, seething at the
slovenliness and indolence which looked as though it had been
pinning her to a bar stool next to the cigarettes and vodka since he
left.

'God, you're not going to start all that again are you?
Seventeen. Did you get the money?'

'No I did not get the bloody money. There's not going to
be any money. Can't you get it into your vodka sodden brain? No
money. Period. And you're on your third pack of cigarettes, I
marked them.'

'You're a mean bastard, Angus. You've let this business fall
apart and you blame me for it. By the way there was a man on a
motor bike hanging around here all morning. When I challenged
him he asked for you.'

'Oh bugger the man … and his motorbike! You're not
listening Betty, you never do. If you'd got stuck in and helped me
instead of sitting round here all day with a glass in one hand and
cigarette in the other we wouldn't be in this position.'

She took another deep lungful of smoke, and blew it out of
the side of her mouth into his face.

'That's revolting.' he said, wincing and twisting away in
disgust. 'If you can't pull yourself together, go into the kitchen and
keep out of sight. By the look of the till and the vodka bottle, which

I also marked incidentally, you've drunk more than you've sold. We'd be better off 'shutting shop' than 'bleeding to death' like this.

While he was speaking she dismounted from the stool and stood, swaying, trying to steady herself by gripping the edge of the bar with one hand and the pink coloured dummy beer pump handle mounted on the counter with the other. For a moment it looked as though she was might succeed but then, suddenly, she lurched to one side and crashed to the floor, wrenching the handle from the bar top as she fell.

It was almost more than he could bear on top of the tension which had been building since he'd left for Rottingdean at crack of dawn. Nothing had gone right there either, he'd lost his way and then, when he eventually arrived, he couldn't find the boat; … now this. He leaned over the bar and looked down at her; she was out for the count, the pump handle still clutched in her hand.

He straightened up and was about to go round the end of the counter to do something about her when he heard the footsteps of someone walking into the otherwise empty bar behind him. He turned and gasped with surprise. It was his brother Rex accompanied, it seemed, by an army of people crowding in behind him. 'Good God, Rex, what are you doing here?' he said, advancing to meet him.

'I came to do you a favour but we'll go somewhere else if we're not welcome.'

'No, no, no.' Angus said, offering his hand. 'It's just I got a shock when you walked in. It's not as if you're a regular visitor. Come through into the other bar and bring your friends. We're refurbishing in here.'

Rex looked around him as he shook hands. 'What's wrong with it? Seems alright to me.'

'It's not the decorations it's the beer delivery system - we're renewing it - and then we're going to do up the bar, get rid of those ghastly pink handles with the hunting scenes on them. We've started already.' he said, pointing to the handle-less mounting. 'We're going to modernise the whole place.'

'Pity, I always rather liked the Olde Worlde look, tasteless but somehow comforting. So where do you want us, we need a drink?'

'Go through into the Sportsman's bar, I'll be with you in a minute.'

As Rex and his party of six went through, Angus quickly returned to do something about Betty. She was still almost motionless but he could see she wasn't hurt, just in a deep alcoholic sleep. He bent down and, taking her by the ankles, dragged her through into 'the office', a little windowless room between the bar and the back hall. Once in there he turned her on her side, put a folded bar towel under her head, and wedged her in place with two armchairs. She was safe enough like that. It wouldn't be the first time for her to wake up between those two chairs, on the same floor, and feeling like death. He pulled the door shut behind him and locked it, pocketing the key, as he went through to catch up with his brother and his friends. While getting their drinks he explained the lack of customers as being due to their not opening at lunchtime until the refurbishment was complete.

Rex's response, which he made by raising his chin in an upward nod of disbelief, was ignored by Angus, who sent the conversation off in a new direction by asking after Eva.

'Eva and I aren't together any longer, Angus; she couldn't keep up and she wouldn't try. I've got another girl friend now, Ginny - Virginia Meddows, she's in the new film.'

'Oh a new film eh? I never got round to seeing the last one, can't seem to find time to get to the cinema these days.'

'We're filming in Bulstrode Park at the moment, that's why we're here.'

'I don't follow you.'

'Well … we lost several days with bad weather, and now we're starting so early and packing up so late in order to catch up, a few of us have decided to stay locally rather than commute up and down to London. I thought you'd like the business. Can you give us six rooms? We won't need food … we have caterers on the set … but we do need to be handy, and where would be more handy than this place?'

'I'm on my own at the moment, Rex, Betty's away today and I've persuaded the staff to take their holidays; there's only me and the woman who comes in to do the rooms.'

'So what are you saying, 'Yes' or 'No'?'

I'm saying 'Yes', provided you understand I can only give you the bar service in here, together with what you find on the Teasmaid tray beside the television in your rooms.'

Rex turned to his friends. 'We're 'in' gentlemen, but my

brother is unable to give us little more than bar service in this room owing to the partial closure of the hotel while he refurbishes it.'

A loudly dressed and rather ruddy faced man of twenty stone whose voice had been consistently heard above all the others expressed the feelings of all of them by shouting: 'Keep the booze flowing Landlord and it'll be fine by us. I'll have a large Remy and a packet of cashew nuts for a start … and room with a King sized bed … and you can stick in a maiden if you've got one to spare!'

Angus forced a laugh then, nodding his agreement to the chorus of similar requests which followed, got on with pulling pints and dispensing brandy instead of brooding over his morning's bungled hunt for Boris's boat.

He didn't get away from the thirsty and progressively voluble assembly until nearly five o'clock. When he did, he found Betty in a state of extreme anger, she was sitting up in one of the chairs smoking, and glowering at him as he approached. 'You locked me in, you rotten bastard!'

'And I'll do it again if you don't get a grip on yourself. Go upstairs and get yourself sorted … and no more drink - please. Rex is here with a load of friends. They're staying for a few days.'

'Rex here … with us … what do you mean?'

'I mean what I said - Rex's bloody here with bloody us. It's a hotel in case you haven't noticed. And keep clear of the guests until you're presentable … and no more drinking. We'll be full for the next three or four nights so for Christ's sake pull yourself together.'

Betty thought about arguing but then, inexplicably changing her mind, dropped her belligerence and started to cry. 'I'll do the breakfasts.' she mumbled through tears which trickled down her cheeks and dropped unheeded from her chin.

'There's no need,' he replied, beginning to feel sorry for having bullied her. 'I've already told Rex we're not catering at the moment. Get a good night sleep and we'll talk properly in the morning. But listen, Betty, we have to get things understood between us. I have to have promises from you which won't be broken this time or we're finished.'

She nodded, bit her lip, and without saying another word shuffled off to bed. As she passed him she paused and let out a long drawn out sigh … but he ignored her. For a while after she'd gone he stood there thinking, it was surely over between them.

He turned off the light and returned to the Sportsman's bar to find the party had gained even greater momentum and the big guy was in the driving seat.

Rex rose to meet him as he entered; 'I've served them more to drink Angus, made a list of what I poured on a bit of paper and left it on the till - you can put it down to me. Now grab yourself one, and come over and sit next to me. I want to know what's going on. Where's Betty for a start? *You* haven't split up have you?'

'Not yet … but we're heading that way. Keep it to yourself though. We might patch it up.'

'What's the problem?'

'She's drinking too much.'

'And leaving you to run the place on your own - how long's this been going on?'

'Long enough, but look here Rex why have you suddenly taken an interest in our affairs? You've hardly been near us in years?'

'I know I haven't … and you know why.'

'Because Dad left this place to me while you got the lousy shares?'

'Exactly … they turned out to be worthless. Stupid man had all his eggs in one basket and when the company went down a few weeks after I got the stock I practically lost the lot while you had all this.' Rex waved his hand about to illustrate what he perceived to be the unfairness of his father's will.

Angus was quick to reply 'I know Dad didn't do you any favours … but he didn't do me any either. His judgement was just as flawed regarding this hotel as it was when he invested in the stock you got. I've been having trouble ever since the motorway opened and the new hotel came on stream, but I never had the resources to mount a defence. We're all but going under at this very moment. No Rex … I'm not any better off than you … Dad left me damn all as well.'

Rex thought about what he'd been told for a moment or two and then he started to laugh. 'Rich isn't it? It looks like 'Good old Ginger Brett' wasn't so 'good' after all. I wonder what his friends would make of it?'

'Which friends?'

'The lot he used to always be talking about, the LM

'something-or-other' lot.'

'Club ... the LMS Club.'

'Yeah. They probably thought he was loaded when he came into a hotel within a year or two of leaving college, and all the time he was frittering it away and no one guessed.'

'Well I certainly didn't, he had me completely fooled. I only discovered the real position we were in when it became mine. Honestly Rex, I never saw the accounts until I owned the place. I got a hell of a shock when I got a look at them.'

'He must have drunk it all.'

'Or given it away, remember how 'generous' he was?'

'You're right ... 'Have it on the house.' Jeez, I can hear him saying it now. No wonder they all liked him ... he bought his popularity.'

'Lucky Mum never found out.'

'Maybe she did.' suggested Rex, scratching the fashionable stubble covering his chin.

'Nah, she'd have flattened him if she had.' Angus replied. 'So, tell me, what's happened between you and Eva?'

'Nothing's happened, not for her, and that was the problem. I kept finding her opportunities but she didn't capitalise on them, never pushed herself. She was stuck firmly to the bottom rung of the ladder. In the end I got fed up trying.'

'You were friendly with her brother Sandy as well at one time, weren't you? Played a bit of golf with him. And what about their old man ... 'Uncle Jock'. Remember how Dad tried to get us to call him 'Uncle'. Huh, I wonder if he's still in the land of the living.'

'Well, I can tell you ... he isn't; he died recently. Saw it in The Times.'

'Go on? He was one of them as well wasn't he - one of the LMS lot?' Angus said, reaching for Rex's glass.

'No more for me, I have to go over my lines for tomorrow's shoot. But yes ... you're right Eva's father was one of them. D'you still have that old photograph of Dad's with them all in it?'

'Standing in the street with drinks in their hands? It's hanging in the office.'

'I must have a look at it tomorrow. I expect they're all six feet under by now.'

'Yeah, they probably are.' Angus lied, thankful Rex seemed not to have given much recent thought to their father or his student friends and, clearly, had never seen the envelope. 'Which is fine,' he thought, 'but it puts me into a bit of a dilemma … one which might eventually force me to choose between two equally distasteful alternatives … tell him or kill him!'

The Public Desk,
Richmond Police Station
Thursday 5th October 5.45 p.m.

The man stood at the widow waiting for attention. He was there a long time while several policemen, on important duties he assumed, walked backwards and forwards across his vision without any of them stopping to ask what he wanted.

Then he noticed the sign, it said: 'Ring for attention'.

He did so, and Police Constable Ernest Roundtree immediately left what he was doing and came across to answer the summons. 'Can I help you, Sir?'

'I hope so.' the man said. 'I want to report someone for running into my churns in his car, and spilling a load of milk.'

'I see Sir. If you'll wait a minute I'll take the details.' He turned to desk behind him and picked up the large ledger on which he'd been working and, swinging back again, laid it on the counter. 'Now Sir,' he said taking a pencil from his pocket. 'What's your name please?'

'Arnold Kingsley.'

'Address?'

'White Rock Farm, Top Moor Road, Scotton.'

'And what's the problem Sir?'

'Well … a month ago yesterday, this man …'

'A month ago … you've left it a bit late in the day haven't you Mr Kingsley? It's difficult to follow anything up after a month.'

'Aye, well, he promised to pay me for the damage you see. 'I've not got enough cash with me to do it now,' he said, 'and I've left my cheque book at home, so I'll send you one when I get back … how about a hundred quid?' It was a fair settlement, so I agreed. He gave me his address and drove off. But the cheque hasn't arrived and I want you to get my money for me, if you can.'

'I see Sir. We don't usually collect debts you know ... tell me what actually happened?'

'He was in a hurry I reckon. It was on the fourth of September. He went to do a U-turn and banged into my milk churns waiting for the creamery tanker to pick them up. Spilled the lot, he did, and split one churn open right down the seam.'

'I see ... back on the fourth of September was it? And he offered you a hundred pounds in compensation?'

'Yes, he did ... but he never paid me.'

'Well ... I suppose we might get him under the Road Traffic Act for 'careless driving', but we have no power to make him pay you what he owes, that's a civil matter. Maybe we can scare him or shame him into coughing up. What was his name again?'

The farmer took a grubby, well handled, piece of paper from his pocket and read out what was written on it, 'Joe Lyons, Corner House, Coventry Street, London.'

'And his car?'

'What do you mean?'

'The registration number of his car - you got it, I suppose?"

'Oh no, I never noticed ... didn't think I needed to when he admitted fault and offered to pay.'

'Pity. What sort of car was it?'

'Damned if I know ... a silver one.'

'You don't know the make?'

'No, I should have looked, shouldn't I? ... Can you get my money d'you think?'

'It'll be difficult Sir, the name and address sound fishy to me, but I'll pass the information to the right authority and wait to see what they turn up.'

After the farmer had gone, Constable Roundtree dated the entry, closed the book, and grinned ... 'No chance, you silly old sod.' he muttered under his breath, and went back to what he'd been doing before he was interrupted.

The Nineteenth Hole,
Woodcote Park Golf Club, Epsom, Surrey.
Friday 6th October 2006. 5.00 p.m.

Mungo raised his glass thoughtfully as he listened to his playing partner Bill Simpson, victor that afternoon in their monthly head to head on The Old Course. Since their last meeting Bill had been promoted to the rank of Commander and transferred to Scotland Yard as National Criminal Investigation Coordinator. They'd known each other for fifteen years or more, having met when competing in local golf tournaments at the time when Bill was in charge of Sussex CID, and Mungo was in the process of taking over from his father.

'It's too difficult Mungo,' said Bill 'I really can't get involved at this stage … much as I'd like to. I'm only brought in when there's evidence things are spilling over from one county's jurisdiction into another. I mainly go in to ensure the most efficient use of resources, to cut out duplication, to sort out areas of contention and all that sort of thing. You wouldn't believe how much time and effort people waste in squabbling over unimportant piddling little side issues.'

Mungo nodded, civil service attitudes getting in the way of efficiency were well known to him. He had hoped Bill would be able to help advance D.I. Sherman's investigation into Dudley's unexplained death but, after what he'd just been told, he could see his high level connection wasn't going get him any further. With his thoughts drifting to the 'never to be forgotten' image of Dudley's body on the mortuary trolley he nearly missed Bill's next remark. 'I do know Ronnie Sherman slightly as it happens, they call him 'Tank' behind his back, not a bad description actually, and I've met him a few times. I can't interfere but I've already given him a ring and asked him to keep me in the picture as a favour.'

'I'd be thankful for anything which will advance the investigation, Bill, as will Boris.'

'Oh Boris ... Yes ... What's he up to these days?'

'Boris is up to nothing except keeping his head down and living the quiet life.'

'What does he do?'

'Do! ... Boris! ... He does nothing ... well not much. He lives on an ancient converted MTB, a wartime motor torpedo boat, moored up a dirty old backwater near Rottingdean. But as to 'doing' - well, it's just odd jobs really, bit of gardening, bit of painting. He's general handyman for anyone who can't or won't spend money going to a proper contractor.'

'He sounds like an over grown schoolboy ... is he?'

'He's a hopeless dreamer, Bill.'

'Married?'

'Boris married? Not likely, he's thinks he's God's gift to women. Says he has the responsibility to keep as many of them as happy as he can. There's no way he'd ever restrict himself to one of 'em. Father used to worry about him at one time but he doesn't even remember him now. I just wish Boris'd pull his weight and help me keep the business going for the sake the rest of the family especially 'the old man' and my three aunts, all of whom are totally dependent on me and the dividends. To tell you the truth, I could give him a boot up the backside when I think of him swanning around in his bloody boat, leaving me to - ah, you don't want to hear all this. Look, are you OK for next month? Got your diary?'

'Mungo I have you pencilled in already. Four weeks today ... how's that?

As Mungo reached for his pocketbook to check the date, his mobile telephone rang. He flipped open the cover and when he saw the name of the caller he turned to Bill. 'It's my secretary, if you don't mind I'll take it. It might be something about Dudley. Maybe Sherman's rung, he said he would.'

Bill nodded and signalled his willingness to leave Mungo to take the call more privately, but he was waved back to his seat. As the conversation went on Bill saw Mungo's face getting paler and paler - it was obvious something was amiss. By the time he'd finished, he was drumming his fingers on the table and staring at them. And then he slowly looked up. 'It was Miss Pink … Now Boris has gone.' he said, returning his 'phone to his pocket.

It took a moment for the words to sink in and for Bill to think of a response. 'Gone? What d'you mean gone? Gone where?'

Mungo smiled weakly 'He's not gone anywhere, he's dead.'

Bill shot up straight he got such a shock 'Dead? … Boris dead? Christ! What's going on?'

'Don't know. They rang looking for me …'

'Who did?'

'Sussex police … he was found in the river.'

'Did they say what happened?'

'They didn't know. It was this morning, he was taken to hospital but they said he'd been dead for hours. He died sometime last night apparently.'

'My God what a shock, I'm so sorry. Are you going down there?'

'Yes, I'm going to go now. I have to ask for Detective Chief Inspector Reynard in the Major Incident Suite at the Police Station in Sussex House, Brighton.'

"Foxy' Reynard? I know him, in fact he used to be my sergeant once, best tutor I ever had. I mightn't be able to interfere in Dudley's investigation, but I can stick my nose into Boris's without upsetting anyone. I know them all down in Brighton 'nick', and none better than 'Foxy' Reynard. Come on I'll drive you.'

Sussex Police Major Incident Suite
Sussex House, Brighton
Thursday 5th October 2006. 6.30 p.m.

Commander Bill Simpson greeted his old friend and mentor D.C.I. 'Foxy' Reynard with a mighty bear-hug and a protracted shaking of his hand, much to the astonishment of the desk sergeant who knew nothing of their former connection, and who couldn't wait to tell the rest of the relief what he'd witnessed. Mungo was then introduced and the three of them went through into the informal interview room where they seated themselves in tub chairs around a coffee table bearing bottles of mineral water and drinking glasses.

Bill Simpson started the proceedings by apologising in case Mungo had deemed the effusiveness of his reunion with 'Foxy' Reynard inappropriate, and then he handed over to the local man.

Mungo responded with a nod of impatience which curtailed further social chat and brought them quickly to the purpose of the meeting - Boris's death.

'I'm afraid I can't tell you much beyond the bare facts at this stage Mr Melchitt.' said Reynard. 'Early this morning, Mrs Sarah Burke, one of your brother's neighbours, on her way to collect her morning paper, saw his body floating in the water near his moorings.'

'She knew it was him immediately?'

'Suspected ... from the clothing he was wearing. Anyway, he was too far out for her to reach him, ten feet or so, so she jumped in to pull him out. Others, nearby, who heard her call for help were quickly on the scene and, by the time she'd got him to the bank, there could have been five or six people on hand to help haul him ashore. Several of them recognised him.

'That'd be Sally Burke, I've met her, and her husband, they're moored downstream from Boris and were often on his boat when I called. If she said it was Boris then it certainly was.'

'Oh we have no doubt the body is that of Mr Boris Melchitt, no doubt at all, several others present at the time his body was recovered knew him as well.'

'Did anyone see what happened?'

'No one has come forward to say they did. The plain truth is ... we don't know what caused him to fall in at this juncture. As far as ...'

Commander Simpson held up his hand to stop any further expansion of the morning's happenings until he'd told Reynard about Dudley's death, exactly a month earlier.

'Dear God! I didn't know; I'm so sorry Mr Melchitt. So your youngest brother Dudley met his death in a fashion not dissimilar to the way in which your middle brother, Boris, seems to have met his. You don't mind if I call him Boris?'

'Not at all, Boris and Dudley - call them by their Christian names, it's simpler.'

'Now I see why you've come, Sir.' Reynard said looking at the commander. 'Are you involving yourself in the other case too?'

'No I'm not,' the commander answered. 'I'm not involving myself in either at this stage; I just happened have finished a round of golf with my friend Mr Melchitt here, when he got the urgent call to come to Brighton to see you. We were in the bar at the time and naturally, once your name was mentioned, I offered to drive him down.'

'Was there any sign of Boris having sustained a blow to his head?' asked Mungo.

'There was a contusion all right. It was still bleeding slightly when they pulled him out. I saw the trail of blood down his neck a couple of hours later after I got there. What makes you ask?'

'Any sign of a weapon?' asked the commander, not waiting for Mungo to answer the question.

Reynard shook his head, 'We haven't found a weapon, yet, but I have a search team combing the bank and I hope to get a couple of divers there first thing in the morning. Maybe, between them, they'll find something. In the meantime though,' he turned to the commander, 'I'd appreciate it if you put me in touch with whoever's handling Dudley's death, we ought to be conferring. I mean it's a mighty big coincidence to have two brother's die in such similar circumstances and not be connected, and it immediately brings the possibility of murder into the equation in both cases.'

'The other inspector is already convinced Dudley was murdered.' said Mungo, 'He was hit on the head before he drowned. And I'll not be in the least surprised if you find out it's what happened to Boris as well.'

'Which,' Commander Simpson said, 'means we have to be prepared, not only to look for a connection between the two deaths but to make sure that, whatever the cause of all this, it doesn't extend to you.'

'Me!' exclaimed Mungo, visibly shocked.

Reynard pursed his lips and nodded. 'I'm afraid so, it looks as though someone doesn't like the Melchitt family.'

'Any chance you could involve yourself Commander?' Reynard asked. 'With your weight behind us we'd have a better chance, provided 'What's-his-name' agrees.'

'Sherman … D.I. Ronnie Sherman. He's stationed at Richmond, up in Yorkshire.'

'Right then, provided he's prepared to work with someone he doesn't know ...'

'But I know you both - you'd make a great team. Look, I'll take Mungo back home when he's confirmed the identification of Boris's body. And I'll ring Ronnie Sherman in the morning to see how he's progressing. If I decide to intervene and set up something between the two of you, I'll have to clear it with your station commanders first. Is that alright with you Foxy?'

'Yeah, no problem.' said Reynard, rising to go when the other two did. 'And, in the meantime, I'll concentrate on looking for witnesses, and trying to find a weapon - assuming he didn't just hit his head on something as he fell.'

Later, as they drove back to pick up Mungo's car, the full horror of what had happened began to sink in.

'I don't know how I'm going to break this to my aunts, Bill,' said Mungo, 'they're all getting on a bit.'

'I'd have thought you'd be more concerned about how your father will take to losing a second son.'

'Ah, dear old Dad, he lives in another world most of the time these days, he's got Alzheimer's … he'll be the least affected.'

And Mungo was right, not because his father didn't understand, but because he and his aunts came to the conclusion he'd be better off left in ignorance. The aunts were surprisingly stoic from the start though, especially Violet and Rose, and, being so remarkably controlled, they wound up being the props upon which Mungo progressively found himself leaning.

The Malt House, Point Hill, Lewes. Sussex. Sunday 8th October 5.25.a.m.

S andy McPhee had been up since a quarter to five. He'd filled a flask with strong black coffee and made some sandwiches, which he'd packed in a small rucksack and left at the kitchen door. Then, with a mug of hot chocolate in his fist, he reached for the biscuit tin but before he opened it he changed his mind and pushed it away again, his appetite vanquished by the tension that was gripping him. When the mantelpiece clock struck the half hour he drained his mug, pulled on his leathers, and went out to the garage, seizing his rucksack on the way.

It was dark outside with only an occasional glimpse of the street lighting showing through the trees. The purposely well-oiled door hinges made no sound as he opened them to reveal the dark shape of a Honda motor cycle he'd rented for the weekend from Hire-A-Bike Ltd. of East Croydon. Like the previous ones it was the most silent transport on the road, with an engine 'guaranteed' to give out no more than a whisper at thirty miles an hour.

He checked the petrol level for the umpteenth time, tested the false number plates he'd made up were adhering to the real ones underneath with the double sided sticky tape, pulled on his heavy black gauntlets, and pushed the bike out of the garage.

He knew the gravel of the front drive was noisy so he shoved the bike along the edge of the lawn until he got to the gate, where he switched to the tar macadam footpath as far as the corner. He'd been as near silent as it was possible to be, and there'd been no sign of anyone having seen or heard him. Even when he started the engine the noise was barely audible. He paused briefly to gather his thoughts then, climbing aboard, he let out the clutch, drove off the path, and pulled away. Never travelling at more than fifteen miles an hour until he got to the main road, he made so little noise he was fairly sure no one had heard him. The motorway was 'out of bounds' to him because of the bike's engine size and, as he didn't want to attract the attention of a police patrol by risking driving on it, his whole journey was going to have to be on the secondary highways. No disadvantage. At any time of day or night, within a radius of twenty miles of Heathrow, there'd be people on their bikes and motor bikes travelling to and from their work on those roads; the chance of his presence on them being remembered was zero.

He went via Croydon, Kingston-on-Thames, Hampton, Hayes, and Slough, arriving at the entrance of the car park of The Mede Manor Hotel, Beaconsfield just before seven. There were five cars parked in it. One, the Saab, he knew from a previous Sunday afternoon's scouting run he'd made, belonged to Angus Brett. The little Ford probably belonged to Angus's wife, and the others were more than likely those of the hotel's guests.

So far so good, after that it was just a question of waiting and watching. But first he had to get the Honda down to the station car park and lock his overalls and helmet in the luggage box. Once he'd done that he could hoist the rucksack onto his back and walk the half mile back to a hiding place in the evergreen shrubbery, in the hotel's garden, which he'd noted the last time he was there. From this position he'd have good view of all the comings and goings and be in a better position to fine tune his plan ... 'I'll need it to be a damned sight better than the last one though.' he thought, 'Where the hell did those bloody joggers come from? And why didn't I spot them before I was on top of them ... Women!'

Wandsworth Borough Council Roads Dept., Harmondsworth Street Yard & Depot, London. SW18 1AB. Wednesday 11th October 2006. 11.30 a.m.

Eddie was rooting about in a 'grave yard' for pieces of unwanted street and public park furniture which, despite having once provided pleasure and service to the citizens of Wandsworth, had almost come to the end of their useful life. He was there looking for something suitable to use as the focal point he was trying to create on a new roundabout on the Portsmouth sea front, but he was also hoping to achieve a little goal of his by getting his hands on a particular lump of stone to use as the centre piece on his own rockery at home.

The same man who was in charge when he'd worked there in the early days of his career was still the boss, and he got a great welcome. 'Have a look round Eddie. If you see something you like, get your manager to make us an offer.'

Eddie nodded, and set off to search amongst the stacks of lamp posts, park railings, manhole covers, and stone statuary, few of which were ever likely to be used again.

He'd spent four months working in the yard ten years previously. Keeping it orderly had been his principal duty and, during the dark wintry days he'd become familiar with the location of every single one of the two and half thousand items stored there. On one occasion, when rooting out a Victorian wall-mounted Lion's head drinking fountain which had been in the yard since the Blitz, and was wanted for a re-furbished school playground, he'd come across a rather oddly shaped, partly sculpted, stone. He was never quite sure what it was meant to be ... indeed he wasn't sure it was meant to be anything. It looked as though it was just a piece half finished work ... yet somehow he knew it wasn't ... and it fascinated him. Usually he saw it as a sleeping baby penguin slumped into its down, its beak tucked into its breast, but on other occasions it was more like the head of Grenadier Guardsman buried beneath his Busby. It was strange the way the two foot high barely shaped piece of rock could at one minute appear to be just a lump of stone and the next - a penguin. It all depended on the angle from which it was observed.

On the back, chiselled into the surface where a signature would normally be found, there was another curious feature, the outline of a frog.

Over the years since he'd first seen it he often thought of that rock. One day he was going to have it.

Squeezing between the stacks of timber, stone, and iron, he got to where the rock used to be. To his relief it was still there. Nobody appeared to have touched it since he'd last done so himself a good ten years earlier. Next to it was another old favourite of his, an unnamed and slightly damaged white marble statue of a ship's helmsman on a massive black basalt pedestal. It had been there so long it had moss all over it but in every other respect it was perfect for the roundabout He asked the foreman the probable price. At the same time he asked how much they'd want for the stone.

'An old bit o'granite, y'say? Take it if you want it.' the foreman replied. 'I didn't even know there was one there. It must have come in with a load of stuff when they widened the road up on Lavender Hill'.

Eddie didn't enlighten him, didn't tell him it had been there for years, listed as 'Stone with frog on it'.

'Are you sure?' he asked 'For nothing?'

'Yeah, it's just a bit o'stone isn't it? Tell you what - you can have it if you buy me a pint.'

Some fancy manoeuvring with the forklift got it onto the little council truck he'd driven up in, and his next-door neighbour helped him to unload when he got home. The weight had broken a spring and wrecked the rear shock absorbers, the cost of repairing which he'd have to bear, but, despite the potential expense he'd landed on himself, he'd a huge grin on his face when he and two neighbours manoeuvred the stone down a couple of hefty planks and into his garden.

Richmond Police Station Canteen
Monday 16th October 2006. 8.40 a.m.

D.I. Sherman wouldn't miss a 'Monday Special' even if it meant crawling from York to get it. Eating a serious 'man's breakfast' at least once a week was as fundamental to his mental health as it was detrimental to his physical well-being.

Mrs Armitage, the station cook's 'Monday Specials' were talked about throughout the Yorkshire constabulary. Any officer who could possibly justify being within a reasonable drive of Richmond town would make their way to the Police Station canteen between seven and eleven, on as many Mondays as they could manage, to join the throng of local coppers queuing for a treat none of them would get at home.

Two fried rashers of bacon, two fried eggs, two halves of fried (not grilled) tomatoes, two slices of fried bread, a spoonful of fried mushrooms and another of baked beans - a dieticians nightmare, a policeman's lifebuoy, just the thing to carry a man through a tedious week.

Placing a tray bearing his 'Monday Special' on the table, at which D.S. Bellamy was already seated, a mug of coffee before him, D.I. Sherman drew back a chair and sat down to examine the feast in front of him with unashamed relish.

'Your Mrs'd have fit if she saw you putting that away,' said Bellamy.

'Malc, she isn't going to know is she? Anyway you can't talk; I can see your plate. You didn't leave much.'

Sergeant Bellamy ignored the taunt. 'I've been thinking about the photo over the weekend Ronnie, and I've remembered where I saw the guy before. I knew his face was familiar.'

'Go on,' said Sherman, 'I was thinking about him as well and, what's more, I've remembered where I saw him an' all … on the billboards over the road … he's a film star.'

'A film star? Bollocks. The man in the picture was in the station a few weeks ago, I spoke to him myself. He was in about a vehicle theft he said he'd witnessed. There'll be a report in the book. I sent a mobile car but we never found them, and then when I looked into it further no one had reported the loss of a vehicle like the one he described anyway. I just thought he was one of those 'nutters' who get a kick out of calling us out.'

'And the court gives them nothing if we catch 'em. But I still reckon the man in the photo's like the fella on the billboards, I even took the print over and checked it. It's the same guy - if it's not I'll eat my hat.'

'Not on top of your breakfast you won't, Ronnie, you'll explode!'

'We'll check 'em both out. You follow up the man who gave the false report … and I'll go to the cinema. How's that? Fair division of duties?'

'No … but I suppose I don't get a say in it?'

'Bull's eye!. Now shut up or this grub'll get cold. Get yourself another coffee if you want.'

'No, I've had enough.'

'Go on … we'll have no time for lunch; we'll be too busy investigating the man in the photo and checking the Super's old case files that 'Records' are sending up. How did you get on with the call to London Transport?'

'Oh yes … I meant to tell you. Going by the serial number, they said the ticket was almost certainly issued from a machine at Monument tube station two days before the Super was killed. I think it must mean at least one of the possible suspects came up from London.'

'Which is only an hour or so from Rottingdean by my reckoning, I must remember to tell Foxy about it when I see him.'

Sussex Police Major Incident Suite
Sussex House, Brighton
Tuesday 17th October 2006. 1.30 p.m.

Re: Melchitt, Dudley (04.09.06) and Boris (05.10.06)

Present, Commander Simpson, D.C.I. Reynard,
D.I. Sherman, D.S. Bellamy and D.S. Groves.

Commander Simpson, having introduced the officers present, explained that the murders of Dudley Melchitt and his brother Boris within such a short time of each other had brought him quickly to the conclusion the two incidents were connected. 'Under such circumstances,' he said, 'and until such time as they prove to be totally independent of each other, I intend to call regular meetings like this one at which we can exchange information on progress made in both Richmond and Brighton. The meetings will alternate between these locations.

For the moment, both investigations will continue to be the responsibility of the CID in the area in which the bodies were found. But this arrangement will be reviewed should new evidence dictate it might be more productive to run everything together. For the purpose of today's meeting, I want you, D.C.I. Reynard, and you, D.I. Sherman, to give us a run-down of your cases. Let's have no ceremony. Ask all the questions you want but keep it as snappy and as informal as possible. You'd better start Ronnie, your incident was first; you can 'kick off'.'

Sherman, a policeman of the old school and never comfortable with the familiarity of address suggested by the Commander, stood up, went over to the flip chart on which he'd already written his bullet points, and started his summary in his normal manner. 'Right Sir, here's where we are at the moment. Speak up ... '

The commander pursed his lips and gave slight shake of his head at the disregard of his request for a less formality, but the mild censure was ignored and Sherman continued uninterrupted. 'Speak up if you want me to expand at any point or of you have any questions. And Sergeant,' he said, giving a little upward tip of his chin, 'stop me if I miss anything out.'

Bellamy, teeth clamped, noisily sucked in a deep breath and nodded.

'Right then,' Sherman went on. 'Two boys out for a picnic with their parents were fishing for sticklebacks in the shallows of the River Swale just west of Richmond where they found the body of Superintendent Dudley Melchitt jammed in between two rocks. He'd been fly fishing for trout just before he died. The post mortem report we received the next day confirmed he'd died by drowning, following a blow to his head.

Our first thought was he'd lost his footing on a slippery stone and fallen into the river hitting his head on a rock as he fell. Our second: he'd been attacked and then fallen.

A lump on his head we noticed when we pulled him out seemed to confirm the possibility of either theory. However, the post mortem later revealed he also had bruising on his throat and the side of his neck, leading us to wonder if, having fallen, he'd had his head shoved under the water and held there. The pathologist found nothing to further contradict or substantiate this possibility so we are left with three possible causes of death, drowning following an accidental blow to the head, murder or manslaughter by drowning following a deliberate blow to the head, or murder by manual drowning. Have I missed anything Sergeant?'

'Don't think so.' replied Bellamy.'

'Any witnesses?' asked Reynard, who got quite a surprise when Sherman nodded.

'It's possible. We have some photos shot by a man from the top of the opposite bank. They appear to have been taken just prior to the incident and show Superintendent Melchitt in the water, fishing, and there's a man walking along the bank in his direction. We're checking to see if this man's local, because both the sergeant and I have a strong feeling we've seen him before. We've circularised the pictures around the town, in every station of all nearby jurisdictions, and in a couple of local newspapers. However, no one has come forward yet. And that's all we have ... the photos will probably be the only physical evidence we'll get, after all it's six weeks now since the incident took place.'

'Don't forget the guy in the bushes.' Sergeant Bellamy whispered.

'Oh yes there was one other thing. It's on one of these pictures - hand them round Sergeant. If you look carefully, you can just make out what we think might be a man's face showing through the leaves of a bush farther down the bank. He appears to be watching the walking man. We don't know who he is and, to tell you the truth, we're not even sure it's a person at all, it could be just a shadow pattern formed in the leaves. So that's it, apart from something which may or may not be relative to our case, a very new London Underground ticket, not even damp when we found it.'

'Interesting, and where was it discovered?' asked Reynard.

'Glad you asked, Chief Inspector, it was picked it up just under the bush we think's hiding the third man, maybe he came from London. Anyway, we also have for you the statements taken at various interviews with family and neighbours etcetera. You'll find them all self-explanatory. Sergeant Bellamy will pass them round and, if after looking through them you have a query, the Sergeant or I will try to answer it.'

'Is that all?' asked the Commander, clearly unhappy at the dearth of information and lack of progress, not to mention informality.

'It's all we have at the moment, Sir, I'm afraid. No decent leads other than the photos and the ticket, and they aren't much. Furthermore, we discovered no reason for the Superintendent's death when interviewing his neighbours or family, other than a rather vague inference Mungo made concerning the villains his brother had put away in the past. I'm having checks made on this angle in 'Central Records', and I've contacted every place in which he served. Maybe something'll turn up, but it hasn't so far.'

The Commander's disappointment was becoming more and more obvious as he slowly shook his head from side to side and the room fell silent at this pointed, if unspoken, second admonition. After a moment he looked up again, sniffed, and turned to Reynard. 'All right, Foxy, your turn, what have you got?'

'We haven't made much progress yet either, Sir,' said Reynard, another man who was having difficulty in taking on the less respectful ways sweeping through the force. 'Of course, we're still at the early stages,' he continued, walking over and Cello-taping a map of the creek on top of Sherman's notes. 'but I'll give you what I've got ... alright?'

'Yes, yes, get on with it.' the commander grunted.

'Right ... well ... we had a report, a week ago, of a man's body being seen floating in a back water ... here.' he said pointing to the spot with his finger. 'By the time we got there he'd been pulled out. He was Boris Melchitt, brother of the man we've just been hearing about, though we didn't know that until later. Several people who were there knew him. Our post mortem confirmed what seemed obvious; he'd been drowned, but ... '

'Don't tell me he'd had a bang on the head as well?' exclaimed Sherman.

'He'd been hit so hard it fractured his skull. If he hadn't fallen in and drowned he'd have died anyway.'

'So this one's definitely murder is it?' the Commander asked, practically beaming and rubbing his hands.

'One hundred per cent. There are no stones or rocks round there he could have fallen on, and the bottom's all mud.'

'Any witnesses Guv?' asked Bellamy.'

'Not one.'

Sherman held up a finger. 'Time he was found and time he died?'

'Found at eight thirty. Died seven hours earlier, around one o'clock in the morning; he was full of beer.'

'Drunk?'

'Not according to the landlord of The Barge Inn, where he'd spent the evening playing cribbage with another regular customer, Conor Burke, the man who lived on the next boat. His wife, Sally Burke, was the one who found the body on her way for the morning newspaper.'

Sherman sat back in his seat and folded his arms over his chest. 'No witnesses eh? That'd be too much to hope for?'

'True, but it's early days.' said Reynard

'Nobody hear anything; it *was* night after all?'

'Not a peep.'

'What about forensic?' asked Bellamy.

Reynard shook his head. 'Not a thing so far.'

Sherman leaned forward and, unfolding his arms, began to rub his knees. 'Could the weapon have floated off?'

'Yes.' replied Reynard. 'We've thought of that and we're searching farther down but, unless we find something with blood on it we going to make little progress, there's thousands of bits of wood, old fencing posts, branches of trees, even cuts of waste wood thrown overboard by weekenders doing a job on their boat. No, there's no end of potential weapons, we'll just have to hope one of them has some of Boris's DNA on it.'

'What about the bottom of the river, anything there?' asked Bellamy.

'No Sergeant. We had divers in the next morning but all they brought up were a few bits of an old bicycle, a dolls pram, and a selection of empty beer cans and lemonade bottles, none with blood traces on them.'

'Any local gossip?' asked the commander.

'Not much, we've copies of everything, which was said, for you. Sergeant Groves will pass them round.'

'Family and friends?' Sherman asked. 'Anything there for us?'

'Friends? He didn't have many; he was a bit of a wanderer. He'd only been on our patch for a year or so. As to family well, put it this way, the family are all in one household, his elderly father, his three great aunts, and his brother Mungo, who you know about already. His father doesn't know what's going on half the time, nor does one of the aunts. The other two are fairly OK, but neither have any idea why Boris was killed.'

'What about Mungo Melchitt?' asked Sherman. 'What d'you make of him?'

'He couldn't suggest any reason, he's as baffled as we are. Maybe the commander can fill us in a bit more. You know him well don't you, Sir?'

'I do.' the commander replied. I've known him for years. They're a very close family, too close maybe. Most families I know don't have so many elderly relatives all living in the same house. Poor old Mungo serves as shepherd to the lot of them, looks after them all very well too.'

Sherman saw a chance to fill a few gaps in his knowledge. 'Has he got a wife … he didn't mention one to us?'

'Mungo has no other close family and, like Boris, never married. He's always lived at home with the previous generations. In recent years, instead of them all looking after him, it's been the other way round. On top of that, as chairman and managing director, he runs the family publishing business up in London.'

'I see.' said Sherman, 'So there's no money problems?'

'Not as far as I know,' the commander replied, 'and, as the aunts all obviously dote on 'the boys', as they still call them, and his father is virtually immobile, I cannot imagine the family being involved in either death. Better confirm this all the same because there are cousins and so on, some of whom are said to be nasty bits of work according to Mungo. Best if you take that on Foxy, it's handier to you. Sergeant Groves'd better interview the aunts - you know - woman to woman ... the aunts'll be less intimidated.'

Reynard smiled. 'Than they would be if I talked to them, you mean?'

'Is that all then?' asked the commander, ignoring Reynard's question, 'Everyone happy? ... Ronnie?'

'Yes, fine, Sir. I'll be on the 'phone to D.C.I. Reynard every couple of days or if anything breaks.'

'Foxy?'

'I'm happy, Sir.'

'Sergeant Bellamy - any more questions from you?'

'I don't think so, Sir.'

'And what about you?' he asked, turning to Sergeant Groves. 'You haven't said anything at all.'

Lucy Groves smiled, and her whole face lit up. She couldn't compete with heavy weights like this, had little or no chance in a debate when they were all shouting their heads off, so, in attempt to convince and to compensate, she'd found a way of working away quietly on her own. She painstakingly collected and analysed evidence, drew information out of reluctant witnesses, and with an inborn ability to tell truth from fiction was more often than not the first to come up with a credible solution. 'I'm fine, Sir' she said, shoving all her papers into a brief case and rising to go.

'You driving straight back Ronnie?' the commander asked Sherman as they shook hands.

'No Sir, we're going to call on Mungo at home before we head north. We're seeing him at five.'

The commander nodded, and turned to D.C.I. Reynard. 'Any point in you going as well, Foxy?'

'No, the four of us are off to the canteen now to have cup of tea together while we sort out a few things and then I'm going back down to Rottingdean, I want to talk to the Burkes again. Sergeant Groves is going chase up the Records Office for some old case files of Dudley's for which D.I. Sherman's been looking, and which haven't turned up yet. We're hoping there might be something in them relating to both investigations; after all, if Dudley's is a vengeance killing it's just possible Boris's death is part of it. Once she has all the information she can summarise it for both teams. Afterwards she's going to talk to the old aunts.'

'OK Foxy,' said the commander, still trying to encourage more familiarity in his command. 'But keep Ronnie and his lot in the loop won't you? We don't want any duplication.'

Reynard, once all the others had gone, relaxed his normal stance and patronisingly putting his arm round his younger boss's shoulders, 'Take it easy Bill, we'll get there.'

Simpson froze instantly, his lips pursed, and a serious look on his face, leaving Reynard to wonder if he'd overdone the familiarity. He hadn't. It was just the Commander's way of having his bit of fun at Reynard's expense and, a moment later, his face wrinkled up into a smile and he winked.

St Anne's House
Horsham Common, Sussex
Tuesday 17th October 2006 6.15 p.m.

M ungo was still on his way home when D.I. Sherman and D.S. Bellamy got to the house. Violet opened the door to them and, after they'd identified themselves, conducted them through to the drawing room where Rose and Daisy were sitting in silence as they concentrated on their tasks, Rose was knitting a pullover for Jonathan, Daisy was bent over a piece of embroidery she was working for a charity auction. It was a tranquil scene of out-dated gentility, hardly one to have an association with murder.

'Mungo won't be long, I'm sure, Inspector.' Violet said, after she'd introduced her sisters. He rang me to say he expected to be home before you arrived. He must have missed the fast train, in which case he'll not be here for another twenty minutes. We could give you some tea while you're waiting if you'd like.'

Bellamy smiled his 'Yes'.

Sherman voiced his, 'That'd be very nice Miss Melchitt, we've a long drive back up to Yorkshire after we've spoken to your nephew and a cup of tea would set us up fine. But, before you go out to make it may we say, Sergeant Bellamy and I, how sorry we are for the trouble which has descended on your family. We didn't know your nephew Mr Boris Melchitt but of course Superintendent Melchitt was our boss, and a damned … sorry … a very good boss he was too, a fine man to work for, and a great friend to have. We miss him ourselves so we can understand how upset you must be to have lost him and how painful it must have been when his death was so quickly followed by Mr Boris's.'

'We still can't believe it's all happened Inspector, and that's the truth.' Violet replied. 'We keep expecting to see Dudley or Boris walk through the door.'

'I'll get the tea, Violet,' Rose said, her lips tightening as she fought back the tears.

'I'll help you.' whispered Daisy, feeling in the pocket of her cardigan for her hanky and scurrying after her.

When they'd gone Sherman asked Violet how Mr Melchitt senior had taken the double disaster.'

'Jonathan? He doesn't know what's happened.'

The inspector raised his eyebrows in surprise. 'You haven't told him?'

'There wouldn't be any point Inspector, he's not capable of understanding anything and, even with something as disastrous as having two sons killed, he wouldn't remember what we said, not for even a minute. No, Inspector we decided to leave him in ignorance. He never asked about them when they were alive in recent times, so there seemed to be little point in risking upsetting him when we knew he'd immediately forget whatever we told him.'

'You're probably right. Alzheimer's isn't it?'

'He's in a bad way I afraid.'

'You're talking about my father I assume.' It was Mungo, whose arrival they'd not heard.

'Yes Mr Melchitt. We were just offering our condolences to the Miss Melchitts.'

'Very kind of you Inspector. Any progress?'

'I wish we could say there was. I'd like to have been able to tell you we had something concrete to go on but we haven't - not yet anyway. There *is* one thing though, a photographer who set his camera up to take a picture of the river just where the superintendent was fishing, caught him in the shot by pure chance. In the photograph, which came into our hands recently, we've noted a second person walking along the bank. Now, he may or may not have anything to do with Mr Dudley's death but we'd like to talk to him all the same. Give Mr Melchitt the photo Sergeant. Let's see if he can recognise the fella.'

As Mungo took the picture the tea arrived.

'Shall I come back?' asked Rose, hesitating on the threshold with Daisy behind her when she saw them grouped together looking at something in Mungo's hand.

'No, no, it's all right, we're just bringing Mr Melchitt up to date. Tea now would be fine … thanks.'

Mungo handed Sherman the picture back, but he was shaking his head as he did so. 'Never seen him before in my life, I'm sorry if you've come all this way and drawn a blank.'

'Don't worry Sir, we're used to disappointments. Anyway we've been down in Brighton exchanging information with the officers investigating Boris's death. We're convinced the deaths of your brothers are not coincidental so it's going to be a joint effort between the two forces from now on to try to get to the bottom of both murders. I expect you know this already, you're a long standing friend of Commander Simpson's I believe.'

'Correct. We've been playing golf together for longer than I care to remember, right back to when he served in Brighton himself.'

As they sipped their tea, Mungo gave the policemen more information on Dudley's life outside the force, but none of them could envisage any leads coming from such a very unremarkable background. By the time their cups were empty the conversation had all but dried up and Sherman decided they'd better be on their way. As they made for the door he sprang a final question, 'Do you know Rex Brett, Mr Melchitt?'

Bellamy turned to look at the D.I., his eyes wide open with surprise at his sudden change of tack bearing in mind they were still guessing themselves. He was just as astonished by the answer Mungo gave. 'Rex Brett? Yes, I know of him *of* course, he's an actor isn't he? Why are you asking?'

'Oh, his name came up, that's all.'

'I seem to remember my father and his father were friends years ago when they were students. I think I might have even met Rex as a child, I probably did. He had a brother as well, I think, but I'm not sure.'

'And your own brothers, Dudley and Boris, d'you think they'd have known him? Any connections you're aware of - especially if there was one between Rex Brett and the Super?'

'I don't think so … No I'm sure of it. I doubt if they'd seen the Bretts since childhood … if at all.'

'Pity Jonathan can't help.' said Violet. 'He was the one connected to Rex Brett's father. They used to call him 'Ginger'; I remember meeting him once. Yes, I'm sure your poor father would have been able to help but …'

'They were a wild lot.' said Daisy, giggling as she came out of her shell. 'They had a secret society!'

As soon as Sherman heard her words his ears pricked up. 'What sort of secret society would that be Miss Melchitt?'

'Don't mind what Daisy says, Inspector.' Violet answered. 'She has a wonderful imagination. I believe it was only a student's drinking club. We weren't supposed to know.'

'It *was* a secret society.' insisted Daisy.

'Well thank you ladies, I'll bear everything you've said in mind.' Sherman answered, 'And now we must be off. We've a five hour drive ahead of us so we need to get cracking'.

As they drove away Bellamy was laughing at the little cameo in which they'd just taken part … but Sherman wasn't, not crafty old Ronnie Sherman … he was talking quietly to himself. 'Secret society eh? There could be something in this.'

Belvedere Crescent, Islington, London N1 1QB
Tuesday 24th October 2006 11.00 a.m.

Mrs Flower's job as minder and cleaner of Henry Byrd's house was hardly onerous, and was quite well paid considering how little she did. She'd arrive at about ten usually, and was well gone by twelve. In the short time she was there, she'd have dusted the mahogany furniture, swept the front steps, and washed the black and white tiles covering the top one. She'd also have stopped two or three times 'to get her breath back', made tea, and read the Daily Mirror she'd collected at the corner shop as she walked the half mile from her home.

There were few callers, bar the men who came to read the electricity and gas meters, and almost no post, other than advertising leaflets, all of which she stuck in a drawer in the hall chest. She knew how to turn on a radiator and change the setting on the boiler so she was never cold in winter. Sometimes, during the school holidays, she might bring her twelve year old granddaughter with her for company but usually she was alone.

On the day Eddie and Sophie called she was without the child and they found her mopping the black and white tiles. As they started to mount the steps towards her, she looked up.

'Well, well, well, look who the cat's brought in! I 'ope yer no' expecting ter see Mr Byrd, 'e's still away, though I did 'ave a card from 'im lars' week tellin' me 'e'll proberly be 'ome fer Christmas.'

'That's a pity.' said Sophie, looking at Eddie and shrugging her shoulders. 'All the way from Gatwick, and we've drawn a blank. Pity we didn't ring ... but we didn't know your home number or your address.'

'Have you a telephone, Mrs 'F'?' Eddie asked.

'I gotta mobile, but I never remember the number. Come inter the kitchen and I'll give itcher.'

As they followed her down the hall to the back of the house, she asked Sophie if it was her first visit to England, since they'd met in March. Sophie told her she'd been back twice, and would be back again before the end of the year, maybe even over the Christmas holiday if she was scheduled.

'Scheduled?'

Sophie suddenly remembered she'd told Mrs 'F' she was a reporter. 'That's right. I've changed my job I work for British Airways now. I'm a trainee air hostess.

I see.' said Mrs 'F', obviously not believing her. 'So you ain't metcher Dad then, butcher's found yer bruvver. I 'eard yer'd been over to Angie's after yer lef' me lars' time, I s'pose she putcher in touch wiv each other?'

'She did, and we've seen each other twice since.'

'Yew don't live rahnd 'ere no more do yer?' she asked Eddie, who was standing over at the kitchen window looking down into the back garden.'

'No, Portsmouth, I picked Sophie up at Gatwick and we've driven up this morning. Tell me what's that old stone in the garden.'

'The big one on top of 'is rockery?

'Yes, it's mounted on a sort of base.'

'I's notta base, i's a plimpf. 'E's very fussy abaht me callin' itta plimpf. Whatcher reckon i' is then? 'E says itza toad bu' I fink 'e's seein' fings.'

Eddie tapped his chin with his forefinger as he pondered over her response then surprised her by asking if he could go out into the garden to look at it more closely.

'Of course yer can,' she replied, 'the back door's open.'

Sophie, puzzled at Eddie's sudden interest in the lump of granite, followed him out.

Mrs 'F' stayed behind and put the kettle on.

When they were outside Sophie asked what was so special about the stone but Eddie wouldn't elaborate, he just said he'd tell her all about it later, when he'd checked something.

By then they were close to the bottom of rockery which, on closer inspection, she could see had a narrow spiral path winding, up through overgrown and leafless shrubs to the stone, prominently sited at the top, on a fine cut stone pedestal. The carefully arranged tumble of boulders either side of the path must have been put there to create a natural look but, in that urban walled garden, they seemed ridiculous.

'What are you looking for?' asked Sophie, as Eddie climbed the path, stepped behind the lump of granite stone, and dropped to his knees.

'Tell you later.' he said, putting his finger to his lips. 'Just come round here first and look at this.'

She climbed up the path to crouch next to him. He was pulling off the ivy, which was mostly obscuring the surface of both the rock and its mount, and was pointing to a strange looking protuberance on its surface.

'Looks like a frog to me.' she said.

'Yeah ... me too.'

'Is it the toad she was on about?'

He smiled and winked. 'Later. I don't want her to see me looking at it too closely, she might tell him.'

'Tell him what?' asked Sophie, still baffled, quite unable to make head or tail of his comments.

'Did yer find 'is old toad?' asked Mrs 'F', standing at the door as they came back in again, and cackling at the sheer absurdity of her own question.

'No I found an elephant!' replied Eddie, winking at Sophie again and grinning from ear to ear.

'Oh yeah?' answered Mrs 'F', 'Yer tea's ready ... i's on the table and, if yer wai' a minute, I'll find some biscuits.'

'Don't worry about biscuits Mrs 'F'.' said Sophie, pulling out a chair and sitting down.

'Speak for yourself.' added Eddie, 'I'd love one. Got any Jammy Dodgers?'

'No I 'aven't. Custard Creams do yer?' she asked, taking down a tin from the dresser and opening it.

As Eddie picked out a couple of Custard Creams from the Afternoon Teas and Bourbons and started to munch, Sophie came back to the matter of her father's return. 'Do you have the date my father's coming back?'

Mrs 'F' didn't answer, she handed Sophie the postcard.

On the front was a picture of a red and blue parrot, on the back, apart from his message, was a Mexican stamp. It gave her a strange feeling … this was the first time she'd ever seen her father's handwriting, other than when he'd signed the back of the photo.

Dear Mrs F,   I'll be back for Christmas.
Please make sure there's enough oil in the tank,
and enough coal in the cellar.
I'll let you know my exact arrival date and time
in a week or two. Regards,   Henry Byrd.

'Mrs 'F' … did you ever hear of the LMS Club?' asked Eddie, out of the blue.

Sophie swung round at his unexpected question.

'The what?' Mrs 'F' asked.

'Ah nothing … I just wondered.' replied Eddie, who followed her negative inference by getting up from the table and suggesting he and Sophie had 'better be on their way' if they were to be at Angie's before one.

They left soon after that, with Mrs 'F' waving from the top of the steps and expressing the hope she'd 'see them again soon'.

Once they were out of sight she returned to the window and stood, peering out into the garden until her eyes watered. 'Wha's 'e up to,' she muttered, ''s only a flippin' stone?'

Melchitt House, Golden Square, London W1F 9JB
Wednesday 25th October 2006. 12.05 p.m.

Mungo was at his desk. Opposite to him were Justin and Jarrold. It was just after midday and the atmosphere was extremely frosty all round.

The twin brothers had arrived unannounced at Golden Square early in the morning just as Mungo was sitting down in conference with his senior staff, including the new recruit, Simon Carey, the man he'd poached at such expense from a competitor. By attracting someone like him, a man with reputation for getting the best out of his authors, and who'd managed to persuade six of them to cross over with him, Mungo had sent ripples round an industry which had always frowned on such practices. He did himself but, after the poor results of the previous year, he'd had to adopt strategies previously scorned by him, in the interest of survival.

The telephone never stopped once he'd done it as, one after another, his trade friends rang to remind him he was breaking ranks. His rivals, on the other hand, told him bluntly that having opened the door he shouldn't expect any support from them if bait was trailed in front any of *his* employees.

Coming on top of the stress of having to cope, first with Dudley's death, and then with Boris's, he was ready to throw in the towel and take off on a long holiday. But there was too much going on for him to do so, he had to support his father and aunts, he had to be available to the police in Yorkshire and Sussex, and he still had to be in the office every day.

Things had quietened down at home a bit though, thanks to Aunt Violet who'd been a tower of strength. Rising above the air of gloom which permeated the house, she'd managed her brother and her sisters without them knowing they were being managed.

Mungo had told Miss Pink that once the editorial conference started he was only to be interrupted to take emergency calls from home or from the police. It was this instruction, which had prevented her from announcing Jarrold and Justin, who'd arrived saying they needed an urgent meeting with him.

Sitting in the waiting room, drumming their fingers on the table and drinking cup after cup of coffee, had driven from their minds any thought of offering Mungo their condolences. It hadn't improved their tempers either and, by the time they were conducted into Mungo's office, they were incandescent with pent up rage.

'You'll regret mucking us about like this Mungo.' said Jarrold, 'We've been out there waiting to see you for nearly two hours and you didn't have the courtesy to give us five minutes. Who the bloody hell do you think you are? You don't own the company you know. You don't even have any shares - you're just an employee. How dare you treat us like this?'

'Oh shut up Jarrold,' Mungo replied. I haven't time to talk this sort of nonsense with you, we have some tricky problems to resolve here you know that damned well. I told you at the AGM I'm doing my best to get us back on track, and *it's* why I instructed Miss Pink not to allow anyone to interrupt the meeting. You should have telephoned. What do you want anyway?'

'We have a buyer for the company.'

'Not interested.'

'What d'you mean, 'Not interested'? It's not up to you - we'll call an EGM. When the other shareholders hear the proposition we have, they'll go for it.'

'I doubt it. Don't forget … while I have no shares, I do hold a lot of proxies.'

'The owners of those shares will swing their proxies to us when they hear the proposition. We'll be making your precious aunts wealthy beyond their dreams, and leaving you and your father out in the cold. We *will* be able to force it through y'know.'

'Try it. Call your damned meeting. Do what you like. I'm fed up with your constant meddling in things you're incapable of understanding. What do you know about the publishing business? Nothing, not a single thing. All you've ever done is sell dodgy cars from a back street shed.'

Jarrold leapt from his seat, his face suffused with anger, and threw a punch, but it was short of the mark by a foot because of the width of the desk. It surprised Mungo though, who was left sitting ashen faced at the ferocity of the attack. Justin was fairly shaken by it too. Usually the back seat man, he grabbed Jarrold's arm and dragged him away leaving a string of curses and abusive threats trailing in their wake.

On his own at last, Mungo absentmindedly stirred a third lump of sugar into the cup of tea which, with a plate of sandwiches, had been slipped in front of him by Miss Pink.

In doing so he created a little trail of endlessly circling bubbles. They seemed to symbolise the way his thoughts were hurtling around his head. So much to worry about. Every day something new to pile on the agony. What would be next? When would it stop?

34, Primrose Mansions, Islington.
Wednesday 25th October 2006. 1.30 p.m.

Angela was in the kitchen loading the washing machine, Wayne was in the sitting room day dreaming.
"Ere. Wayne.'

'Wha' ?'

'You ain't forgo' tha' job yer was doin' fer me?'

'Sortin' out them old geezers?'

'Right ... yer've forgo' 'aven't yer?'

'No I 'aven't. I'm workin' on i'.'

'Don't look like i' ter me.'

'I'll ge' i' sorted - don' worry Ange.'

'When?'

'Soon.'

'It's always 'Soon' wiv you Wayne, never 'Now'.'

'Ah Ange, fer Chris' sake. I'll do 'em when I'm ready.'

'Which will be?'

'Which will be bloody never if you don' stop naggin'.'

' 'Ere, 'av yew got Garf in there ?'

'I'm readin' the paper ... Garf's your problem.'

'No Wayne, yew're my effin' problem. Why don't yer get orf of yer fa' backside and go an' look for 'im, 'e's yours as well as mine. And anyway I'm up ter my neck in your mucky cloves.'

''Ere 'e is ... under the table. 'E's eatin' the cat's dinner.'

Angie rushed in from the kitchen steam, fists bunched to hit the first thing she could reach, preferably Wayne. And then she dissolved into laughter, Garth was slumped across Wayne's knees. He was fast asleep.

'Gotcha!' said Garth with a grin on his face the width of the Mile End Road.

'So wha' abah' tha' job then?'

'I'll try an' do i' this week Ange ... promise.'

The Mede Manor Hotel,
Beaconsfield, Bucks.
Thursday 26th October. 2006. 9.15 a.m.

I t was Rex's last day there. Filming hadn't started until quite late the previous afternoon because of rain, and then it had gone on well into the night before the final 'wrap' was called. Later in the day the whole 'show' would be moving back to London. In consequence of his late night, Rex was still half asleep when he rolled downstairs for breakfast.

Betty was waiting for him. 'Come on Rex, all the others went ages ago. What do you want to eat?'

She wasn't exactly bright but she was sober, for she'd taken to heart what Angus had said to her - threatened her with - on the day, a week earlier, when Rex and his pals had turned up unannounced. In fact that day had been a major turning point for her in many ways. Since then, much to her surprise, she'd been able to resist the temptation of alcohol, though not of cigarettes. She'd even found herself beginning to wonder if, despite the tell-tale signs known to her as a publican, she was, after all, not heading for alcoholism but solely for nicotine addiction.

It had been a good moment when she'd dared to think she was on the mend, but painful to remember that the change had been induced by the combination of Angus's angry threats and her feelings of shame. They'd preceded the 'no holds barred' talk which had followed the day after she'd collapsed behind the bar clutching the pump handle. It had been heart to heart stuff for the first time in months; prior to it, she'd have abused him with curses so vile she'd often amaze herself. But on that morning the ice had started to melt, the slow haul back to a civilised approach to each other had commenced, and they were talking again instead of shouting.

'Just toast and a cup of coffee for me.' Rex said, as he took a seat at the kitchen table and picked up the newspaper she'd just laid down 'Is Angus about?'

'No, he's gone into the town … to the bank. He spends half his time there these days.'

'I see. He told me you were having problems, that the business had gone slack since the motorway came.'

'I suppose he told you we're refurbishing too - we're not - we're going bust. Our customers have all but disappeared, taken themselves to the new place on the motorway or the other pubs in the town. We're finished.'

'What happened?' Rex asked, as he poured coffee from the cafetière Betty had just filled and lifted a slice of hot toast from the chipped Claris Cliff toast rack.

'We left it too late, plain and simple. Weak as our finances were we were over confident, thought ourselves invincible, and didn't go with the times by modernising when we should have done. We just refused to believe what was staring us in the face, that the good times were vanishing, thought we could go on for ever as we were. Talk about King Canute trying to halt the tide, Rex, that was us, only it was the tide of change we couldn't stop. And now it's sweeping us away. We've run out of cash. It was always tight, right from the start. We've had to let all the staff go except one cleaner. If Angus doesn't get a promise of some relaxation of the position the bank's been taking today she'll be gone as well, and we'll be in the 'you know what', waiting for the bailiffs to arrive.'

'I can't believe it.'

'I can hardly believe it myself. It seemed so solid, so permanent. Shall I make more toast?'

'No thanks I've lost my appetite. I know the problems are yours not mine but I spent all my life here before I went to RADA, remember? And I've a lot of happy memories of the place. I certainly wouldn't want to see them soured by what's happening now. Why didn't Angus talk to me I might have been able to help.'

'Pride. After your obvious disappointment when he got the place, there was no way he'd ever admit to you he'd squandered it. And that's what he's done. Me too, I confess it. As to asking you for help, I think it's too late. I hear him mumbling on about a possible lifeline, but I don't know. It's something to do with that old gang of your father's I think.'

'Gang. What gang? I don't know of any gang.'

'Yes you do.' she said walking through to the office and taking the photograph from the wall. 'This lot, The LM something or other club.'

'Oh them … LMS. It says it on the back … The LMS Club. My God that photo takes me back.' said Rex, reaching for the frame. 'I wonder where they are now, all of them. This picture must be nearly fifty years old.'

'He's been trying to track them down recently, I know. This one's dead, killed in an accident.' she said pointing to Roly. 'I don't know about the rest, and he didn't tell me what he thought they could do to help anyway. To be honest, we've been through a pretty sticky patch ourselves, on a personal level, if you know what I mean. Seems to be a bit better at the moment but we still don't have a lot to say to each other so I don't know what he's up to. As far as these friends of his father's …'

Rex, whose eyes had drifted to the headlines of the paper as she spoke, held up his hand to interrupt her. 'Here's a coincidence … isn't one of the guys in the photograph called Melchitt?'

'I don't know, look on the back, I can't see without my glasses.' said Betty, slipping the photograph from the frame and handing it to him.

He turned the picture over. 'Ah, only their nicknames, but there's one here called Ghandi, and I could swear his surname was Melchitt, same as these two guys in the paper who've been murdered. I wonder if they're related; I wonder if one of the dead men is actually Ghandi? I mean, Melchitt's an unusual name.'

Just then Angus walked in and the matter was forgotten as Betty and Rex peered at his face to see if they could work out how he'd got on at the bank. From his silence they concluded the interview had not been a success.

'There's still some coffee in the pot.' said Betty, trying to initiate a conversation, as Angus went through to hang up his coat - but he ignored her. 'And Rex'll be off soon, all the rest of them have already gone.' As she spoke she turned to Rex, her forefinger to her lips, her eyebrows raised, begging him not to mention their conversation. When he winked his agreement she nodded, and slipped the photograph under the newspaper.

'I will have another cup, if there's one left.' said Angus, with a more encouraging smile.

The rest of the morning, until Rex left, passed by quite

quickly and Angus unexpectedly continued to thaw. Betty was unable to see why his earlier silence over the morning's meeting had given way to normal behaviour, but she happily accepted it. Even Rex noticed the drop in tension, and purposely avoided bringing it back by not asking questions on the current dire position.

Somewhat surprised at having discovered something of her old self in their time of crisis, Betty kept making attempts at guessing what might have happened to bring about Angus's change of mood. It hardly had anything to do with the bank or he'd have said so … it had to be something else. Had he got some sort of assurance or backing from his father's former friends? Was it something totally different, something new which he was keeping as a surprise? Or was it the calm before the storm?

34, Primrose Mansions, Islington.
Friday 27th October .2006. 7.05 a.m.

Wayne had got up at seven; early for him for a weekend, and quite an event. He hadn't shaved but he never did until Saturday evening came round, and he hadn't been too close to soap and water either. He was standing at the cooker, frying himself two eggs to go with the four slices of badly burned fried bread which awaited them on a fat spattered plate beside the smoking pan. He had a West Ham Supporters club mug in his hand full of hot sweet tea. From time to time he supped at it noisily.

Garth stood beside his father, clutching the leg of his jeans, a half empty baby's bottle dangling from his mouth. Angie was at the table, bleary eyed and bad tempered. She'd been awakened at dawn by the cries of her children and given them both a bottle to shut them up. Garth had quietened down but Lance had rejected his and continued to scream. Eventually she'd capitulated and got up. Still half asleep, she was absentmindedly giving him his breakfast while leafing through the pages of a mail order catalogue she'd propped against the teapot. He was sitting astride her thighs facing her, his back to the table, forcing her to sway from to one side to the other of him, in order to see the pages properly.

With her attention taken by the illustrations, she didn't notice the child was ejecting his food as quickly as she spooned it in, gobbing it out in a slimy mess which dribbled down his chin to slither into the tray at the bottom of his red plastic bib.

Instead she was totally lost in a world of flimsy silken nightdresses and, with a wry smile on her face, contrasting them with the elephantine yellow tee-shirt she was wearing; a present from Wayne the previous Christmas advertising a new 'Two For The Price Of One' key cutting service on offer from a local locksmith.

Wayne's skill with the eggs appeared to be better than the one he'd exhibited with the fried bread, for they were perfectly cooked and unbroken as he slipped a spatula under them and lifted them on to his plate with a great 'Yeah!' of satisfaction.'

'Are yer goin' dahn there t'day then?' asked Angie ignoring the triumphant exclamation. Wayne, at the table by then, didn't answer in words; he just gave her a brief nod.

'On the train, or on Reg's bike?' she asked.

'Bike. Reg's is lendin' it ter me - he carn ge' off.' he replied, with an eggy smile.

'You be careful Wayne.'

He grinned again and poked a crumb of crusty fried bread from between his teeth with his knife. 'I'll be orlrigh'. I'll only be a few hours.'

'Don't ittim!'

'Jesus, Angie, make your flippin' mind up … I'm doin' this fer yew. If I' wasn't fer yew goin' on abah' tha' crowd all the bloody time I wooden be goin' a tall, I'd still be in bed.'

'Promise me you won' ittim.'

'Me … 'it an old geezer … oo d'yer fink I am?'

Angie nodded, apparently satisfied with his re-assurance, and turned back to her world of imagined glamour. Clearly Lance wasn't satisfied though; he opened his mouth and let out a yell.

'Whassermarrerwiv'im?' asked Wayne, piling his dirty dishes in the sink.

'Nuffin' 'e finks yer taking Garf and 'e wants ter go.'

'Well 'e ain', and nor's Garf, itsa one man job. I'll be in and out like a flash.'

As he spoke he pulled on the leather jacket he'd borrowed, picked up the keys of Reg's Harley Davidson, and headed for the door. 'Righ' then, I'm orf.' he said.

St Anne's House,
Horsham Common, Sussex.
Friday 27th October 2006. 3.00 p.m.

Ghandi Melchitt sat just inside the open French window staring vacantly out into the garden. It had been sunny for most of the morning, and warm. The blankness of his expression might have been taken by some to be the mirror image of the apparent blankness of his mind - but nobody really knew - not even his doctors.

His sisters, who doted on him and fussed over his welfare every waking minute, had often wondered about this. Did he know what was going on around him or did he not? Was his brain churning away behind his inscrutable expression and just failing to show it?

Violet was of the opinion his mind, other than when it was responding to a few obvious bodily demands was, to all intents and purposes, dead. She couldn't believe he had any reasoning ability left, or that his dementia hadn't effectively gnawed away his spirit. For her, the permanent lack of expression on his face was proof enough of this and, in consequence, she never made any pretence of treating him as though he'd somehow simply been temporarily discommoded of a few useful functions. She never, ever, patronisingly pretended to converse with him. When she was on duty she topped him up with food and drink at regular intervals, made sure he was sitting or lying down comfortably, and kept him warm. That was all. She was a fully paid up member of the 'no nonsense' brigade

Daisy was totally different, disagreed with Violet absolutely as far as their brother was concerned and, in truth, thought just about the opposite in every respect. She talked to him incessantly, asked his opinion on every subject under the sun, and genuinely believed she saw a response to her words in his eyes. Maybe this was because she was a natural chatterbox and, like others of that genre never actually needed much of a verbal response. She was utterly convinced she was the only one to treat 'dear Jonathan' properly.

Rose was somewhere in between. She tended him with a degree of affection which was lacking in Violet's more mechanical approach yet managed to avoid Daisy's sycophancy. Ever the compromiser in the family, her way of ministering to him would have been no surprise to Jonathan were he able to sense it. Maybe he did.

Rose had gone shopping in Horsham and intended having lunch with an old school friend. Violet had had an early snack at home with Daisy, and then walked over to the Public Library to change everyone's books prior to going to a committee meeting of the Woman's Institute. Daisy was left in charge of Jonathan. She'd fussed around him as usual. First she'd settled him in his chair in his study and given him the paper to read - he'd let it slide to the floor. She reprimanded him, and brought him down to the sitting room where she sat him in his favourite arm chair with the jigsaw tray on his lap. Then, when his head dropped to his chest and he started to snore, she woke him up, 'tut-tutted' him, and led him over to the old Queen Anne chair standing just inside the open French windows. The sun shone straight into his face, she 'tut-tutted' again, told him to 'sit still for a minute' while she went upstairs to get his sun hat.

She never knew what prompted her to glance down onto the terrace from his bedroom window just as she was taking his sun hat down from the top shelf of his wardrobe. But what she saw, before she fainted, was her brother, lying face down amongst the water lilies in the ornamental gold fish pond, and a man, running as fast as he could towards the orchard at the bottom of the garden.

When she came to, a few seconds later, she hauled herself to her feet with the aid of a bedroom chair and looked out of the window again. Jonathan was still where she'd last seen him, but the man had disappeared.

She hurried downstairs to the terrace, all the time trying to puzzle out what might have happened, worried to death she might be too late to save him.

When she got to the side of the pool, she kicked off her shoes and jumped in. The water was barely a foot and a half deep. She waded over to where Jonathan was lying in the cascade spilling from the basin at the foot of the ornamental fountain. He was completely still and she feared he was dead. Even so she made a worthy attempt to save him, bearing in mind her eighty odd years of age. Drawing on an inner strength she never knew she had, she shed her normal twittering approach to crises, grabbed him by the collar and dragged him, floating, behind her, to the side of the pond where she sat on one of the bull nosed flagstones which edged it. Then, having braced herself by placing her legs apart she pulled him closer, hauled his upper body out of the water, and kept him there by draping his arms over her thighs, his head cradled in her lap.

And that's how they found her twenty minutes later, Violet and Rose, they'd met at the Public library and come home together. The minute they opened the front door they sensed trouble, when they hurried through the house, and out to the garden, they saw her. She was rocking to and fro, humming softly, and picking strands of water weed from Jonathan's hair.

Melchitt House Publishing,
Golden Square
London W1F 9JB
Friday 27th October 2006. 2.15 p.m.

Mungo had been badly shaken by the angry exchange he'd had with Jarrold two days earlier and, in consequence, had been unable to seriously concentrate on anything worthwhile since, choosing instead to stand most of each day staring out of his office window.

Miss Pink often found him like that. In times of stress he seemed to find consolation looking down on the ordered layout of the Square, an inspired garden oasis protected from the bustle going on all around it by a shroud of densely planted evergreen shrubbery, silver trunked beeches, and peeling planes; a strong sense of the country brought to London's heart. Not that he'd seen much of it, for he was thinking, his mind concentrating on trying to devise a way in which he could excise Justin and Jarrold from his life. This was no time to have business worries on their account; getting rid of them or, at least, having them side-lined, was a priority. Unfortunately no practical plan immediately came to mind, though a few tempting, if impracticable, ones had.

And then, after a long period when his brain seemed to have been reluctant to engage in any sustained way, he began to have an inkling of what he might do. Instead of preparing a defence to their attack, the obvious thing was go on the offensive himself and attack them. He couldn't imagine how he'd do it, but the refreshing surge of exhilaration which the very thought induced was enough to make him rub his hands together gleefully. He would no longer wait for them to wipe out his business … he would try to think of a way of eradicating theirs.

Not normally a person who would take pleasure in thought of destroying anything, let alone a man's livelihood, he found himself smiling at the prospect of Jarrold begging him for mercy, and laughed outright at the possible answers which he might be tempted to give.

He turned from the window and walked over to a cabinet which wasn't often opened. He knew there was a bottle of 12 year old malt whisky inside, and though he seldom drank when he was on his own, he picked up a glass and poured himself a modest measure. Then, taking it over to his desk, he pulled pencil and paper towards him.

Ten minutes later, with his pad still blank, the telephone rang. It was Aunt Violet. What she told him had him racing out of the building in search of a taxi as fast as his legs would carry him. With luck he might just make the 15.10 'two stopper' from Victoria.

St Anne's House,
Horsham Common, Sussex.
Friday 27th October 2006 4.35 p.m.

The house was still when Mungo entered it. For a moment he thought there was nobody else there but then, on his way through the morning room to the scene of the accident, he came across two of his aunts, Violet and Rose. They were sitting on the sofa in total silence while in their minds they re-ran the early afternoon's tragic event as told to them by Daisy.

She was in bed, unable to free herself from the feeling of guilt she'd worked up, and blaming herself for Jonathan's death. She'd broken down the minute Violet and Rose appeared and found her sitting on the edge of the pond nursing his head. 'It's all my fault, it's all my fault,' she kept saying as she rocked to and fro, and no amount of reasoning would comfort her. Eventually the doctor gave her a sedative and sent her to her room.

Violet and Rose, strong at the start, had by then also sunk into a trough of remorse and were blaming themselves for having left Daisy to look after Jonathan on her own, but they'd pulled themselves together when Mungo got home.

Earlier they'd reacted mechanically and made tea for all the strangers who came, but once the ambulance had gone, and the police and the doctor had followed it down the drive, their adrenalin dried up. Thoroughly deflated, they'd collapsed on the sofa and wept on each other's shoulders. Mungo's arrival had somewhat restored them.

'Oh Mungo, Mungo.' they both wailed as he crossed the room and enclosed them in a tight embrace.

'Where's Aunt Daisy?' he asked.

Violet freed herself and resumed her seat. 'She's all right, she's in her room, the doctor's given her a sleeping draught. She's better off up there … it's all been too much.'

Mungo nodded slowly. 'Where's Father now?'

'They took him away in the ambulance, dear, for a post mortem.'

'A post mortem? What on earth for? Surely they don't think Aunt Daisy killed him.'

'No of course they don't.' said Aunt Violet, by then more composed as she perched on the arm of the sofa. 'They have to confirm his drowning, and anyway nobody knows what happened for sure. Daisy left him sitting in a chair inside the open French windows in the sun, but when she realised how strong it was she went upstairs for his hat. For some reason we can't fathom he must have gone outside, tripped, and fallen into the pond.'

'But what on earth prompted him to go out in the first place. Did Aunt Daisy know? Could she suggest why?'

'No, she has no idea, but she did get a glimpse of something odd, there was someone running down the garden and into the orchard just before she saw poor Jonathan, face down in the lilies.'

'Father didn't call out, then?'

'If he did she didn't hear him. She could have been on the stairs at the time; on her way up to the bedroom to get his hat.'

'Any chance the man she saw pushed him in?'

'I don't know. She wasn't even sure if it was a man, could have been a woman. Oh it's all so confusing Mungo, we'll just have to wait until she's recovered.'

'You're right of course. Go and lie down for a while both of you; I'll telephone the detective chap down in Brighton and let him know what's happened, there may be a connection. Though if there is, I'm blessed if I can see what it might be.'

James McPhee and Son,
Stockbrokers,
3, Lombard Street, London EC3V 9AA
Monday 30th October 2006. 10.30 a.m.

S andy was having a terrible morning. There was no more cash left in the deposit accounts, and the first of the letters, which would eventually become a flood of them, had arrived, Charles Wintergreen, one of his father's oldest friends, and a client for the last thirty years, had been on the 'phone wanting to know why his half year report hadn't arrived and had asked for a replacement copy to be sent to him. Sandy was sure there'd be more requests in the same vein within the week. He'd have to try to gain a bit of time by spoofing, tell the clients he was in the process of shifting funds to get better rates, that he was in dispute with the bank over interest due, or that he'd been ill and unable to compile the reports … anything.

His elbows were on his desk, his chin was in his hands, and his expression was blank, when his secretary came into the room. 'I don't suppose you've thought about Christmas presents for the clients yet, Mr McPhee?'

He looked up in astonishment. 'Christmas presents, Barbara? In October? What on earth made you think of Christmas presents at this time of year?'

'It was just an idea I had.'

'What idea?'

'Well, I understand we usually send the clients a bottle of whisky or wine or something.'

'Ye … es.' he said, frowning suspiciously.

'Well I thought a book might be nice this year.'

'Did you?' he said, swaying his head in disbelief.

'Sorry I spoke. I was only trying to help.'

She was only nineteen, just out of Pitman's Secretarial College, keen as mustard and trying to stand out. Little did she know! But she was all he could afford these days, he hadn't had a real secretary since Miss Cavendish, his father's long suffering 'Girl Friday' retired two years previously. Since then there'd been a procession of youngsters, all like Barbara - schoolgirls. Poor kid, she hadn't a clue ... books ... Christmas presents ... with the problems hanging over his head, who cared about Christmas! 'I'll think about it Barbara,' he said, 'thank you for the suggestion, it's a very good one. Now will you make me another coffee, this one's cold.'

At his apparently friendly response she decided to continue in greater detail and, forgetting his request for coffee, beamed a smile and went into her well-rehearsed speech. 'My Dad's friend writes thrillers, you see ...'

Sandy, accepting he'd get no coffee until she'd said her piece, sat back folded his arms across his chest and tried his best to look interested.

'... and I thought ... if we bought a load of this man's books, and my Dad can get them at twenty five off, we could get the author, my Dad's friend, to sign them, dedicate them to the individual clients. Wouldn't that be a good idea? ... Better than an old bottle of whisky.'

Sandy nodded, 'A very good idea Barbara, I'll think about it ... now what about my coffee ... please.'

As she primped out of his office in her impossibly high heeled shoes he smiled again, got up from his desk, and walked to the window. Sometimes looking out to the London skyline gave him inspiration, and he needed one now if ever he'd needed one.

'Books ... what next?' he thought, 'Wonderful to be in fictional world where you could simply make up what you want ... Make up what you want! ... My God that's it ... that's how I'll do it, how I'll buy more time. I'll write up fictional accounts and delay the disaster looming until the other plan delivers the goods.'

He clapped his hands together, went back to his desk and pulled a ruled sheet of accounting paper towards him.

Outside St Anne's House,
Horsham Common, Sussex.
Wednesday 1st November. 2006. 10.30 a.m.

She'd arrived from Tobago the day before, spent the day resting at the Gatwick Holiday Inn, and was waiting for Eddie when he arrived. He'd agreed to accompany her on her attempt to interview Ghandi Melchitt, and to do so he'd taken the day off and driven up from Portsmouth in his 'new' transport, an eight year old white Ford Fiesta van with 'only' 77,000 miles on the clock, and the reputation of being a 'reliable good runner'.

Soon after greeting each other in the hotel foyer they'd driven off to a nearby Little Chef roadside restaurant, a more affordable alternative, for a cup of coffee. There, they worked out how they'd make best use of the day - one on which they hoped to find out more about their father. Before they got down to business though, Sophie gave Eddie a present - a pineapple.

'Wow!' said Eddie 'Never had one of these before. I love the stuff but I've never had the guts to buy one, I wouldn't know what to do with it, I get it in tins.'

Sophie smiled. 'Well this is the real thing Eddie. It's out of my garden.'

'You'd have a job growing one in any of the gardens I work in!' he replied with a giggle. 'So … are you still on for Ghandi? I've found out exactly where he lives … on the map.'

'Oh yes I can't wait. Let's hope you bring me more luck this time.'

'Than what?'

'Than the last time I tried it, when I got to Jock McPhee's house … he was dead.'

'Of course, you said so in the letter you sent me before you flew back. Anyway, you'll be alright today, it couldn't happen twice.

Now what're we going to say to him?'

'We can work it out on the way, but first bring me up to date on Angie and Wayne. Have you seen them since I was here last and, more important again, do you know if this father of ours is in the country or not?'

'No, and no.' he said, as the waitress came over for their order.

'What do you mean - 'no and no."

'I haven't seen Angie or Wayne, and I rang Mrs Flower yesterday, and there's no change, he's definitely not coming back until Christmas.'

'So he's still in Mexico painting?'

'I suppose he is, I didn't ask. He's not in this country anyway ... which is the main thing.'

'Right. We'll have our coffee and get straight down to Ghandi's place then ... see what we can dig up there. Afterwards, we'll just have to wait until Henry gets back ... maybe another call on Mrs Flower would be worthwhile, to find out if she knows any more about his movements. We can call on Angie at the same time.'

'Fair enough, let's head for Horsham, then.'

Half an hour later they were sitting at the gate looking at the front of Ghandi's house.

Outside was a hearse.

'I can't believe it,' Sophie exclaimed, 'this is the second time this has happened. Let's hope it isn't him.'

It was, of course.

Sophie had barely got out of the car when she saw one of the undertaker's men standing just inside the gate lighting a cigarette, he told her the funeral about to take place was that of Mr Jonathan Melchitt who, he said, had died as the result of a fall three days earlier.

As she turned to speak to Eddie, who'd remained in the car, a man appeared at the front door of the house shouting, 'If you're Press you can go away.'

It was Mungo. 'This is a family matter and we don't want newspapers sticking their noses in.' he yelled.

Sophie held up her hand in a gesture of re-assurance. 'We aren't from a newspaper; we came to talk to Mr Melchitt.'

Mungo, not satisfied they weren't reporters, walked towards them. 'I'm Mr Melchitt, what do you want? It's a very inconvenient day to give an interview, my father has just died.'

Eddie got out of the car to stand beside Sophie as she spoke, 'We've just heard about Mr Melchitt's fall. May we say how sorry we are … it was him we were hoping to see.'

Jonathan shook his head, obviously not believing them. 'About what?' he said.

'We are trying to find out about our father.'

Mungo laughed. 'And what makes you think he'd know? Don't be daft. You've got the wrong man.'

'Someone told us they once knew each other.' said Eddie, coming to Sophie's 'rescue'. 'From what they said it seems they were fellow students at one time … we're just asking so we can find out more about our own father.'

'Well, I don't know your father so I can't help.' Mungo said, 'Why don't you ask him … have you lost him?'

Eddie threw up his hands in a gesture of helplessness. 'We might just as well have Mister, 'cos we've never seen him … ever.'

Mungo looked at his watch and, realising the funeral procession should have been on its way said: 'Look, you've got here too late by three days to talk to my father and we have to go now, we're five minutes behind.'

Sophie and Eddie both nodded. 'Maybe we could come back another time, and talk to you?'

Mungo, quickly assessing them again, saw a dark skinned girl with a West Indian accent and a young white skinned Londoner. He couldn't imagine any father of theirs would have had the slightest connection with his. 'I don't think there'll be much point. I can't believe I'll have anything to tell you even if you do come back.'

Eddie nodded again, accepting Mungo's refusal, and climbed back into the car.

But Sophie stood her ground, and then she dropped her bombshell. 'Not even if we said his name was Henry Byrd?'

That changed Mungo's attitude. 'Are you telling me your father was Henry Byrd? Never. I've met him I think and, yes, he was a great friend of my father some years ago, but I find it hard to credit he was the father of you two. Be that as it may, I've must go. You can ring me if you're ever in the district again and I'll tell you as much as I know about him … but I don't think I'll be telling you much, because I don't know much. The man who really knew him was my father and, obviously, you can't ask him now.'

'That's true,' Sophie said, clearly disappointed. 'and it's what I feared when I saw the hearse. It was the same when I called on Mr George McPhee.'

'Jock McPhee? He's dead too?'

'Yes he is, and my father and yours both knew him. He died after a stroke about a month ago.'

'Died of a stroke did he? Didn't drown? Well that's a change'

'What do you mean?'

'Ah, it was a silly thing to say, it's just … well … my two brothers have both died very recently and, like my father, they died by drowning. As a matter of fact, I've begun to wonder if anyone dies any other way these days.'

'I'm so sorry, we had no idea. We wouldn't have come if we'd known. They were accidents I suppose?'

Mungo thought for a moment before drawing a visiting card from his top pocket and giving it to Sophie. 'I wish it were … just a series of unfortunate accidents,' he said, 'but it's beginning to look unlikely. The police haven't been able to find out what happened yet. But look Miss 'er … I've got to go. You can call me the next time you're down this way and I'll pass on to you whatever I know of Henry Byrd, which is practically nothing.'

'Alright,' Sophie answered, 'and thanks for talking to us, it'll probably be in a month or so.'

With his brief parting remark ringing in her ears, Sophie went back and got into the car, Eddie was already at the wheel. 'So much for the good luck you said you'd bring' she said to him as she took her seat. 'Anyway, there's no point in hanging around here any longer, let's go and see if Angie's in. And we might try calling on Mrs 'F' again.'

As they drove away Eddie asked what Mungo had said about accidents as he'd been unable to hear from inside the car.

'There's something strange going on down here, Eddie, two of his brothers and his father have all lost their lives by drowning … and the police don't seem to know why.'

'In the same accident?'

'No - they're not even sure they were accidents.'

'Blimey.'

'He even asked me if Jock McFee had been drowned when I told him he was dead. Anyway, it doesn't look as though we're going to get any more help from the Melchitts than we did from the McPhees. It'll be funny if the deaths are connected.'

'Very funny.' said Eddie, but he wasn't laughing, he was thinking about a lump of granite.

'Penny for them.' offered Sophie, but he still didn't reply, he was wondering if he ought to tell Sophie about the stone he'd just put on top of his rockery in Portsmouth, and about a curious tale Angie had once related to him.

The Alexandra Suite, Dolphin Square, Pimlico, London SW1V 3LX. Monday 6th November 2006. 11.00 a.m.

Rex had been up for hours pottering about, Ginny was still in bed. 'Rex ... Rex.'

The noise of the water powering through the shower rose must have been obscuring her call for she received no answer.

'Rex ... Rex.' she screamed.

Still there was no answer.

Finally she put the telephone down on the bedside table, climbed out of the bed, walked, naked, across the bedroom floor and banged on the door of the en-suite bathroom. 'Rex ... Rex, there's a policeman on the 'phone, he wants to see you later on today.'

Rex must have heard her because the shower was turned off and a moment later the door opened and he stepped into the room, his steaming body dripping with water. 'What?'

'It's a policeman from Yorkshire or somewhere,' she said, 'he wants to meet you, to interview you.'

'What on earth for?'

'I don't know, darling, he didn't say,' she replied, holding out the 'phone, 'talk to him yourself.'

Rex grabbed a towel from the rail just inside the bathroom door, wrapped it around himself, and took the handset from her. Once she'd handed it over she minced her way back to the bed confident that, irrespective of any diversion arising from the policeman's call, he'd follow her.

He didn't though, he stood still, where he was, while the policeman spoke, then answered, 'But I've never been to Richmond in Yorkshire ... Richmond in Surrey, yes. I lived there once, a few years ago, but I've never been to the other one, or anywhere near it as far as I can recollect.'

As the policeman continued to talk, and Rex continued to listen, the towel was suddenly snatched from his waist. Ginny unfazed by the possibility the call could have been about anything serious, had decided to get back to her own agenda.

Rex waved her away impatiently and signalled he wanted the towel back. She shook her head, so he turned away from her and walked back into the bathroom leaving her sitting on the edge of the bed sulking.

Three minutes later he re-appeared. He'd put on his underwear and having replaced the telephone and avoided her grasp as he passed, went straight his wardrobe to pick out a shirt. He had a puzzled look on his face, 'Damned funny that, he wants to talk to me about a murder; they think I might have been a witness. I told the guy I'd never been to the Yorkshire Richmond but he was still very insistent on seeing me. He's driving down to Brighton sometime today and he's going to try to find time to come here later on, around six. He said he'd ring again in an hour to give me a more definite time. It's very strange.'

Ginny, back in bed and still plotting as to how she might recapture his interest, hardly heard what he said as she leaned back against the pillow, her arms beseechingly outstretched towards him, 'Rexy … Dar…ling.'

But he wasn't to be diverted so easily. 'No Ginny,' he said, as though he were addressing a naughty child and not a voluptuous young woman ready for action, 'not now. My agent's coming for a 'conflab' in half an hour and I don't want to be all out of breath! Get some coffee ready for us would you? And when I'm finished with him we'll go to Wheeler's for lunch. I've got to be at a production schedule meeting in Wardour Street at three, and back to see the policeman at six.'

'So who's dead anyway?' asked Ginny, accepting defeat and abandoning her scheming.

'Oh, someone, he didn't say … a man.'

'That's not much help, is that all?'

'All until he sees me, I suppose.'

'I mean, when did it happen, for instance?'

'Oh yes, he mentioned a date, it was several weeks ago, the 4th of September I think he said.'

'And does he think you did it? That's hilarious.'

'Not to me it isn't.' he replied tetchily. 'Are you going to make coffee or not?'

Ginny climbed out of the bed, drew a flimsy, transparent wrap over herself and went through to the kitchen, speaking as she went. 'You were on location down in the New Forest around then. You could hardly have seen a murder taking place in Yorkshire from there. Didn't you tell him?'

Rex paused as he was about to tuck his shirt into his trousers. 'You're right, I'd forgotten. So whoever they *are* looking for … it can't be me.'

'Ring him back.'

'No, I want to know what it's all about now. It'll be interesting to hear what he has to say.'

The sound of water going into the kettle almost drowned her reply, 'You didn't slip up to Richmond between scenes and slit someone's throat did you?'

'No I didn't.'

'Want any flakes?'

'No.'

'Toast?'

'No.'

'Anything … you know … anything?'

'No, Virginia Meddows, you nympho, I just want coffee.'

'OK.' Ginny replied cheerily, draping herself in a Film Star pose around the edge of the door and winking.

The Coffee Pot, Cecil Court, London WC2N 4HX Monday 6th November 11.55 a.m.

Eva couldn't wipe the smile from her face; she'd landed a job for the first time ever without any help from Rex. She was to play the Fairy Godmother in 'Babes In The Wood', the Coliseum's forthcoming Pantomime.

Seated in a window seat of a small café in the narrow thoroughfare linking St Martin's Lane and Charing Cross Road, and content to watch the non-stop stream of people hurrying along the alley, she scooped up a huge blob of creamy froth from the top of the Cappuccino, put it in her mouth, and sucked the spoon pensively. Life was good again. Her script lay on the table before her. 'Here we are,' she said to herself, opening it to a marked page.

'The Babes, lost in the forest, lie exhausted and frightened on a bank covered with dead leaves at the base of a giant oak tree ......

Enter Fairy Godmother (flash and smoke)

F. G.   'Sleep now my babes, for though through the woods with wicked men you go ... I will be with you ...'

'Oh my God!' Eva stuttered out loud, unable to prevent herself from blushing at the sheer awfulness of the lines she was going to have to deliver. But then, smiling at her own pomposity, reaffirmed to herself her intention to properly mark the occasion of getting her first job on her own.

'I'll have an hour browsing in the bookshops in Charing Cross Road,' she murmured, 'and then I'm going to Wheeler's Fish

Restaurant in Wardour Street ... where I haven't been since I was with Rex ... and I'm going to have Fillet of Sole Veronique, a few spears of asparagus dripping in butter, and a nice glass of ice cold bubbly.' With her mind made up she spooned up the rest of the froth, drained the cup, and set off - a grin of self-satisfaction on her face for the first time in months.

Perusing the stock in the Charing Cross Road area's bookshops had always been an attraction when she'd been in the vicinity. With time on her hands to explore, and the letter confirming she'd been awarded the part in her hand bag, she couldn't have thought of a better way to spend a morning than rooting around in a second hand bookshop.

Not that she bought many books, for those which would fit into her collection of good condition, hard backed, children's stories with stand-up illustrations weren't very often found. Her forty one book collection had taken fifteen years to assemble. Seldom did she have time, or money, to spend on her hobby but today she felt lucky. Maybe she'd look back one day and see the day she got the job in Babes in the Wood had been the day she'd put behind her the double misery of losing Rex, and being unemployed - the day she'd embarked on a new phase of life and started to redevelop her independence.

She'd been browsing the bookshops for an hour when she struck lucky in Unsworth's where, having quickly glanced through the stock on the barrows outside, she'd gone into the shop and made for the Second Hand Section (Children). The first volume she picked up was an American edition of Jack and the Beanstalk, published by McLoughlin Bros, New York in 1889. It was in near perfect condition, its stand up illustrations as new, and at twenty two pounds, a bargain. She paid for it with a fifty pound note and, pocketing the change, made her way through to Wardour Street.

The minute she went through Wheeler's door she saw them ... Rex and Virginia Meddows. They were sitting at table in the middle of the room. He had one arm round her waist, holding her tight to himself while pouring an oyster into her open mouth with the other hand.

'The bastard.' Eva muttered, as her anger mounted, 'he used to do that with me!'

She felt sick. She felt furious. She turned straight round and went home. The day was ruined. She could kill him!

The Alexandra Suite, Dolphin Square, Pimlico, London SW1V 3LX. Monday 6th November 2006. 6.15 p.m.

As soon as Inspector Sherman, accompanied by Sergeant Bellamy, followed Rex into the apartment he began to have second thoughts, by the time Rex had introduced himself, the doubts had turned to certainties. This was not the man in the photograph; he'd made an idiotic mistake.

'So what can I do for you?' Rex asked, leading them into the sitting room. 'I've already told you I wasn't in Richmond, or anywhere else in Yorkshire, on the day you mentioned … the 4th of September wasn't it? Tea?'

'No tea, thank you Sir.' said Sherman, beginning to feel really uncomfortable. 'We … 'er …just 'er … just have to clear something up. We're seeking the help of a man who might have witnessed a murder. He appears in a photograph we have which was taken moments before the incident. Now it may be he was about to become involved, but it may equally be that he had no involvement whatever. It's possible he was simply walking past and was gone before anything happened.'

'And you think the man was me, do you. Why? I've told you I wasn't there. In fact I was down in the New Forest - making a film, I was on the set all day. There are dozens of people who can vouch for me.'

'Well, Sir … said the inspector, struggling to extract himself from the embarrassment he was feeling.

Sergeant Bellamy rescued him. 'It's like this Mr Brett, people often confuse the identity of a person we're seeking with that of someone whose face is familiar to them, someone like you for example, someone famous. I can see it's what might have happened in this case. A genuine mistake seems to have been made, and we must apologise for interrupting your day.'

'No need to apologise Sergeant. I can give you the names of the people I was with if you like.'

Bellamy was about to say 'No', when the inspector, still feeling foolish, interrupted him. 'Thank you Sir, perhaps you'd write them all down ... just for the record ... so we can eliminate you from the enquiry.'

Rex nodded and, taking a used envelope from the table, started to write names on the back of it. 'I've never been involved in the real thing though I have been both victim and murderer more than once - on the stage.'

Sherman nodded. 'Is that so, Sir ... really?'

'Yes, several times ... so who died?

'Tragically, the victim was one of our officers - Chief Superintendent Dudley Melchitt. He was in a river, fly fishing, when somehow he fell into the water and was drowned.'

'And who's the witness you're looking for?'

'Well,' said the D.I., taking the photograph from his pocket and tapping it, 'here he is, walking along the bank towards the victim - you may have seen have this picture in the newspapers or on the television. We have no idea, as yet, whether he witnessed anything or not. He might even have been beyond the victim when the attack took place. If he was, then the noise of the water would have masked any other sound.'

As the inspector spoke, Sergeant Bellamy took the print and handed it to Rex, who brought it to the window to get better light. His back was to the police officers, which was just as well, for he recognised the man in it immediately, it was his brother, Angus.

'It's not very clear, is it?' he said, trying to hide the surprise the picture had given him.

'No ... but unfortunately it's the only one we have, and we're just hoping it'll be good enough for someone who knows this man to recognise him.'

'Hmm ... he does look a bit like me, I suppose.' Rex conceded, as casually as he could. 'So if that's all ...'

'Yes, Sir, that *is* all.' answered the D.I., making for the door.

Sussex Police Major Incident Suite
Sussex House, Brighton
Tuesday 7th November 2006. Late morning

That you Ronnie? … Foxy here. I was hoping I'd find you in. How are you?'

'I'm OK. I was about to telephone you. How are you getting on … making any progress?'

'Not much … but there's been a couple of developments … that's why I'm ringing.'

'About Boris or Dudley?'

'Neither, about their father, Jonathan.'

'You told me it was an accident when you rang.'

'Well, it probably was, but the pathologist found an abrasion under the hefty grey locks he was sporting, and it set us wondering …'

'If it was another case of a clout on the head and a drowning … and was it?' asked Sherman, snapping his fingers at Bellamy then stabbing one of them towards the other telephone, indicating he should be listening in.

'It might have been. Whoever's doing this has got it in for the Melchitts in a big way, the whole lot of 'em.'

'Have you spoken to Mungo recently?'

'I've seen him, and I'll be seeing him again, but I wondered how you got on with him when you called. You were going there after you left here last time.'

'And we did.'

'So?'

'So nothing, not a bloody thing. Sorry I should've told you.'

'Don't worry …. anything on Dudley?'

'Maybe … I went to see Rex Brett yesterday.'

'Oh did you? That must have been an interesting call. How

did you get on?'

'I'm not sure ... the guy in the photo wasn't him, I knew it the minute I saw him face to face. On top of that he reckoned he could produce a string of witnesses who'd confirm he'd been filming down in the New Forest all day.'

'So you've ruled him out? Good thing, a high profile suspect always buggers everything up.'

'Hmm.'

'You don't agree?'

'Oh, I do agree. High profile wallas bring a load of unwelcome attention. Having a film star as a suspect would be just about the last thing I'd want. No, I'm glad he's not the man we're after, but ...'

'But what? What's the problem?'

'The problem is, I'm quite certain he knew who the man in the photo really was.'

'Go on ... and did you ask him?'

'No, but I will.'

'You should have pushed him when you were there. He's had time to think now.'

'I know I should have. But to tell you the truth, Foxy, I got a bit rattled when I realised the gaff I'd made in telling everyone I'd recognised him as the guy in the photo. I just couldn't get out quick enough. It was only later I realised his denial didn't have the ring of truth.'

'Was Bellamy with you?'

'Yes, he was.'

'What did he think?'

'Well he thought I was wrong in the first place, he has his own theory. He reckons the guy's a local man, I mean local to Richmond. You'll remember he told you, the last time we were with you, that he's sure he spoke to him quite recently - in Richmond nick.'

'Oh yeah, I do remember ... the incident of the *stolen* car which *wasn't* stolen?'

'Right. Anyway I'm going to call on Brett again next time I'm down. I might even chance going there without letting him know I'm on the way. So, how're your two cases doing? Any sign of a motive? Anything which might help us up here?'

'I wish I could say there was, but no link has surfaced.

We're at a dead end really as regards motive. As to the cases themselves ... well, take the old man first because it may turn out to be the easiest. We've done some reconstructive tests and it's beginning to look as though the injury to his head could have been sustained when he fell. The lip of the fountain's bowl is only five feet in from the edge of the pool and we're wondering if he didn't simply crash into it as he went down. The pathologist took scrapings from the abrasions around the main wound. They may have grit in them and, if they do, he'll check to see if it's the same sandstone as the basin. Assuming it is, we'll be going off the idea of him being attacked.'

'What d'you think he did then - trip? Or was he pushed? From all accounts he spent most of his life sitting wherever he was put. So why was he out there, he was hardly taking a stroll in the garden?'

'Unlikely. No, we haven't been able to work that one out yet, and there's ...

'The guy who the old girl saw sprinting down the lawn into the orchard? Yeah ... what about him?'

'He's the one we're concentrating on at the moment, and we've had a bit of luck there. The Melchitt's orchard's a new one - a sort of a project of Mungo's. It's a fenced off section of the paddock in which the three brothers used to keep ponies when they were kids. The young trees are still not much bigger than bushes and they've still got a good few leaves on them. Once the bloke got in amongst them he'd have been invisible from the house and, with no one after him, he'd have had more than enough time to make his way through them and trot across the paddock to where his Harley Davidson was parked inside the gate opening onto Nightingale Lane.'

'He had a motor bike? How d'you know that?'

Foxy grinned, 'Couple of youngsters larking about with a football lost it over the hedge when one of them kicked it too hard. It landed on the bike, tucked out of sight behind the bushes and only visible to them when they climbed over the gate to get it. Their mothers made them come into the station to tell us.'

'And did they see the man?'

'Oh they saw him alright - couldn't have missed him. He came running at them, cursing like hell; scared the wits out of them. They grabbed their ball and ran.'

'Get a description?'

'Not really, except he was big, dressed in black leathers, and had a helmet on.'

'Ha, fat lot of use that is. So what d'you reckon happened then, if the old man didn't get thumped?'

'Dunno. Maybe he saw the guy coming towards him all dressed up like bloody space man, and went for him. We'll know when we catch the bugger.'

'Fair enough. And what about Boris? You didn't hear of a motor cyclist lurking around in the bushes down there as well I suppose!' asked Ronnie, grinning and winking at Bellamy as he spoke.

Foxy laughed, 'Cheeky, cheeky. But the laugh's on you, mate, because there was a bike there, and we've some lovely tyre marks to prove it. It wasn't a Harley though, more of a lightweight, a two stroke maybe. Look, I've got to go. I'm in court today. Ring me when you've seen Brett again.'

'Will do.' replied Sherman, pausing a moment in thought as he replaced the handset, and then starting back in surprise as a sudden gust of rain laden wind lashed across the window. He crossed to it and looked up towards the cloud enshrouding the moorland above the town. 'Might be a few fish on the move if the rain comes down and the river floods.'

34, Primrose Mansions, Islington.
Wednesday 8th November 2006. 10.30 p.m.

Angie was reading the paper when Wayne came in from the pub. His friend, Reg, was with him. Both the children were in bed asleep, though Garth had been up and down on numerous occasions, 'a drink of water', 'a monster under the bed', 'too hot', 'too cold', the usual parade of excuses and Angie was fed up. The last thing she wanted was Wayne to arrive as he did, half drunk, and accompanied by his 'mate' Reg, a lazy slob who never stopped belching.

'Anyfin' to ea'?' asked Wayne, flopping down at the kitchen table opposite to Angie, and signalling Reg to sit next to him. 'Me an' Reg's 'ungry.'

'So?' asked Angie, not taking her eyes from the article she was reading.

'So, is there anyfin' to ea'?' repeated Wayne.

'Look in the 'fridge.'

'Reg, mate, 'ave a look will yer?'

Reg heaved his huge bulk from the chair, which creaked with relief as he rose, and went over to open the refrigerator. Apart from some cartons of milk and a couple of baby's bottles ready for Lance during the night there was little else other than three eggs and half a pound of sausages.

'Damn all here.' he said, as he went back to torture the chair again.

'Didn't you do no shoppin' terday?' asked Wayne.

'Didn't you do no earnin' terday?' replied Angie, sticking her tongue out and cocking a snoot at him.

Wayne ignored the insult. 'Ain' there no bread n'cheese then, we ain' 'ad nuffin?'

Angie fixed him with a fearsome look before answering

him. 'Bread's in the bread bin Way ... ayne, wha' a surprise! And there ain' no cheese, 'cos there ain' no money, no' until Friday when I'll be paid, I s'pose yor wages is all dahn the Nag's ... as usual.'

Wayne nudged Reg. 'Come on mate le's go an' ge' some chips. Wha' about you Ange?'

Angie stared him straight in the eye for as long as she could without grinning and then burst out into great guffaws of laughter 'Look in the oven, you plonker.'

Wayne, not the sharpest knife in the drawer, gave her a quizzical look of incomprehension ... and then it dawned on him ... she was joking. 'In the oven?'

'Ye ... es ... Way ... ayne ... In the effin' oven. There's a shepherd's pie there. Yer can si' down again Reg, there's enough for all of us.'

Reg did as he was told, he wasn't going to risk messing with Angie, he'd seen what happened to those who did. Wayne remained as he was, he didn't like being mocked in front of his mate, but he stopped worrying when he saw the look of total incomprehension on Reg's face, clearly the man had no idea what was going on. Re-assured his standing had not been seen to diminish under the onslaught of Angie's wit, Wayne bent down and pulled a nicely browned shepherd's pie from the oven. 'Where'll I put i'?' he asked.

'I'm tempted ter tell you.' Angie whispered, under her breath. 'On the bloody table where d'you fink? An', by the way, did yer see this bi' about old Melchitt in the paper? ... 'e's dead, drowned in 'is goldfish pond. I tole you not ter hittim.'

'I didn't ittim.'

'Yew sure?'

'Course I'm sure. I never touched 'im.'

'Yew shoved 'im then.'

'I didn't. 'E went fer me, stupid old geezer.'

'Yew'll be forrit when they catch yer ... yer'd betta ge' yerself a good brief.' she cackled.

28, River View Gardens,
Richmond, Yorks.
Saturday 11th November 2006 4.00 a.m.

D.I. Ronnie Sherman woke with a start. 'A secret society … I'm bloody sure that's what she said.'

His wife, Daphne, awakened by his mumbling, rolled over to face him. 'What is it Ronnie?'

'Nothing,' he replied, 'I've just remembered something that's all … go back to sleep.

'You sure you're alright?

'Yes … sure.'

Daphne patted his hand and turned away from him, struggling to re-enter her dream where she'd exited it. In two minutes she was enjoying an entirely different one. Not so Ronnie. He couldn't do that and it infuriated him. Sliding out of the bed, he put on his dressing gown, and went down to the kitchen to make himself a cup of tea. As he waited for the kettle to boil he turned on the television only to find England were all out for a hundred and ninety three. 'Damn Aussies!' he said, turning it off again.

Rocky, disturbed by the noise and the start-up flickering of the fluorescent ceiling light, looked reprovingly from his basket, and growled. 'Sorry mate.' Ronnie said, walking over to pat the dog's head, 'You go back to sleep … I'm going to do a bit of thinking about 'secret societies'.'

With his mug of tea sitting on the stove, he settled in the old basket chair beside it. Some of his best work was done in that chair in the early hours of the morning. Not that day though for, most un-typically, he almost immediately 'dropped off', all thoughts of 'secret societies' shoved into in cold storage for another day.

Sussex Police Major Incident Suite
Sussex House, Brighton
Monday 13th November 2006. 2.00 p.m.

Detective Chief Inspector Reynard was at his desk in a fixed partition office at one end of a large open plan area. Before him a couple of dozen desks were corralled together in small groups, separated by shoulder high royal blue partitions. They were in use by a team of detectives working on other cases, plain clothes men and women clustered together and hunting for solutions to a number of crimes recently committed in Sussex. Next to Reynard's office was that of Detective Inspector Jack Crowther, his opposite number. Reynard's team had the two Melchitt cases to solve and a missing girl to find. Crowther and his squad were up to their necks in a series of Post Office robberies.

Opposite to the offices, at the other end of the room, was the Incident Display Wall. It was divided into two sections - one for each team - and was covered with photographs, diagrams, sketch maps, time lines, and notes, some circled to highlight the importance of the data displayed.

Sergeant Lucy Groves knocked on Reynard's door. When he looked up and saw who it was he beckoned her in. 'Take a seat, Lucy. I have to make one 'phone call and then I have a good hour to talk with you about the Melchitt cases, fancy a coffee?' He nodded towards a Cona coffee machine bubbling quietly away on the top of his filing cabinet and pulled out a drawer crammed with packets of chocolate biscuits. A creature of habit, he only extended hospitality when he fancied a snack himself, which was at ten in the morning and four in the afternoon. Everyone in the nick knew, and they all competed to be on hand at the moment his stomach sent out the call for sustenance. Get it right and you were in for a treat, mis-time it and you got nothing. Sergeant Lucy Groves had looking at her watch since ten to ten and, on the hour, she was straight in with her eyes on the coffee pot.

'OK. So where are we?' asked Reynard opening a pack of Hobnobs and tipping some out onto a plate.

'Well, Guv,' she answered, picking one up. 'We're only making slow progress. As far as Jonathan Melchitt's death is concerned I reckon we ought to discount our original thought about his being hit on the head before he fell. It makes little difference to the investigation whether he was knocked out before falling, or whether he was simply pushed. Provided he didn't jump into the fountain of his own accord it probably comes down to one of two options, murder or manslaughter.'

'Not our problem then, the DPP can decide the charge based on the Path report, added to what we dig up. Don't matter to us whether he was hit, pushed, or slipped, we still have to find who did it - if anyone did.'

'Of course Guv, and the same in Boris's case.'

'Precisely. We may have a good reason for thinking Boris was clobbered before he was chucked in but, as with his father - and Dudley for that matter - it'll help us if we find out the 'whys' or the 'whos'. What we have to do now is break each case down and classify the evidence under one of the usual headings.'

'I agree … leave the 'Hows' to one side and concentrate on the 'Whys' and 'Whos.'

'That's it, a logical and incremental approach on two fronts. Let's see what we know about the 'Whys' in the two cases we have.'

Groves nodded and drained her cup. 'Being both part of the same family'd be the first obvious thing.'

'Yes, and …?'

'And they may have had common enemies, common friends, and common interests.'

'Common enemies I like. Common friends… less probable, but not impossible. Common interests … hmm … like what?'

'Money.'

'Ah. That's an idea … yes. Supposing there's a lot of dosh in the family and there's someone within it who needs money … we may have a possible motive there.'

'Yes, but there's a snag as well, from what we know of the wills, the aunts were just as well off as Jonathan Melchitt was, and far better off than either Dudley or Boris, but *they* weren't killed.'

'They weren't killed *yet*, you mean?' said Reynard.

'OK ... so they might be next! But what about Mungo, to what extent does he benefit?'

'Well the deaths of his father and brothers give him effective control of the firm as long as his aunts stick by him, because he now has the same shareholding as each of them.'

'But aren't there problems with some of the other shareholders - his cousins for example. They'd like to see the back of him, isn't that what he told you?'

'Yes' said Reynard, 'he did, but I cannot see how the killings would profit the cousins. Jonathan's death, together with Dudley's and Boris's, strengthened Mungo's hand, it didn't weaken it. No I think you can rule the cousins out from what we know but ... the trouble is you see ... if we leave them out, I don't like what's left.'

'You mean Mungo?'

'Indeed.'

'I can't believe he did it, Guv.'

'Well then, we must leave him to one side for the moment as well. Maybe I'll call and see him again ... try to draw him out a bit more. In the meantime refresh my mind about your conversation with the aunts.'

'Guv, they really are lovely people and there is no possibility whatever they could be involved.'

'That's a very sweeping claim.'

'It is, but I'll stand by it. They're far too old and far too frail for a start, and to think of them, or one of them, driving backwards and forwards across the country to bash a nephew on the head is quite ludicrous.'

Inspector Reynard raised his eyebrows, 'Ever hear of a surrogate killer?'

Sergeant Groves bent over laughing at her boss's question, but quickly sat up again and straightened her face when she realised he might be serious. 'Sorry Guv, the whole idea of them being involved in murder in any way is just too far-fetched for me. In my view there's not the remotest chance they'd have killed anyone, or had them killed.'

'Nor in mine. I just couldn't resist seeing how you'd react ... so where are we now?'

'Further testing of Mungo's innocence, One. And search for other motives, Two.'

'Other way round, we'll concentrate on motives I think. Find the 'Whys' and we'll soon uncover the 'Whos'.'

'So what d'you propose?'

'I propose we go back to the start of our interview notes and pull out anything we don't understand, or don't know enough about. Maybe, as we go through everything again, we'll stumble on a pointer, because we certainly need one. You get on with that, I'm going up to Richmond tomorrow to see D.I. Sherman and I'm going to run over to Rottingdean now, this morning, to see what's been happening there. D. C. Best's been doing a 'house to house.' Maybe he's stumbled across something else in addition to what he mentioned on the 'phone yesterday.'

"Next' Best, Guv ... is he on this too? If he is, he's more likely to have stumbled over a something than stumble across it.'

Before Reynard could think of a suitable answer, she'd gone. He shoved his papers in a folder and went out to his car.

Driving through the back roads to Rottingdean he went over everything again in his mind ... he'd missed something ... there had to be a clue there somewhere which would unlock the mystery ... what the hell was it? Who on earth was killing all these people - no one he'd met so far fitted the bill. It had to be someone who hadn't yet come into his orbit. Mungo was his only hope for a lead because the old ladies clammed up as soon as he appeared on the scene. He decided to call on him on his way back to Brighton and have another go at him. Seven o'clock ought to do it; he ought be home by then.

On board the 'Caveat Emptor'
Blackwater Creek, Rottingdean.
Monday 13th November 2006. 4.30 p.m.

To say Boris's boat was 'tatty' would be the understatement of the year; inside it was a shambles of cheap DIY self-assembly furniture placed haphazardly wherever there was enough space to take it. Boris had called it 'work in progress'. The only sections which were anywhere near reasonable were the galley and the tiny storeroom off it in which he seemed to have been living, for there he had a camp bed and a deck chair. Everywhere else inside was a nightmare, and almost impossible to penetrate. Outside it was poor too, the paint, peeling off since decommissioning fifty years earlier, had permitted rust to gain the upper hand.

Boris had only owned the appropriately named 'Caveat Emptor' for a year, and he'd clearly been trying his best to make up for the long periods of negligence by many previous owners when he began to tackle the outside. A few had tried and, like them, he'd started by slapping paint onto the worst affected areas once he'd de-rusted them. Unfortunately however, as none of them had ever been able to obtain the same shade of grey which had been used originally, the result achieved made the boat look as though it had been painted by the members of the local Patchwork Quilting Club.

D.C.I. Reynard sat in the deck chair, D. C. Best was on a five gallon drum which, from its label, had once contained Sunflower oil, and must have been obtained from the local Fish and Chip shop. He'd piled a couple of folded blankets on top of it to increase both comfort and height.

Between them, and supported on a four more drums, was

half a sheet of plywood, its surface covered with the papers they were discussing.

'This the lot then?'

'Yes, Guv, as far as I can see.'

'And they all came from different places around the boat did they?'

'Not really. I found one box on top of the locker in the kitchen which he'd been using as a food cupboard, and I found another two in here. The one from the kitchen was full of letters ... they're in this pile. I don't think they'll be much use though, they're all to do with the local branch of Barclay's Bank and a publishing company up in London called Melchitt House - must be the family business I reckon.'

'It is. Did you come across anything interesting?'

'I wish I could say 'I did' but I can't, the bank statements show he was *just* in credit, but there was little movement and nothing fishy in them I could see. The stuff from Melchitt House was even less informative, accounts for the last three years trading, a few letters calling meetings, some advertising literature, and two invitations to book launches - all pretty harmless.'

'No tax returns, share certificates, dividend payment slips or anything like that?' asked Reynard.

'Nope.' replied Best.

'OK. And what about rest of the stuff you found.'

'There is no 'rest'; everything I found is in these piles. They're quite interesting actually, because they tell us a bit about how he lived.'

'And how was that?'

'Frugally, very frugally. He appears to have existed on the proceeds of his odd-jobbing, and a three monthly payment from The Melchitt Trust. I knew you'd ask about it so I've done a bit of telephoning in advance to get the story.'

'Which is?'

'Which is ... his grandfather, an old guy called Oscar Melchitt, left money in trust for all five of his grandchildren, Boris, Mungo and Dudley, plus two cousins of theirs, Jarrold and Justin. They can't touch the capital which will eventually go to the last of them to survive. Until then they each get quarterly cash payment of a few hundred quid.'

'Only a few hundred pounds, are you sure?'

'Yeah, unless one of them dies, then his share is split between the others.'

'That gives us a possible motive, well done!'

Best looked up from the notes from which he'd been reading and shook his head. 'I doubt it … it was only a matter of a thousand a year each.'

Reynard hauled himself out of the deck chair, bent over, and started to massage the back of his thighs. 'Didn't go in for comfort in this boat did he?'

Best didn't answer, he smiled instead

'So there's definitely nothing else?'

'No Guv, everything's on the table, plenty of interesting information … but I can't see it getting us far.'

'Go on then … summarise it for me.'

Best rubbed his knees, seeing the D.C.I. dealing with his discomfort had made him conscious of his own.

'Right then, this lot all clipped together are cash register dockets for things he's bought for his boat and for his odd-jobbing. Over there you have pre-printed invoices torn from one of those triplicate books you can get in any stationers. He's rubber stamped his name and address on the top and they're all marked 'Paid'. They're copies of what he's been using to bill customers and they're for all sorts of jobs, plumbing, joinery, and painting in the main. As far as I can see all the work was on boats.'

'Any company registration numbers, VAT numbers, or anything like that on 'em.' Reynard asked.

'Nah, this is small time stuff … pocket money.'

''Fiddle de Dee' business you mean.'

'Yeah, probably, but it's too small to provide a motive, and far too small to be of interest to the Inland Revenue. The guy was living on buttons. Look around you Guv … nothing here worth killing for.'

Reynard nodded. 'OK, so is that the lot?'

'Yeah, apart from a few odds and sods - personal correspondence from people overseas who he'd met on his travels. Nothing else for us that I could see.'

'Stick 'em all back in the boxes then and put them in my car. I'll go over them later, see if I can spot anything. And what else have you found on the boat?'

'Nothing Guv.'

'OK, so tell me what you've discovered on your 'house to house' interviews.'

Best pulled out a different note book and flipped over the pages. 'Summary first?'

'Oh yes, please, I don't want to be here all night but, hang on, let's make ourselves a hot drink, I'm freezing ... and see if you can find how his lighting works, it'll be dark soon.' As he spoke he swivelled round and looked out of the long narrow window. The night was drawing in fast. 'No forget it; let's find a 'caff'.'

'We needn't do that, Sir, I live quite near - we'll be more comfortable at my place and I'll soon have the kettle on.'

'Oh ... I don't want to disturb your household.'

'Disturb my dog you mean,' said Best, 'I live alone - apart from him.'

Fifteen minutes later they were sitting in D.C. Best's kitchen with a steaming mug of tea in their hands and ready to start again. 'Algy', Best's black Cocker Spaniel, having checked out the smell of Reynard's dog on his trousers, was leaning against his legs having the top of his head scratched.

'You have to appreciate the lay of the land, Guv. The side of the creek opposite where we were today is all boggy, and there's no housing there only a bunch of water birds, swans, mallards, geese, and so on. There're no people, it's too soft underfoot. On the side we we're on it's different; the ground is a few feet above the water level and quite dry once you get away from the bank. The land, all the way from the estuary to the first bridge in fact, is covered with bungalows.'

'I saw that, how many of them did you get to call on?'

'Every one between the creek and the main road. None of the dozens of people I spoke to had any information of interest, bar two women who I met on the road just as I was finishing off. They'd been out for an early morning jog on the day of the murder.'

As he spoke he went pick up the teapot from the draining board with the intention of topping up their cups but Reynard was impatient. 'Forget that for a minute, what did they say? Did they see anything or what?'

The D.C. took his time; he'd been waiting for this moment since his boss arrived. 'Well ...' he started, but just as quickly stopped again when he saw there was almost no milk in the jug.

'Just a tic Guv, there's a bottle on the front step.'

Reynard was going frantic. 'Stuff the bloody milk constable. Tell me what they said.'

'Well they didn't see anything actually happen.'

'Tell me what they damned-well *said*, man.' Reynard shouted, as he pounded the table with his fist.

'They said, as they left the river bank to go home, a man drove along the footpath on a motor bike - a small motor bike. I think you know about it. It was a Honda one of the women reckoned. It was like her son's.'

'Ah, the motor bike, yes, someone in Forensics was talking about tyre tracks yesterday ... and the man?'

'It was half seven in the morning, barely light, but they were sure he had black leathers on and was wearing a black helmet with the visor down, everything squeaky clean and looking as though it was brand new.'

'Now we're getting somewhere.'

'... and I checked the tyres on this year's edition of several different models of Hondas at a dealer in the town and took a print of each type on a piece of card. The one from this year's 50cc Honda is the same as the one on the photo of the cast taken by our boys when they were at the crime scene.'

Reynard's displeasure at having been strung along by the young constable showed. 'You saved the best 'til last, didn't you? It should have been first, this isn't a pantomime. You're a bright young man Best, but don't ever try pulling a trick like that on me again, this isn't a drama school.'

'I'm sorry Sir, it was stupid. But I was so excited when I compared the prints and realised what I'd found, I suppose I wanted to impress you. I hadn't planned to dramatize it - it just came out like that. I apologise, Sir, it won't happen again.'

'It had better not.' replied Reynard, cooling down when he heard the contrite response and almost smiling by the time he said, 'It's not a bloody game you know.'

By then it was getting on for six and he knew he had to be off. As he left, he instructed Best to go back and look for the weapon again. 'Get yourself a pair of rubber boots and check the boggy side of the river; he could have thrown it over. When you've done that go back round all the bungalows on the routes the motorcyclist might have taken to get where he was when those women saw him. See if anyone can think of a local man, a hefty guy probably, who matches the description of the fella who did the bike hiring and, if they can, see if they can provide you with a bit more detail. Ring me when you're done.'

'Will do Sir,' said Best, going back into the house to prepare a meal for himself and Algy.

St Anne's House,
Horsham Common, Sussex.
Monday 13th November 2006. 7.15 p.m.

Mungo was on the point of putting his key into the front door lock when D.C.I. Reynard drove in through the gate. The car was unmarked and he couldn't see who the driver was until he got out. 'Ah, it's you Inspector, you're a late caller, 'I'm hardly back myself. I presume it's me you've come to see?'

'Yes it is, if you can spare a few minutes.' Reynard replied.

'Certainly I can.' said Mungo, opening the door and ushering Reynard into the hall. 'Just wait here a minute will you? I'll tell my aunts I'm back, and then we can go to my study.'

When he opened their sitting room door Reynard could see the backs of the heads of two of the old ladies, the third was out of sight. Mungo told them he was home, and had Inspector Reynard with him.

'I hope you won't be too long,' one of the women said, 'Rose's just gone down to the kitchen. We'll be eating soon.'

'Go ahead without me. I'll get mine later.' Mungo replied, as he came out to conduct Reynard upstairs to the study. 'Whisky?' he asked, as they went into the oak panelled room.

'Not for me thanks.' answered Reynard, 'but have one yourself, don't mind me.'

'I will, but take a seat and tell me what I can do for you. Have you any progress to report?'

'Well … not much. I'm actually here to ask a few more questions, a few loose ends to be tied up … know what I mean?'

'No I don't know what you mean.' said Mungo, with a hint of impatience. 'What questions?'

'Well, we understand you and your brothers and cousins

have all been benefiting under your grandfather's will. Is that right?'

'Yes, we all share the annual dividend from a trust he set up for us. It's not a lot, five thousand a year between five of us - three of us now I suppose - with Dudley and Boris out of it.'

'It's not the sharing of the dividend which troubles me Sir; it's what happens to the principal on the deaths of the beneficiaries.'

'The principal remains intact until the penultimate death Inspector. After it the trust is wound up and residual value goes to the last survivor.'

'Just what I thought. And what do you think the value would be at the moment?'

'The value would be, give or take a few hundred, one hundred thousand pounds after expenses.'

'Again … what I reckoned - it's been delivering a fixed five per cent return hasn't it? That's a lot of money, Sir.'

'It is Inspector … but not enough to kill for; it's not enough for that surely?'

Reynard nodded. 'I'm afraid it is. 'I've come across plenty of people who've killed for well under a hundred thousand pounds; it depends on how desperate they are.'

'By people, I suppose you mean Jarrold and Justin. I know I told you they were being difficult, and I'll go further - they need cash so badly they're currently scheming to force the sale of the company to get it - but it's a long way from committing murder Inspector, and I just don't believe they, or anyone else in the family, would contemplate so heinous an act, let alone commit it. You must look elsewhere.'

'Well if money is not a motive, what is? We can't seem to get a line on any other thing which suggests motive, unless it's vengeance. Can you think of anyone who might have a serious grudge against your family?'

Mungo shook his head. 'No I can't … I've racked my brains and I can't.'

Reynard pinched his nose thoughtfully, got up from his chair and started to pace about the room. 'The trouble is Mr Melchitt … where will it stop?'

'Where indeed? Am I going to be the next, or one of my aunts? God forbid anyone would harm them … I can't imagine they'd have an enemy in the world.'

'But they're all well off aren't they?'

'In their shareholdings, yes, but they've no cash to speak of; not that they need any, I pay for everything.'

'And those shares will go to you one day I dare say. It'll make you a very rich man.'

Mungo swirled the last of the whisky round in his glass before taking it down in one noisy gulp and placing the empty glass in the exact centre of the occasional table beside him with exaggerated precision. 'I ought to be offended at the way you seem to be driving this conversation Inspector, but I'm trying not to be. The idea of my killing off the other members of the family one by one, in order to inherit their wealth, is so ludicrous I'm tempted to laugh. I didn't kill any one, get that straight. And you can forget any sort of family involvement as well, it just won't wash.'

'I'm sorry Sir; I have to ask the questions.' Reynard replied, getting to his feet.

'Do you?' asked Mungo, pointedly unconvinced by the inspector's apology. 'Then you shouldn't be wasting your time going down blind alleys.'

Reynard didn't like that; he shrugged his shoulders and made for the door. 'I'll be getting along then,' he said, 'I'm going to Richmond tomorrow. I'll give you a call when I get back.'

Mungo nodded but he was stern faced and, as they walked to the door, the frostiness was glaringly evident. When they parted they didn't shake hands.

Richmond Police Station
Tuesday 14th November 2006. 3.00 p.m.

Richmond Police Station
Tuesday 14th November 2006. 3.00 p.m.

D.I. Sherman, watching from his window, saw D.C.I. Reynard arrive, park his car and walk into the building. 'Bang on time … great.' he muttered, pulling on his jacket which, until then, had been draped cross the back of his chair, straightening his tie, and going back to sit at his desk in readiness for his visitor.

He'd spent most of the morning getting his notes in order. With the two most recent deaths having taken place down in Sussex, and only Superintendent Melchitt's on his patch, he was already sensing a shift in the centre of gravity. In addition, with such a long standing personal friendship between Commander Bill Simpson the boss of CID Coordination, and Mungo Melchitt the head of the family of all three deceased men, it was obvious the control of the combined operation to track down the killers was shifting southwards into Reynard's area of responsibility. Sherman's last chance to play an equal role and not slide into the position of second fiddle would be to secure a conviction, or a significant break-through, without delay. Superintendent Dudley Melchitt's killer had to be found - and pronto!

Reynard, on the other hand, with plenty of time on the long drive up to Richmond to think about the two cases which were *his* principal responsibility, the deaths of Jonathan and Boris Melchitt, was also concerned about something else …pride.

With two of the killings in his brief he had twice the opportunity to grasp the initiative in a case which could one day be legendry in the annals of detection, but he also had double the chance of making an embarrassing cock-up. Whatever about those conflicting considerations he had to keep one step in front of Sherman, or risk yielding pride of place.

Driven by such a competitive frame of mind, both men had not only sharpened their own determination but made damned sure their teams were clear as to the fate awaiting them should they not secure the first conviction.

When Reynard entered Sherman's office, they both deliberately tried to put these thoughts to the back of their minds. Even so, as they advanced towards each other to shake hands, an outsider might have thought they did so more like boxers on the point off battle than police officers cooperating together on a case of triple homicide.

'So, Ronnie ... anything new?' asked D.C.I. Reynard, taking the chair which Sherman had placed for him and dropping his document case onto his knees.

'There is as it happens - something new cropped up this morning - though whether it'll be of any real importance I'm not sure. Bellamy's out hunting up the details now ... he'll be back later and we'll know then.'

'Some new forensic? ... A witness?'

'Possibly a witness - not of the incident - but of one of the men involved.'

'The man on the bank? Don't say it's someone who's going to confirm it was Rex Brett after all.'

'Leave it out, Foxy, it *wasn't* Rex Brett, I knew it the minute I saw him, I just got it wrong, you needn't rub it in. No, this opens up a new line altogether. It might refer to either of the men in the photograph, and it might refer to neither of them, that's what Bellamy's gone to find out. It all started when I got a slot in the briefing session which 'Uniform' hold at the start of each shift. I was asking everyone present to think back again to the day of the Super's murder and to try to remember any little thing out of the ordinary which happened. They all shook their heads and I thought it was the end of it but half an hour later a young copper came knocking on my door.'

'He'd seen something, had he?' asked Foxy, sitting forward in anticipation.

'Not him - a local farmer ... well, not so local actually, a chap from about four miles out of town. He'd been in about a fortnight ago to report a man who'd damaged some milk churns of his, six weeks back. It seems the guy who did it drove off promising to send a cheque to cover the damage but it never arrived and the farmer's asked us to get him his money.'

'Some chance!'

'Exactly. Anyway this young copper had been on the desk and he'd taken down the details. When I'd asked them all to think back, he'd remembered the guy coming in and went to check the date he'd logged the complaint, hoping he'd also written down the day on which the actual incident had occurred.'

'And it turned out to be the day of Dudley Melchitt's murder.'

'It did, and the timing's right too. Now … the business with the churns might have nothing whatever to do with the murder but, in the note our laddie logged, he mentions the farmer thought the car involved was silver, which just might be the break through we've been waiting, remember the photographer who took the picture also mentioned a silver car.'

'So he did.' said Reynard, bending to pull the papers from the file at his side. 'I have his statement here somewhere. Hang on a minute while I find it.'

'Don't worry I've my copy in front of me.' said Sherman. 'Listen to this, 'Statement of Mr Tony Bloxham, chef … da da da da …' here we are - 'a man scrambled over the parapet and ran across the bridge. He almost collided with my car. I jumped out to remonstrate with him but he was fifty yards away by then and getting close to a parked vehicle, a silver one, which was facing in the opposite direction, and in which he took off.'

'Yep, that's it. Maybe you're goin' to win a coconut. Let's hope it turns out to be the same car in both cases.' said Reynard, leaning back to stretch and yawn.

'Sure you don't want a break before we get down to business?' asked Sherman, noting his visitor's tiredness. 'I'd prefer to wait until Bellamy gets here if it's all the same to you. His input is important.'

'What I'd really like is a shower to wake me up. I've been up since five. Do you run to one in this nick.'

'Every 'mod con' here, Foxy. Come on I'll show you. And I'll have the coffee ready by the time you get back. Are you staying overnight?'

'I haven't decided yet. I won't either, until I see how we get on today.'

When Reynard returned to Sherman's office half an hour

later, he felt fresh as a daisy. As soon as he entered the door he smelled the coffee, and he couldn't miss the gleeful look on the faces of the two people sitting waiting for him, Sherman and Bellamy. 'So, was it the car?' he asked, already guessing the answer from their expressions.

'I think so.' answered Bellamy, rising to take Reynard's proffered hand. 'Seems this vehicle was driving away from the scene of crime so fast he missed his turn and decided to risk a quick 'U-turn' to get back to the junction he'd shot past. He misjudged the turning circle though, and his bumper clipped the leg of a stand on which there were a couple of full milk churns waiting for the creamery tanker. They came crashing down, spilling the contents. One of the churns hit the vehicle and it split down the seam. He'd have driven off if the farmer hadn't appeared just then by pure chance, on his tractor, and blocked his escape. Apologies were offered and accepted apparently, when the man offered a hundred quid in compensation. He didn't have enough cash with him, said he'd left his cheque book at home, and promised to send the money on by post the next day. The farmer took down his address, shook his hand, and the man drove off.'

'Never to be seen again ... you're all a bit naïve round here don't you think?'

'Not really, Sir.' Bellamy replied, smiling as he said it. 'Unlike you Southerners, we Northerners generally stick to our word. Farmers are always doing deals on the shake of a hand.'

Sherman, who'd said nothing up until then, grinned when he heard the sergeant answer the gentle rebuke and asked him if he'd made any progress with the car registration number, and if the farmer had recognised the man in the photograph.'

Well,' Bellamy replied, 'he didn't recognise the guy in the photograph so, bearing in mind he was close enough to the driver to give a positive identification, I think we can say the driver was not the man on the bank.'

'But he could have been the guy in the bushes couldn't he?' said Sherman, drumming his desk with his finger nails,

'Certainly.' Bellamy replied, 'I thought that too.'

'So,' said Reynard, 'back to the 'reg' number ... why didn't he write it down when he took the address?'

'He's kicking himself he didn't, but it doesn't matter much

because I had a bit of luck; his fourteen year old son was with him on the day in question, and he'd spent his time examining the car while his father and the driver were arguing. I spoke to the lad this morning.'

'And ... go on man don't spin it out.' said Sherman rising to his feet in anticipation of a major revelation. 'What did the boy say?'

'It was a silver 'Y' reg, Volvo C40, drop head.'

'And the number ... what was the bloody registration number?' Sherman almost screamed.

'The boy's forgotten it. All he could remember is it contained a double K, his initials, his name's Keith Kingsley.'

'Bloody hell. Why didn't he remember the whole effin' thing?' cried an exasperated Sherman.

Bellamy shook his head, but Reynard offered a useful observation when he said, 'It mightn't be enough to find him, Ronnie, but it'll be powerful evidence to nail him with if we ever come across him. We must be thankful for small mercies.'

It seemed an anti-climax when, a quarter of an hour later, they got down to the main business of the day, acquainting each other with progress made on all three cases and updating their files.

'I'll go first if you like.' said Reynard. 'Let you guys get your breath back.'

Sherman and Bellamy nodded and Reynard got stuck straight into it. 'Right,' he said. 'The case of Boris Melchitt ... let's start with him. Ask your questions and act as devil's advocates as we go along will you?'

They nodded again and took up their pencils.

'OK ... cause of death. The medical experts have come to the conclusion he was alive but probably unconscious when he entered the water and subsequently drowned. We're still unable to say whether he was hit, rendered unconscious and fell into the water all in one movement, or whether he'd been hit a short time earlier and then staggered a short way before toppling in.'

'Does it make a difference?' asked Bellamy.

'It might do in the hands of a clever brief. In the first instance it'd be hard to dodge a charge of murder or manslaughter, but in the second case, particularly if there was a time interval of say ten minutes or so between the blow and the fall, it might be possible to argue the two incidents were unconnected, which would make a problem for us. Anyway, though it's out of our hands, we must keep in mind the possibility we might have to face the same difficulty in the other two deaths as well: hit first ... fall later.'

'That'd be a bit of a bugger wouldn't it?' said Bellamy. 'It'd double the number of cases we have to investigate if each consists of two incidents.'

Sherman shook his head. 'We'll face it when we come to it Malc. It won't be our decision either way ... so what's next Foxy?'

'Weapon, we've found nothing. We've hunted everywhere but there wasn't a sign of anything. The 'Path' lab told me we should be looking for an iron bar or something similar - a jemmy say - or one of those hexagonal section shaped things you use to lever the nails out of a packing case.'

'Not a lump of wood which's since floated away?'

'That was my first thought but no, I'm convinced the 'Path' boys know what they're talking about.'

'Anyway, 'Motive' is next ... but we haven't progressed far with it either.'

Sherman, who'd been examining his finger nails, looked up. 'Could be something to do with the family, you said so yourself the last time we were talking.'

'True, I did, and I still think it might be, but I've not found anything worth looking into.' answered Reynard. 'Problem is, it involves two generations. I mean what other than a blood relationship might connect poor old Jonathan Melchitt, a half demented dodderer, with Mungo or Dudley, two forty odd year olds in their prime? I've written off the nephews as suspects, they never had a quarrel with either Jonathan or Dudley, only with Mungo and he's still alive. Incidentally did you find any old lags recently released who might have been looking for revenge on Dudley?'

'No, can't say we did.' Sherman replied. 'We've checked a good few mind you, and we're still looking.'

'So a family motive is still the favourite, even though there's no evidence. I'm delving as tactfully as I can, but it's like walking on glass and I've ruffled Mungo's feathers already. I didn't mean to but, as recently as last night when I saw him, he gave me a blast of the 'chilly winds'. Put me right in my place.'

Sherman was incensed. 'Well stuff him. We have to ask the questions - how else will we find out who's responsible. Doesn't he want to know?'

'He's scared he's set for the high jump, that's what I reckon's rattling him … not us.' said Bellamy.

Sherman let their thoughts take over for a while, before re-starting the conversation by asking Reynard what was next.

'A bit of evidence and a couple of possible witnesses,' Reynard replied, 'two women joggers who were out on the path which runs alongside the creek. What they told D.C. Best might tie in with the evidence relating to Jonathan's death.'

Sherman's bushy eyebrows shot up so far they almost disappeared, so vigorous was his response. 'Really!' he exclaimed, leaping to his feet 'You've got evidence connecting the two killings?'

Reynard shook his head. 'Down Fido! You're getting ahead of me. I said 'might'. What we have is a motorcyclist in each case.'

'Probably the same man.' said Sherman lowering his eyebrows again and resuming his seat.

'We have tyre tracks at Boris's murder scene, good ones; I think I've mentioned them before. But we now also have two joggers who saw a man in black leathers and wearing a black crash helmet riding what, from their description, might have been a Honda two stroke. They were only a few hundred yards away from where Boris was attacked and passed face to face.'

'Brilliant.'

'No … he had the visor down. But they were able to tell me his gear and his bike all looked new.'

'Pity about the visor.' said Bellamy.

'That's not all.' Foxy went on. 'I've bright young copper doing the leg work down there and he went one better, he trotted off to the local Honda dealer and took a print of the tyres of all the current models and, guess what, he thinks he's identified the bike, he reckons it's a crimson and cream Honda 50cc, this year's model, and only out a few months.'

Sherman started to rub his hands together. 'Any chance of tracing it … you didn't mention registration number.'

'I only got this late yesterday afternoon. My constable's going round to see the joggers again today to see if he can …'

'Jog their memories?' said Sherman, grinning hugely and slapping the table with the flat of his hand.

'You could be right … we'll know tomorrow.'

Bellamy stood up. 'I'm ready for more coffee. Who else

wants some?'

'I think we should buy Inspector Reynard a pint don't you Malc?' said Sherman.

Bellamy faked a pained expression. '*We?*'

After the pints and the pies had been consumed in the back bar of The Raby Hunt Inn, next door to the police station, they returned to the office and resumed their deliberations.

'I'll finish by telling you what we have regarding the Jonathan Melchitt case ... there's no weapon, no motive we can discover, little enough evidence, and no forensic. On top of that I'm far from sure it wasn't simply an accident.

The newest info I have concerns the man who Daisy Melchitt saw running down the garden and into the orchard. We have two witnesses, young lads who were kicking a football in the lane which runs behind the Melchitt property. They'd gone into Melchitt's paddock, to get their ball, which had bounced over the hedge and stopped beside a gold coloured Harley Davidson motor bike, tucked into the back of the hedge, out of sight of the road. As they went to pick it up a man emerged from the orchard running towards them at top speed. He was roaring and shouting as he ran and frightened the wits out of them to such an extent they leapt back over the gate and ran back home as fast as their legs could carry them.'

'Did they get a good enough view of him to recognise him if they saw him again?'

'Not really. He had a helmet on.'

'Ah, another helmeted man ... any idea who he is?' Bellamy asked.

'None whatsoever ... we'll just have to keep asking.'

Sherman, struggling to keep awake as the effect of the lunchtime beer and the stuffiness of the room began to overwhelm him, rubbed his eyes and yawned. When Bellamy saw his boss on the brink of losing the battle to keep awake, he got up and opened a window.

Reynard, also noting what was going on took a less kindly view, 'Sorry if I've been boring you, Ronnie.'

The sarcasm pained Sherman, who tried to turn the whole episode into a joke by sitting up ramrod straight and lifting his eyebrows.

But Reynard wasn't amused and showed it when, instead of laughing, he asked if they had any questions.

Sherman, anxious to appease, shook his head, and thanking Reynard for his comprehensive update asked if wanted a final word on Boris or Jonathan before he began his report on Dudley's murder.

'No I don't.' replied Reynard testily and then, like Sherman before him, immediately regretted what he'd said and stuttered. 'Er ... yes ... sure ...maybe I do, I just want to say ... in my view, we're still missing a major piece of the jigsaw ... an essential element which will probably tie the puzzles together. The trouble is, we don't know what it is, so we don't know where to look. If we don't stumble on it by pure chance now, I reckon we'll still be looking come Doomsday.'

'Maybe it's the secret society Mungo's old aunt Daisy was spoofing on about the last time we saw her.' suggested Sherman, trying to be helpful.

Reynard frowned. 'What secret society? You've never mentioned anything about a secret society to me.'

'She was rambling I expect. Violet tried to shut her up.'

Reynard looked at his watch. 'We'd better get on or we'll not be finished before the light starts to fail.'

Unable to understand what the light had to do with their discussion, Sherman carried on. 'Right, fellas, let's get on with the case of the death of Superintendent Dudley Melchitt

'OK, the cause of death has been established to be drowning as we all know. However, when I was talking to the pathologist yesterday in connection with another matter, he told me, in his opinion, the sequence of events in the Super's case was: first the attack, second the fall into the water and third the drowning as a result of being held under. Now, bearing in mind what the Brighton pathologist said, we have to think in terms of a similar situation having taken place here.'

'Of what?' asked Reynard, who had not quite followed Sherman's drift.

Bellamy provided the answer. 'It's the time gap Guv. There's a good chance that, with a sufficient interval in time between the blow to the Super's head and his actual drowning, there's a possibility there were two separate incidents. If this is the case we'll have to allow for a totally new scenario with two people involved - one who hit and ran - and one who finished the job off.'

Reynard, who'd been shaking his head in disagreement all the time Bellamy was expounding the new theory, raised his hand to get the sergeant's attention. When he didn't get it, he interjected with his own view. 'You've made an interesting interpretation of the facts, Sergeant, if I may say so, but it's a bit too fanciful for me. I'll go for your suggestion that the initial attacker 'hit and ran' leaving Boris to stagger along and fall in a few minutes later … but in Dudley's case I can't see a third party, on seeing him crawling out of the river, shoving him back and holding him under until he drowned. No, that's not a starter for me.'

'What about the guy in the bushes then?' challenged Bellamy. 'What was he up to? What makes you think it couldn't have been him who rushed in, shoved the Super under and then make a rapid exit in the silver Volvo we've been hearing about. It's possible.'

'Possible yes, just about, but I don't buy it.' said Reynard.

Sherman, listening with righteous amusement as the other two provoked each other, tapped the desk top. 'To continue gentlemen … Weapon: none found … but the pathologist gave me the benefit of his opinion on the subject too. He reckons the weapon was round, and about an inch in diameter. He discounted it being a stone or rock despite his original contention it had been. He based his view on the fact he found no stone residue in the wound. Nor did he find any wooden matter. As a result he's swinging round towards the idea the weapon was made of metal, which brings us back to the findings in Boris's case.'

'A jemmy or something similar, you mean?'

'Exactly. Now, as to motive, we have no idea at all yet, nor have we any progress to report on the only bit of forensic we found so far - the ticket. However we do have the important evidence regarding the silver car and the milk churns.'

'Remind me of what happened when you went to see Rex Brett.' said Reynard, shooting off at a tangent. 'Maybe he was driving the silver car.'

'Not a chance,' replied Sherman, 'his car's yellow. I made a right idiot of myself there. I had to bail out as quickly as I could as I've told you. No, the guy on the bank definitely wasn't him.'

'But the guy in the bushes might have been.'

'On what evidence? We couldn't make out the details on

the blob in the bush, even if it was a face.' said Sherman. 'Anyway, Rex was filming on the day concerned - I told you, and ...'

'Listen, Guv.' begged Bellamy, patiently, 'The guy walking along the bank is absolutely definitely the guy I spoke to on the front desk, not Rex Brett, or his double. I'm dead sure he's the bloke who came in on the day of the bogus car theft.

'So we can forget Rex Brett, can we?' said Reynard.

Sherman nodded, 'Apart from the niggling memory of the look on his face when he first saw the picture, yes. He knew who it was alright.'

'Why don't you go back and ask him?'

'I doubt whether I'd catch him out again Foxy, it was the surprise he got which made him nearly give himself away.'

'It must be twenty to or twenty past.' said Bellamy, looking at his watch when he realised the room had gone quiet.

Reynard and Sherman consulted their own to check if the old belief sudden silences usually occurred at twenty to or twenty past the hour, but all three showed five to four.

Fifteen minutes later they'd packed up and were shaking hands. 'See you in a month then Foxy, if not before. I'll 'phone if anything crops up.' said Sherman, shaking Reynard's hand, as Bellamy nodded his farewell.

'Fair enough.' Reynard replied, saluting them both with a wave of his forefinger.

When he'd gone, Sherman suggested to Bellamy they should go back to The Raby Hunt Inn, to discuss the day's proceedings.

'D'you reckon we're being shoved aside Guv?' asked the sergeant, when they were settled at the bar with pints of beer in front of them.

Sherman paused before answering 'Are we being elbowed out d'you mean? Yes, I reckon we are Malc, but we're not giving way are we? We ... are ... not ... effin' shifting until the Super's killer is locked up in one of our cells.'

Bellamy looked thoughtfully down into his beer, and nodded. 'Whatever you say, Guv.'

Golden Square,
London W1F 9JB
Wednesday 15th November 2006. 3.00 p.m.

Mungo had crossed from the office, to cut through the gardens and exit on the other side where he knew there was a letter box. In his hand was a plain brown stamped envelope. On the front he had printed the address in bold letters with a felt-nibbed pen,

Department of Inland Revenue
Company Taxation Division
Somerset House, Strand, London WC2 1LB

He picked up the single piece of paper and took a final glance at what he'd printed.

Melchitt Classic Cars, Crawley.
V.A.T. Returns on sales?
Mileages on cars for re-sale?

He replaced the sheet in the envelope, sealed it, and dropped it in the box. 'Now Mr Jarrold,' he said to himself, as he walked back to the office, 'see if you can talk your way out of that one. It'll keep you and Justin off my back even if you aren't on the fiddle… which I bet you are.'

'First time I've seen you looking so cheerful for a while Mr Melchitt.' said Miss Pink, when he returned.

'Well it's the first time in a while I've felt so cheerful, Miss Pink.' Mungo replied.

The Mede Manor Hotel,
Beaconsfield, Bucks.
Thursday 16th November 2006. 12.30 a.m.

Rex drove his Jaguar into the car park, still wondering if he was doing the right thing. Was he going to make the biggest mistake in his life in accusing his brother of being involved in murder? He had no proof; he didn't even have the photograph the inspector had shown him.

When he got to the hotel, he drew up at the back alongside the untrimmed privet hedge and way beyond the half dozen cars already there: Angus's Saab, Betty's Ford Fiesta, a smart suburban saloon, and two huge 'Chelsea Tractors' - housewives out for a pub lunch probably, and an hour or so of character assassination.

Hardly had he stopped and pulled on the handbrake than his nerves began to get at him. He sat back, opened the window, and forced himself to belch, hoping it would rid him of the anxiety which he could feel creeping up on him.

It didn't.

He tried again and nearly made himself sick.

All the time he was wishing he hadn't come, wishing he was anywhere but where he was.

He belched again … disgusted at his own disloyalty. How could he suspect Angus of being involved in anything as heinous as murder? And how the hell had he convinced himself he ought to tackle him about it?

A young man came out of the hotel, got into the saloon and drove off. Rex hardly noticed him as he sat, keyboarding the driving wheel with his fingertips, struggling to recover his composure and trying to decide what to do.

And then he made his mind up … he was going home. It

was nothing to do with him what Rex got up to and, whatever it was, it couldn't be murder. How could he ever have thought so? He turned on the ignition, drove out of the car park, and headed for the motorway; by the time he got to it he was smiling.

Betty wasn't smiling though, she'd seen him, and she was still wearing a puzzled look on her freshly made up face.

To be fair, she couldn't be dead sure it was Rex who'd driven in, she'd spotted the yellow Jaguar coming into the car park alright and, as the only person she knew with a yellow Jaguar was Rex, she'd assumed it was him. But, by the time she'd run upstairs to fix her face, and raced back down again to greet him, she'd been just in time to see him disappear.

'What's the matter?' Angus asked, when he saw the surprised expression on her face, but she didn't reply, because she wasn't entirely sure herself.

Rex, in the meantime, bowling back down the M40 towards London, was already beginning to have second thoughts about having run away. He should have tackled his brother head on, asked him when he'd last been in Yorkshire.

Sussex Police Major Incident Suite
Sussex House, Brighton.
Thursday 16th November 2006. 1.45 p.m.

D.C.I. Reynard had found a message waiting for him as soon as he came in. It was from D.C. Best, the young detective in Rottingdean who'd been ferreting around for anything which might impinge on the Boris Melchitt case.

Hoping he'd unearthed something of significance, Reynard ploughed his way through the paperwork on his desk, and rang the young constable.

'I've found some interesting new information about the Honda from the local franchise holder.' Best told him.

Reynard, resisting the temptation to start cross-examining on the telephone, told Best he'd meet him at his house, around twelve thirty. And as soon as he'd put the phone down, he rang the Melchitts, asking whether Violet, Rose, and Daisy, would 'give him a few minutes' if he drove over. He offered to see them all together in the hope this would fend off any resistance they might have to holding an interview in the absence of Mungo.

He arrived at St Anne's House in time for coffee and sat at the kitchen table with the three old ladies fussing around him offering biscuits and cake. They assumed he'd come to tell them of some advance in the matter of Jonathan's death.

'I'm afraid I have nothing new to tell you, ladies.' he said, 'We're making progress but it's very slow and we have to double check at every step, which is why I'm here today, as a matter of fact. We've recently interviewed two boys who were playing football in the lane running behind your paddock on the day Mr Jonathan died. They say they saw a man come running out of the orchard. I want to know if it was the same man you saw Miss Daisy.'

Daisy looked pleased to be singled out and answered him without having to think too hard. 'Well, let me see, he was a tall bulky man in a black leather jacket and he was wearing high black boots with straps down the side.'

Reynard scribbled down her answer and then asked her if she'd seen the colour of his hair or remembered any other distinguishing feature.

'Well ... er ... Mr Reynard.' she said, unsure of the correct form of address, 'I couldn't see the colour of his hair because he was wearing a big shiny helmet.'

'Pity, any chance you could guess his age?'

Daisy shook her head. 'Not really I only saw him from the back. Thirty to forty I should think not younger, he was a bit too stout.'

'That's brilliant Miss Daisy.' he said. Then, as he returned his note book to his pocket, he asked her to telephone him if she thought of anything else.

'Certainly I will ... is that all?'

'For the moment.' he replied, 'Don't bother to get up I'll let myself out.'

As he was about to leave the kitchen he turned back again. 'Oh yes, there was one more thing I've just remembered, Miss Daisy. When D.I. Sherman, the policeman from Richmond, was here you told him something about a secret society but, for some reason, I never got the full story from him. Would you mind repeating to me what you said?'

'Oh, I'm not sure I can remember, Mr. Reynard, I don't know much, it's a secret Jonathan never allowed us girls into.'

'I see ... so it's a sort of male thing?'

'We don't know anything about it at all, except he used to refer to it as the LMS Club. It was all years ago when he was still a student.' said Daisy, suddenly jumping up from her chair and shooting out of the room.

'It'll be defunct by now, I expect.' said Violet.

Rose obviously agreed. 'Yes, yes, yes.' she said.

Just before Reynard departed Daisy re-joined them; in her hand was a photo of the LMS club. 'Here they are,' she said, 'Jonathan and his friends; this is the secret society I told you about.'

'Ah.' replied Reynard, politely reaching to take it.

Violet snatched the photograph before he had it though,

and she gave her sister a disapproving look, 'The Inspector doesn't want to be bothered with that nonsense Daisy,' she said, as she ushered Reynard out into the hall.

When he left them, they were crowded in the front doorway waving; visitors to St Anne's House never saw themselves out.

Rottingdean was a good hour away, and Reynard was hard put to get there by one let alone twelve thirty.

Best was at his front door waiting. In the kitchen the sandwiches were ready and the kettle was on the boil. 'So what've you got for me?' asked Reynard, as they walked through.

'The guy in the local Honda dealer's I spoke to you about previously rang me up yesterday afternoon, Sir. Obviously he'd been thinking of our earlier conversation.'

'And what did he have to say?'

'He thinks there might be some significance to the fact the joggers both remarked on how the bike, the leathers, and the helmet, all looked new.'

'Yes, they did, so what did he deduce from that?'

'Well they could've been newly purchased of course, but he thought it just as likely they'd been hired.'

'Well, well, well.'

'So I've been making out a list of firms within a twenty five mile radius who are in that sort of business.'

'Any luck?'

'I haven't contacted any of them yet - I thought I'd better run it by you first.'

'Well done, another feather in your cap, we'll make a real detective of you yet. Start ringing them the minute I've gone.'

Best gave his boss an enthusiastic grin. 'I'll get straight down to it once you've left, Sir, but I'd like to take you back up to the scene of crime first, if you've time, I think I've found something up there as well.'

'Pour me some tea, I'm dying for a cup … and what's your first name?'

'It's Norman, Sir. But everyone calls me 'Next' … you know - 'Next' Best - I've been 'Next' since I was at school.'

'Ah, I see, yes …right … I think I'll stick to Norman.'

Best laughed. 'That'll be you and my Mum then, no one else calls me Norman.'

After they'd had their snack lunch they both got into Reynard's car and went back to the crime scene, still cordoned off, and still guarded by a uniformed officer.

'OK, Norman. What have you got to show me?'

Best conducted the inspector over to where the tyre marks had been found, and then walked on a few yards to a bush at the side of the track. Behind it the grass was still showing signs of having been trampled down, and stamped into the clay were two cigarette ends. 'What d'you think Sir?'

Reynard stooped, levered one of them out with his ball point pen and dropped it into a polythene sachet. 'I think, Norman, the famous 'Scene of Crime' team have something to answer for. Well done again.'

Before driving back Foxy rang his wife, Cathy. He'd had a good day and he'd come to a decision so momentous she didn't believe it when she heard it, a night out at The Pavilion Theatre, assuming there were any tickets available.

'Oh, lovely.' she'd replied, deciding not to remind him she'd been suggesting the very same outing for weeks.

The Mede Manor Hotel, Beaconsfield, Bucks. Thursday 16th November 1.50 p.m.

Rex was back in the hotel car park again. As he'd got closer to London he'd become more and more ashamed at his own cowardice. Eventually, as he'd been about to leave the motorway, he'd convinced himself he ought to go back and do what he'd intended from the start, tell Angus he knew he'd been at the scene of a murder and see what response he got.

The same cars were still in the car park when he got back; obviously the ladies were having a long session. He parked alongside one of the 'Chelsea Tractors', a Shogun, which made his Jaguar seem minute by comparison.

As soon as he entered the bar he spotted Angus, he was in a corner snug, reading a newspaper. Before him was a cup of coffee. In another corner grouped around two tables which had been pushed together, were six or seven women. They were all talking at once. There was no sign of Betty.

He went over to Angus who rose and thrust out his hand. 'What a surprise, are you filming again? Do you need the rooms?'

'No, we're not shooting this week we changing location … I've come to see *you*.'

'*Me*? That's a surprise. It's sunk in has it?'

'Sunk in?'

Angus, walked over to the bar carrying his empty cup and saucer. 'Yes, sunk in … the fact I didn't do any better than you did when Dad left me this place.'

'Oh I'm not worried about that anymore.' Rex said, 'From what I gathered the last time I was here you got a bummer same as I did.'

'Worse.'

'What d'you mean worse?'

'Well, your shares plummeted, but they still had a value of some sort; this place was in debt when I got it. You wound up with 'penny' shares but I got a bucketful of mind boggling debt, this place isn't worth a jot and we could lose our home.'

What Angus said, and the vehemence with which he'd said it, stunned Rex, and he stood in silent thought as the implications sank in. It seemed to be a much poorer scene than the one Betty had outlined and it didn't look as though they'd much chance of getting their heads above water without an injection of cash. He was no accountant, but even he could see that. As he pondered on what Angus had said, he forgot about the racket the women were making. When he finally came back to earth, he pointed to the spirits dispenser. 'What'll you have?'

'Nothing for me thanks, Rex. I've stopped drinking to help Betty, she's packed it in. Have whatever you want ... go on ... take your pick.'

'So there is *some* good news.' said Rex, giving his brother a 'thumbs up' sign then moving behind the bar and pushing a glass up to the Bell's whisky optic. 'I was afraid she might have lost the battle ... I was wrong.'

Angus smiled. 'It's what I was worried about too, but she's really trying her best. She's cottoned onto herself at last and ... so far so good. It all started getting better after you were last here, maybe you triggered it.'

'I doubt it.' replied Rex, taking the top off a split of soda water. 'Hey, d'you remember how we used to pinch drinks down here when we were kids?'

'Not half. And I remember the belting Dad gave us if he caught us. I've still got the marks!'

Rex glanced across at the women who, having recognised him when he came in, and spent a good five minutes nudging each other, were by then back up at full volume. 'Regulars are they?' he asked.

'Too regular. Bloody nuisance really, they come here twice a week at one o'clock. They order three plain cheese sandwiches between the six of them, stay two hours, and drink one bottle of 'house white'.'

'You wouldn't make much out of them, then.'

'It doesn't cover the cost of washing the glasses. I'd get rid of them entirely but for the fact that without them the place would be completely empty and what casual caller would stay in a place to be on their own.'

'Don't you get anyone else in at all?'

'Only in the evenings, and at weekends if there's a rugby match. The bar in the local club was damaged by fire a couple of months ago and I let 'em use this place while it's being repaired.'

'But that's only one day a week. How do you survive for the rest of the time?'

'We don't.'

'Jesus, I didn't think it was so bad. Does Betty realise how dodgy things really are?'

'Well I've told her often enough, but she puts up a protective mental barrier which filters out all the bad news. I don't think the true situation's registered at all. Anyway I'm not going to worry whether she understands or not if it helps her get off the drink, I've more than enough to be concerned about with the business; in fact I'm desperate. I've got to get money from somewhere, I've got to - I'd kill for fifty grand!'

'Jesus, don't say that.' replied Rex, moving back behind the bar again to stiffen his resolve, having finally remembered why he'd gone there. Anyway … how much is a double these days?'

'Oh shut up, his brother replied. 'Have a treble if you want … 'on the house' as Dad used to say.'

'Aye, and a pity he did … if the customers had paid for their own drinks you wouldn't be in this mess. Who ever heard of a publican losing money?'

'I did.' said Angus with a wry smile. 'Me … I'm losing my flippin' skin.'

Rex splashed some soda water into the double measure he'd drawn for himself and Angus made himself another cup of coffee. With their drinks in their hands they moved back to the sunny corner they'd started in.

Before Rex got a chance to edge towards the question he'd come to pose though, Angus put one to him: 'So what brings you here today if you're not filming?'

Rex didn't say anything, he was afraid to ask Angus about Richmond, worried he'd be putting at risk the rediscovered friendly attitude, while Angus, mistakenly sensing embarrassment in Rex's silence, tried his best to encourage him. 'Come on chum … spit it out ... I've opened up to you haven't I?'

Still Rex held back.

'Oh, for Christ's sake Rex, what is it?'

Rex looked him straight in the eye. 'Have you been up in Yorkshire recently ... Richmond for instance?'

For a moment there was dead silence ... and then Angus spluttered out his answer. 'What on earth has Richmond got to do with what we're facing?'

'Have you been there?'

'No I haven't. What sort of bloody question is that? What are you on about - Richmond - which one?'

'I'm talking about the Richmond in Yorkshire ... Have you been there recently Angus?'

'You're off your chump mate ... I've told you I've never been there ...well, not in years ... why?'

'Because the police have been questioning me about a murder which took place in Richmond a few weeks ago, they have a photograph taken at the scene a few moments before the killing took place. You're in it!'

'Now I know you're mad. You come down here with all this friendly brother malarkey and all the time you're trying to trap me in to saying I was somewhere I wasn't. What the hell are you up to?'

'I'm not up to anything Angus. I'm trying to find out why the police have a picture which looks so like you it has to be you, walking along a river bank where, they told me, a man was attacked and bludgeoned before he fell in the river and drowned. If it's not you on the photo you've nothing to worry about but ... ah hell! ...' For a moment he was lost for word then, drawing a deep breath, he went on, 'Look here Angus ... I won't lie to you ... I came specifically to ask you if you'd been in Richmond ... I admit it. In fact I came earlier on today, but I lost my nerve and drove off.'

'Was it you Betty saw?'

'Probably, I was here for the first time just before half twelve. But listen, if the man in the photo isn't you, and I believe you when you say it isn't, then why don't you go to the police before they come looking for you. That way they'll see how wrong they've got it.'

'Stuff the police, it wasn't me. They can't do anything. Who got themselves killed anyway?'

'Well there's another funny thing, it was a guy called

Melchitt. Dad knew a man of the same name I'm sure, he's one of the guys in that photograph of him and his pals which always hung in the office.

'It still does. But I don't remember anything about them, or if any of them are called Melchitt, and I haven't been in Yorkshire since I was in the corps at school. I went up there then - once - to the army camp at Catterick. If the picture was taken up there it's someone else, not me. Anyway ... I'd better get on if you've nothing more sensible to talk about.'

Rex wished he hadn't gone back, and rose with his hand held out in an attempt to heal the breach. But, when Angus ignored the gesture and angrily turned away, he let his hand fall to his side and walked out to his car.

As he drove back to London he was seriously troubled, Angus might have denied it was him in the picture but ... deep down ... Rex knew he was lying.

Sussex Police Major Incident Suite
Sussex House, Brighton.
Friday 17th November 2006. 7.30 a.m.

T hat you Ronnie? … It's Foxy.'

D.C.I. Reynard had been 'in' since seven, the best time of the day to get things done without interruption. He knew Sherman held similar views and chanced he'd be in his office too. It was a short conversation but one long enough to give each of them the opportunity to inform the other of the results of work undertaken since their meeting earlier in the week. In the course of it, he told Sherman he'd got DNA from a cigarette end found close to where Boris had been assaulted, and it would be held as possible additional proof of the nearby presence of any suspect they picked up.

'Good, it'll be the same as the double K number plate being useful to confirm the presence of a suspect brought in in connection with Dudley's killing.' said Sherman. 'And, by the way, I've heard from London transport again. They've confirmed what they told me before, about the ticket coming from dispensing machine at Monument station. Now they've gone further, it was scanned through an exit machine at Victoria Station, at three thirty five pm, two days before Dudley was killed. Victoria is the main line terminus for trains serving towns in the south including Horsham, I believe.'

'That might be useful, Horsham is Melchitt country. Yes… it's a bit tenuous Ronnie, but all these little things add up eventually. By the way, I collected a couple of useful bits of information myself yesterday, the Honda motor bike, a 50cc model we think, used by Boris's attacker might have been hired complete with all the gear. I've man working on it as we speak. And you'll be pleased to hear I also saw Daisy Melchitt yesterday on a trumped up excuse which I hope has put her off the scent.'

'Oh, yes. What about?'

'Your secret society.'

'Daisy's you mean. And did you get anything?'

'I did, I got the name. It's called The LMS Club. Jonathan joined it when he was a student fifty years ago. I can't imagine it has any relevance now.'

'Did Daisy tell you what sort of club it was?'

'She said it was 'drinking'. Violet and Rose agreed.'

'LMS ... hmm. I wonder what the initials stand for?'

'I've looked them up on Google. Quite a few societies with the right initials came up but none of them seem relevant to me, want to hear them?'

'Yeah, read them out.' said Sherman

'OK, there were six societies, here they are: the Latin Mass Society, the Life Modelling Society, the London Mathematical Society, the Leongatha Medieval Society, the Live Musical Society, and the Liverpool Malaysian Society. There was only one club, the LMS Railway Club.'

'Can't see any connection there except the last one and it's only of use to us if they shortened the title by dropping the word 'Railway'. The LMS was the old London Midland and Scottish railway wasn't it? Maybe they're all train spotters.'

'Can you see Mungo Melchitt standing on a railway bridge, in rain, watching for a train to go by ... I can't.'

'Ask him.'

'Don't worry I will.'

'Is that it then?'

'For now ... have you got anything else?'

'No, but I'm driving down to tackle Rex Brett again soon, maybe this week, why don't you come?'

'OK, I will if I'm free. I'll ring you tomorrow.'

The Mede Manor Hotel,
Beaconsfield, Bucks.
Saturday 18th November 2006. 11.00 a.m.

Sophie had flown in the previous day and stayed overnight at The Holiday Inn, Gatwick, as before. Eddie had collected her after breakfast and they'd driven to Beaconsfield, it had taken two hours. Once there they found they had to wait, for it would be another hour before the hotel opened, according to a man who was taking a short cut through the car park to a gate into his back garden pushing a wheelbarrow.

'You'll not get in before twelve thirty.' he said. 'You could in the old days, when they were busier. But now, with all the bar trade lost to The Jolly Farmer and The Roebuck, and the B&B business to The Motor Inn, they don't open before twelve thirty. 'Do y'know what,' he added, shaking his head, 'I often wonder whether it's worth his while opening at all.'

'He must be well past it anyway?' Eddie replied.

'Right ... right ... yes, I suppose.' replied the man, vaguely, seeming not to have understood what Eddie had said.

'Sorry mate, it was meant to be a joke.' Eddie replied, 'But to spend hours getting here from Gatwick and then find it's shut ... well ... it's frustrating.'

'Have you tried banging on the door? He's there, that's his car, the Saab. He could be in the cellar. She'll be 'lying down' I expect, she does a lot of that.'

'She's not well?'

'Betty? No, she's not. She spends half her time getting sozzled and half getting sober. Poor Angus has a hard time.'

'Angus?' said Eddie. 'But, isn't his name Rory?'

'No, Rory was Angus's father - 'Ginger' they used to call him. Yes, old Ginger's real name was Rory, he died ages ago. He'd never have let the place fall apart like this.'

'Who's Betty then?'

'Betty's Angus's wife.'

'Oh, I see and is Rory's, I mean Ginger's, wife alive?'

'Greta … no … she went off with an Italian count thirty years ago when Angus and Rex were kids. There's just Angus and Betty now. You know about his brother, Rex, I suppose?'

'The film star? Yes, what about him?'

'Nothing. Just he's Angus's brother that's all. He never shows his face around here these days. I used to go to school with him, but he wouldn't give me the time of day now … Here look, I must be off, hope you can raise them. Go and give the side door another good thumping … it might wake 'em up.'

As the man continued across the car park, Sophie walked over to the door he'd pointed out and tapped repeatedly on it with her key ring. For a long while nothing happened, and then she heard a man's voice calling, 'I'm coming, I'm coming.' She turned and beckoned to Eddie who was still thinking about the information they'd just been given, especially of the news that since Ginger's death the hotel had been steadily failing.

When the door finally opened they were confronted by a tall man in shirt sleeves, who they assumed to be Angus. 'What the hell do you want?' he asked, 'We're not open yet.'

'Sorry to disturb you Mr Brett, but we've driven all the way up from Gatwick to see you and when we found you closed we didn't know what to do. A man walking through the car park suggested we knock on this door.'

'Knock on it, yes, not wreck the bloody thing. What do you want anyway?'

'We want to know if you can spare a few minutes to tell us something of your father.'

'Are you joking? My father? He's dead - died a long time ago - what's it all about? … Ah, you'd better come in I suppose, I think I've left a tap running in the bar.'

As they made their way down the semi dark corridor, they were hard put to see where they were going but eventually they came into a large square atrium style hallway with a glazed roof. Off it were several doors, two of them led to toilets, others to the bars, the dining room, the office and, presumably, the Brett's private quarters. Each had an identifying brass plate on it.

The minute they entered the Sportsman's Bar they spotted the woman. She was standing at the counter facing them, pouring coffee into a cup from a glass jug, and blinking as the smoke from a cigarette clamped between her teeth curled up into her eyes.

'Turn the tap off would you Betty.' Angus said, quickly twisting round again and whisking them back through the hall into the Saloon Bar, 'We'll leave her to get on with it,' he added, without explaining what he meant ... but they guessed after what they'd been told by the man in the car park.

As they entered the bar, Angus indicated a bench seat in the window. 'I'll give you five minutes and then I have to open up, after that there'll be no time to talk to you ... we're on our own and Betty and I will both be busy ... now what is it?'

'I'll keep it as brief as I can Mr Brett. I'm the daughter of a man called Henry Byrd, Eddie is his son ... we have different mothers as you can see.' she said, placing her hand on Eddie's to let the different colours of their skin demonstrate the point. 'Years ago, when our father was a student, he and a group of friends were members of a club called the LMS Club. We think your father was a member as well.'

'Was he? He died a good while back now. I don't know much of his early life, and I've never heard of this ... this club. In fact I'd almost forgotten he was once a student.'

'What about our father then: Henry Byrd ... he was known as 'Dicky'. Did he ever mention him?' she asked.

'Not to my recollection.'

'Or Ghandi Melchitt, or Jock McPhee, or Frog La Tour. Ever hear of any of them?'

'No, who're they?'

'Well, we think they were all members of this LMS thing as well but if you've never heard of them ... '

'What's it all about?'

Eddie was about to answer but seemed to change his mind and sat back, leaving Sophie to do it. 'We've never met our father, Mr Brett.' she continued, 'He abandoned both our mothers as soon as he knew they were pregnant.'

'Ah.' said Angus. 'I see.'

'As a matter of fact,' Sophie went on, 'Eddie and I have only become aware of each other's existence quite recently, and we're trying to find out as much as we can about this man who's been influencing our lives since we were born.'

'Why don't you ask him?'

'Because,' she said, 'he lives in Mexico, and only comes back to Britain occasionally.'

Angus began to grin. 'I get it … and you're going to nail him next time he comes, right? Can't say I blame you, but I can't do much to help either.'

'Yes, so it seems … more's the pity … but remember, we thought we'd be talking to your father.'

'Well, you're out of luck,' said Angus, 'by quite a long time … maybe he'd have been able help you, but not me … I can't.'

Sophie nodded.

'You mentioned someone called Melchitt?'

'Jonathan Melchitt,' said Eddie, 'they knew him as Ghandi. He died three days before we got to him.'

In the background Betty's step could be heard, followed shortly by sound of her voice. 'Angus, are you ready? I'm going to open up.'

'Coming.' he shouted back, and rose from his seat. 'I have to go.' he said, 'Can you find your own way out?'

'No problem.' Sophie replied, 'Pity you knew nothing.'

When they got to the hall Rex went through to the Sportsman's bar but Eddie, pointing to the door marked 'Gentlemen', said to Sophie: 'Go on, I'll catch you up.'

'No, I'll wait here.' she replied, looking at the labels on the other doors: 'Ladies', 'Sportsman's Bar', 'Saloon Bar', 'Private', 'Office'. All of them, except the one marked 'Office', were shut, but *it* was standing invitingly open.

She couldn't resist the temptation and gingerly stepped in. It was a tiny room and almost totally dark inside apart from a narrow shaft of sunlight which was leaking past her from the hall. Opposite she could make out a desk with a chair behind it. Hanging on the wall, behind the desk, and spotlighted by the beam of sunshine, was the photograph she knew so well.

She stepped across to get a closer look. 'Hmm' she said to herself, '… and he says he's never heard of them!'

Approaching Beaconsfield, on the A 355. Wednesday 22nd November 2006. 11.30 p.m.

Sandy McPhee was in the saddle again and, having passed through Slough, was entering Beaconsfield. The road, wet after the evening's rain, was slippery under a covering of leaves and he had to motor carefully until the town's lights came in sight. He'd hired the bike the day before in Banstead, more awkward to get at this time, but far enough away from Redhill and East Croydon, where he'd hired previously, for anyone to spot a connection. He'd spent the late afternoon disguising the number plates and generally getting ready.

The early part of the day had seen him in the office, writing greetings inside Christmas cards which, with the books, would be posted to the company's most valuable clients. He was delighted with the change, and had already convinced himself it had been his idea when he discovered a book cost less than a bottle of whisky, and the delivery charge was half as much. Whether the clients would react to the financial fiction of their annual reports as well as he hoped they'd be responding to the literary fiction of the novels, he was less sure. To be lost in a gripping story written by a well-known author and dedicated to them personally was one thing. To be bamboozled by the stock exchange jargon he'd employed to disguise the dodgy arithmetic in the report was another. In fact, most of his clients probably didn't read their reports with any understanding, and he'd have every chance of getting away with it for a few more months if only he could get his hands on a hundred thousand pounds.

The Honda's engine gave out no more than a whisper as he motored into the deserted car park and left it out of sight behind

Betty's Fiesta. Not much chance anyone would be looking out, Betty would be in bed, passed out probably, Angus would be clearing up … going through what had become his regular routine of 'washing up and putting away' before taking the rubbish out to the refuse bins, and then following her upstairs. With no staff to help him since he'd paid off the last cleaner a week earlier, it would be around half past midnight before he'd get to bed himself.

Sandy knew all this from recent clandestine visits he'd made. In consequence, he got quite a shock when he realised there were still two shadowy figures evident in the lights of the bar, obviously they must have had a rare late night function of some sort and were still finishing off.

Spotting a row of beer casks below the window he climbed up on one of them and, peering through the partially frosted glass, was just able to make out Betty as she replaced glasses in the racks over the bar. Angus was vacuuming and straightening the tables and chairs. Obviously they were nearly done. Soon she'd be off to bed, and he'd be on his way out with the refuse.

He stepped to the ground, flattened himself to the wall beside the door, tightened his grip on the foot long stonemason's chisel he was holding in his right hand, and prayed it would be Angus and not Betty, who'd be bringing out the rubbish.

When the door opened at last, and he sensed someone was about to come out, he lunged forward and brought the chisel down with all the force he could muster. It was Angus, and he dropped like a stone into a dozen empty bottles lined up on the step.

Betty heard the crash and rushed out to investigate. Sandy got such a surprise when she appeared - he hit her too.

He didn't hang around after that, but raced back to the motor bike as fast as his legs would carry him, leapt into the saddle, and roared out of the car park.

12, Whitby Street, Scarborough, Tobago.
Thursday 23rd November 2006. 5.30 a.m.

Sophie glanced at her watch, turned over, pulled the cotton sheet and the single blanket over her head, and tried to get back to sleep. After returning from Gatwick late the previous night she needed more than four hours to combat the tiredness and the jet lag. How frustrating then to find she was still wide awake and ready for a new day when it was only half past five in the morning, local time. Two more hours before the street noises were usually awakening her, pity no one had told her body! She sighed, clamped her eyes shut and tried again.

An hour later she was up. There was a tinge of orange coming into a sky which was still almost black and she sat before the open window, a mug of hot milk in her hand, watching the dawning day.

How strange these trips to London were turning out to be. She'd been partially prepared for England in advance of them by the visual impact of television programmes of course, but she was also beginning to discover a puzzling feeling of familiarity too ... even with people she'd never met before.

Was this the English half of her responding to unseen resonances? She couldn't fathom it out.

Sitting in the semi dark she allowed her mind to roam back over what she'd seen and the people she'd met. Most of all she thought about her newly found half-brother Eddie. Finding him, let alone discovering he was as keen as she was to dig out everything he could about their father, had been an amazing bonus.

She'd started off with anger in her heart but already it had been partially replaced by a wider curiosity. She was beyond just wanting to find out why her father had abandoned her mother so she could somehow punish him, she wanted to know everything about him … but she was still a long way from doing it.

Recalling her recent visits to England prompted her to think of the original residents of Whitby Street who might have sat at this same window thinking of the family they'd left behind, wondering if they'd ever see them again.

'Whitby', obviously chosen by the first settlers to remind them of home, brought her to wonder about her other half, the half which was not from an old English fishing port but from some remote riverside village in one of the great rain forests of West Africa. Did her relatives from there pine for home and family too? They must have done. But where her English settler ancestors had some prospect of returning to their families one day, her African forebears had none.

The sun was up by then, and her untouched cup of milk was cold. She yawned and glanced at her watch again. Still only six o'clock. Carefully balancing the mug on the window sill she climbed back into bed and, surprisingly, went straight to sleep.

When she awoke it was midday.

Just for the hell of it she rang Eddie.

'Guess who?' she said.

'No idea.'

'I can hear a steel drum band outside.'

'Bloody hell! … Sophie!'

She thought it was nice having a brother … in a couple of weeks she'd be seeing him again … What would come next?

The Malthouse, Point's Hill, Lewes.
Thursday 23rd November 2006. 5.30 a.m.

S andy was home again, and utterly exhausted. His physical tiredness combined with the stress of the previous hours had numbed him and, in consequence, the journey back had left little print on his memory. He didn't know how he'd found his way back to Banstead to return the motor bike and leathers, or how he'd driven home in his car from the car park at Lewes station afterwards. It had only been when he was climbing up the narrow stairs into the loft over the garage to hide the helmet he had any recollection of what he'd done since leaving the hotel.

But why had Betty come on the scene? She'd messed the whole thing up by appearing out of nowhere like that and now he had another death to count against him if he got caught, blasted Bretts! It had been bad enough when gone up to Richmond to research Dudley, and Angus had appeared out of nowhere; now Betty had got in the way. Lucky he'd decided to follow Angus that day in Richmond all the same, *and* realised what he was up to. God dammit, there was he, working out how to eliminate Dudley, and along comes Angus and all but does it for him! Boris was a different matter. Even so, unless the two women joggers remembered seeing him and told the police they'd done so, the coppers would have a job finding him. Dressed in black like every other motor cyclist in the country, and riding a bike which was only one of tens of thousands, it would be nigh on impossible to track him except by the registration number on the bike, and he was safe enough there with false plates stuck over the real ones.

'Anyway,' he decided, 'I think I'll leave it for a while before I tackle the next one … let things cool off a bit.'

The Metropolitan Police Station,
202-206, Buckingham Palace Road,
London. SW1W 9SX.
Thursday 23rd November 2006. 11.30 a.m.

Foxy Reynard was there first. With not much over an hour's drive as against Ronnie Sherman's four, he'd even had time to put in a couple of hours at his desk before he left and was, by then, in the canteen at the nearest police station to Rex's flat, reading the paper, a rare treat.

'Been here long?' asked D.I. Sherman, as he walked in and sat down beside him.

'Twenty minutes, it's given me a chance to catch up with the news outside the little world in which I live.'

'I'll have a quick cup of tea and a Jimmy Riddle then we can go, if you like.'

'No rush, I'm with you all day if needed.'

With their cars parked in the station compound, they walked down to Dolphin Square buoyed up with the prospect of catching Rex out by surprise, hoping to trick him into telling them why he'd been so shocked when the photograph had been produced on the previous occasion. But when they got there he was out. Virginia Meddows opened the door and, made up like the film star she was, she stopped them in their tracks.

'Oh, it's you again Inspector! He's not here ... he shot off to Beaconsfield leaving a note, that's all I know.' she said, accelerating into an over-elaboration of her own morning in which they hadn't the slightest interest. 'I've been with my trainer since ten, Rex was here when I left. He told me this morning he wasn't going out all day, that he was going to read over a new script his agent's sent him. He must have changed his mind. I've been down at the gym. I spent some time in the exercise room and then had a swim. Afterwards I went for a coffee with a girlfriend before I came home. I was hardly through the door when you rang the bell.'

'Must have been an emergency if he's gone off at such short notice.' said Reynard, fishing for information.

'Oh you don't know Rex, he's always darting here and there without telling me. Getting a note is quite unusual.'

'Any special connection with Beaconsfield has he?' asked Sherman, who was already mentally adding up the hours he'd wasted driving down, and the additional ones he'd be wasting driving back … and all his own fault, which made it even more irritating, for he'd been the one to suggest calling on Rex without giving him any notice. So busy was he in chastising himself he nearly missed her reply, 'He comes from Beaconsfield. It's where he was brought up. The family have a hotel there.'

'Do they still have it?' asked Reynard.

'Not his parents,' Ginny replied, 'his mother and father died some time ago, his brother Angus runs it now, with his wife. Rex's been seeing a bit more of them recently, though for a while they were almost out of touch. He gets very busy y'know, Rex. He has to travel a lot … America and so on … Hollywood … you know how it is?'

'We didn't realise he came from Beaconsfield, or that he had a brother.'

'There they are,' said Ginny, 'in the photo on the mantelpiece. It was taken outside the hotel the day Angus and Betty got married.'

Reynard went over and picked up the framed picture. Ginny crossed to his side and pointed out who each person was. 'That's Rex's dad, Ginger, as I said he died a while back. And that's Rex, doesn't he look young? He was best man. And Betty and Angus are between them. Angus is *so* like Rex isn't he?'

'Yes, Miss, he certainly is, are they twins?'

'No,' said Ginny, 'there's a year between them.'

'Even so …' Sherman replied, straight away seeing why Rex had paled so markedly when he'd seen the picture of the man on the bank. 'So this is where he's gone then, is it - the Mede Manor Hotel in Beaconsfield?'

'That's right, the old meany, he might have taken me, we could have had lunch out.'

'Well we won't detain you any longer Miss, you've been very helpful.' said Sherman.

'I'll tell him you called shall I, when he comes back?' asked Ginny, as she escorted them to the lift.

'If you don't mind, yes, it would be helpful. He has my card, but here's another, in case he's lost it.'

'What now?' asked Reynard, as the lift descended.

'How far's Beaconsfield?'

'Not too far to catch a killer!'

'Right we'll take our own cars and then we're independent. We'd better have some lunch back at the nick first though; we mightn't get a chance later. We'll get on our way after we've eaten, try to make Beaconsfield by three.

Right.' said Reynard, but Sherman, relishing the prospect of securing the first arrest, wasn't listening.

By the time they pulled up outside the Mede Manor Hotel it was nearly half past three. They were staggered to see all the activity going on, people in different sorts of uniforms, others in white disposable overalls, plenty in plain clothes, and all threading their way backwards and forwards through a congestion of ambulances and police cars.

As Sherman started to get out of his car, a uniformed policeman, who'd been guarding entrance to the car park, came over to him. 'You can't stop there Sir, you'll have to move down the road. Nobody is being allowed in; we have a major incident.'

Reynard, not to be put off, having pulled in behind Sherman's car, got out and walked up to the constable, yanking out his warrant card as he did so. 'What's happening?'

The P.C took the card and examined it. Then, glancing down at Sherman, still in his seat, searching his pockets for his own identification, asked 'You together?'

'Yes we're here to interview the owners of the hotel in connection with some cases we're working on. Can we pull in somewhere?'

'Yes Sir, stick your cars over at the back, where you're not blocking anyone.'

'What's going on?' Sherman asked.

'Two people dead, Sir, they might be the people you came

to see.'

'Mr and Mrs Brett?'

'Don't know any details, just that it's a man and a woman. You can ask for D.I. Lightfoot, or Sergeant Birch, they're both over there somewhere.'

They picked their way through the vehicles and were just about to go into the building when two ambulance men walked past carrying a stretcher on which there was obviously a corpse.

The men loaded it into one of the ambulances standing with its doors open. Hardly had it been put in than a second one was slid in beside it.

'Looks like they didn't want to talk to us, Foxy.' said Sherman, with half a smile.

'Bit extreme though!'

A short dark haired man in a blue suit, who'd followed the second stretcher out, demanded to know who they were. When they showed him their warrant cards he responded by showing his own and introducing himself: 'D.I. Lightfoot, Buckinghamshire CID ... Greg.'

Once the introductions were over Lightfoot, puzzled at finding two other detectives so far away from their own patches, asked why they were there.

'Anywhere we can go inside to talk?' Sherman asked, determined to establish the seniority of his case. 'We're already both on murder enquiries, mine, the first one, took place near Richmond up in Yorkshire, D.C.I. Reynard's, the second, was down in Rottingdean ...'

'In Sussex.' said Reynard, nudging his way in to complete the sentence and making sure Sherman didn't succeed in side-lining him, an officer of senior rank. 'The two victims were brothers and we've been cooperating with each other because we believe that, apart from the obvious blood relationship between the two victims, the cases may be linked in other ways. We saw two bodies going past just now, who were they?'

'Hang on.' said Lightfoot, 'I'm asking the questions! They were the owner of the hotel and his wife, Angus and Betty Brett. Don't tell me their deaths are linked to what you're investigating?'

'They could be ... they probably are. We wanted to talk to Angus Brett in the hope of getting something which would have confirmed our belief he was our killer.'

'Good God Almighty, that means we'll have three counties involved - it'll be a nightmare.'

'Well yes, it might be.' Reynard answered, 'But clearly you have to sort out what's happened here before we cross that bridge. Commander Simpson up in the Yard put the two of us together, maybe he'll think it appropriate you join forces with us as well, once you've have had a chance to work out what's been going on. By the way is there a Mr Rex Brett knocking around, he'd be Angus's brother; we want to talk to him.'

'Yes, he's in the office, calls himself a film star … the stuck up so and so.'

'Oh … that's a bit …' interrupted Reynard, with a mock frown of censure.

'He's too big for his damned boots, Rex, I've known him for years - I used to go to school with him.'

'Oh, so you're a local man then?'

'Born and bred in Seer Green a couple of miles away. We both went to High Wycombe Grammar School … lots of the boys from round here did … still do.'

'And did Angus go there as well?'

'Yep … a year ahead of me and Rex.'

'Maybe we'll also be interviewing you in that case!'

'That's a laugh.' said Lightfoot. 'Come on we'll go inside. I've taken over the Sportsman's Bar for the moment, we can talk there. So who're these brothers you're investigating, I might know them if they were friends of the Bretts.'

'They're called Melchitt - one was my Super - Dudley Melchitt.' Sherman said.

'And the other one, my victim, was his brother Boris. He was killed near his boat, down in Rottingdean.'

'Never heard of them. Cause of death?'

'Drowning.' said the two inspectors, simultaneously.

'These two here, were bashed on the head. We found the weapon - a stone mason's long chisel … no prints though.'

'Well I'm damned, 'said Sherman. 'ours were hit as well … before they fell into the water.'

Lightfoot held up a finger to halt the conversation when he'd spotted his sergeant waving at him. 'Look you guys, you'll have to excuse me - I've got to get on - there's a queue forming up over there to talk to me. Go and have a chat with Rex if you want, he's in the little office off the hall we came through, he's going through his brother's papers.'

They found Rex sitting at the desk. He was holding a piece of paper in his hand, but looking into the distance blankly. Before him were stacks of computer printouts and accounts ledgers.

He showed no surprise at seeing Sherman, and rose as the two policemen entered. 'Ginny rang me to tell me you were on your way, but I'm sure you weren't expecting to walk into a catastrophe like this?'

'We were not Sir, and I don't suppose you were either? D.C.I. Reynard and I would like to offer our condolences. We can talk to you another day if you're too shocked.'

'No, no, ask away. I can't vouch for what I'll say in reply to your questions though ... because I admit I'm shaken.'

'Well it's not surprising Sir, we'll try to restrict it to just one or two important queries if we can.'

'We hadn't been close y'know ... not for years ... not since Dad died. And then, quite recently, we realised life was too short to carry a grudge, and Angus and I have been rediscovering our relationship. It was all a misunderstanding anyway you see - over Dad's will. Ach, what am I rambling on about ... what do you want to know?'

'Thank you Sir,' Sherman replied. 'Actually we weren't aware of the tragedy here until we arrived just now; we came about your brother. Him and the photograph of the man on the riverbank I showed you last time.'

Rex bit his lower lip and nodded.

'You recognised him didn't you?'

'How did you know?' Rex asked, tapping the desk top with a pencil he was holding.

'Instinct, nothing in particular ... I just did.'

Rex nodded. 'He's dead now anyway so it doesn't matter anymore.'

'What was your brother doing up there, and what might have prompted him to attack Dudley Melchitt?'

'I have no idea. I've been worried sick about his involvement ever since the day you called. I even drove down here to ask him about it, but when I got here I chickened out and set off for home. I was about half way back when I changed my mind and returned, determined to clear the matter up once and for all but when I asked him about being in Yorkshire he denied all knowledge of ever being there, or of hearing of anyone called Melchitt. I knew he was lying.

'You knew he was lying ... how?'

'Because Dad *did* know a man called Melchitt, he often mentioned him. They'd been student friends.'

'Him and Superintendent Melchitt?'

'Your officer who died? No, not him, another Melchitt. This was ages ago - forty years or more, and anyway, the Melchitt my Dad knew wasn't a policeman - at least I don't think he was.'

'Why d'you think Angus didn't recall him?'

'I'm damned sure he did. We both used to hear stories of Dad as a young man in college when we were kids. I remember him telling us about some outrageous pranks he and his pals used to get up to. That's them in the photo.' Rex said, swinging round to point at the frame hanging behind him.

'May I see it?' asked Sherman, not waiting for permission, before lifting it off the wall and taking out to look at it in the better light in the atrium. Almost immediately he called to Reynard. 'Come out and look at this, Foxy, it's that L.M.S. crowd again.'

'Blimey, you're right,' Reynard answered, as soon as he saw the photograph. 'I got a brief look at one like this before ... the day I called on Mungo's aunts.'

Sherman winked, 'OK,' he whispered, 'let's see what the film star has to say.'

Reynard walked back to the office and stuck his head inside the door. 'Can we have a word please?'

'Certainly.' Rex replied rising from the desk to join them.

Reynard stabbed his finger on the framed photograph which Sherman was holding. 'We've come across this crowd before, who are they?'

Rex took the picture and looked at it closely for a moment, trying to remember the names. 'Well, it's Dad and his college pals isn't it? That's him at the end.' he said, pointing to his father. 'He used to be called Ginger, and I can tell you who two of the others are, this one's Ghandi Melchitt, we once bumped into him and his family at the Zoo, I was about twelve. That one's Jock McPhee, I was sort of engaged to his daughter, Eva, for a while but I only ever met *him* three or four times. I don't know the other two.'

'Thank you, Sir, very helpful.' said Reynard, 'Now there's just one more thing, I see you're going through your brother's papers. Did you come across anything connecting him to Richmond or Rottingdean?'

'No, not so far, but I haven't really started yet, the stuff on his desk is all to do with the hotel and 'er ... 'er... ' he trailed off into silence as the enormity of the situation confronting him began to sink in.

Realising they'd get no farther they left him and went looking for D.I. Lightfoot. But they couldn't find him and soon they were in Reynard's car assessing the way the day had turned out.

'Looks like you're case is practically complete then, Ronnie,' said Reynard, 'It's clear Angus Brett killed Dudley Melchitt. All you have to do now is tie up the loose ends.'

'Maybe,' said Sherman, less convinced than Reynard by Rex's report of the conversation he'd had with his brother. 'We're still missing something, and I've the guy in the silver Volvo to explain, he's involved somehow, Bellamy's finally convinced me.'

'Fair enough. You keep digging. I'm going to try to track down these other guys in the LMS Club, I'm sure that's where the answer lies.'

'And how are you going to do it?'

'With this little address book I've just borrowed.'

'You crafty old bastard, you nicked it.'

'No I didn't, I borrowed it ... he'll get it back, it's an old one, might be his Dad's with a bit of luck.'

4, College Close, Wimbledon Hill, London. SW18 6DE
Friday 24th November 2006. 11.30 a.m.

Three days to go, no wonder Eva was unable to settle in her little bed-sitter just off Wimbledon Common, the opening of the pantomime was only a few days away. She'd had her lines and all the dance routines 'off pat' for a fortnight but, despite having been a pro for over twenty years, and despite having first night nerves on countless occasions during all that time, it never got easier. Every time she thought of her first entrance her knees turned to jelly and, when the possibility of 'drying' in the middle of her first speech came to mind, she shook like a leaf.

All morning she'd paced up and down, made cup after cup of tea, nibbled and thrown away numerous half eaten biscuits, and yet her stomach was still churning. In desperation she flung on a coat and went for a walk on the common, hoping the fresh air would blow away her anxiety.

It was slightly foggy on the open land, less so when the path brought her into a grouping of leafless birch trees. Maybe it was being amongst them which set her off. Before she realised what she was doing, she was dreaming of her entrance again.

Flash. The babes are sleeping on a bed of leaves.
Flash. A mist swirls about them.

I appear; I'm all in white and silver. I stand on my points like a ballerina. I mustn't wobble.

I wave my wand slowly over them and then thrust it threateningly towards the hobgoblins, who are stealing up on the children.

'Begone foul fiends and leave these children lie.
Begone I say for should I hear their cry
Or call for help, then surely will I fly
To hold them safe in my embrace,
And lead them to a safer place.
Begone. Begone I say.'

God Almighty! In her four years at RADA, and sixteen years on the stage she'd played in every conceivable form of drama from William Shakespeare to Tennessee Williams, acted anything from a girl of sixteen to a woman of ninety, appeared as a tart, a toff, a mother, a mistress, a communist and a capitalist, but never, never, in all her life had she been involved in anything half as pathetic as this pantomime. She'd had so many 'real' parts she couldn't remember them, and now she was reduced to this rubbish. And it was all down to Rex, it was his entire fault. She kicked a small stone in fury and, without looking to see if there was anyone near enough to hear her, cursed him at the top of her voice ... 'Bloody Rex ... Bastaaaard!'

She felt better for saying it, for shouting it out to the world, and then she realised there had been someone within earshot after all, a woman with a beagle hound had just appeared from way down the path beyond the trees and was looking anxiously towards her. 'Are you alright dear, you seem upset?' the woman said.

It reminded her of the occasion when the child with the ice cream had spoken to her down on the seafront at Hove, the day she'd failed the audition. 'I'm fine thanks,' she said, 'just practising my part, I'm an actress.'

'Oh, sorry I ... 'er ... 'er, I hadn't realised ... sorry.' the woman said, not at all convinced by Eva's explanation.

By the time she'd broken out of the trees and into the mist she was talking to herself again: 'Now what?' she said, 'It's too cold out here and I can't sit in that rabbit hutch of a bed-sitter for the weekend, what'll I do? I know! ... I'll go 'home' for a couple of days, haven't been there since Dad's funeral a month ago. That's what I'll do. I'll grab a few things and drive down to Lewes after lunch. No point in ringing Sandy in the office, he goes off to play golf on a Friday, I'll try his mobile.' As she walked she pulled out her telephone from her pocket and rang his number. No answer. 'Thought so,' she mumbled, 'I'll send a text and hope he gets it before he goes 'home'. Doesn't matter if he doesn't it's my 'home' too, to hell with him.'

She arrived at two. The traffic had been light and she'd done the trip in under an hour, including a stop to pick a few items of shopping: milk, bread, butter, and half a dozen eggs.

The gate was shut … 'Unusual.' she thought. There was no sign of his car in his regular parking place at the side of the house, or in the garage. 'He must have gone away for the weekend.'

She dug into her handbag and found the Yale and the Chubb keys. Two minutes later she was inside. The house was warm. She went over to a radiator and felt it; it was warm too, probably just switched off after the mid-day boost. 'It'll not be on again until five.' she muttered to herself as she went through into the kitchen. 'Everything tidy in here, plenty in the fridge, dish washer empty. Ah, here's a note on the table … it's from Mrs Flint, I wonder how long it's been here.'

> Dear Mr McPhee
> We need more washing up tablets for the machine and we need furniture polish and vacuum cleaner bags. I'll get everything for next Tuesday you can pay me then. Don't forget to order more central heating oil - we're very low.
> Yours faithfully
> Alice Flint (Mrs)

She boiled the kettle and made a mug of coffee, took it through into the sitting room and, for the first time, felt the absence of her father. She'd been so used to coming into the room and finding him sitting in the big button back chair doing the Times Crossword, she'd been subconsciously expecting to still find him there. 'I suppose Sandy'll take this place over like everything else that's left.'

Her father's will had been shown to her when she was down for the funeral. It was straightforward, the business and the house had been left to her and Sandy equally, but Sandy had told her not 'to hold her breath' because the company was nearly insolvent, and the house was hocked up to the hilt. 'We'll get nothing.' he'd said.

'So what happened to all the money?' she'd asked.

'Gone.' he'd answered, but he'd refused to expand.

Between her very deep grief at her father's death, and her very acute anger at the way Rex had treated her, she hadn't felt inclined to pursue Sandy on the point then, and she hadn't seen him since. She wished she'd come down and forced the information out of him. Not that she'd have believed him, whatever he said; he couldn't possibly be right, the money couldn't all have gone. What had he done with it?

She sat in her father's chair. She'd always been 'Daddy's girl'. Running her hands along the rich velvet fabric, she imagined herself sitting on his knee and smoothing the skin on back of his hands. It didn't sadden her strangely, a comforting warmth came over her instead. Draining the mug she walked over to one of the side tables bearing photographs of the family. All except one ... she'd forgotten about it ... it was one of her and Rex on deck of a cross channel ferry, they'd been going to France on holiday. 'Bloody Rex again, I'm going to get rid of him.' she decided.

She unclipped the back of the frame, took out the picture and tore it up, casting the pieces into the waste paper basket standing between wall next to the fireplace and the side of her father's chair. He used to open his mail when he was in that chair, dumping the envelopes into the basket, ready to be burned when the fire was next lit. As she tore up the photographs, she remembered others in her bedroom, dozens of them, in albums. Deciding to destroy them as well, she went upstairs to fetch them.

When she returned, she set about removing all the prints which had Rex in them, tore them into little bits and threw them away. He could burn with the rest of the rubbish!

Then, thoroughly pleased with having got rid of all the irritating images she sat back, closed her eyes and started to think of revenge. She never heard the car drive up, never heard a thing until the front door bell rang and startled her.

She went over to the window and looked out. Two strangers were there, a man and a woman. Smart, neatly dressed, business-like - but not business people.

She answered the third and more insistent ring.

Each held out a pocket sized folder containing an identity card and photograph.

'D.C.I. Reynard and D.S. Groves.' said the man. 'Is this the home of Mr George McPhee?'

'Was.'

'Was? What do you mean?'

'He died recently.' Eva couldn't miss the look of disappointment on the man's face, or the strange glance, he gave the woman? What could that be about, she wondered?

'Recently?' he said, 'oh dear … sorry.'

Eva nodded, 'I'm his daughter … why did you want to see him? Maybe I could help?'

'Maybe you could … can we come in?' asked the man, who continued to question her as they went through into the sitting room. 'And your name is …?'

'I'm Eva McPhee. As I said I'm George McPhee's daughter, his only one as a matter of fact. I have a brother, an older brother, his name's Alexander but we all call him Sandy.'

'Perhaps I should explain …' the policeman replied.

'I wish you would … you have me quite worried. What did Dad do to interest the police?'

'Nothing as far as we know, we just wanted to ask him about an old friend of his.'

'Oh, I see … who's that then?'

'His name was Melchitt.'

'Sorry I've forgotten yours already.'

'I'm Detective Chief Inspector Reynard, Sussex CID. My colleague is Detective Sergeant Groves. We're enquiring into the death of three gentlemen called Melchitt.'

'A car accident, I suppose, there are so many these days, aren't there?'

'You suppose wrongly, Miss McPhee,' said Reynard, 'we're investigating a murder and two suspicious deaths, though we expect at least one of these will prove to be a murder as well.'

'Crikey.'

'Have you ever heard of anyone called Melchitt, Miss McPhee?' asked Groves.

'No I haven't,' Eva replied. '… as far as I know.'

'Do you think your brother would know them?'

'I have absolutely no idea. I don't live here myself, haven't for twenty years or more, but Sandy does. We only see each other occasionally these days, I work all over the country, I'm an actress.'

Groves paused for a moment tapping her forehead 'Got it!

I thought I'd seen you before. You were in something in Worthing last year, weren't you, a play, The White Sheep of the Family, if I remember correctly. Am I right?'

'Preistly's crime comedy? Yes, I played the daughter.'

Reynard cleared his throat to catch the two women's attention, and take them away from the blind alley towards which they appeared to be heading. 'Back to your brother then ... when do you expect him to return?'

'He gets home around round seven most evenings, I think. I've only just arrived here myself, I tried to contact him in the office before I left, but I got no answer. That's no surprise mind you; he often plays golf on Fridays. I left a text message on his mobile to say I'd be here when he got home.'

'Did you get an answer?' the inspector asked.

'I didn't look.'

'Would you mind doing so now?'

'No, of course not, my handbag's upstairs.'

'Your handbag?'

'I think Miss McPhee means her mobile telephone's in her handbag, and it's upstairs.' explained Groves, still slightly smarting from Reynard's mild rebuke.

'Oh right,' said the inspector with a smile, and shaking his head as he thought of the tortuous and often unnecessary complexity of his some women's speech. 'Will you get it please? Go with her Sergeant.'

'I don't need to be shepherded round my own house thank you Inspector.' Eva said, stiffly.

'No of course you don't, but we're in a hurry and the Sergeant may help you find it more quickly. Go on Sergeant fast as you can.'

As soon as they'd left the room Reynard dropped to his knees and, reaching under the chair on which Eva had been sitting, picked up a piece torn from a photograph. Almost exactly in the middle of it was the face of a man.

He'd spotted the fragment as soon as he'd sat down. More important though, even at that distance, he could see it was Rex Brett.

When the women came back into the room Groves was

shaking her head. 'No answer Sir. There's been no answer to Miss McPhee's text.'

'We'll have to call here again then. I'll leave a card Miss McPhee. Would you ask your brother to telephone me when you see him?'

'Certainly I will Inspector.' said Eva, remaining standing in a clear indication she wanted them to go. 'Is there anything else?'

'Just one thing, yes. I picked this piece of a photograph up when you were upstairs; it was underneath your chair.'

'Oh I've been clearing out some old snaps this afternoon. The waste paper basket's full of pieces of photos I threw in, I must have missed it with that one, thank you.'

She held out her hand to take it, but he held on to it. 'Really.' he said, 'Do you know who the gentlemen is?'

'Yes, of course I do Inspector. He's a friend of mine. His name is Rex Brett, you've probably seen one of his films.'

'I'm not sure I have, but would you mind having a look at a photograph I have here?'

He opened his brief case and pulled out the copy of the picture showing the man walking along the bank Sherman had given him, and handed it to her. 'Now, Miss, is this Rex Brett?'

She took the photo from him, saw immediately it was Rex's brother, Angus, and was about to say so, when it dawned on her the inspector had given her a chance to make Rex sweat a bit. It might be childish to resort to pointing the police in his direction compared with what he'd done to her, but she knew how sweet it would feel. Bending down, pretending to examine the photograph in the better illumination of the table lamp, she slowly nodded her head. 'Yes it's Rex alright. Why do you want to know? What's he done?'

'It's just routine.' Reynard replied, indicating to Groves they should be on their way. 'We want to talk to anyone we think may have a connection with the enquiry and ... oh yes ... would you let your brother know we need to speak to him sometime soon.'

'Certainly, of course I will.' she said, as they left.

Richmond Police Station canteen.
Friday 24th November 2006. 5.00 p.m.

D.I. Sherman was in the canteen explaining to Sergeant Bellamy, over a plate of egg and chips, what had happened down in Beaconsfield the day before. 'We're all but done here I think, Malc. It's pretty obvious Angus Brett killed the Super. Bit late in the day to find out 'why' perhaps, and maybe we'll never know for sure after what's happened since. However, ignoring Eva McPhee's star performance when she tried to divert poor old Foxy with some frivolous information which he was telling me about this morning, we still have a convincing identification by Rex Brett, who's prepared to say Angus was the man on the bank, and that he did know the Melchitts.

'What about the chap in the bushes then, I thought you'd agreed he was a possible starter, are you going to ignore him now?' asked Bellamy. 'Don't forget we have strong evidence concerning the accident with Mr Kingsley's churns.'

'Don't worry, Malc, I'm not forgetting him. But I think you'll find he's peripheral, Angus was the murderer and I'm going to prove it. You stay with the man in the bushes if you want but all you'll wind up doing is eliminating him.'

'Fine by me, Guv ... you take Angus and I'll continue with the other guy because I'm damned sure I spoke to him. If I don't get his complete story I'll never have him out of my mind, maybe he was up doing a bit of scouting. And we can't ignore young Keith Kingsley either, don't forget he also identified him. On top of that, I've still got the Underground ticket to sort out. Yes, I'll stick with the chap in the bushes.'

D.I. Sherman stood up, grinned patronisingly, and in doing so closed the conversation. 'OK, you do your thing, Malc, I'll do mine. Let's get on with it.'

Sussex Police Major Incident Suite, Sussex House, Brighton. Wednesday 29th November 2006. 6.30 p.m.

Foxy had called into the office on the way home to see if there were any messages for him. There was only one, an e-mail from Detective Constable Norman Best.

Re, Boris Melchitt. ... Guv, I have two new bits of information to add to the pile.

Firstly, I was back at the SOC to have another good look at those tyre prints after I'd noticed what I thought might be a flaw in one of casts or, hopefully, a cast of a flaw in one of the tyres. It looked to me as though there could be a piece missing out of one of the treads. The depressions on the clay made by the tyres were dried out and crumbling but, even so, I could still see what looked like a fault quite clearly. Looking back along the track, I quickly found the mark again - not so distinct this time but quite definite. The distance they were apart corresponded exactly to the circumference of a Honda 50cc wheel. I have attached the photograph for you to see for yourself.

Secondly, I've been on the 'phone constantly trying to track down the firms which might have hired the bike out without any success, though I have narrowed the field down quite a lot. One thing has come to light, none of the companies I spoke to will hire a helmet. Apparently they won't take the risk of being accused of a hiring a faulty helmet in the event of injury. Seemingly a weakness can develop even if a helmet is simply dropped. The hirers I spoke to keep out of trouble by not hiring helmets at all, so it's possible our suspect has a helmet ... but no bike or leathers of his own.

Norman Best.

34, Primrose Mansions, Islington.
Wednesday 29th November 2006. 11 30.p.m

Wayne and Angie were nearly asleep when she remembered something she'd intended to tell him.

'Wayne.'

'Wha''

'I saw somefin' in the paper.'

'Tell me termorrer, I'm tired.'

'Did yer know tha' geezer's sons was murdered?'

'Melchitt's? Yew jokin' … murdered … when?'

'Just afore yer went dahn there.'

'Well it weren' me.'

'Yew sure yew never 'ittim?'

'Tol' yer, didn' I? Go ter sleep.'

'Eddie's comin' up termorrer. 'E rang me.'

'Oh yeah.'

'Wayne.'

'Now wot?'

'If you didn' ittim, maybe he got done by the same geezers wot killed 'is sons.'

'Maybe I'll win the fuckin' lottery. Go ter sleep.'

'Wayne.'

'Wot?'

'Garf's cryin', i's your turn.'

'Yeah, yeah, yeah, in a minute.'

'Now Wayne.' She said, putting her feet to his back and shoving him out of the bed. 'Now, or 'e'll wake Lance up.'

Wayne reluctantly picked himself off the floor and went through to his sons who, by then, were both bawling their heads off. Angie grinned, drew the duvet over her head, and shut them all out of her mind.

Sussex Police Major Incident Suite, Sussex House, Brighton. Thursday 30th November 2006. 7.00 a.m.

D.C.I. Reynard was at his desk at crack of dawn. All day long, the day before, he'd had a strong feeling things were coming together despite the fact two more murders had been added to the list. The encouraging flow of information coming forward had once again triggered the sense of excitement which developed when a reasonable prospect of success was showing its hand.

On top of that, what he was about to attempt might propel him forward even faster for, with the aid of the address book he'd 'borrowed' in Beaconsfield, he was hoping to track down the last two members of the LMS Club or their families: Dicky and Frog.

He raced through the pile of paperwork and messages on his desk, made the appropriate responses, then rang D.I. Lightfoot to ask him the one question he should have asked the day before.

'Did anyone come forward to report a motor cyclist acting suspiciously in the vicinity during the last few days?'

'I don't think so but maybe the report just hasn't got to me yet. Why?'

'Because there was one seen on the river bank, when Boris Melchitt was murdered.' Reynard replied, 'A guy on a crimson and cream Honda 50 cc wearing black leathers and a shiny black helmet. And we had another sighting of a motor cyclist when Jonathan Melchitt died. It might be the same man, and it might not. This time the fellah was also in black, but he was on a gold coloured Harley Davidson … a big man.'

'No, I've just asked my sergeant as you were talking, and we've not had any motor cyclists reported. I'll mention it at this morning's briefing though, and get the guys to ask around … see what they can find out.'

'I'd be obliged if you would, Greg.'

'No prob.' I'm glad you rang though, because I was about to telephone you, we might have got lucky with a witness who popped up after you'd gone - a local.'

'Really? Did he actually see the attack?'

'Ah, no ...he didn't; I'm never that fortunate. This man was walking through the car park to his back gate, which opens off it. It was the day before yesterday, mid-morning, there were two people at the back door of the hotel, trying, but failing, to get in.'

'You mean breaking in?'

'No, no, trying to get a response to their knock on the door. They were looking for Ginger Brett, Angus's father, who's been dead for years.'

'And they didn't know.'

'Apparently not, anyway this guy told them to give it a good hard wallop or to try hitting it with a coin or a key. He reckoned Angus was probably down in the cellar checking the beer delivery pipes and out of earshot. Betty, he assumed, was more than likely getting stuck into her first bottle of the day.'

'Oh, she liked a taste or two did she?'

'It was more than a taste, from what I hear.'

'And what happened ...did they get in?'

'Well, the girl gave the door a good whack with her fist first, and then with a key. A few minutes later, just as the guy I spoke to was departing, Angus appeared and began shouting at them for hitting the door so hard.'

'And what made the witness suspicious?'

'Their attitude. They'd driven up from Gatwick, they told him, and implied they weren't going to go away until they'd found out something they wanted to know about Ginger Brett, Angus's dad. Determined they were, and angry, he said, but to tell you the truth, I couldn't help feel he was making a meal of it.'

'Could he recognise them again?'

'Oh he could do that alright, they were a very distinctive pair, both in their twenties. The girl was black and the man was white - though they said they were brother and sister. He thought the man was a Londoner, but she wasn't - he reckoned she was a West Indian.'

'Your witness didn't make this all up, did he?'

'I doubt it; he'd have known who I am.'

'Lucky you, I wish I could find something as positive to go on in my cases.'

At that moment Sergeant Groves walked into his office, Reynard said goodbye to Lightfoot and turned to her, 'I want you to come up to London with me, Lucy, we're going to hunt for suspects.'

Groves smiled. 'There must be twelve million people living in London Guv, how're we going to find them?'

'We're going to knock on their doors, that's how.' he replied waving the little red book at her, and winking.

His confidence prompted her to ask how he'd got it.

'I borrowed it yesterday, didn't I? So, now that we know where all the people in the 'famous' photograph live, or have lived at one time or other, we're going to try our luck. It may take all day, it may take several days. Make sure you've settled anything else urgent you have on your plate, and we'll start. I'd like to be knocking on Mr Henry Byrd's front door some time today.'

'Wouldn't you ring first, he mightn't be there.'

'No, take 'em when they least expect it. Don't give 'em chance to think the way Ronnie Sherman did with Rex Brett.'

'OK … ten minutes and I'll be ready.'

The commuter traffic had thinned by the time they hit the motorway and they were standing on the doorstep of Eight Belvedere Crescent at ten to eleven waiting for someone to answer their knock. Mrs 'F' did. Reynard showed her his warrant card and introduced himself and Sergeant Groves.

As he spoke, the puzzled look on Mrs 'F's face was quickly replaced by one of anxiety.

'Wha's 'appened?' she asked.

'Oh, there's nothing to be concerned about.' Reynard answered, well used to such a reaction. 'We want to talk to Mr Byrd, that's all. He does live here doesn't he?'

'When 'e's 'ere, 'e does, but tha's not very offen, and 'e ain' tere now … 'ain' been 'ere for mumfs.'

Trying to hide his disappointment, Reynard asked where Mr Byrd was.

'Mexico.'

'Mexico! Is he on holiday?'

'Nah, 'e's been there since lars' Christmas, 'e's a pain'er … spends 'arf 'is life there pain'in' pitchers.'

'And you are?'

'Yer'd betta come in, carn talk out 'ere. I'm 'is 'ousekeeper. I come in full time when 'e's at 'ome and par' time when 'e's not.'

As they entered the sitting room Reynard's attention was immediately taken by the picture over the fireplace.

'That's one of 'is. Bit saucy innit? Know wha' I mean?'

Groves answered before Reynard got a chance to open his mouth, 'I wouldn't have it over my fireplace.'

'Me neiver.' answered Mrs 'F', with a chuckle.

'So, Mrs … 'er … 'er?' asked Reynard.

'Flower. Ada Flower. Y'can call me Mrs 'F' everyone else does.'

'Right then Mrs 'F', if Mr Byrd isn't here is Mrs Byrd in, or is she with him?'

'There ain' no Mrs Byrd. Never 'as been.'

Sergeant Groves, who'd continued to stare at the picture in spite of herself, asked, 'Is he a successful painter. I mean this place is rather more than the average artist's studio.'

Mrs 'F' laughed. 'This all come from 'is old auntie wo' brought 'im up … 'e's loaded. None of it comes from pain'in', bu' I fink 'e does make a tidy bit outa tha' as well … 'E 'as exhibitions, yer know … some gallery place up Wes' … King's Road, I fink. Everytime 'e comes back from abroad 'e 'as a great big box of canvases wot foller on la'er. 'E'll 'ave pain'ed them all in the year 'e's been away. A few weeks after 'e ge's back, 'e 'as 'is exhibition. Does the same every year … 'ere for two mumfs … away for ten.'

'Not a bad life. I wish I had it.' Reynard said, crossing to the fireplace.

Groves thought he was going over to take a closer look at the naked woman in the picture and turned to Mrs 'F' with a grin. 'Men!' she whispered, throwing her eyes to the ceiling.

But Reynard didn't notice the by play because he wasn't actually interested in the picture at all, he'd spotted something else. 'Oy, oy, oy, what have we here … it's them isn't it?' he said, 'reaching for a photograph at the back of the mantelpiece. 'It's that LMS lot again, isn't it?'

'What … 'er … oh yes … them. I thought it was them the

minute we came into the room.' Groves stuttered, unable to stop her face reddening.

Reynard gave her a look of disapproval and cast his head to one side, he hadn't been fooled. Then he turned back to Mrs Flower. 'Who are these men Mrs 'F'?'

'Wha' is i' wiv tha' photo. Everyone keeps astin' me abah'dit'. First there was tha' young black girl an' 'er bruvver - now you lo' ... I don' know 'em ... none of 'em.'

'You've had others enquiring?'

'Yeah, I jus' tole yer ... a young black girl an' her bruvver. Said they were 'is kids. The boy defini'ly was, 'e was 'ere a few mumfs ago ... but Mr Byrd couldn't 'ave had a black girl for a daugh'er - now could 'e?'

'What were their names? When did you see them last? Come on Mrs 'F', this is important.'

'Orlrigh', orlrigh', wha's the 'urry? Eddie's 'is name but I carn remember 'ers ... no 'ang abah', I fink I can ... yers, it was Sophie. She's been 'ere before as well ... back in the spring. Come 'ere from Trinidad, she said.'

'Trinidad ... not Mexico?'

Mrs 'F' went scarlet with indignation. 'Oo d'yer fink I am ... I know wha' people from the West Indies look like, we've plenny of 'em rahnd 'ere, and I know wha' Mexicans look like. I'm not schtupid.'

'Really, Mrs 'F' ... and what do Mexicans look like?' he added, without thinking.

Mrs Flower started to cackle. 'Like flippin' Mexicans, of course ... them fellas wiv the big 'ats.'

Sergeant Groves, seeing the thunderous look on the inspector's face, and fearing his response, asked Mrs 'F' if she could describe either of the two callers.

Mrs 'F' paused for a moment while she worked out whether she was still being teased then, coming to the conclusion she wasn't, replied: 'She was abou' twenny free, I'd say, 'e was more. And she was dead interested in them fellas in the pitcher. Fought I didn' notice, but she'd been fiddling wiv the photos while I was gettin' 'er a cuppa tea.'

'How did you know?' asked Reynard.

'Because I know exac'ly where them pitchers all go. Blimey I dus' 'em often enough ... The girl puttit back in a differen' place.'

'May we borrow it Mrs 'F'. Sergeant Groves'll give you a receipt.

''Snot mine ter lend ... Go on take it then - but be sure ter bring i' back.'

'Was she staying round here?'

'Nah, Ga'wick.'

'And that's where she was going back to was it?'

''Ere, will I get paid fer all this? You coppers arst a lorra questions don' cha?' she said, smiling at the same time.

'I'll put your name in the hat.'

'Will ya? Right then ... I sent 'em rahnd to Angie La Tour's ... tha's what I done.'

'Who's she?' asked Reynard.

'See this fella,' replied Mrs 'F', pointing to the picture of Roly on the photograph. 'La Tour's 'is name, she's his daugh'er.'

'And can you tell us where she lives?'

'Near my place. Fir'y Four, Primrose Mansions. I's no' far from 'ere. Look, I berra gerron. 'Ave yer finished?'

'I think we have for the moment Mrs 'F', but I'm sure one of us will be back when we've thought over what you've told us. When do you expect Mr Byrd to return, any idea?'

'Christmas. 'E sent a postcard ... Tha's i', ... back o' the man'elpiece.'

Reynard picked up the card with the parrot on it, the one Sophie and Eddie had read, and glanced at it. 'I'll leave you my 'phone number, maybe you'll ask him to contact me.'

'Yeah, orlrigh'. Wha's this all abah' then?'

'It's about murder Mrs 'F'.' said Reynard, and waited for the explosion.

'Wha'! Murder. Stone the crows - yer shoulda tol' me.'

Reynard made no answer and, leaving Sergeant Groves to thank Mrs 'F', he touched his forehead in a farewell salute and made for the door.

St Anne's House,
Horsham Common, Sussex.
Thursday 30th November 2006. 11.30a.m.

Mungo was in his father's study, sitting at the desk. The room had always been his father's private place, his sanctuary, a space solely for him - as was clear from the way people referred to it, 'Daddy's study', when he was child, 'Your father's study', when anyone else in the household was talking to him about it, 'Father's study' when he mentioned it himself.

Even after his father became senile, and knew no different, it remained there for his exclusive use. His proprietary right to it was respected by all - fiercely so by Aunts Violet, Rose, and Daisy who would have frowned at Mungo's boldness in sitting where he now sat had his father been alive. And they wouldn't have been too slow in voicing their displeasure either. The odd thing is, Mungo would have taken their criticism without a murmur of complaint. It was yet another example of the strange way in which the Melchitts related to each other, and it would have made him a laughing stock amongst his business associates, had they known.

The room was hexagonal in shape and took up the whole of the upper floor of a rather silly turret, grafted onto one corner of the granite house by a past owner with more money than taste. The ground floor had been given over to his sisters by Oscar, Mungo's grandfather, as a private sitting room for them; Jonathan had endorsed the situation when he became head of the family. Now it was Mungo's turn to carry on the tradition and he had every intention of doing so.

The walls of both rooms were panelled in dark oak, giving them a sombre look. In the case of the 'Ladies Sitting Room' a certain relief had been introduced by a profusion of flowers - the arrangement of which was Violet's preserve. The floral theme was continued in the pattern of the curtains, chair covers and cushions which Rose had made, and a number of Daisy's delicate, even whimsical, water colours completed the scene. Each aunt had her own escritoire standing before a window and an armchair before the fireplace. By common consent there was no television set.

Upstairs, 'Mungo's Study', as it had currently become known, retained the Spartan look, having a huge partner's desk placed so it's user, if sitting at it, would be facing anyone coming in. There were a few glass fronted book cases and other smaller pieces of furniture which looked as though they were there 'for show', and a business like pair of olive green metal filing cabinets on top of each of which, in an attempt to disguise or soften their appearance, stood a bronze facsimile of one of Rodin's Ballerinas. Every other bit of free wall space was adorned with framed photographs of groups of people posing in front of schools or colleges, though there were a few individual ones of men in sporting poses, or holding trophics. Amongst them, was the one of the LMS Club.

The coffee he'd brought up had gone cold and he pushed it to one side. All morning he'd been reading papers from his father's deed box which he'd collected, first thing, from the bank where it had been in safe keeping. As he digested the information contained in each document he'd tried to familiarise himself with the various aspects of his father's life which they revealed. A lot were well known to him. Some were not. The papers now lay in three heaps before him ready for a second reading.

In the first pile was his father's will, the details of his portfolio of bonds and shares, and a copy of the Memorandum and Articles of Association of Melchitt House Publishing. In the second were documents relating to St Anne's House, and to various investment properties in Brighton. The third pile was small, consisting of two envelopes only, one of which had been inside the other with a single sheet of paper on which was a hand written agreement signed by several people whose names were familiar to him, 'Frog' La Tour, 'Dicky' Byrd, 'Jock' McPhee, 'Ghandi' Melchitt and 'Ginger' Brett - the members of the LMS Club.

Across the top of the sealed flap of the smaller envelope, in his father's distinctive hand was written,

Not to be opened in my lifetime - Ghandi Melchitt.

He went to the first lot of papers again and quickly leafed through them, returning most to the deed box when they were read. There was some work for the solicitors there but, other than one thing, nothing which couldn't wait. The exception, and it contained no surprises for him, was his father's will. It was simple, and in many respects a repeat of Oscar's. His whole estate, bar a few bequests which between them didn't add up to more than ten per cent of the total, was left to Mungo, Boris and Dudley. It was to come to them in equal shares provided they agreed to continue to maintain a home for Violet, Rose, and Daisy, each of whom got fifty thousand pounds.

Mungo had breathed a great sigh of relief when he'd first read it for, while he'd never doubted its contents, the document confirmed that, as a result of the deaths of Boris and Dudley, he would inherit all his father's shares. Henceforth he'd have a holding equal to the combined total held by Justin and Jarrold. Any further harassment by them could be fought off with confidence, for his aunts had long ago not only assured him of their proxies but of the majority of their shares when they died. He didn't know how large the majority would be ... the fact it was a majority was enough.

The second pile had held no surprises either. He knew all about the properties in Brighton, indeed he'd had dealings with many of the tenants from time to time since his father's illness. All in all, it looked as though his personal fortune was going to increase by another two and a half million pounds once the hands of The Chancellor of the Exchequer had come out of the till.

He shoved everything back into the deed box except the agreement of the LMS Club and the sealed envelope. So interested was he in these two items he completely missed a very important point: following the murder of Boris and Dudley and his subsequent inheritance of their shares, he'd be propelled to the top of the list of suspects in the eyes of the police. What he should have been doing with some urgency was compile two alibis, instead of which he was getting all excited over an amusing document dating back forty or fifty years.

'Lu ... unch!' shouted Aunt Daisy, by then recovered from her state of shock. 'Mu ... ngo ... Lu ...unch.'

Reluctantly he put down the envelope which he was just about to open and went downstairs.

34, Primrose Mansions, Islington.
Thursday 30th November 2006. 2.00 p.m.

D.C.I. Reynard and Sgt Groves stood outside Angie's flat and rang the bell. When she came to the door she had Lance in her arms; he was sound asleep. Half hidden behind her Garth, standing on one leg and swinging the other backwards and forwards, held onto her skirt to steady himself. Groves tried smiling at him at him but he remained stone faced.

'Are you Angela La Tour?' asked Reynard, showing his identification and proceeding to make the introductions.

'Yeah.' Angie replied, not unreasonably coming to the conclusion that Wayne's luck must have run out.

'Daughter of Roland La Tour?'

She raised an eyebrow. 'Yeah, why?'

Reynard ignored her questions and continued with his own. 'Does your father live here?'

Angie laughed at him. 'My Dad died years ago. 'E did live 'ere up until then …Wots this all abah'?'

'It's a long story. We're investigating a death and your father's name came up in our enquiry, that's all.'

Angie, having by then realised the arrival of the Old Bill on her doorstep probably had nothing to do with Wayne on this occasion, relaxed a little. Of more importance was to get them away from her front door before her neighbours saw them, she took the easiest way out. 'Berra come in.'

They went through the hall and into the kitchen. It was full of steam as usual, and smelled of fried bacon.

She pointed to the table and they sat at it while she cleared away the dirty crockery by piling it in the sink with a load of baby's bottles waiting to be washed

'I can see you're busy,' said Reynard, 'so I'll be as quick as I can. Have you ever heard of a man called Jonathan Melchitt, he was a friend of your father's years ago, according to information in our possession.'

Alarm bells started to ring loudly in her head again as soon as she heard him say 'Melchitt', but she didn't react, hoping he knew nothing of Wayne's little trip down to Horsham on Reg's Harley Davidson.

'Melchitt ... Melchitt ... it sahnds familiar'. She rolled the name round as though she was trying to recapture the occasion on which she'd heard it before, amazingly rediscovering most of her 't's' and some of her 'h's' on the way, and switching to the 'posh' accent she reserved for visitors and telephone answering machines. 'Hmm, yers, Melchitt, I fink I've gorrit. Just a minute will yew.'

She plonked Lance on Grove's unsuspecting lap and shot out of the room. A minute later she was back. In her hand was the photograph. She'd taken it from top of the television in the sitting room and handed it to Reynard. 'I knew I knew the name Melchitt ... look on the back.'

Reynard glanced at the signatures with which, by then, he was so familiar, Ghandi Melchitt, Ginger Brett, Dicky Byrd, Jock McPhee, Frog La Tour..

'I've seen one of these before, more than one, this is your dad isn't it?' Reynard said, pointing to the bearded man in sandals.

'I was only a nipper when 'e died. 'E was run over by a bus, right outside the school 'e taught in.' said Angie, sniffing, and taking a screwed up tissue from her apron pocket to dab at her eyes.

Reynard was inclined to laugh at her overt and artificial plea for sympathy but made a few quiet murmurings instead. 'And what did he teach?'

'Art. 'E was sculptor but 'e taught drawing and paintin' at the school.'

'Bit like his friend 'Dicky' then.' Reynard said, tapping the photograph again.

'Maybe ... I don't know much abaht them.'

Lance gave a volcanic burp, causing Sergeant Groves to start in alarm; and when a trickle of yellowish baby food emerged from his mouth and began to dribble down his chin, she panicked and turned to his mother for help. Angie giggled at the policewoman's inability to deal with such a simple thing as a baby's gastronomic turbulence. 'Ere, give 'im ter me. You aven't 'ad no kids yet 'ave yer?' she said, patting Lance's back.

Groves shook her head, embarrassed by her inadequacy. Reynard was highly amused, in other circumstances he might have teased his young sergeant, but this time he didn't, he was thinking of another angle.

'How well d'you know this one ... Henry Byrd ... 'Dicky' he's signed himself?'

Angie shrugged her shoulders. 'I met 'im once, he lives near 'ere, round in Belvedere Crescent.'

'We know where he lives, we were there earlier. What about the girl from Trinidad; what d'you know about her or the man she was with, the man who might be her brother?'

Relieved to be escaping from the dangerous subject of Jonathan Melchitt, Angie laughed again. 'You met 'em, then?'

'No. Mrs Flower told us about them. She said she'd sent them round to you. Who are they?'

'They're who they say they are, 'enry Byrd's son and daughter. E's their dad but they've got different mums.' Angie replied and, when she saw Reynard's puzzled expression she began to giggle. 'It's easy, 'er mum was a West Indian ... from Trinidad, 'is mum was English ... from Clapham ... and guess what? She was my mum an' all!'

'Good Grief.' said Reynard, reaching up to scratch his head. 'What sort of a family have we got here? Let's see if I've got it right ... Eddie is Sophie's half-brother and they're both Henry's children - so what are they to you?'

'To me? Well, Eddie's my half-brother as well, isn't 'e ... because of our mum? But Sophie's no relation o' mine.'

'It's going to take some time to get my head round all this. It's a bit complicated isn't it Sergeant?'

Groves, looking apprehensively at Lance, who had started to explode at the other end, hardly heard what he'd said, but nodded. For a moment Reynard appeared to be on the point of asking another question but then, seeming to think better of it, glanced at his watch instead. 'Time to go.' he said, beckoning his sergeant with one finger. Groves gave a weak smile and leaned forward to ruffle Garth's hair. Then, standing up, made for the door, keeping as far as she could from Angie ... and the over-powering stench of Lance, who was grinning at her.

As they climbed into the car, a gold coloured Harley

Davidson appeared from around the corner and drew up at the foot of the stairs leading to the flat they'd just left. Two men dismounted, both well built, both well over six feet, and both dressed in black leathers and wearing helmets!

'Hello, hello, hello. What have we got here Sergeant?'

Groves was already ahead of him. 'I think Angie knew a bit more than she let on, Guv.'

'And I think you're right. Come on … we've some unfinished business up there in Thirty Four. If we go back we might get lucky.'

When they returned to Angie's flat the door was still open. They didn't bother to knock but walked straight through into the kitchen. Wayne and Reg were taking off their leather jackets, Angie was filling the kettle, Garth was peeling the wrapper from a red lollipop and Lance, not at all happy at being strapped into his high chair, was bawling his head off and smacking the baby food on his plate with a plastic spoon.

Reynard strode quickly across to block the back door. Groves stood her ground in the entrance from the hall. Their rapid action took Angie and her two companions completely by surprise. 'What the bloody hell?' said Wayne getting to his feet and advancing towards Reynard, his fists bunched ready to strike.

'Sit down.' commanded the D.C.I., pulling out and flashing his warrant card.

Wayne, stopped in his tracks by the authoritative tone, and the appearance of the card, quickly assessed his options before abandoning all thought of aggression and, much to Sergeant Grove's relief, did as he was told.

'They was 'ere just now Wayne.' Angie explained. 'They was arsting about Dad.'

'Oh yeah.' Wayne replied, visibly relaxing when he realised he wasn't the focus of the inspector's attention. 'Wha' abah' tim?'

'We're interested in all the friends and former friends of a man called Melchitt, who's been murdered.'

'Well you're on the wrong track if you're looking for Angie's dad … 'e's dead.' said Wayne.

'Yes, so we've discovered. It's a pity because we were hoping to talk to him about one of his old friends, the father of the murdered man. I don't suppose either of you ever heard him mention anyone called Boris Melchitt?'

'I didn't.' said Angie.

Wayne, shook his head. 'Me neiver.' he replied, dismissively shrugging his shoulders and reaching across the table for the tin of biscuits Angie had moved as far as possible from him. That he'd been expecting to be questioned on an entirely different topic was obvious to Reynard, he could see it in the man's face and he smelled blood. 'Do you own the gold coloured Harley Davidson motorbike you arrived on?' he shouted, banging his fist in the table.

Wayne jerked back in his seat at the unexpected aggression, but still said nothing.

'Well?' demanded Reynard. 'Do you own it?'

'No, I do.' said Reg.

Reynard ignored him and continued to press Wayne. 'You borrowed it from this man, didn't you? Where were you on the 27th of last month - you were in Horsham weren't you?'

'Christ I don't know … work probably.' replied Wayne, having found his voice again. 'I'm a bus driver. You can get my roster from the depot.'

Reynard came round behind him, bent down so close he could almost smell him, and whispered in his ear, 'I hope you're right son, because … if you're not … I'll have you. We've a description of the man we're looking for and it fits you exactly, so does the description of the motor cycle. I'll ask you one more time, were you in or near Horsham on the 27th of October. Come on I want an answer.'

Wayne's bravado suddenly evaporated, tough as he looked, he was a weakling when it came to anything like this. For a second or two he made an attempt to remain silent … but then, without warning, it all came rushing out. 'It was them fuckin' kids wasn't it? I never done nuffin'. I never touched 'im. The silly old bugger ran at me and tripped over. Arse over tit 'e went. Next thing I knew 'e was in the bloody pond and I bloody scarpered didn' I? I never done nuffin. It's the troof.'

Angie watched his capitulation with horror, then went for him with her fists, screaming, 'You did, you 'ittim you liar, you silly, stupid, effin' liar. I knew i'.'

Reg ignored the mayhem and never said a word. He'd been helping Garth unwrap his lollipop, and was busy picking bits of sticky paper from his own fingers with his teeth and spitting them out on the floor.

It was another hour before they left. The car which had brought two up from Brighton took three back, Wayne, having been arrested on suspicion of involvement in the death of Jonathan Melchitt, was on his way to Brighton for further questioning and possible charging.

St. Anne's House,
Horsham Common, Sussex.
Thursday 30th November. 2.15 p.m.

A ll through lunch Mungo had been wondering about the envelope. He'd hardly been able to listen to Violet and Rose as they twittered on about nothing of any great importance. He'd have to start thinking about them a bit more seriously in the future though, he'd seen old people going down like ninepins once the first one died, and they were older than his father. Not that his father had been all that old - seventy odd - nothing really. Violet was nearly eighty six, Rose a couple of years less, but they were sprightly enough. Daisy was a good bit younger, yet she was the one who was failing. Maybe he should engage a housekeeper. There'd be resistance of course, but they oughtn't to be on their own, not after what had happened.

'Finish the bread and butter pudding Mungo, I made it especially for you.'

'I couldn't eat another morsel, Aunt Rose, even though it *is* my favourite. You finish it, you like it too.'

'No, I've had enough,' she replied.

'Me too.' added Violet. 'We're going into town Mungo. We haven't a thing in the house. Will you be alright on your own … we won't be late?'

'Alright on my own, I *am* forty seven you know! 'I'll be fine, Aunt Violet, do you want me to drive you?'

'No Rose'll drive.'

'I'm going up then.' he said, and returned to the study … and the envelope. It lay in the middle of the desk.

He knew, somehow, it was going to be important and he sat

looking at it for a long time before opening the top drawer and taking out a paper knife.

The agreement which had been with it, and on which he'd been pondering, had been signed by all of them. It was too vague to be of much help in discovering anything of consequence about the club but, before opening the envelope, he glanced at it once more.

Latchmere Cricket Club
Burns Road, Battersea
22nd May 1957.

The L.M.S. Club

We the undersigned do solemnly resolve we will uphold the rules of The LMS Club contained in the accompanying envelope which may only be opened by our executors on our demise.

The LMS, as defined in the rules, is the only body authorised by us to make the details public.

We charge our descendants and executors to abide by the above resolutions and observe the rules, as will we.

Mungo, unable to take the paper he held in his hand seriously, smiled to himself as he took the envelope, slit the flap, and drew out a second sheet.

It was also headed with the name of the cricket club. He scanned it quickly trying to grasp its meaning but, once he'd read it through, he concluded it to be the product of a crowd of inebriated students: comic book stuff, with secret agreements and solemn resolutions, a load of gibberish which must have been written in a pub and more than likely after they'd drunk enough to float a battleship. His father must have kept it, as he had the photograph, to remind himself of the days of his youth. It was a souvenir, nothing more. And then he read it again more carefully, immediately seeing a possible connection to the disasters which had befallen his family. Without any further thought of complying with the undertaking made by his father, or the plea he should do the same himself, he picked up the telephone and rang his friend, Commander Bill Simpson at New Scotland Yard, who was out. His secretary promised to get a message to him.

'Tell him something's turned up.' said Mungo.

'May I say in what connection?'

'Just say the Melchitt deaths.'

Ten minutes later the commander rang back. 'What's happened Mungo? My secretary seemed to think your message was important enough to hunt me down.'

'Glad she did, Bill. If what I think may be behind all these terrible 'goings on' I may be in danger myself. I know you said it to me the last time we met. I didn't believe you then, but I now have every reason to think you might be right.'

'What the hell's happened?'

'I've found something - a letter - an agreement ... Oh it's all too complicated. When can we meet?'

'Well, I'm on my way to the airport - I'm going to attend a dinner in Brussels, an E.U. thing. I'll not be back until the morning. Contact Foxy Reynard if you're worried about your safety. I'll ring him anyway and tell him to put a man up at the house.'

'No. I'll wait until you get back. I'm not sure enough of my ground to ask for protection, and anyway my aunts would be worried to death if they thought we were in danger. I mean, I might be seeing a threat which doesn't actually exist.'

'So you might, but listen, I'd trust Foxy with my life so take him into your confidence, he won't bite you if it all turns out to be false alarm ... Go on ring him.'

St Anne's House,
Horsham Common, Sussex.
Thursday 30th November 2006. 7.00 p.m.

Reynard had hardly seen Wayne into a cell before he was called to the phone. It was Mungo, ringing to tell him he had new information which might indicate the possibility of more killings. He dropped everything and drove straight over to Horsham, deciding, on the way that he wasn't quite ready to reveal anything of Wayne's arrest.

As soon as he got there, Mungo conducted him to the study. On the desk was the envelope he'd found in his father's deed box. So much had happened he could hardly credit he'd only just opened it for the first time that morning.

'I'm grateful for your coming over so quickly Inspector; I just hope you won't feel your journey has been wasted by the time you've read these two pieces of paper.'

'I doubt whether that'll be the case Mr Melchitt. From what you told me on me telephone you may have stumbled on something which'll prove relevant to all our investigations.'

'Before we start Inspector I believe I was a bit short with you the last time we met, when we talked about my grandfather's trust and the way it worked. I have a lot on my mind but it was no excuse for my unmannerly behaviour to you, I apologise.'

'I took no offence Mr Melchitt, forget it. I know how the tensions build up and how lack of progress can be so frustrating. Now … what have you to tell me?'

'I hardly know where to start … it's a long story and started back when my father was a young student at London University. He and some friends made an agreement regarding something they jointly owned. In this agreement … well you'd better read it yourself inspector … here.'

Reynard took the envelope, read the instruction on the front of it and turned it over. When he saw the signed instruction written across the seal he put it down again and sat back with his arms folded across his stomach. 'Very dramatic Mr Melchitt.'

'Yes, isn't it? replied Mungo. 'Schoolboy stuff, you might say, but I had to give you the opportunity to make your own mind up regarding the real relevance, if any, of what you'll find they call the LMS Club.'

'I understand. May I read what's in the envelope?'

'Oh do, do. That's why I asked you to come? I hope, indeed I think you'll see, as I have done, how an innocent bit of fun has become unexpectedly transformed into an incentive to murder people. It's harmless enough at first sight as you will soon discover, but when you consider what's happened to the Melchitts and now, I understand, to the Bretts, I think you'll appreciate how apprehensive I am regarding my own safety and that of my aunts.'

'Well let's have a look.' said Reynard, as he withdrew the letter and the second envelope from the outer one.

When he drove back home two hours later he wasn't sure whether he should be laughing or worrying.

Sussex Police Major Incident Suite, Sussex House, Brighton. Friday 1st December 2006. 7.22 a.m.

Reynard hadn't slept a wink, he'd been up since six and was in at seven. It was looking as though the back of the Melchitt investigations had finally been broken.

Sherman had identified Angus Brett as Dudley Melchitt's probable killer and *he* had Wayne Tyler in a cell downstairs held for his likely involvement in the death of Jonathan Melchitt. One of these two would surely turn out to be responsible for Boris Melchitt's death as well.

Best of all though, after his talk with Mungo the previous evening he now had a possible motive for most of the deaths, including those of Angus and Betty Brett.

There was a massive complication in the offing however. As a result of reading the papers Mungo had shown him and, adding the information he'd gained during his visit to Angie La Tour, he could see there were still seven future potential victims and, bizarrely, each was also the possible killer.

Bearing in mind what had been happening, it was obvious any of the deaths so far could have come as direct result of the agreement made by the members of the LMS Club, and that the killer could be any one of the seven suspects.

The only person who didn't fit the pattern was Angus's wife Betty, and he assumed she'd stumbled on her husband's killer by chance and been murdered to preserve his identity.

His immediate priority was to use the compelling new information to identify the killer from amongst the seven people whose names he'd printed on a slip of paper:

Rex Brett
Mungo Melchitt
Sandy McPhee
Eva McPhee
Eddie Parsons
Angie La Tour
Sophie Sweetman

He rang Commander Simpson, catching him on the way to the airport in Brussels. As soon as the normal courtesies had been exchanged he'd blurted out the information he'd got at Mungo's the previous night. 'So my recommendation, Sir, is that we change our tactics immediately, put the maximum effort into preventing more deaths, and only when we have everyone under guard or some sort of surveillance, do we risk going back to our hunt for the killer.'

'Absolutely. Start getting something together now. I'll come to you straight from the Heathrow. Put a watch on all the seven people on your list. We need to be aware of what every single one of them is up to at every waking moment. I want to know about it if one of them picks his nose. Clear?'

'As crystal, Sir. I've been borrowing a few bodies from other enquiries and other divisions. Most of the seven are down on my patch, or up in London. We'll have everyone under observation by my people, in plain clothes, sometime today.

'OK, you seem to have it covered. What about the enquiries into the deaths which have already taken place, anything new there?'

Reynard gave the commander a précis of each case and a promise to be at the Brighton Police Station to meet him when he arrived from the airport. He then rang D.I. Sherman and acquainted him with the new facts as well. 'I thought you'd like to know I got a guy for Jonathan's death yesterday. I have him here and I'll be questioning him this morning ... if I can find time.'

'Great. Was it the man who ran into the orchard?'

'It was, I had a bit of luck, Groves and I were searching out the members of the LMS Club, and when we were talking to Frog's, that's Roland La Tour's, daughter, Angie, this guy turned up. He's her boyfriend.'

'So, the little red address book came in handy then, you crafty old sod?'

'What red book?' Reynard asked, innocently. 'Don't know

what you're talking about.'

'Who is he anyway, and did he kill old Melchitt?'

'His name's Wayne Tyler, late twenties, bus driver, lives in East London, no record of significance, just a few cases of football hooliganism and two of 'drunk and dis…' He's not bright; I reckon his wife, Angie Latour, egged him on. She's got a bit more backbone than him. What we don't know is why. But I'm sure it'll turn out to be something to do with this LMS Club crowd, especially in light of this new information.'

'Yeah … did he hit Melchitt, d'you think?'

'Says he didn't touch him at all. Says the old man leapt out of his chair and went for him but tripped, staggered over to the pond and joined the goldfish.'

'D'you believe him?'

'I don't disbelieve him. Anyway, we have to find out why he did it, especially as he's not on the list. It might mean Jonathan's death's un-associated with the others … or with the LMS Club. In fact, the more I think about it, the more I'm inclined to think that's the case.'

'OK, so what's the most likely reason Tyler was there?'

'Up until last night I would have said robbery, but why go all the way to Horsham to do that unless it was to steal some particular item. I'm going to have a go at wheedling it out of him later on today.'

'Good luck, let me know how you get on. Any news on Boris's case?'

'I'm hoping to get to Rottingdean this afternoon after trying Sandy McPhee again, but I have to see Bill Simpson at two so I'm not so sure when I'll get down there. By the way …'

'What's that young copper you have down there been doing, did he find anything?'

'Young D.C. Best? Well, he's been trying to track down the company which hired out the bike - assuming it was hired. He hasn't been back to me. How're things at your end?'

'No change. I still reckon Angus did it, but Bellamy's got this fixation on the man in the bushes, I suppose he may be connected. If we could only eliminate him we'll be better able to pin the killing on Angus. Not that it'll matter much now, he's dead anyway. Have you been speaking to Greg Lightfoot lately?'

'Not yet, I'll be talking to him next. If he has anything of consequence to say I'll give you a bell.'

'Don't worry, you have enough on your plate, I'll be calling him during the morning. Is that it then?'

'Yeah, I'm done.'

Ten minutes later Reynard was talking to Lightfoot and repeating what he told Sherman. Lightfoot had no news and it was left that they'd talk again if there was any new development. Reynard asked him to keep a special lookout for any reference to the LMS Club which he described as being the link between the three Melchitt deaths and that of the two Bretts. He never mentioned 'borrowing' the little red book.

'You were wondering if it was a student's drinking club when you were here. Still of the same opinion?'

'No. Whatever it is ... it's much more; it has to do with their youth alright and it's connected, would you believe, with the ownership of a stone.'

'A what?'

'Yeah, I know ... a stone, a bloody stone.'

'A precious one?'

'That, old son, is what I'm going to have to find out isn't it? And the person who has the key to it all, Henry Byrd, lives in Mexico for most of the year. He's there now, but he'll be back at Christmas. I hope to see him when he returns to London. Maybe then we'll see a way through the mist.'

By ten, Reynard and Groves were tackling Wayne, who was accompanied by the legal aid duty solicitor. They spent over three hours questioning him but at lunchtime they still had nothing worthwhile beyond what they'd extracted in the first ten minutes. It had been a soft interview because Wayne indicated, from the start that he intended to plead guilty to 'Intimidation' and nothing else.

Reynard had begun with an aggressive statement and a short sharp question. 'You killed him Wayne, a poor old man, so frail he couldn't blow the top of a rice pudding and you belted him and shoved him into the water when it must have been obvious he couldn't swim. Why did you do it?'

'I didn't.'

'OK let's start at the beginning ... why were you there in the first place?'

Wayne thought for a bit before answering. 'Angie tole me ter go down and give 'im a few verbals.'

'Why?'

'Because 'e's a stingy old bastard wot made loads o' money out of 'er Dad and wouldn't give 'er a tosser when she was skint.'

'You went to frighten him?'

'No I didn't ... well ... yes I did ... but I'd no idea 'e was such an old dodderer till 'e come charging out of the 'ouse screaming blue fuckin' murder.'

'And then?'

'And then 'e tripped and went head first inter the flamin' water. Shook me I can tell you.'

'What's the LMS Club?'

'The what?'

'LMS Club.'

'Never 'eard of it.'

'What's the stone?'

'What stone?'

'The one the LMS Club own.'

'Look 'ere boss I ain't got no idea what y'talkin' abaht ... notta clue.'

And that was as far as they got, despite spending hours going over the same ground again and again. Wayne couldn't be shaken, and Reynard was sure he was telling the truth.

'So what'll it be?' asked Groves.

'Oh I don't know it's up to the coroner ... 'Accident' or 'Misadventure' I expect.

'And what'll happen to Wayne Tyler.'

'He'll get a roasting, not much more. Angie will give him some stick though ... he'll probably wish he was inside.'

At around two o'clock Reynard was greeting Commander Simpson. A full review of all the deaths took place in Reynard's office and, once the commander had digested everything he'd been told, and agreed the plans for future action he'd been shown, he left, while Inspector Reynard and Sergeant Groves set off on another attempt to interview Sandy McPhee.

They got to his house just before three. There were no cars visible and no one answered the door when they knocked. 'Have a look round the back Sergeant; we didn't get a chance to do it the last time. I'll check the garage.' Reynard said, tightening his scarf around his neck and turning up his collar against the driving rain. 'Go on, go on.' he urged, 'Let's get this over with. If we don't find anyone here we might as well go down to Rottingdean.'

Groves set off to circle the house by walking along the brick path which not only ran right round it but also linked a number of semi-circular terraces. On each of them stood cast iron urns and ornate terracotta planters full of leafless geraniums or withered petunias. The beds were no better, un-trimmed shrubs fought with roses which hadn't been pruned for years. Weeds had taken over all the intermediate space. All in all it told a story of neglect and disinterest.

As she worked her way round she stopped at each window and peered in, but she saw no sign of life and little evidence of anyone living there. The place was tidy, over tidy actually, and showed none of the negligence apparent in the garden. Even the kitchen, which did seem to have been in current use, gave the impression of being a show place. The only thing she could see confirming someone had been there recently was a single mug, rinsed out, and standing upside down on the draining board. The curtains were drawn in the room they'd been in previously, the one they were in when they'd interviewed Eva, so she couldn't see much of it. All in all it looked like it was the home of someone living alone, and spending as little time there as possible,

Reynard had no more success than Sergeant Groves, the garage was shut and locked, as was the workshop behind it, and the door which he assumed led, via a narrow stairway, to the hayloft above it. He managed to see into the garage through the dirt and the cobwebs covering the glazed upper half of a side door. Inside was an old car, a black Austin Princess. It was covered in dust and its tyres were flat. Apart from the vehicle and a dozen petrol cans the place was empty, while the wooden shed round at the back of the garage only had gardening implements in it.

When they met at the front of the house they gave the door one more knock, and when it wasn't answered they got into the car and headed straight for Rottingdean.

On board the 'Caveat Emptor',
Blackwater Creek, Rottingdean.
Friday 1st December 2006. 2.30 p.m.

D.C. Best had been half expecting them since lunchtime. He'd suggested meeting at his house as it was so cold on the boat but Inspector Reynard had said 'No'. He was never a man to get too cosy with his staff - didn't want a promising young man like Constable Best getting above himself by allowing him closer than an arm's length. Foxy Reynard, like Tank Sherman, was old school, a man who believed everyone had their place, and he wasn't comfortable sitting at the kitchen table eating ham sandwiches with the young constable every time they met. Canteens and other junior officers were for that!

'What have you got then?' asked Reynard, as Best opened his folder. 'And while you getting your stuff in order I'd better tell you we have two more murders that're likely to be connected to the deaths of the Melchitts'

'Who're they Sir?" asked Best.

'Name of Brett, husband and wife, killed on their own backdoor step in Beaconsfield sometime early the day before yesterday.'

'That'd be Thursday ... '

'Yes Thursday the 23rd ... why?'

'Might tie in with something I found out.'

'Really ... so what have you got for me?'

'Plenty.' was the confident reply. 'I found five companies who might have hired out the Honda and the leathers, and called on them. I got a better print of the defect in the tyre, in case it turns up again, and I have a partial registration number the joggers remembered.'

'OK.' said Reynard. 'Tell me about the hire companies first … where are they for a start?'

'They're all between here and London; I stretched out my search when I couldn't find one in the original zone we picked. There's one in East Croydon, one in Cheam, one in Sutton, one in Banstead and one in Redhill. Now it's obvious he could have got the bike anywhere in the UK, or even France, but I had to start somewhere and these are what came up that are within a reasonable distance.'

'OK, and what happened, did you see any of 'em?'

Best drew his oil drum seat closer to the makeshift table they'd set up on the previous visit and lay down his papers 'Oh I saw them all alright, went yesterday, took me all morning.'

Sergeant Groves who'd been shivering since they'd arrived spotted a bottle of Bovril on the shelf over the kettle. 'Anyone for a hot drink?'

'I'll make it Sarge.' said Best, half rising.

Sergeant Groves went over to fill the kettle.

'Forget it' barked Reynard. 'Let's get through what D.C. Best has to say first, then we can go down to the pub and get warm before we go back to see if Sandy McPhee's turned up. Carry on Constable …'

Sergeant Groves shrugged her shoulders, shivered violently, pulled on her gloves and, with an expression of resignation, resumed her uncomfortable seat.

D.C. Best waited until she was settled and then cleared his throat and carried on. 'Right, Sir … as we don't know who we're looking for I had no picture to show the people I spoke to. Nevertheless I did make some progress because the first place I called had hired out a new 50cc Honda and a set of leathers on the day before Boris's death. The girl in the office remembered the man clearly and she was able to give me a good description of him. I used this description when I went to the others, and in one of them it was recognised.'

'Really? This is sounding good. Go on.'

'It dodgier from here on unfortunately, Guv. The first company is the Banstead branch of a firm in Wembley and they send all their paperwork over there by post, weekly. As of this morning the batch of papers we're interested is still in the post, and won't be delivered until Monday. I had to settle for the man's description to make any progress.'

'How did he pay?'

'Cash in both cases.'

'Driving Licence. He must have shown one.'

'Yeah, that's what I thought, and he did, but neither could give me the details. The first lot had 'em with all the rest of the paperwork which is in the post, we'll get it on Monday, but the other crowd, a bit of a 'back street outfit', if you know what I mean, only had a tick in a box on their form to confirm they'd actually *seen* a current licence and I couldn't make out the name of the hirer because someone had spilled coffee all over it. They gave him a new Honda as well.

'Didn't they keep a note of his driving licence number, they can't do that ... I'll have them sorted!' said Reynard crashing his fist on the table and sending Best's papers flying. 'The flamin' idiots,' he said, 'so we're no farther on then?'

'Well we are a bit, Guv.' Best replied, trying not to show his disappointment at Reynard's apparent failure to recognise the progress he'd made. 'When I called round to the address given to the second hirer - it didn't exist!'

Reynard started to nod, this was better, 'Yes, yes, yes ... so, we have a man who looks as though he doesn't want to be traced hiring a Honda motorcycle and a similar set of leathers from two different hirers within striking distance of Rottingdean.'

'And of Beaconsfield Guv ... after what you've told me today ... we can include Beaconsfield.'

'So we can.' answered Reynard, rubbing his knees.

'Getting cold Guv?' asked Groves, hopefully.

'No, no, no. Just thinking ... so it looks as though we have a description of the man but we still don't know who he is. Correct? And we'll have his licence in a day or so. You've done well again, Constable, we'll have that hot drink now; where shall we go?

'My local, Sir, The Barge Inn ... five minutes away.'

'Evenin Next.' said the landlord, as they came in, 'What're you having ... it's a cold night?'

Best looked at Reynard, who grinned as he answered, 'D'you know what ... I fancy Bovril?'

The landlord wasn't sure how to react to such an unlikely request, but he knew Best, and he'd seen Reynard around since

Boris's murder so he realised he was 'Police' as well and decided to assume the order was genuine.

'Same all round is it?' he asked, half smiling in case it wasn't.

Best and Groves nodded but Reynard wasn't finished. 'And a few slices of toast would go down very.'

' 'Er ... right.' the landlord replied, returning a few minutes later with three steaming glass mugs of the beef extract drink and a plate piled high with hot buttered toast.'

'So much for the hiring then ...' said Reynard, reaching for half a slice dripping with butter.

'No, no. But there is one more thing ... neither company hired out a helmet. Remember I told ...'

'So you did, what else have you got?'

Best dug into a file he was holding 'I have the print of the tyre fault. Not much use on its own, I know; but it might turn out to be a helpful bit of corroborative if we find something else.'

'Yeah, excellent again. And 'er ... 'er ... oh yes, the registration number.'

'Well Sir ... they only remembered a bit of it unfortunately, so don't get too excited.'

Reynard took another piece of toast, 'Try me.'

'It's just that the two women joggers are both fairly sure the registration started with a letter K.'

Reynard's eyed nearly popped out of his head. 'A letter K? That's amazing, we've had a K crop up before.'

Both Groves and Best looked puzzled.

'Where's that then?' asked Groves.

'Bloody Yorkshire Sergeant, that's where.' Reynard exclaimed, slapping his knee. 'You've done it again haven't you Constable, you've saved the best until last.'

By the time Reynard had explained about the milk churn incident they'd finished their Bovril, polished off the toast, and were starting to put on their coats.

'Can I get you anything else?' asked the landlord.

'Give D.C. Best a large 'whateverhelikes' next time he comes in, give me the receipt ... and here ... keep the change.' said Reynard, laying a twenty pound note on the bar.

Sergeant Groves winked at Best, waved at the landlord, and followed the D.C.I. out.

As they drove up to Lewes they reviewed all the factual and circumstantial evidence they'd accumulated in their investigation. The amount was piling up and the recognition of the rapidly improving position was clearly reflected in grins of satisfaction widening on their faces.

'So what's behind it all Guv? Is it the people in this LMS Club thing d'you think?'

'Might be; Mungo spilled the beans last night. Want to know what he said? If I tell you, don't laugh.'

By the time he was finished a look of total disbelief had replaced the sergeant's earlier grin. 'There must be more to it, Guv.' she said. 'Four dead, for something so childish.'

'You may be right Sergeant, but it's clearly not childish to whoever's doing the killing.'

'I thought you had Angus down for it.'

'What, and murder his wife and commit suicide afterwards by hitting himself on the head with a stone mason's chisel - I don't think so. But it looks like this LMS thing is a serious matter for the laddie we're after.'

The Malthouse, Point Hill,
Lewes, Sussex.
Friday 1st December 2006. 6.00 p.m.

There was still no sign of anyone when they arrived at Sandy McPhee's house for their second visit of the day, which brought a string of curses from D.C.I. Reynard. 'Give the door a good thumping while I wait in the car.' he said.

As Sergeant Groves raised her hand to grasp the knocker a vehicle swung into the drive, its lights silhouetting her against the door. Reynard, whose car was facing into the garden hedge, looked into his mirror but the un-dipped headlights dazzled him and he had to put up his hand to shade his eyes. By the time he'd got out, the newcomer had driven round to what must have been his regular parking place in the shadows at the side of the garage. Next thing Reynard heard was the sound of a car door closing and, soon afterwards, a man emerged from the darkness and approached him; a small square shouldered man wearing a tweed cap, a black waterproof windcheater, and carrying a golf bag.

'You looking for me?' he challenged.

Reynard flashed his warrant card. 'If you're Mr Alexander McPhee - yes we are.'

'Ah, police … you'd better come in.' the man answered. 'I'm Alexander McPhee, but everyone calls me Sandy. My sister told me you'd be calling.' He nodded to Sergeant Groves who stood aside to let him get to the lock with his key. When he'd opened it he went in first. 'Hang on 'til I turn a light.' he said, affably. 'Been waiting long?'

'No, we've just arrived,' answered Reynard 'but we were here earlier this afternoon.'

'Sorry about that, I've been playing golf.'

'Right … right. Can you spare us ten minutes?'

'Just about; I'm going out for dinner.'

'We'll try not to keep you too long then.'

As they'd been talking they'd moved into the sitting room, where McPhee went over to the window and drew the curtains across. 'Keeps the cold out.' he said with a laugh, walking back and putting a match to the fire. 'Soon have you warm ... 'er ... 'er ... '

'Detective Chief Inspector Reynard and Detective Sergeant Groves - Sussex CID.'

'Ah yes ... would you like a. drink ... I'm having one?'

'No thank you Sir. We just want to ask you a few questions and then we'll go.'

'Fair enough. What about you, my dear?'

'Not for me either.' snapped Groves, bristling at his patronisingly posed question.

Ignoring her frosty reply, or probably not even noticing it, he said: 'Right then, so it's just me.'

Waving them to the sofa, he poured a large measure of whisky for himself and took it over to a fireside chair which was clearly his preserve.

Reynard decided to play the 'wait in silence' ploy and said nothing. Groves, who was used to his ways, did the same. McPhee, hanging on until he couldn't stand the tension any longer, broke first. 'So ... Inspector ... you want to talk to me about the LMS Club, according to the telephone call I received from my sister.'

'Yes I do, but I've found out a bit more about it anyway, from another source. What I really want to ask you about is something slightly different.'

'Fire away Inspector.'

'Where were you on the 24th of last month?'

'I beg your pardon.'

Reynard repeated his question.

'I don't know. How should I know?'

'Perhaps you'd check.'

'But I thought you said this interview was to do with the LMS Club.'

'It is to do with the LMS Club. Where were you Sir, on the 24th of November?'

'I haven't a clue Inspector. Really I must protest. Why do you want to know?'

'Just answer the question Sir - if you would.'

'I can't; I don't remember. The office probably, I'm there most days. I'll get my diary, it's on my dressing table upstairs, it should tell me.'

Reynard was enjoying McPhee's discomfort 'Go and find Mr McPhee's diary Sergeant.'

'Really Inspector.' Sandy said, his face beginning to redden. 'I must protest. Oughtn't you to have a warrant or something to search my house?'

'We're not searching your house Sir; we're just trying to establish your whereabouts on the date I mentioned ... your diary might help.'

'I'll get it.'

'No Sir, I need you here.' said Reynard, jerking his head sideways to indicate to Groves she should leave the room and go to get the diary, hoping she'd realise he really meant 'have a good look around'. Even before she'd gone Reynard was firing another question. 'While Sergeant Groves is getting your diary would you tell me where you were on the 4th of September last ... or the 24th of October if you can't remember that far back?'

'Inspector I don't know, I really don't - it's ages ago and I can't just recall where I was without giving it a bit of thought. What's it all about anyway?'

'We're enquiring into the deaths of a number of people with whom we believe you have a connection.'

Sandy leapt to his feet. 'I have no idea what you're talking about - I think you should go.'

'Sit down Sir. When you've answered my questions we'll leave. Or maybe you'd rather come with us and we can do it all at the station. It's up to you.'

'But I don't want that woman poking about in all my private things upstairs. Your behaviour is disgraceful. You can be sure I'll be taking this to your superiors.'

'That is your prerogative, Sir. So ... is it to be questioned here or at the station?'

'Am I under arrest?'

'No Sir, you are not.' answered Reynard, biting back the word 'yet' which he'd been inclined to add. 'So if you sit down again we can carry on.'

Sandy didn't sit though; he went to the side table and poured himself another whisky. He pointedly didn't offer one to

Detective Chief Inspector Reynard.

'Have you a motor cycle?'

'Sandy stopped in his tracks and swung on the D.C.I. 'Have I a what? ... Are you mad?'

'A motor cycle - a crimson and cream 50 cc Honda, probably?'

'No I do not. Look this has gone far enough. You can get out of my house I'm calling my solicitor.'

'That'll be to ask him to join you at the station then.' replied Reynard.

'You've got a fucking cheek Inspector and, by God, you'll rue the day you came here. Now go.'

'I'll go, but only when my men arrive. They'll be staying here until further notice.'

'What for, for God's sake?'

'To protect you, Sir. We have a dangerous killer at large and you are known to be one of his targets.'

'Me. This is ridiculous. Why me?'

'Because of your connection with the LMS Club.'

'I don't understand.'

'Oh I think you do, Sir.'

Sergeant Groves came back into the room shaking her head. In her hand was Sandy's diary. 'Here you are, Sir.' she said, as she handed it to him.

Sandy put it on the table without opening it as Reynard continued, 'You see, Mr McPhee, I have the names of seven people in my pocket ... they're all connected with the LMS Club, and they all have to be protected. Yours is one of those names.'

'But I've never disguised the fact I knew about the LMS Club.' said Sandy, beginning to relax as he felt himself less in the spotlight than he'd been only minutes earlier. 'It's all a damned silly joke anyway ... something dreamed up by my father and his friends years ago; it has no relevance now. Anyway they're all dead as far as I know.'

'Not all, Henry Byrd is still alive.'

'So who are these seven people?'

'Oh I'm sure you'll be able to work out who they are, if you know what the LMS Club is, Mr McPhee. The important thing is every one of them, including you, is in danger, which is why I'm having a man here twenty four hours a day, and another who'll accompany you wherever you go; I'm doing the same for the other six too. Once my people get here I'm leaving. You could let us take you into protective custody until everything is sorted out if you like.'

As Reynard's last few words sank in, Sandy's hopeful thoughts began to evaporate again. 'No I don't think I want that. Who authorised this plan?'

'Commander Simpson, the CID national coordinator. He's up in Scotland Yard. Do you want to talk to him?'

Sandy shook his head.

'I'll ask Sergeant Groves to take a look around then, she can make sure everything's locked which should be locked, check there's no one about who shouldn't be about, see nothing's amiss … all that, and in the meantime we can continue our conversation.'

Sandy remained silent as he felt everything closing in. How had they got on to him? What had led them to his door, or was it after all as the inspector had said, and they were simply protecting everyone. If that was the case he'd better play along with them.

'Your keys Sir … may we have your keys? Sergeant Groves will check all the doors of the house and the outhouses.'

'Oh very well.' Sandy replied, begrudgingly handing over a bunch of keys he took from his pocket. 'I doubt if you'll find anyone hiding here, I'm sure I'd know if there was anyone skulking around. Who are you expecting anyway? You must tell me who they are Inspector, so I can look out for them myself.'

'Well Sir, I'm sure you'll appreciate we can't release the names of the people we suspect until we can prove our suspicions. We'd be in serious trouble if we were wrong … as I'm sure you will appreciate. For this reason we won't be giving your name to any of the others.'

Sandy sat for a moment digesting what D.C.I. Reynard had told him, balancing it with what he knew.

Reynard took the opportunity to cross to the window and pull back one of the curtains. 'Just keeping an eye on who comes in.' he said, spotting Groves on her way to the garage. 'Ten minutes more and we should be off.'

As he returned to his seat Sandy spoke, 'I can't have a man trailing all round London with me Inspector, it's not a practical arrangement.'

'Well it might only be for a few days with a bit of luck …

have you ever hired a motorcycle?'

'There you go again. Why would I want a motor bike, I can't even ride one.'

'That's what puzzling us, Sir. How far is it from here to Beaconsfield?'

'Are you completely mad? What's Beaconsfield got to do with me?'

'We don't know yet. We're hoping you'll tell us. What about Rottingdean, do you go down there much? What about the 'Caveat Emptor' ... or Blackwater Creek?'

'Can I ring my solicitor please, you're trying to bully me and I won't have it.'

'It's your telephone Sir, you can ring who you like. Who do you know up in Richmond?'

Sandy looked at him blankly.

'In Richmond, in Yorkshire, Sir ... know anyone up there do you? What were you doing up there in September?'

Sandy got up, filled his glass to the brim and was about to sit down with the telephone in his hand, when Sergeant Groves stuck her head round the door and beckoned Inspector Reynard to join her in the hall.

'He's our man alright.' she whispered, much more calmly than she really felt. 'I found a box in the hay loft over the garage. Inside there's a black helmet with a dark visor, a pair of black gauntlets, and three sets of false number plates. One set would fit over those on his car and the other two sets would probably fit a motor bike. There was a coil of double sided tape there as well. It looks to me as though he used the tape to stick the false plates temporarily over the real ones.

There's also a load of loose letters and another blank set of motor cycle plates. He quite clearly made up different plates for each outing. And ... wait for it ... he's used a double K in making up one car number plate I found, and a single K at the start of one of those for a motor bike which also looks as though it's been used. There must have been a sale in Ks going on when he was setting this all up because he's still got about eight of them left! On top of that, I also saw tyre marks in the dust on the garage floor which look about the size of a motor cycle; I'm sure if we search we'll find some of them have the fault D.C Best came across.'

'That's brilliant ... more than enough to charge him. You

did well to spot so much, so quickly.'

'Thank you Guv, but that's not all.'

'You have more?' asked Reynard, his voice rising in parallel with his excitement.

'You didn't see his car when he came in?'

'No, his lights were dazzling me and he drove it round the side anyway, I couldn't see much from where I was parked.'

'It's silver!'

'It's not!'

'Yes … and it's a Volvo!'

'Don't tell me it's a 'Y' reg, C40, drop head?'

'I cannot tell a lie Guv! He must have used his car to go to Richmond and travelled on a motor bike for the others.'

'We have him!' exclaimed Reynard. 'I'll charge him and then we can get down to corroborating everything.'

They went back into the room together and, from the stern looks on their faces, Sandy knew the worst. He got to his feet hesitatingly, 'What …?'

'Alexander McPhee I'm arresting you on suspicion of being involved in the murder of Boris Melchitt and others on various dates in September, October and November of this year. You do not have to say any ….'

As Reynard's voice droned on, Sandy hardly heard the familiar phrases; he'd slumped into his chair and was staring disconsolately into the fire.

When Reynard finished his ritual he reached out a hand. Sandy grasped it and, pulling himself to his feet, took one last look around; somehow he knew he'd never see the place again. Then he meekly walked out to the car between his captors.

On his way back to Brighton, Reynard rang Commander Simpson on his mobile. 'I've just spent the last hour at Sandy McPhee's. I'm bringing him back to Brighton with me, as I speak, having just charged him with complicity in Boris Melchitt's murder, which I think we'll be able to prove fairly convincingly.

I also think he killed Angus and Betty Brett, and possibly even Dudley Melchitt as well, we have a number of indicators pointing us in that direction.'

'Tremendous work, Foxy.' said the commander. Please pass

my thanks and congratulation to all concerned. You'll telephone Lightfoot and Sherman?'

'Oh I'll certainly will Sir, sometime tonight, though I don't know how happy Ronie'll be to hear I've beaten him to it.'

'He'll live! So ... no loose ends?'

'Just a couple, I still don't know much about a flippin' stone which keeps cropping up and might be at the root of the trouble, and I've still not met three leading members of the cast, so to speak: Henry Byrd and his two children, Sophie and Eddie, the West Indian girl and her half-brother from Portsmouth. Maybe, when I've spoken to them, I'll be able to piece together the whole story. They're my priority now.'

It was after midnight when he got home to his bungalow in Malvern Gardens, and crept into the bedroom in the dark so as not to disturb his wife's sleep.

Unfortunately for him she was waiting for him to get back so she could unburden herself. 'Where have you been? I thought you were never coming home - I've had a terrible day, the boiler won't light and the man only serviced it yesterday. He can't come again for a week - I could kill him.'

'I'll ring him in the morning, Cathy,' said Foxy, wearily, 'I've had a bit of a day myself.'

Belvedere Crescent, Islington, London. N1 1QB
Monday 11th December 2006 1.30 p.m.

Henry Byrd sat at the head of the table. On either side of him were his two children, Sophie and Eddie. Through the glazed double doors, linking the dining room to the sitting room, Sophie could just see the picture of her mother over the fireplace. The offensive facial expression which had so upset her when she'd first seen it seemed to have mellowed into one of parental concern, and the leer had almost become a smile.

Outside the window, in the garden, a light covering of early snow had encrusted the stone perched on the top of the rockery.

Eddie was looking at it out of the corner of his eye.

Mrs 'F' had left an hour before. She'd let the visitors in when they'd arrived, conducted them into the sitting room, and then gone to the kitchen to fetch the tray of coffee which Henry had asked her to prepare. That had been at eleven, and from then until he rang for her again at twelve, and asked her to bring the salad lunch things to the dining table, all she'd heard was the muted murmur of his voice coming from behind the closed sitting room door. It was only when she'd brought the food into the dining room, and looked through the glass of the dividing doors, she'd got the opportunity to see them. Henry had his back to the fireplace heating his backside, smoothing it with the flat of his hands and rubbing the warmth of the fire into a body unused to the cold.

He dominated the room from the position he'd taken, but he would have dominated it wherever he'd been standing, a powerfully framed man of six and a half feet, steel grey hair brilliantined and brushed flat to his scalp and with a smooth shaven somewhat florid complexion. His dress was quintessentially English: Cavalry twill trousers, Harris Tweed sports jacket, Old

Cranleighan's tie knotted tightly into the cutaway collar of his pristine white shirt, and highly polished brown leather brogues. A military man if ever there was one, and nothing like the popular perception of an artist.

That he'd deliberately chosen his stance in order to control what he anticipated might be an uncomfortable interview was not immediately obvious. That he'd done so to head off any thought of their taking him to task over the past was equally unclear. But the fact his children were so mesmerised simply by the sight of him was immediately apparent to Mrs 'F' in the few minutes she'd surreptitiously watched from the next room. During the whole time she'd not heard Sophie's or Eddie's voice once. Where were the fireworks she'd been expecting? She went back to the kitchen bearing an expression of undisguised disappointment.

Right from the beginning, Sophie and Eddie had lost their way. Unprepared for the paralysing effect their father was having on them, they'd listened in silence, their questions unasked. Had they had the opportunity to think about it they might have begun to understand why their mothers had been unable to resist him. Years before, when he'd have been in his prime, his effect on all who met him must have been devastating; no wonder impressionable young girls capitulated.

He'd started by repeating the guidelines he'd insisted on before accepting their request for a meeting. Only a cruel and selfish man would treat his children as he was treating them, but all his life he'd put himself first and it didn't look as though he was about to change.

The meeting had come about after Mrs 'F' had spoken to him of Sophie's initial visit when she'd been on her own, and of her more recent one, when Eddie had been with her. She'd expected Henry to turn them down but, inexplicably, he hadn't, and she'd been sent straight round to Angie's to get Eddie's number and set a meeting up. From then on it had been a matter of finding a date when one of Sophie's trips to England coincided with one of Eddie's days off.

The atmosphere had been tense from the moment they'd been conducted into the sitting room. An outsider would never have believed this was the first meeting of a father with one of his children and only his second with the other. His cool almost resentful greeting had set the style from the start, and he'd shown little sign of relaxing it as the time ticked past.

'Pleased you're here' - 'Only seeing you to clear the air' - 'We'll not meet again' were his opening three phrases. They were delivered staccato fashion in tones which brooked no contradiction. 'I am not interested in opening channels of communication with you. I don't know you ... you don't know me; it's a situation which will continue.'

Sophie wanted to ask why he'd agreed to see them in the first place if he didn't want to build a bridge, but her courage failed her and she remained silent.

'You may have an image of me in your minds and find me a disappointment,' he continued, 'that is your problem, not mine; I have no preconceptions of you. I live my life the way I want to live it. I depend on no one and no one depends on me. I have no intention of changing the situation. Be sure you understand one thing in particular, you will no more be coming into my life than I will be intruding into yours.'

'Thank God.' Eddie muttered quietly.

'What did you say?' Henry barked, stabbing a finger towards him and glowering.

'Er nothing.' replied Eddie, wishing he'd never come, regretting he'd allowed himself to assume he and Sophie could ever awaken the conscience of the self-opinionated freak glaring at him.

'Right then.' Henry went on, once he'd cooled down a bit. 'Let's get one thing straight. You will not attempt to contact me again. This will be the only meeting we will ever have ... do you both understand?'

They nodded and, once he sensed their agreement to his strange and stringent conditions, his attitude began to soften. 'I do acknowledge you to be my children however and, for your information, you are my only children. I never sought to see you or your mothers because I never turn back. I did however always make sure you would never lack a financial safety net.'

'This is something new' Sophie thought, looking at Eddie to see if he was showing any sign of understanding what had been said, but he seemed just as puzzled.

'Your grandfather has access to ten thousand pounds which

he can release to you should you fall on bad times Miss Sweetman. If he has not used it on your behalf before you marry, it will come to you then as a wedding present.

Similarly,' he said to Eddie, 'I have made an arrangement with your foster father, and you too will get the money if he has not had to call on it. Hopefully he hasn't.'

Puzzlement had turned to astonishment by the time Sophie found her voice. 'I never knew; I really didn't. Grandpa never told me and I'm sure Mum knew nothing about it.'

'My trust in your grandfather has been vindicated then.' said Henry. 'He is my uncle don't forget, and he knew that for you to benefit he had to keep the secrecy of the understanding we had made. And you, Sir,' he continued, turning his gaze to Eddie, 'I assume you have no knowledge of the arrangement I made with your foster father.?'

Eddie shook his head, his voice also having failed him he was so surprised.

Emboldened, Sophie chanced trying to press him on the most important reason for her being there. 'Why did you do this for me and leave my mother with nothing, that's what I can't forgive … or understand?'

'I am not a monster Miss. Your mother knew what she was doing when she opened her door to me, so to speak … whatever she may have told you. It was her choice and her risk. The fact she ignored advice I know for sure she got from friends and family alike, is her business. On the other hand, however surprising you find it, I do feel some responsibility for you; you had no choice in the circumstances of your birth.'

'Similarly, Sir,' he said to Eddie, 'Your mother knew what sort of person I was from her first husband Roland La Tour, a friend of mine for years. She ignored what she knew in her heart would happen, believed she'd be able to change me into someone she wanted me to be, and couldn't. You had no part in this; you were the consequence of it. That's why I provided the safety net.'

At that point, with his children's spirit drained, he changed his tack again. 'Go through into the dining room now, I'm going to speak to Mrs Flower.'

Not long afterwards, as they took their places at the table, they heard her steps in the hall, and then the noise of the front door shutting. When Henry had told she could go she'd been furious, she'd wanted to be there for the afternoon session, to be on hand when the explosions took place. Instead of which he'd told her to go home, and was on his way back to the dining room by the time she was putting on her hat and coat. She left in a rage, still mumbling angrily to herself.

Henry pushed the wooden salad bowl towards Sophie, who helped herself from it, and slid it back. As he started to serve himself she thought she sensed a further relaxation and decided to test it. 'That painting of my mother ...' she started.

'You like it?' he asked, 'You can have it.'

She got such a surprise at his response she lost her tongue, from which he deduced she didn't like it.

'Ah, I see ... it makes you uncomfortable.'

'Well it's ...'

He almost smiled, 'Immodest?' he asked, and without waiting for an answer, turned to Eddie. 'I don't have an equivalent one of your mother I'm afraid, or it would have been yours for the taking.'

Eddie broke his bread roll and started to butter it. 'Pity, I haven't as much as a photograph of my mum.'

Henry wasn't listening; he was tapping the table in annoyance at himself, 'Blast! I forgot to offer you wine,' he said, standing up and going over to the trolley on which there was a bottle of Pouilly Foussé in an ice bucket. 'What about you Sophie, will you have some?'

'Why not,' she replied,' noting his use of her Christian name for the first time. 'If this is to be our 'Last Supper' I might as well have a glass of wine to go with it!'

Henry smiled. 'Eddie?'

'Not for me. I'm driving.'

'Quite right.' said Henry, bringing over Sophie's glass, and his own. 'Perhaps you'll have water instead?'

'Yes I will thanks.' Eddie replied, wondering if he was also sensing a change. Before he had time to work out what it might mean though, Sophie blurted out the question she'd been pondering on for the previous ten minutes.

'Why are you so afraid of us?'

'Me afraid of you?' exclaimed Henry, 'I'm not afraid of you or anyone else.'

'Well, in that case ...' said Sophie, risking all by pressir home her temporary advantage, 'why do you hide yourself behind all the bluster?'

For a moment she thought she'd gone too far, sure she had when she saw the reddish tinge on her father's face become scarlet and start to spread from his collar up to his hairline. For a while after that there was complete silence then, much to their surprise, he burst into laughter.

It was enough for Eddie; he put down the glass from which he was sipping, pushed his chair back, and rose to go - a rapid exit was called for and he was responding. Sophie had stretched her luck too far.

'Sit down young man.' Henry commanded, his spluttering reduced to a grin. 'She's made of sterner stuff than you. You'd better ask her how it's done.'

Sophie was trembling. She too had thought she might have been pressing him too hard yet, instinctively, she knew she was right. Here was a naturally shy man putting up a shield of aggression to hide what he perceived to be a weakness in himself. It wasn't an unusual response, there are many who react in a similar fashion.

Henry drained his glass and reached for the bottle to top it up. Sophie's put up her hand when he went to do the same for her. 'Sure?' he asked

She nodded.

He turned to Eddie. 'Changed your mind?'

'No. I'll stick to water.' he replied.

Henry sat for a moment, thinking, and then drew in a big breath. 'Start again?'

Sophie smiled, so did Eddie. The change in the atmosphere had gone beyond all recognition in a matter of a few minutes and she couldn't help but wonder what would have happened if she'd kept her mouth shut. So busy was she analysing her own audacity, and the consequence of it, she nearly missed his next remark.

'I'm not a very good painter you know. I'm more a journeyman than an artist. I could never draw d'you see. I was never as good as a draughtsman as old Roly for example - and he was a sculptor!'

'So why do you keep painting?' asked Sophie, certain by then the bluffness and distancing of himself seen by others as bad tempered arrogance, was just his way of defending himself against hurtful comments regarding his shyness and artistic shortcomings.

'I don't know, and that's the truth … I like the cachet which goes with it I suppose, the romantic way in which artists are seen by those who don't know better. I have money, luckily, left me by my father and my aunt; it helps. I don't actually have to work - that's been my cross in a way. I never had to try … so I didn't. I've been a 'rolling stone' and I must have been good at it, because I've gathered little moss.'

'Talking about stones.' said Eddie, plucking up his courage at last. 'What's the one on the rockery all about?'

Henry stared at him for a moment, slowly shaking his head. 'You mean you don't know?'

'Know what?'

'About Roly's work.'

'Roly La Tour?'

'Yes, Roly … 'Frog' we called him … a very talented man, a real artist, a man who saw what others couldn't see.'

'I'm sorry,' said Eddie, 'I haven't a clue what you're talking about. I know almost nothing about him.'

'Ah, well Roly was a friend of mine when I was at college, we were drinking companions but beyond that, as different as chalk and cheese. He was poor, and spilling over with latent ability. I was comfortably off and, as I've said, more or less talent-less.'

'You're being hard on yourself.' Sophie said, surprised to find she was beginning to feel slightly sorry for him.

'Tell me about Roly La Tour then.' asked Eddie, getting back to the point. 'I only know what people who lived round us said … that he was 'a self-indulgent drunk'. I know he was tight when he fell under the bus.'

Henry began rocking his head from side to side again. 'Show me an artist who doesn't enjoy his tipple, Roly was no worse than most. There was a crowd of us; we all liked our pint and our pudding.'

Eddie leaned towards him 'What crowd?'

'We called ourselves the LMS Club.'

'Oh them, yes, we've heard of them alright. We even know who they are. In fact we tried tracking a few of them down to find out more about you.'

'Really? Did you? And how did you come across the LMS Club may I ask?'

'We didn't,' said Eddie, 'Angie did, Angela La Tour, Roly's

daughter, my half-sister. She found something about it after her father died. And now she's going for them.'

'Oh her, yes ... I know who you mean. But why is she 'going for them', why does she want to do that?'

'She's got a massive, ton weight, grudge against the LMS Club.' said Eddie, 'She reckons they diddled her dad out of a load of money ... you included.'

'Does she really? How does she make that out?'

'Well, she says you lot bought his sculptures from him on the cheap, before he became famous and, later, when he became well known, you sold them for thousands and gave him nothing. She also says, when she was having a rough time after Roly died, none of you would help her.'

'She's wrong there, I never sold mine. Anyway she didn't make the right approach. She was too belligerent the day she called here and I sent her packing.'

'She's having tough time.' said Sophie.

'Is she? Well, maybe I'll think about it again. By the way the police were on to Mrs Flower just before I got back. They wanted to know about the LMS Club as well. They're going ring again today apparently ... an Inspector Reynard I believe. I wonder what he wants ... have you any idea of the reason for their interest?'

'I don't,' Eddie replied, 'but we discovered several of your LMS friends had died, when we went looking for them.'

'I went to Jock McPhee's wake.' added Sophie.

'Jock's dead? Good God! How did you know *him*?'

'I didn't know him; I was just trying to get information about you. The day I went round was the day of his funeral that's all. He'd died of a stroke.'

'And, the day we went to see Ghandi Melchitt, we found he'd died three days earlier, fallen into his goldfish pond and drowned.' Eddie added.

'So poor Frog's gone, and now Jock and Ghandi have gone as well. That just leaves Ginger and me.'

Sophie shook her head. 'It doesn't, Ginger died a while ago. You're the only one left.'

'What about their sons and daughters?'

'Their children?' asked Eddie, 'Well ... we've met some of them, but we don't know much about them. One was killed recently; I read it in the paper ... one of the Melchitts.'

'And you don't know what the LMS Club is?'

'No, I've said so. What is it?'

'What *was* it, you mean? It all goes back to our student days. More wine Sophie - it's a long story.

'Not for me.' she replied, as she continued to marvel at the amazing change in her father's attitude: pompous, monosyllabic and taciturn when they'd arrived, he was so voluble and affable by then he couldn't be stopped, she could hardly credit it.

Then, just as Eddie was reaching for the jug to top up his water, Henry sparked into action again, and stood up.

'Let's go through to the comfortable chairs.' he said, walking round the table and opening up the dividing doors. 'I think it's time to explain the 'ins and outs' of the LMS Club, I'm going to remove the cloud of mystery which seems to have gathered round it. It's complex mind you … you may even think it's silly … but everyone appears to want to know what it is, or was, so I'll start by telling you. Anyway I expect I'll be telling this policeman chap later.

I remember it as if it was yesterday, though it's all of forty years ago now. Ginger Brett and Ghandi Melchitt were at school together, in the same form actually. When they left and went up to London University they moved into a flat over in Battersea. I was in a bed-sit at the time in the next street. George McPhee was in the same house, in the room adjacent to mine, but we were all at different colleges.

The local pub was, and still is, called The Latchmere. It's right beside Battersea Park, where Latchmere Wanderers, a local cricket club, of which Ghandi and Ginger were members, used to have a pitch. It was a club without a clubhouse and the landlord let them have a room to change in. He charged no rent, taking his reward from the additional business which came his way after every match and practice session - a quid pro quo which suited everyone.

Obviously I'd already got to know George through living in the same house as him, and we'd often go down to The Latchmere at weekends for a drink. On Saturdays, during the cricket season, the place would be packed with players and their supporters. It was inevitable that sooner or later we'd join them, and when we did they dubbed us the 'pavilion members' because instead of playing, we drank.

After a match one evening, the opposing team and a crowd of their supporters came in. Roly La Tour, an art student studying sculpture, a man who none of us had ever met before, was with them. Somehow he got detached from the friends he arrived with, and joined us. After that he began to come to The Latchmere on a regular basis. We often teamed up on a Saturday night. Then, one day, Ginger told us the house next to the one he and Ghandi lived in had become vacant and was up for re-letting, it was one of those 'two up and two down' Victorian terrace ones. He suggested the five of us should get together and rent it. We thought it a great idea and within a week we'd moved in.

It worked out well considering how different our backgrounds were and how different our, how shall I put it, 'financial circumstances' were as well. Jock, Ginger, Ghandi and I were all fairly well placed for cash, but poor old Roly, who by then had become 'Frog' to us because of his French sounding name, was always broke. He struggled permanently to keep up with his share of the rent and the living costs. Lucky for him, the rest of us turned a blind eye to the frequent instances on which his contributions were late. Anyway, all went well until the day Ginger suggested playing cards. Rummy turned to Whist, Whist turned to Poker, and soon we were at it every night. The stakes were low at the start, and our gambling didn't get out of hand.

Actually it never got out of hand for four of us but Roly, the one who least could afford it, always seemed to lose. His debt to each of us grew and grew until it was obvious that not only would he never be able pay it off, he wouldn't be able to afford his share of the rent or the living costs either. It was a terrible time for him, but also for us, he felt guilty for having no money; we felt guilty for having so much … well so much more than him anyway.'

Eddie got up and walked around the room slapping his thigh. 'Leg's gone to sleep, sorry.'

'Maybe you don't want to hear all this.' said Henry. 'I just thought …'

'But we do, we want to hear everything, both of us.' Sophie replied. 'Don't we Eddie?'

'Of course we do … take no notice of me.'

Henry waited a moment while he gathered his thoughts again and then went on, 'It was Jock, I think, who came up with the solution we eventually adopted - an arrangement based on something he'd been learning in his studies called a Tontine Agreement. We concocted our own variation in which we waived

Frog's debts and share of rent, until the end of his course, which still had two years to go.'

'And where did the LMS Club come in?' Eddie asked, as he resumed his seat.

'It was all part of it ... Frog, you see, was too proud to accept what we offered without giving us something in return. The only thing he had was a big stone, a sort of experimental sculpture, which he insisted we accept. The agreement covered the conditions of our joint ownership of it.

It was all a bit embarrassing to the four of us at the time because, to us, the sum of money was of such little significance. But the stone - just a lump of granite to everyone else - was the only thing he owned, apart from his clothes and his bicycle.'

'So how did this agreement work?' Eddie asked, 'and you still haven't really told us anything about the LMS Club.'

'Well, *we* were the LMS Club of course, Ghandi, Ginger, Jock and I, *we* were the members; Roly was sort of included when we made him a non-participating associate. In the agreement, the stone belonged jointly to the members in such a way that when one of them died his portion went to the others. The last man standing eventually winding up as its sole owner.'

'LMS - Last Man Standing - yes. That would be with the exception of Roly, of course.'

'Of course ... he wasn't a member, he was an associate

'So,' said Sophie who'd been listening carefully, 'as Ghandi, Ginger, and Jock are all gone, it now belongs to you?

'Not quite.' replied Henry. 'At the last knockings we made it more interesting by changing it to make it a lottery for our children, if we ever had any. So instead of one of us getting the stone; the last of our children would get it.'

Sophie looked at Eddie, and saw in his face the same expression of incredulity which was showing on her own. 'That's ridiculous,' she said, 'what a lot of nonsense over a lump of stone.'

'I agree, certainly I agree ... now ... but that's how it all started.' said Henry, 'and then everything changed when, sometime just before Frog's death, an influential art critic came across one of his works and pronounced it to be that of a genius. In no time his stuff became 'sought after' - all the rage - and the value of the few pieces in circulation rocketed. As a result our LMS agreement was no longer a joke.'

'What's so special about them?' asked Eddie

Henry pinched his lip and thought for a few moments before answering. 'Yes ... ah ... oh dear, it's hard to describe, and I don't know if I can, other than by giving you an analogy.'

'Go on try us with an example.'

'Well, take clouds. When you look up and see those big fluffy clouds moving across each other you must have often thought you could see faces or animals in them.'

'Oh yes.' Sophie said. 'And in wallpaper.'

Eddie nodded enthusiastically, 'I've got plastic flooring in my bathroom - it's got a marble design on it - and I can make out all sorts of things. Sometimes I lose them and then, all of a sudden, there they are again.'

'Right,' said Henry, 'well ... it was like that with Frog's work. He could see things in a stone which others couldn't. Whether it was the contour arising from the way in which it had been split from the bedrock, or whether it was the lie of the cracks, the colours, the striations, or the undulations which made up the image he could see, I don't know. But he'd be stalking round a lump of granite straight from the quarry, and suddenly, without warning, he'd yell out 'I can see it - 'it's a dancing bear', or 'it's leaping dolphin.' When he pointed out what he'd seen most of us still saw nothing but a hunk of rock.'

Sophie seemed to grasp what Henry was saying and nodded her head. 'What changed then? How did he convince people that what he saw was there?'

'He set about slightly emphasising the essential features by grinding a bit off here, smoothing a bit off there, gradually shaping the surface until he'd created a vague outline which anyone, who was prepared to 'work' at it, could recognise. He called them his puzzle stones. All in all, he made about fifteen of them. They're known these days as Frog's Stones or Frogstones because he always signed them by carving a frog into the base instead of a signature. I've got several under wraps in the mews at the end of the garden.'

'Really? And you have one of them on your rockery as well, haven't you?' Eddie said, pleased with himself.

'Well spotted. Did you see it as a toad; if you didn't, go out and try looking closer.'

Eddie smiled. 'The last time I was here I noticed it, and somehow knew it was special. I got Mrs 'F' to let me have a closer look but it was so overgrown with ivy I couldn't make out what it was - I did spot the frog on the back though.'

'It's hard to see, isn't it?'

'How come you have so many?' asked Sophie.

'Luck, just luck really, Ginger, Jock, and I, each had one, Ghandi had two. We bought them off Frog not long after we'd left college, while he was still struggling and desperately broke. The others couldn't see anything in them, and only took them off him to help him out. I was the one who could see what Frog saw. And when I realised none of the others were able to make anything of them, I didn't have much trouble in persuading them to sell them to me. I never ever thought of them as investments, after all they hadn't been 'discovered' at that stage and had little real value. To me they were simply amusing oddities.'

'And where's the original one, the one the Last Man Standing will get?' asked Eddie, 'Is that it in the garden?'

'No. The original one was there at the start alright, in fact I was deputed to look after it, but it got stolen. I never told the others, I just replaced it with the first one I bought. They wouldn't have noticed. I fact they probably think I still have the one that started it all off.'

'The others may not have realised what had happened but surely Frog would've.' said Eddie.

'Of course he would, no doubt of it, because he was the one who stole it.'

'What?'

'Carted if off, him and another guy; I saw them do it from an upstairs window.'

'Why didn't you stop him?'

'I didn't have the heart ... after all it was only a bit of granite at that stage. I thought he'd taken it because he had no money to buy another lump. I simply put up one of the others and said nothing.'

'And presumably he didn't either ... how odd.'

'Not really, we never met again. We all went our different ways, and none of them ever called here. We simply lost touch. I suppose they think it's still here.'

'They're going to get a shock aren't they?'

'Well, if what you've told me is correct they're all dead so it doesn't matter, and their children wouldn't know it's a different stone because they never saw the original. The Last Man Standing, whoever it turns out to be will still get a Frogstone - it'll just be a different one to the one which started it all off.'

'And what happened to the one he took, the original one, do you know?' asked Eddie, gripping the edge of his seat.

'I really have no idea where it is. I did hear, years ago, it had been put up in front of an insurance building in Wandsworth. But when they widened the road the buildings were demolished and I have no idea what happened to it afterwards, I mostly live abroad you see. It was all before Frog's work became valuable, so it wouldn't have been seen to have any significant value.'

'And what was that particular one supposed to be?'

'A baby Penguin, asleep, with its beak tucked into the down of its chest,'

'I wonder where it is now.' said Sophie.

'As I said … I've absolutely no idea.' Henry answered. 'In someone's rockery I suppose, not recognised for what it is.'

Sophie nodded.

But Eddie didn't.

By then it was beginning to get dark outside, which prompted Sophie to look at her watch. They'd been there for hours and she knew she ought to be on her way back to Gatwick to catch her flight home. There was just time for her to pose one more question. 'So, what are these Frogstone things worth?'

Henry grinned as he answered. 'Around a hundred thousand pounds I suppose.'

Sophie gasped. 'That's a lot of money for a few stones.'

'A hundred thousand pounds each!'

'Each?' she repeated, her voice rising to a shriek.

'Yes, each. You'll be getting mine in due course.'

'We will? How's that?'

'Because I've left them to you jointly in my will … call it my 'conscience legacy' - the last act of the Last Man Standing of the original five. You'll be getting a Beefeater, a Polar Bear, a Winston Churchill and a Barn Owl between you … but not the Toad in the garden, that'll be for the last man standing in accordance with the rules of the LMS Society! The paperwork for the ones I own has already gone off to my solicitors, I posted it this morning.

As Henry's startling revelations began to slowly sink in,

Sophie, already anxious regarding the time left before she'd need to be at Gatwick, glanced at her watch again - time to go. Reluctantly she rose from the sofa. Eddie absentmindedly followed suit, his brain was in turmoil with the thoughts of a Penguin in his back garden worth a hundred thousand pounds, and the inescapable fact that, as things stood Angie, who needed money most of all, was destined to get nothing.

As they were going out into the hall to put on their coats Henry suggested they might 'call again sometime'. It was hardly an enthusiastic invitation but, undeniably, it was considerable improvement over the way they'd been received when they arrived - perhaps as much as they could expect on the first day of a new found relationship. They promised they would, and meant it, smiling inwardly at their own earlier feelings, which still slightly prevailed.

At the top of the steps they paused, awkwardly, facing him but reluctant to close the gap. And then, swiftly, they shook hands and went down to the street level.

When they reached the bottom, they turned. He was standing quite still watching them. And he'd shrunk, his military bearing seemingly replaced by the stoop of an old man. Not that they took much notice of that … they were more interested in the beaming smile on his face, it embodied a multitude of emotions, and every one found a resonance in them. They climbed into the car, wound down the windows, and waved. The last they saw of him he was still grinning.

He stood for a moment staring after them and then, when the sound of the telephone ringing in the hall caught his attention, he swung round, straightened his shoulders, and marched back inside to answer it.

It was Detective Chief Inspector Reynard.

The towns, villages, and establishments
mentioned in this book
are a mix of the real and the imagined.
All the characters are fictitious.

Lorenzo Tonti devised the first Tontine scheme.

The Pardurmon Society to which this book is dedicated
has seven members.
They are all my grandchildren

Once again I would like to thank best-selling author
David Rice
(Shattered Vows, The Pompeii Syndrome,
The Song of Tiananmen Square etc.)
for the encouragement he has given me
in presenting Eddie's Penguin.

Alan Grainger 2009

The Author

Alan Grainger is an Englishman who emigrated to Ireland at the time when everyone else seemed to be going the other way. He got seduced by the lifestyle, married an Irish woman, and never went back. They have three children and seven grandchildren.

His business career ended unexpectedly early when his company was taken over, and a whole new world of opportunity opened up.

Ever since then, other than when he's watching rugby or cricket on television, he has been travelling, painting and writing. His journeys have taken him all over the world, provided him with much of the background material which features in his books, and allowed him to choose authentic sets against which he can tell his stories.

The following books of fiction, by him, are available from Create Space, Amazon, and other on-line booksellers, or by ordering from book shops.

The Learning Curves

Divided from his father, and frozen out of his home in Ireland by his new stepmother, sixteen year old Jimmy O'Callaghan runs away, resolving never to return. With no one to guide and support him, he finds himself with little option but to learn about life and love as best he can. He's aided in his quest for enlightenment, success and happiness, by an unlikely collection of worldly people, the sort of people he would never have encountered, let alone befriend, at home in Templederry. Starting off with the few pounds he'd stolen from the till in his father's pub the night before he left, and with little appreciation of how big a risk he was taking, his personality, determination and charm ensure nothing is ever beyond his reach.

This book is the first of The Templederry Trilogy, and is partly set in the rural Irish town of Templederry, County Tipperary. It is followed by Father Unknown and The Legacy

Father Unknown

Sometimes volatile relationship between two brothers, Dick and Roger Davenport, is demolished forever when they find out something previously unknown to them about their beginnings. In the aftermath of violence which follows their discovery Dick, strongly supported by his grandfather Archie, sets off in a new direction, one which brings him to Ireland on a journey of more surprising discoveries.

This book is the second of The Templederry Trilogy partly set in the rural Irish town of Templederry, County Tipperary. It is preceded by The Learning Curves and followed by The Legacy.

The Legacy

When an heir hunter turns up looking for Charlie O'Callaghan and finds he's been dead for years, he tells O'Callaghan's son and daughter, he has information which might connect them, through their late father, to an unclaimed legacy. He asks them if they'd like him to process their claim, but they think his fees are too high and decide to do the job themselves. It's a choice they regret when they discover their father was not the man they thought he was.

The Legacy is the third of The Templederry Trilogy partly set in the rural Irish town of Templederry, County Tipperary. It is preceded by The Learning Curves and Father Unknown

The same author's three murder/mystery novels featuring Detective Chief Inspector 'Foxy' Reynard, are also available from Create Space, Amazon and other on-line booksellers; or by ordering through bookshops.

Eddie's Penguin

When a young girl's quest to find the father she has never met becomes entangled in a police investigation into a series of seemingly unconnected murders she has no idea the information she digs up will ultimately lead to the uncovering of the last bit of the jigsaw the police are struggling to put together. Detective Chief Inspector 'Foxy' Reynard who makes his first appearance in this murder/mystery story leads the team, from Sussex CID, who eventually solve the mystery and the crimes.

Deadly Darjeeling

When Nelson Deep, wealthy tea merchant, is found dead in his study in bizarre circumstances and Detective Chief Inspector 'Foxy' Reynard is called in, a solution seems inevitable. Such an assumption, however, makes little allowance for the dysfunctional and self-centred attitudes the D.C.I. uncovers as he attempts to unravel the strange relationships prevailing within the Deep family.

Deep & Crisp & Even

The body of a young woman newspaper columnist is found part buried under the snow, and Detective Chief Inspector 'Foxy' Reynard is called in. As his investigation into her death proceeds, it becomes increasingly apparent there was more to Rosaleen Sommerton than met the eye

Alan Grainger's spy thriller/saga **Blood On The Stones** is now available from Create Space, Amazon, and other on-line booksellers.

It's the story of two young men, once close as brothers, who fall out over a girl when they are in their twenties and go their separate ways. Their vow 'never to meet again' is forgotten though, when they find themselves face to face in the course of an attempted royal assassination.

All this authors' books are available in a variety of e-book formats

Proof

Made in the USA
Charleston, SC
12 January 2016